DOWN THE DARK STREETS

DOWN THE DARK STREETS

WILLIAM W. JOHNSTONE
and J. A. JOHNSTONE

PINNACLE BOOKS
Kensington Publishing Corp.
www.kensingtonbooks.com

PINNACLE BOOKS are published by

Kensington Publishing Corp.
119 West 40th Street
New York, NY 10018

ISBN: 978-0-7860-4444-3

First Pinnacle paperback printing: May 2022

10 9 8 7 6 5 4 3 2 1

Printed in the United States of America

Electronic edition:

ISBN: 978-0-7860-4445- (e-book)

CHAPTER ONE

"I'm not going to hurt you, but if you don't do exactly what I say, I will kill you."

Anne glanced at the oxygen tank by her bedside. The steady hiss of air through the cannula came to a sudden and alarming stop.

I can't breathe!

She didn't dare open her mouth to express her profound terror.

Anne's gnarled hands clutched the sheet across her chest. Her lungs felt on the verge of collapse. The room swam around her as she gasped for air, her hips aching as she writhed on the bed.

"Don't you move. I'll be right back."

The door closed, and Anne heard the lock click into place.

If she could only reach the valve on the oxygen tank. It was only a few feet away. Not much more than a long stretch across her night table.

Not for the first time, Anne cursed the withered husk that was her body. Her ninety-one years hadn't always been easy, and four bouts of cancer over the last twenty of them had left her brittle and bound to her sickbed. Some days, she prayed for the black, painless emptiness to where all souls must eventually pass.

Not today.

Not like this, desperate for air, mouth opening and closing like a fish on land, trembling with fright and . . . and anger. Yes, Anne was furious.

Furious at her tormentor.

And, perhaps even more so, furious with herself.

You can breathe if you just calm down, she admonished herself. Closing her eyes, she took as deep a tremulous breath as she could, willing her legs and arms to cease their useless struggling. All that was doing was getting her tangled up in the sheets, and if it continued, she'd be sealed up like a mummy, and then there would be no hope at all.

She listened for the sound of approaching footsteps on the other side of the door. Again, she knew it was futile. Her hearing aids mocked her from their perch on her dresser—all the way across the room. They might as well have been on the dark side of the moon.

The Dark Side of the Moon. Oh, how her son Jimmy used to play that album over and over when he was in high school. She and Herbert (and how she wished he were here right now to save her, and not in the ground these past twenty-six years) begged him daily to turn the volume down. This was when Jimmy had started to change. He was no longer their little, timid boy who looked at them with wet eyes when they told him he'd have to take the public bus to school in seventh grade. This was the Jimmy who oftentimes turned the volume *up* instead, slamming his door in their faces. His hair had grown long and shaggy, and good grades and the track team were no longer priorities in his life. All he cared about was that awful music and that trashy girl who worked in the bowling alley, Dana Grogan. She knew what that Dana girl was all about, and her heart broke as she watched her rebellious son led down the road of premarital sex and drinking in the woods and smoking pot.

Instead of heading off to college, Jimmy and Dana had hopped in an old Impala and simply drove away. They'd seen him a dozen or so times after that awful day, until he simply stopped coming around, or even calling. A postcard would arrive in the mail every few years, usually including a request for money and a note of where to wire it.

The men in her family, in her life, had left her long, long ago. Her vitality had followed suit.

Anne turned her head and looked at the door. It was still closed.

There was no way of defending herself. She was painfully aware that she was more helpless than a newborn kitten, at the mercy of anyone who stepped into her room.

She just wanted air.

If she could breathe properly, she could think straight.

And then what?

Anne didn't know.

All that mattered was getting oxygen into her lungs. It was funny. All the things she and Herbert scrimped and saved for, the clutter and trips and amusements that seemed so important at the time, all of it paled compared to something as simple as fresh, clean air.

It hurt like the dickens to grasp the edge of the mattress and roll herself onto her side. Her vision was almost as bad as her hearing, but she could see the hazy shape of the tank with enough clarity to make her chest ache.

Swallowing hard and dry, she stretched her right hand out with fingers that looked like they belonged to someone else, someone unearthed from a long-sealed tomb, fluttering uncontrollably, seeking the cold metal of the small handle atop the oxygen tank.

Almost there.

She leaned into the night table. Her arm weakened, collapsing onto the collection of pill bottles, knocking over the glass of water.

No!

She felt the vibrations of feet rushing up the stairs well before she heard the *thump-thump-thump* along the landing. The door opened with a crash.

"What have you been up to?"

Anne's heart skipped several, painful beats. She was too weak to even lift her arm off the table.

"You'll get that once you've done what I asked you."

When Anne tried to speak, all that came out was a gargled hiss. Resting on her side compacted her lungs. Now even taking the smallest breath had become a chore.

"What a state you've gotten yourself in. Well, I can't have you like this."

When the woman went to grab her, Anne tried to recoil, but her movement was so faint, she was sure it wasn't even noticed.

Placed on her back and pulled into a sitting position, Anne's head bobbed as her pillows were fluffed.

"There. Better?"

No, you evil witch! she wanted to scream. Her eyes watered from pain and helplessness instead.

"I know you want your oxygen, and I promise, you'll have it in just a few minutes. We just need to get through a few things first."

The woman had introduced herself as Nia Anderson, though Anne was sure her last name was something else, something foreign. She looked Eastern European and had let slip a few oddly accented words from time to time. Nia had come to her through a recommendation from her friend Dolores as a capable elder companion who hadn't once touched the jar of quarters or envelope of twenty-dollar bills Dolores kept on her dresser.

Nia had been coming by once a day, every weekday, for the past year. She helped get Anne showered and clothed, cleaned the house, and ran any errands that needed doing. She was sweet and compassionate and loved to sit with her and watch old movies on TV. She'd even stayed around when the visiting nurse came by to learn more about Anne's medical needs just in case Anne had an emergency and there was no time for medical help to get there.

Anne had let Nia not just into her life, but into her heart. Nia's visits were the highlights of her day. Anne had wished for more children, but God had only granted them Jimmy, then sowed the seeds for him to desert them.

It had been a lifetime between Jimmy—the young Jimmy who loved her—and Nia.

And now this.

Who was this girl standing over her, rifling through an accordion file of papers? The Nia she knew would be making sure she took her medication before doing a load of laundry and setting into the chair next to her to see if there was a Cary Grant movie on TV. She wouldn't be turning off Anne's precious oxygen and threatening to kill her.

Was Anne hallucinating all of this?

It was possible.

It had happened before. Or so she'd been told. The memory was a tricky thing at her age. So much reliance on the accounting of others, so many gaps that couldn't be filled.

Or was this someone who looked like her Nia?

Yes. That was it.

The file slipped from the woman's fingers, and when she bent down to retrieve it, cursing loudly, Anne though her hair looked different. It was a shade darker than Nia's normal chestnut.

And what about that tiny scar above her right eyebrow. Had that always been there?

Anne racked her brain, calling up images of Nia tending to her, smiling when she brought in magazines to read to her, staring into her face when she brushed her hair or tucked her in.

That scar. Where was that scar?

Anne started to cry, frustrated that she couldn't recall the scar or the proper hair color or decide whether she was dreaming or awake. She prayed this was all a nightmare, a fever dream brought on by her pills and flagging health.

"Don't cry," the woman said, suddenly soothing.

"Nia?" Anne gasped.

"Sure. Nia."

Blinking her tears away, Anne looked to Nia as if for the first time that day. Yes, maybe she had been dreaming and was now just coming out of it. Nia smiled at her, dabbing her cheeks with a tissue.

Anne touched the cannula under her nostrils.

Still no air!

"Now, I need you to take this," Nia said, wrapping Anne's arthritic fingers around the pen. "Just sign exactly where I tell you to sign."

Nia placed the bed tray over Anne's lap. On it, instead of her usual nutrition shake and wheat toast with butter and jelly, was a stack of papers.

Her vision went fuzzy as her lungs hitched.

A sharp slap on her cheek brought everything back into focus.

"Stay with me, Anne. If you want your oxygen, you're going to have to do what I say. It'll all be over before you know it."

There was nothing to do but follow Nia's orders. Anne didn't even have the breath to shout—not that anyone would have heard her.

In a shaky scrawl, Anne signed her name wherever Nia pointed. Without her glasses, she couldn't even read what she was signing. Truth be told, she didn't care. She would sign anything just to be able to breathe again and make all of this go away.

When she was done, Nia scooped the papers up and stuffed them back in the folder.

"Wasn't that easy?" Nia said, back to her smiling self. But was that her voice? Her light accent sounded off. Had she said she was Nia? Now Anne couldn't remember, and the not remembering frightened her almost as much as her desperate need for air.

Anne nodded, her body sinking deeper into the bed.

Nia turned the valve on the tank, and the sweet tang of fresh oxygen burst through the cannula.

Leaning over her to adjust the cannula, Nia said, "There, do you feel better?"

All Anne could give in response was a slow closing and opening of her eyes.

"Good. I need you to understand this. You're not going to say a word about this to anyone. I've changed my schedule. For the foreseeable future, I'm increasing my visits to seven days a week. I'll be here every day. And if I find out you talked to someone, your nurse, a doctor, that dried-up old hag Dolores"—Nia's lips pulled back, revealing her too-white incisors—"I'll kill you slowly and painfully. And then I'll do the same to the person you spoke to."

CHAPTER TWO

Seven thirty was *Wheel of Fortune* time, which meant Patrick Knox had to get his tired butt out of his tattered chair and rustle up a ginger ale and some crackers for his wife. It was slow getting up, Patrick's knees popping like firecrackers. There was a time those knees carried him across the finish line of the New York City Marathon. Now, the walk to the kitchen and upstairs was marathon enough, and there was no one to cheer him on.

He opened the refrigerator and took out a bottle of ginger ale for Mary and a seltzer for himself. Tucking a sleeve of crackers under his arm, he trekked upstairs to their bedroom. Mary had the TV on. Vanna White showed the world her latest dress with a smile.

"Oh, isn't it beautiful, Pat?" his wife said.

The formfitting dress was a riot of some glittery fabric, red and white streaks racing up the letter turner's waist and chest.

"You could see her in that thing from space," he said, twisting open the cap and inserting a straw. He held the straw to Mary's lips so she could take a sip.

"Daft old man. What do you know about fashion?"

"About enough to fill the head of a pin," he replied with a light chuckle.

Mary loved all that glamour and gossip on the TV and in those magazines he bought her from the racks by the supermarket register. She'd long since given up trying to clue him in to the latest travails of the movie starlet of the moment. He wouldn't know Jennifer Aniston from the woman who offered tax advice to seniors at the library, and he was proud of it.

"Now, are you at least going to try to solve the puzzles tonight?" Mary asked.

"I always try. It's just that I don't even know what the heck the answers are referring to half the time."

With some difficulty, Mary lifted her hand off the bed, her arm skeletally thin, and patted his hand.

"When did I marry such an old codger?"

Pat smiled. "I resemble that remark." He glanced at the screen. The woman who had spun the wheel asked if there was a J. "A J? No one starts with the letter J."

"Maybe she knows something we don't," Mary said.

The buzzer sounded.

"Or maybe not," Pat said.

For the next half hour, he fed Mary her nightly snack of two crackers, a bit at a time, in between sips from the small ginger ale bottle. Mary figured out two of the four puzzles before the contestants. As usual, Pat hadn't a clue what anyone was talking about.

After the game show ended, he asked her, "You feeling tired, or would you like your pill?"

"I'd better take that damn pill. You look bushed. You need your rest."

"Don't you worry about me, old lady. I'm just hitting my prime."

"Well, then, it looks like your prime hit you right back."

Their bedroom had an attached bath. Pat found the bottle with her sleeping pills on the counter and filled a glass with water. When he saw himself in the mirror, beneath the garish light that made everything look worse (why were these lights even invented?), he nearly gasped. The circles under his eyes were darker than usual, and his bags had their own bags. He didn't like to admit to her how tired he really felt. She had her own worries.

But he wasn't naïve. They both worried about each other, and there was no amount of sugarcoating that could hide it.

With Mary being laid up with the distal muscular dystrophy, unable to walk on her own and her arms and hands so thin and weak, it was hard to maintain normal body rhythms. She often wasn't tired at night because there was nothing she could do to tire herself out. Which meant she'd be up at night and at several points would need his help, including getting to and from the bathroom. So some nights she took the sleeping pill to let him get a good night's sleep.

Pat never minded taking care of Mary. After all, she had given him two children (both boys—or, more accurately, men now) had been by his side through layoffs, illness, deaths, births, relocations, and all of the highs and lows of a life well lived. He knew he hadn't always been an easy mate, but Mary had never flinched. They were each others' rocks in a world seemingly made of gravel.

It pained Pat to the core to see her like this. Mary had been stronger than any three men and prettier than those movie stars she liked to gawk over. She'd always been a ball of nervous energy, flitting around the house like a hummingbird, preferring catnaps to a good night's sleep. How many times had he begged her to just sit still, her tutting at him and dashing off to the corner store or doing extra work she brought home from her job at the Woolworth department store? She did the books for the store, and those books were often laid out on their living room table—a table reserved for her work and special family meals.

"Here you go, my sweet," he said. Pat put the pill on her tongue and helped her wash it down with some water.

After she swallowed, she smiled and lay her head against the pillow. "Remember how much I hated when you called me that?"

"Only when I did it in front of your friends." He adjusted her sheets, tucking her in as best he could.

"That's because it sounded corny and insincere."

"And how about now?" Brushing her hair away from her forehead, he bent over to kiss the tip of her nose.

Mary smiled. "It's sweet."

"I knew I'd wear you down eventually. It just took, oh, fifty-three years to do it."

"If you are anything, it's persistent."

"That I am. That I am. You must be in a good mood, because you usually call me a stubborn old mule."

He changed the channel to a station that played reruns of old comedies. *Welcome Back, Kotter* was on. He didn't like the show when it was on in the seventies, but Mary loved it, saying it reminded her of their watching it as a family when the boys were young.

"You need anything else?" he asked, suddenly feeling bone tired.

"Yes, for you to get ready for bed. I didn't take this pill for nothing."

With a sigh, Pat said, "I think I'll do just that. Let me close up shop downstairs, and I'll slip into something more comfortable."

"Just don't slip down the stairs," Mary said with a light titter.

Pat double-checked the locks on the door, made sure the windows were closed, and turned out the lights. He put on his pajamas, took his own pills—there was never a shortage of pills in the Knox house—and settled into his bed, which was next to Mary's fancy hospital bed that she hated but had become a necessity. It had at first felt utterly alien, sleeping in separate beds, but at least they were still beside one another.

"Whatcha reading?" Mary asked as he turned on the lamp.

He held a battered book he'd checked out at the library earlier that day. "*The Lodger* by Marie Belloc Lowndes. I've been meaning to read it for a long time. Written over a hundred years ago by this British lady."

Mary's nose crinkled. "Is there nothing you won't read?"

"It's a classic. It tells the story of a sorry old couple—you know, like us—who take in a lodger who might be an active serial killer. I could read it to you if you want."

"You stick to your books. I have Mr. Kotter."

Pat chuckled.

He got as far as page two before he fell asleep.

CHAPTER THREE

The town of Woodlean, Virginia, had been home to Patrick and Mary Knox their entire lives, save for that two-year period when his job had forced them to relocate to Boca Raton. They'd hated Florida, from the heat down to the lack of anything to do. Luckily, Pat's manager had been fired, and his replacement saw no reason why he couldn't return to Woodlean.

Since the early twentieth century, Woodlean had been a haven for immigrating Irish, most of them arriving at Ellis Island and taking the Boston Post Road to what they'd heard was a slice of Ireland among the opportunity and grandeur of America. Pat's parents had settled in Woodlean from Cork in 1932. Mary's had arrived from nearby Limerick the following year. Her family moved around the block from Pat, and they'd both attended St. Brendan's Elementary, Pat two grades ahead of the girl who would one day become his wife.

There was a time when hearing heavy brogues on every corner was commonplace. Nowadays, they were few and far between. The children of Pat and Mary's contemporaries had moved off to what they called bigger and better things, scattered across the country like buckshot. Woodlean was not exactly a hotbed of opportunity and excitement. At least, not anymore. It had served its purpose as a haven for the Irish when they needed time to acclimate to a new country. Several generations later, it was still a quaint, safe place to live, but its days were numbered without an influx of youth.

The Knoxes were a dying breed. The town, Pat sometimes lamented, was dying right along with them.

Pat showered, changed, and made sure Mary had everything she needed before heading for his doctor appointment. Driving down the narrow street, he noted the sad shape many of the houses were in, including his own. Paint was peeling, roofs needed mending, gates were off their hinges, and lawns were in dire need of tending. For the most part, the people living in those homes were too old, sick, or crippled to do the necessary upkeep. And with the younger generation hundreds if not thousands of miles away, it wasn't going to happen anytime soon.

Pat kept a to-do list in his head that grew longer with each passing year. Pushing a broom and gathering some leaves were just about enough to take the wind out of his sails but good nowadays.

He stopped outside a gray two-family house. The front porch, just big enough for a couple of resin chairs, was starting to sag in the middle. He honked the horn. The front door opened immediately, and Pat chuckled. Doyle was one of those curtain peekers. Most likely, he'd spotted Pat's Buick as he'd turned down the street, but the man wasn't going to budge until Pat tapped the horn.

The old man waved, donning a tweed cap that was older than Moses and a favorite meal of the moths in

Doyle's house. It had more holes than a cheese grater, the man's bare scalp plainly visible from every angle.

"You're late," Doyle said, slamming the door so hard it made Pat's teeth rattle. The man was a world-class door slammer, though when he was truly angry, he'd turn it on its head and close the door softly.

Pat looked at the clock on his dashboard. "By two minutes. I hope I didn't inconvenience you."

Clicking his seat belt in place, Doyle huffed.

"It's a good thing Dr. Mendelman isn't a stickler for time, or else I would have gotten ready for nothing."

"It's a good thing at that," Pat said, pulling away from the curb. "How's your knee?"

"Feels like someone hit it with a bat, but I can take it."

"You should ask the doctor for one of those cortisone shots. They worked wonders for my shoulder."

"Then they might as well stick me all over. You take away one pain, another just takes its place. Better to just accept it and move on."

Pat turned onto Bridge Avenue. Both sides of the street were lined with stores, the zombies, as Pat liked to call people his age, out and about buying groceries, newspapers, or heading to the Bridge Coffee Shop for a cup and conversation.

"Is that Edna Moore?" Doyle said, pointing at a woman wheeling a collapsible pushcart filled with her day's haul, plastic bags heaped upon one another. Her white hair was windblown, her eyes downcast, concentrating on getting to her next stop.

"Looks like they released her from the hospital," Pat said. "She shouldn't be out like this. She just had a heart attack two weeks ago, for crying out loud." He slowed to a stop, double-parking. Doyle rolled down his window.

Pat called out, "Edna. Edna!"

She either couldn't hear or was willfully ignoring him. He got out of the car and approached her. Edna looked up when her cart brushed against his leg. The poor dear looked terrible, her face gone waxy, beads of sweat on her upper lip.

"Here, Edna, what are you doing about? Shouldn't you be resting?"

Edna squinted at him, and a tiny smile touched her wrinkled face. "Heya, Pat. I was near starving to death in that house. I figured if I was to go out, I might as well get enough to last me a while."

"Doyle, get your butt out here." Pat gently pried Edna's hands off the cart's handle. "Let me take you home."

"I can manage," Edna protested.

"Oh, I know you can. But if I don't do this, I won't get my merit badge."

"We're late as it is," Doyle cried out, still in the passenger seat.

"Doyle, you come help me, or you can walk. Then see how late you are."

His friend was out the door before he could finish. Doyle was paranoid about being late. He made a big production of the whole thing, raising his arms in the air, grunting louder than he had to when they placed the cart in the trunk and muttering under his breath about missing his appointment and in all likelihood being excommunicated by the doctor, and then what would become of him. Pat ignored his griping. If Doyle wasn't complaining, it was time to put the mirror under his nose.

He was relieved that he didn't have to struggle with Edna. He helped her into the back seat and drove the three blocks to her house. They brought her things inside and managed to unpack four of the bags, filling her kitchen table with groceries, before she ordered them out of the house with a big thank-you for a deed well done.

"You call me if you need anything else," Pat said as he stepped out the door.

Edna nodded. "I think I'm set until Armageddon. Thanks, Pat. Please tell Mary I was asking about her and to give me a call."

"I will." He crossed his heart. "Scout's honor."

She laughed as she closed the door.

"I don't know how I'm going to explain this to Dr. Mendelman. Edna knows better than to be out like that. Sometimes it's like everyone around us has regressed to stupid children," Doyle whined all the way to the row of medical offices that had once been family homes.

"I'm sure you'll find a way, and the good doctor will give you a special dispensation for helping a woman in need."

Doyle gave an actual harrumph and slammed the door, tottering his way to the doctor's office. Pat's doctor was in the house next door. Luck shined on him because a spot had opened up right in front of it. It was a good thing, because he was knackered by the time he got inside, said his hellos to the girls who ran the office, signed in, and took a seat under the television. But he had plenty of time to catch his breath. He managed to read most of the paper before his name was finally called.

"Blood pressure's a little high," Dr. Murphy said, swiping at the electronic tablet. He must have hit the wrong spot, because he let out a string of expletives, tapping the screen with his stubby finger before tossing it on the empty chair next to him. "Damn thing is more trouble than it's worth. I want to go back to my regular files, but Kelly is insisting we modernize everything."

Pat, sitting on the crinkling paper of the exam table, chuckled. "From what I can see around here, your daughter is the boss, so you best get with the times."

The doctor smiled. "That's what everyone keeps telling me. So, have you been taking your blood pressure pills?"

"Every day. Your pressure would be high, too, if you had to drive with Sam Doyle. Plus, I had to pluck Edna Moore off the street and get her back home."

"I'd heard about Edna's heart attack. Couldn't have been too long ago. She probably shouldn't be out of the hospital, much less walking around." He shrugged his shoulders. "As doctors, we may be able to save lives, but we're powerless before these insurance companies."

"Ever since the lawyers and accountants dug their claws into the insurance business, it's been a disaster, to say the least."

"Don't forget the politicians."

"I never forget that. That lot of good-for-nothings should all be put on an island far away from civilization."

Slipping his stethoscope into his ears, Dr. Murphy checked Pat's heart. He gave him the usual exam, walked out of the office, and came back with a thick manila folder. Rifling through the pages, he said, "I read over your last blood work, and everything looks good. I just want to double-check it while I have you here. Now, where the hell is it?"

Pat buttoned up his shirt and put his shoes back on while the doctor flipped through the file.

Dr. Murphy opened the door a crack and called out, "Kelly, where did you put Mr. Knox's lab results?"

She was quick to respond, her tone sharp yet loving, "Scanned and uploaded, just like all the results."

"I can't find them."

The pretty young woman came into the examining room, rolling her eyes. She swiped the folder out of his hands and replaced it with the tablet. Standing over her father's shoulder, she tapped away until she found the appropriate file. "See how easy that was?"

"For you, maybe. My fingers don't work with this thing."

She patted his shoulder. "A finger is a finger. You just don't want to learn." She looked at Pat with a smile that could melt the polar ice caps. "How have you been, Mr. Knox?"

"Good as an old man can be."

"Do you fight technology like this one?"

Pat nodded. "With everything I've got."

"I give up," she said, still smiling.

"I wish you would, but I know you won't," Dr. Murphy called after her as she left the room. He turned his attention back to Pat. "Like I said, everything is as it should be at this stage. As long as we keep an eye on that prostate of yours. How are you urinating?"

"Pretty frequently for a while, but it's starting to settle down."

"Still experiencing any burning sensation?"

Pat shook his head. "Thankfully, no."

"Good. You took to the medication well."

"It's my one remaining superpower. 'Takes to medication well.'"

The doctor chuckled. "How's your energy?"

Pat said, "What energy? I need a nap just from coming here."

"You still insist on taking care of Mary all by yourself?"

That was a sore point for Pat. When he was laid low with a blood infection last year, he could barely care for himself. But he knew that his responsibilities to his wife were what kept him going, prevented him from despairing about his own situation. You had little time for self-pity when the woman you loved needed you desperately. He'd beaten the infection, but it had taken a toll on him.

"Of course," Pat said, defiant.

Dr. Murphy put the tablet down and looked him in the eye. "What you need most right now is rest. I can give you pills and vitamin shots, but nothing can replace good old-fashioned R and R. If anything, consider getting someone to come by the house a couple of days a week for an hour or two, just to help out. If it works for you and Mary, you can add more hours. I really think having those moments to exhale will do wonders for the both of you."

Pat was pretty sure if he exhaled, he'd deflate entirely, and where would that leave them?

Instead, he said, "I'll think about it."

"I'll be happy to give you some recommendations. I can have Kelly look into it."

Standing up, Pat shook the doctor's hand and doffed his hat.

"As always, thanks for everything."

Dr. Murphy said, "You're not leaving just yet. Susan has to take some blood."

Pat sat back down. "Fine. Send the vampire in. You keep

taking all my blood, how am I ever supposed to get better?"

"All the more reason to get some help. See you next month."

Waiting for the nurse, Pat rolled up his sleeve. He wondered how many vials she'd take this time. He'd have to cook up a steak tonight to balance things out.

CHAPTER FOUR

"How'd you make out?" Pat asked Doyle. The man scratched at his scalp by poking a finger through one of the holes in his hat.

"Same as always. Just happy I can pay for his vacation house in Florida."

The rest of the drive home was quiet. Pat was too tired to engage in their usual banter, and Doyle seemed pensive. Men their age rarely got good news at the doctor. The best they could hope for was that things were status quo, but the bar for status quo had been lowered considerably.

Well, if and when Doyle was ready to talk about it, he would. There was no need to prod. Pat had learned long ago that he'd rather poke a beehive than Doyle.

"I have to make a quick stop at McDonald's," Pat said. "I promised Mary I'd bring her back one of those fish sandwiches. You want anything?"

Doyle shrugged. "That place will kill you dead."

"After eighty, a cold or a walk up the stairs can bring you to your Maker. I think we can handle a little fast food."

He spied the Golden Arches up ahead.

"Fine. I'll have a coffee then," Doyle said, his arms crossed over his chest.

"Two creams, no sugar?"

"Of course two creams and no sugar."

Pat placed their order at the drive-through, opting for a cheeseburger for himself. He didn't eat McDonald's often, but he was in no mind to whip up lunch. In fact, the burger and fish would carry him and Mary right through dinner. Maybe they'd snack on some pound cake later, during *Wheel*. Doyle lifted the lid of his cup and blew on it.

As Pat made the left onto Doyle's street, he hit the brakes. A splash of coffee landed on Doyle's lap.

"Jesus Christmas, are you trying to send me to the burn unit?"

Pat leaned into the steering wheel, peering out the window. "I wonder what's going on."

A throng of people had gathered outside one of the houses across from Doyle's. A sheriff's car took up most of the road. There was no way Pat could maneuver around it. Besides, there were too many people walking in the street for his comfort.

Doyle forgot about his burned leg. "It's Bridgett Monahan. What on earth happened to her?"

He got out of the car, slamming the door.

Curiosity had Pat putting the car in park and following. Most of the people in the crowd were older, some muttering among themselves, but most staring at the spectacle in wide-eyed wonder.

Bridgett Monahan struggled against the clutches of the sheriff, a burly man with a thick black mustache and dark sunglasses. Pat couldn't tell if he was trying to bring her in or out of the house.

When she spotted Doyle in the crowd, she shouted, "Sam! Please help me, they're taking my house away!"

Another man in uniform pushed his way through the crowd and grabbed ahold of Bridgett. As the crowd absorbed Pat, he noticed the furniture piled on the sidewalk. Someone stepped on his foot. He turned to come face-to-face with William Campbell. The octogenarian was known all around as Onion Breath, and for very good reason.

"So sorry," William said.

"It's fine," Pat said, quickly getting his nose upwind. "Why are Bridgett's belongings out on the street?"

"Sheriff was called in to evict her."

"Evict her? I know for a fact that her husband paid the mortgage off thirty years ago. I was at the barbecue they had to celebrate the event."

William couldn't tear his gaze away from his neighbor struggling against the police. "I don't know any particulars. They shouldn't handle her like that."

Bridgett Monahan was pushing ninety and small as a bird. That being said, she was giving the much younger men a run for their money. No matter how much they tried, they couldn't get her past the threshold of the house.

"Hey you, stop that!" Doyle barked. Everyone else, Pat realized, had been too stunned to speak on the woman's behalf. He saw a lot of fear in the eyes around him.

"Put her down or so help me, I'll call the real police," Doyle said.

"We are the real police. Now everyone, get back."

That only got Doyle to move closer, one foot on the cement stoop. He turned to Aggie Firth, his next-door neighbor of the past fifty years, and said, "Ags, go inside and call the police."

Aggie clutched at her necklace. Pat knew that within her palm was a charm of Mary.

"But he's right, Sam. They *are* the police."

"Please, just do it."

She hurried across the street and into her house, a couple of other women in her wake.

Pat sidled up next to Doyle. Bridgett was beginning to lose her strength. The two men lifted her off the ground while she screamed for all the world to hear. They took her down the steps, but their way was blocked by Doyle and Pat.

"You can't do this to me! Thieves! You're nothing but thieves!" Bridgett Monahan wailed. Her cheeks were bright red, but the rest of her had gone a concerning pale.

Pat felt weak in the knees. He was confused and angry and terrified.

Doyle, on the other hand, only seemed madder than a bull. He jabbed a finger at the sheriff.

"You stop right there," he growled. "You wouldn't treat a criminal like this, much less an old woman."

"I said get out of our way."

Doyle didn't budge. Pat took a faltering step back. He was instantly ashamed of his cowardice.

"What are you going to do? Shoot me? Go ahead. Do it right in front of all these people."

Pat scanned the crowd. If it was made up of young people, he knew there would be cell phones in every hand recording the event. He didn't see one. He had a cell phone himself but had never learned how to take a picture, much less a video, with it.

The deputy, a wiry man with sandy hair and a Vandyke beard, spoke up. "Sir, you're impeding an official in the course of duty. This is the last time we're going to ask you to step aside."

Doyle huffed. "Official duty? Since when is it your duty to cart people out of their homes and throw their possessions to the curb like tomorrow's trash? I'll have your badge . . . after I knock your block off."

A collective gasp went up around them.

"Hit him, Sam! Don't let them take me!"

Bridgett's writhing barely affected her captors. She winced in pain.

"Can't you see you're hurting her?" Pat said.

Now the sheriff, his eyes hidden behind those damn glasses, said, "We have to carry out evictions all the time. This doesn't have to be difficult."

"Oh, so people should just let you steal their home with a smile, huh? I'm sorry if we're making your job a wee bit harder. I'll tell you one thing, if you don't put her down this instant, your day is about to get much, much worse."

Pat reached a trembling hand out to his friend, but Doyle shrugged it away. Sure, Doyle never said no to an argument, but this was something else altogether. If the sheriff was here, there had to be a valid reason. Maybe if Doyle backed off, they could calm Bridgett down and settle things afterward. A lawyer was what Bridgett needed, not a cantankerous old fool.

The sheriff and deputy carried Bridgett down another step.

Doyle bumped his chest into the sheriff's considerable gut. He reached up to pry the man's hands off Bridgett.

"Get your hands off me!" the sheriff shouted.

"Doyle, don't," Pat pleaded.

Bridgett shot Pat a look that made him cringe. He could

see in her eyes that he was just as low as the men who were throwing her out of her house.

Bridgett found her second wind, twisting her arms, trying to slip her wrists out of their grasp. Doyle went to work on the sheriff's wrist. The people behind them cried out, some imploring Doyle to keep at it, others begging him to stop. Terror and indignation fought for control of the crowd.

The sheriff nudged Doyle, both of them losing their footing.

Doyle's plan had worked. At least half of Bridgett was free. However, both Doyle and the sheriff fell down the few hard steps, Doyle landing on his back, the bulky sheriff atop him.

Pat's stomach flipped when he heard a dull snap.

Doyle cried out in agony.

The sheriff jumped to his feet, staring down the crowd.

Bridgett had gone silent. A single word passed her lips. "Sam."

The deputy wrapped his other arm around her waist and carried her down to the sidewalk.

"Doyle!" Pat went to his friend, his knees aching as he crouched down. Doyle clutched his side. His face was pulled into a rictus of pain.

"Something broke," Doyle hissed between his gritted teeth. "I think it's my leg. Or my hip. Jesus, Mary, and Joseph!" He cut his gaze to the sheriff and actually spat at him. "You won't have a job after this, you goddamn fat son of a bitch. I'll make sure of that!"

Pat turned to make sure the sheriff wasn't going to finish what was started. He knelt between the men, feeling helpless and afraid. "Somebody call for an ambulance!"

He noted with thanks as a few people peeled off from the crowd, heading inside and, hopefully, to their phones.

Doyle had tears in the corners of his eyes. Pat had never seen him like this before. It only added to the cold knot of tension in the center of his chest. "We're going to get you help real soon."

"Forget about me. Don't let them put Bridgett in that car. Once they do, it's all over for her."

What did Doyle expect him to do? Even in his younger days, he wouldn't dare take on two men, much less two men with guns.

He was startled from his inner conflict by someone shouting, "I think she's having a heart attack!"

Bridgett's mouth was pulled into a grim line, her eyes squeezed shut. Her body went rigid as a pole, her skin gone a deadly shade of pale. Sweat poured down her face.

The deputy stopped trying to get her in the back seat of the car, instead laying her on the ground. He spoke quickly into the mic attached to a band on his shoulder. Even the sheriff hustled to tend to Bridgett.

Her back arched, and she suddenly went very, very still. Her head rolled to the side, her mouth opening wide enough for her tongue to loll out, inches from the filthy pavement.

"You killed her!" Doyle hollered through pained breaths. "Are you happy now? You killed her!"

CHAPTER FIVE

Pat sat beside Mary in a hardback chair in their bedroom. He couldn't stop his hands from shaking, even with both of them holding onto a glass of Jameson. He hadn't had a whiskey in years. He knew he'd need more than just this one glass if he ever expected to settle down.

"It was terrible. Just terrible," he said.

Tears shimmered in Mary's eyes.

"The poor woman. I just can't believe it. How was she when the paramedics got there?" she asked.

The images of the men working to resuscitate Bridgett Monahan replayed in his mind, making his hands tremble even more. He couldn't dispel the image of the blue pallor of her face or the graying of her eyes.

He hung his head, staring into the amber liquid. "It didn't look good. Not good at all. I wouldn't be surprised to find that she passed before they ever got her in the ambulance. They'll say she died at the hospital because they need a physician to officially make that call, but I tell you, she was already gone."

Mary gasped. She tried to lift her hand to her mouth, the frail limb instead falling onto her stomach.

"I . . . I just can't believe it," Mary stammered. "If Bill was alive . . ."

"It wouldn't have happened. And if it did, it would have killed him, too, seeing her like that."

Pat was both bone weary and wired. He was sure he wouldn't fall asleep so much as pass out. The whiskey would help. He wanted a moment of peace from the unceasing swell of emotions and vivid memories of the afternoon's events. What frightened him was the thought that they would only slip into his dreams.

"And Doyle?" Mary asked, her voice paper thin.

"They think it's his hip. Might be broken in more than one place, from what I heard and the way he was acting. I told him I'd go to the hospital with him, but he made me promise I'd come back home to you. I'll go see him tomorrow as soon as visiting hours begin."

"Do you know what hospital?"

"I made sure to ask. He'll be at St. Luke's."

Mary pushed her head against the pillows and sniffled. Pat plucked a tissue from the nearby box and dabbed at her eyes and nose.

"I'm having a hard time believing any of this is real," she said. "Bridgett was a good woman. Bill did well to provide for her, even all these years after his death. How could this happen? How?"

Pat took a deep breath and shook his head. "I don't know. I don't care what might have happened to put her in that situation. No one should throw a woman out of the home she's lived in all of her adult life. And that she had to die from it? It's not just unconscionable, it's immoral."

Sipping at the whiskey, he stood up to work out some of the nervous energy.

"Can you pass me my rosary beads?" Mary asked. "I want to pray for Bridgett. And Doyle, too."

Pat kept her blue, crystal rosary beads on a small hook he'd affixed to the wall by her bed. He placed them in her hands, her thumb and forefinger rubbing at the beads. She closed her eyes and her lips moved silently. He knew enough to leave her be for a while. Mary coped with bad news by praying. He'd often been proud to tell people that Mary's direct prayers to the Father, Son, and Holy Ghost had saved their bacon plenty of times.

Walking out of the room, he took the stairs one at a time, worried that his knees would buckle or the whiskey would hit him like a freight train, making the room spin. Once he was downstairs, he poured a little more Jameson into the glass and practically fell into his easy chair. The silence of the house was too overwhelming. It invited the sounds of Doyle's hips breaking and Bridgett's cries for help. He turned on the television, not caring what was on, only that it was loud and distracting.

There was a time he might have joined Mary in prayer. Not today. Sometimes, he wondered about a God who could let such things happen. Maybe it was a sin to question their Maker, to doubt his divine plan, but so be it. If that made Pat a sinner, he was fine with it.

Being a sinner felt far preferable to his role as an impotent old man. Sinners had hope for redemption. He wasn't going to get any younger, stronger, or braver.

Not in this life.

When it was time for him to pass on, would Bridgett Monahan be there waiting for him?

"*Why didn't you help me?*"

What would he say? Would he ask forgiveness, or try

to explain that no matter how he looked at it, there was nothing he could have done?

Pat closed his eyes and saw Bridgett's accusatory glare as she struggled against the sheriff and deputy.

If you don't have a solution, you're part of the problem.

"I don't know what I could have done."

Maybe he was right. He'd been powerless to stop what had already started.

It didn't lessen the guilt. Not one iota.

The next day was slow going for Pat. His body cried out for him to stay in bed. Getting Mary situated in the morning had him out of breath. He was just going to have to fight his way through it. Visiting hours at St. Luke's started at eleven. The plan was to pick a few things up for Doyle before heading over.

"I'll be back sometime after noon," he said to his wife, shrugging on a blue flannel shirt.

"Your complexion looks like spoiled cream. Maybe you should stay home."

Mary was propped up in her bed, a fresh sheet draped over her. The television was on low, tuned to the local morning news. They were calling for rain that night, and the slate-gray skies outside the windows confirmed it. So did the swelling in Pat's joints.

"I promised Doyle I'd see him. Plus, I need to get the man some necessities. If I don't do it, no one else will."

Mary rolled her eyes. "That's because he's such a pleasure to be around."

Pat chuckled. "He is at that. I like to think of him as grossly misunderstood."

"Sam Doyle has been playing the part of the bristly curmudgeon since we were in our twenties."

"And practice makes perfect. It takes a special person to understand a special man."

"Now don't go thinking either of you are all that special," Mary said with a playful smirk.

Tucking his shirt into his pants, Pat said, "Oh no, we wouldn't want that. Speaking of wanting, is there anything I can get you while I'm out? I could stop at Beth's Bakery and pick you up a black-and-white cookie."

"I'm not adding to your itinerary. I want you to see Doyle and get right back here for a long nap. I'm not going to be able to rest until you're in that bed. Understood?"

He squeezed her hand. "Clear as Waterford crystal."

The thought of a nap filled him with longing. He knew he could take one right now, even though he'd just woken up an hour ago. The promise of a reward at least should light a fire under his keister.

Searching for Mary's cell phone, he found it on the floor between her bed and the night table. Bending down to get it was no small task. He put it in her left hand.

"In case of emergency," he said.

He'd set the speed dial for both 911 and their next-door neighbor, Anna McCurty. Even though Mary had limited mobility in her extremities, she could easily call for assistance if needed.

"Be careful," she called to him as he ambled down the stairs.

"I'll try."

The air was cold and damp, and there was a chilly breeze that had him shivering underneath his tried-and-true black peacoat. A gust of wind nearly snatched the hat right off his head. The car's heater took forever to warm up. At least the cold had him more awake.

On the way to St. Luke's, he stopped at O'Toole's Stationery. The place had a little bit of everything, which was just perfect. He got a toothbrush and travel-sized toothpaste, a comb, deodorant, the newspaper, and a couple of magazines.

As he was being rung up, he felt someone tap his back.

"I heard you were there, Pat."

He turned to see the stricken expression on Maureen Kennedy's face. Her white hair was piled into a bun big enough to hide two cats within. Her fingers worked nervously on a dainty leather glove.

"Sad to say, I was."

"They say Bridgett passed from the stress."

Pat had yet to hear anything official, but in his heart, he had known it couldn't be any other way.

"It was terrible," he said. "Sam Doyle was hurt, as well. I'm just going over to St. Luke's now to see him." He held up the plastic bag as if to prove that he was on his way and bearing gifts.

Maureen clucked her tongue. "People are saying she was evicted. I don't see how that can be."

"I don't, either. Maybe it was a problem with taxes. Not that that gives anyone a right to do what was done to her."

"It's terrifying. She was all alone in that house, but it was her house. Free and clear. Just like mine. It makes me wonder if it can happen to me."

He patted her shoulder. "I wouldn't borrow misery. I've never seen the likes of it before, and I hope to never see it again."

It was obvious his words did little to alleviate her fears.

She looked furtively around the store and whispered, "I'm thinking it's one of those scams they're always trying to play on seniors. You get a strange call that asks for your personal information so they can access your account at the power company or the bank. In a moment of weakness, you say the wrong thing, and look what happens."

Pat read about the numerous frauds targeted at senior citizens all the time in the paper and AARP's magazine. It was a shame that they had to always be on their toes, the vultures out there waiting for them to drop their guard.

"It could have been that, yes," he said. "But the Bridgett I knew would never give a stranger anything more than her first name, if that."

"She hadn't been well. I saw her at church two Sundays ago, and she wasn't herself. When I walked over to her to say hello, it took her a bit to even recognize me. The poor woman."

That only infuriated Pat more.

"I'm sure we'll learn more soon enough. Don't you go worrying about yourself. You'll be fine."

She struggled to put her gloves on, the leather having a hard time stretching over knuckles deformed by arthritis. "Some days, I feel like all I do is worry."

Chapter Six

The details of why Bridgett Monahan had been evicted from her home never did come to light. Bridgett had no children, and there was no one left to tell her side of the story. That led to worried whispers of speculation in the shops, homes, and church of Woodlean.

All they did know was that Bridgett had not just departed her home but this world, as well. The day of her funeral was bitter and rainy, forcing many of her friends and neighbors to mourn her from their homes.

Pat Knox was one of those friends who couldn't make it to St. Brendan's Church. He'd come down with a terrible cold and could barely make it down the stairs to get food for himself and Mary. He worried that it might be the flu, the symptoms getting worse as it dragged into its second week. What he needed was a doctor, but there was no way he could make it to Dr. Murphy's. Pat missed the days where doctors made house calls, like Dr. Murphy's father had until he retired, oh so long ago. This neighborhood could keep the medical profession quite busy, seven days a week.

What bothered him more than his lingering illness was that he couldn't take care of Mary as well as he felt he should. He knew her sheets needed changing, and she was overdue for a bath. Neither was a task he was up to tackling. He might as well have been asked to build a skyscraper with his bare hands.

"Let me call Anna," Mary said as they watched one of the many court shows on during the early afternoon. "I'm sure we're running low on food."

It hurt to lift his head off the pillow. Pat didn't need a thermometer to know he had a low-grade fever. Even his skin hurt to the touch. "Give it another day. We still have soup. I can make some hard-boiled eggs, too."

When he thought about the walk down to the kitchen and the act of warming up the soup and boiling the eggs, the wind, what little there was, went out of his sails. Later. After a nap. They'd be fine for now.

"You remember when you and I came down with strep throat at the same time," Mary asked, turning her head to see him. Her frail body looked like a bundle of sticks under the sheet, but still she was smiling.

Pat remembered it well. Strep had hit them hard, and the first round of antibiotics didn't work. They'd been laid up and pretty much out of commission for a week. "My throat hurts just thinking about it."

"Johnnie and Joe were ten and twelve at the time. Those boys who refused to clean up after themselves and tracked more mud into this house than a soggy gardener took such good care of us. They washed the dishes, got themselves ready for school every morning, cooked our meals . . ."

Pat chuckled, the act hurting his ribs. "We ate a lot of toast and cereal that week."

"At least they didn't try to make a roast. They probably would have burned the house down."

"With us in it, too sick to make a run for it."

Mary sighed, staring wistfully at the ceiling. "I miss them, Pat. Don't you feel sometimes that we should have moved to be close to them?"

Pat missed his sons very much. Joe, their oldest, had left after college, headed to New York to start a career in advertising. Over the years, he'd changed vocations several times. He was currently in Sacramento, managing the IT department of a company that did something Pat never quite understood. Sacramento seemed to do Joe good. He found a wife there, had two children, and his wanderlust finally exhausted itself. If they'd picked up stakes and tried to follow Joe, they would have either gone broke or crazy . . . or both.

Johnnie went straight from high school into the army, doing a four-year stint at Fort Bliss in Texas. From there, he used the GI Bill to get his college degree at Seton Hall University, going straight from there to Portland, Maine, where he was now the director of sales for a company that specialized in health care research. He and his wife, Marion, had tried desperately to have children, but it wasn't in the cards. There was a time they'd considered adoption, but the cost was so high. In the end, they decided to foster children instead, offering a warm and loving home to children in desperate need of stability and love. At the last count, they had fostered six children, ranging in age from three to thirteen. Johnnie was the more stable of their sons, but Pat could never imagine living through a Maine winter.

Which is why they'd stayed in Woodlean, in their precious home, their doors always open for their family.

It would be grand to have Joe or Johnnie walk through those doors right now and lend them a hand. Though Pat would never say that out loud. Male pride always got in his way.

"We could either freeze in Maine or fry like bacon in Sacramento," he said. "No, thank you. I'm a man of temperate climate." When Mary remained silent, he added, "Besides, this house is as much a part of our family as the boys. Except it can't go out in the world and make its way. It needs us just as much as we need it."

When she looked to him, a lone tear trickled down the side of her face. "For a daft old man, you can say the most wonderful things. I love our home, too. I just wish I could turn back time and have it filled with the sound of our boys clomping up the stairs and asking what's for dinner."

"And those fights. There were times I thought they'd go through the floor." Pat had become a world-class referee, thanks to those boys. To say they were spirited and opinionated was putting things lightly.

Pat fell into a fitful, feverish sleep, dreaming about his sons and missing them so deeply, he at least allowed his dream self to cry.

By the following Sunday, Pat was feeling like himself again and strong enough to go to church. He and Doyle were ushers, but it didn't look like Doyle would be coming back anytime soon. His hip and pelvis had been fractured, and he was in a rehabilitation center—a fancy name for a nursing home—until he was healed and could get around again. Doyle's normal irritation had risen to maximum levels. He was talking with a lawyer about suing the sheriff's department. That wasn't going to be enough for Doyle. He wanted the man run out of town on a rail.

Dressed in his good suit, Pat took his time walking to St. Brendan's. It was only three blocks away, but two of them were uphill. People passed him by, nodding or saying hello, the walk so effortless for them. It had been for him, too, once upon a time.

A little out of breath, he was greeted by Father Biglin.

"How have you been, Pat? Mass hasn't been the same without you."

Father Biglin was in his early fifties, his hair completely gray, making him look older. He'd been with the parish since his graduation from the seminary and word was he'd be named monsignor next year. He was a good man who took his calling seriously but had a kind heart and warm smile.

"I weathered the storm. It's good to be out in the fresh air, I tell you."

"And how is Mary?"

As people filed into the church, the father smiled and wished them a good morning.

"The same. She didn't catch what I had, thank God."

"This is the perfect place to thank him. I hear Sam Doyle is in rehabilitation."

"Unhappily so. I have a feeling they'll send him home soon enough just to be done with him."

Father Biglin laughed. "Knowing Doyle's disposition, I wouldn't be surprised. It will be nice to have my two top ushers back in the game. Well, I have to get ready. It's great to see you in the pink."

The mass began in short order. Pat helped the usual late arrivals to their pews, Father Biglin giving him a wink while Betty Knowles gave the first reading. The day's service was dedicated to Bridgett Monahan as they prayed for her soul in heaven. Pat swooned for a moment, again recalling her last, desperate moments. He found a folding chair in the narthex, where he waited until it was time to pass the basket for the offering.

After that was complete, Noel Simons, one of the younger ushers on the team at just under seventy, whispered to him, "Are you feeling okay, Pat? You look pretty pale."

In truth, Pat was feeling far from okay. The thought of walking back home to where his bed awaited filled him with dread.

He gave a gentle tap on Noel's back. "First day out is always the toughest. Just need more time to get my sea legs."

"Maybe getting a little air might help."

"It might. I'll give it a go."

Walking through the big doors, he was met by a cool breeze and warming rays of the sun. He took a few deep breaths, but he still felt weak and tired. He stayed outside until mass let out, rows of people streaming through the doors. Pat stepped aside, chatting with a few of his neighbors, doing his best to smile through it.

Father Biglin shook hands with everyone he could, reminding them of the Rosary Society's bake sale next week. As the last parishioners made their way out, the priest came to Pat and said, "Noel told me you weren't feeling well. I'll drive you home."

"It's no worry, Father. I'm just three blocks away."

"From the look of you, Pat, it may as well be three miles in heavy snow. Accepting charity is as Christian as giving charity. Just give me a few minutes to pop out of my game day uniform. Wait right here." He dragged a chair outside, setting it directly under a shaft of sunlight. "So you can make Mary jealous of your tan."

Pat was grateful for the seat and the offer of a ride. He almost fell asleep in the short time it took Father Biglin to reappear. He was in his black pants and shirt, white collar around his neck.

"I had to be on the road anyway," the priest said. "The Capitals are playing this afternoon, and I need to get some beer and chips."

They walked slowly to Father's modest Honda. The seat was soft and worn in, so much so that Pat was afraid he might conk out before they made it to his house.

"Thank you very much, Father. The quicker I'm back in bed, the better."

"Anytime, anytime." He handed him a postcard. "I'm not sure you saw this on the bulletin board. There's a company that came to speak to me a few months back called We Care. They have a variety of elder services, and they said they were offering a ten percent discount to anyone from the parish."

Pat looked at the laminated card, but without his glasses he couldn't make out much. It had a picture of a smiling woman helping an equally happy old man out of his wheelchair. You'd think the both of them had just won the lottery, they were so ecstatic.

He said, "Thank you, but I'm still holding my own."

Father Biglin came to a rolling stop in front of Pat's house. "Everyone can use a little help every now and then. You've done an admirable job taking care of Mary, and the house, and anyone who's ever come to you in need. It's time you took care of yourself, and the best way to do that is to give yourself over to someone with as big a heart as your own."

The priest made it sound so natural, so inviting. Allowing someone into his home to care for him and Mary was a line in the sand that he was terrified to cross. Time had taken so much from them. Their independence was just about all they had left. If he allowed this line to be crossed, the only other thing left to be taken was their lives.

"I'll think about it," he said. "Thank you for thinking of us."

"I think about all of you. Don't feel like you'll be alone. Quite a few people have taken We Care up on their offer already, and I've heard nothing but good things. A little rest and some peace of mind can do wonders."

Pat stared at the postcard, then stuffed it in his shirt pocket.

"I promise, I'll talk to Mary about it."

"Good man. And I know Mary. She's the sensible one. She'll talk you into it."

He was right. Mary would insist, especially when it came with an endorsement from Father Biglin. Which was why he was contemplating holding off on telling her about it.

Pat got out of the car and tapped the hood. "Enjoy the game."

"I will if they win. God's a fan of the Capitals, so we have that."

He watched the Honda drive away, looked up at his house—in need of more attention and labor than he could give—and trudged inside, almost asleep before he settled into his easy chair.

The office was quiet for a change. Deputy Sheriff Kenny Carlson remembered when that was the norm. Not so lately. He settled back in his chair and sipped the sludge that passed for coffee. The phone sat in the center of his desk, mercifully silent.

The cup shook slightly in his hand. He moved his head forward to meet the lip of the cup halfway before he spilled any on his uniform.

It had been almost a week since that nightmare with the woman, and he was still a mess. Why the hell did she have to fight so hard? And where did the frail old woman find the strength to do it? He knew the instant he saw that crowd of dinosaurs that things were going to go badly.

They were just doing their job. When a person lost a house, it's not like they could just decide to never leave. Someone had to get them out. That someone was him. The whole eviction process had ceased bothering him years ago. After a while, you become callous to the whole drama. People pled and cried and screamed and threatened, until it was just white noise—a wall of sound between him and his desire to get the job done, go home, and have a few beers.

But no one had ever died before.

The sheriff was madder than a starved junkyard dog. And Carlson, being the only deputy in the department and always around, had to bear the brunt of his anger. Plus, there was all the damn paperwork that Carlson had been ordered to complete. He hated paperwork more than throwing old people out of houses.

His phone chirped, letting him know it was time for lunch. Normally, he'd head to the diner and grab a cheeseburger or BLT, but with all the added stress, he just wasn't hungry.

Instead, he thought of that old man who had broken his hip. Sam Doyle. If that crusty old bastard hadn't shown up, Carlson and the sheriff could have easily chucked the woman into the back of the car and been out of there. There wouldn't have been all that back and forth. Oh, sure, Bridgett Monahan would have hooted and hollered the whole way, but he knew that time spent in the back of a patrol car had a way of quieting people down.

Sam Doyle had killed her.

Not him.

He kept telling himself that over and over. Holding his hand in front of his face, Carlson saw the trembling abate.

Yep.

If there was a God, Doyle would drop dead himself in the hospital, just like most old-timers when they broke their hips. It would serve him right.

"Wasn't me."

He got up from the creaky chair, thumped the desk with his fist, and left the station. He suddenly craved a hot, greasy cheeseburger.

CHAPTER SEVEN

The flu returned and blossomed into a mild case of pneumonia. Just the word *pneumonia* was a dagger of fear that pricked the hearts of every man and woman Pat Knox's age. More often than not, pneumonia meant "welcome to the last exit on the expressway." Pat had to take a taxi the day of his appointment to see Dr. Murphy because he didn't trust himself driving. He was afraid of nodding off at the wheel or not having the reflexes to avoid an accident.

The doctor wanted him to go straight to the hospital, but he refused. Hospitals were rife with disease. With his luck—because the luck of the Irish wasn't always good—he'd come down with something far worse, like that killer MRSA infection that would take a few of his limbs before it finished him off.

Not wanting to do battle with him in his frail state, Dr. Murphy sent him home with several prescriptions and strict instructions to stay in bed. Anna next door had been wonderful, making sure he and Mary were fed and the house wasn't a disaster. But there were limits to what they'd ask of her, and they felt terrible for imposing.

It was even difficult for Pat to read, his concentration was that fuzzy and limited. Days and nights bled into one another, the steady blather from the television his and Mary's sole distraction. One night, Mary wept, asking his forgiveness for being, what she felt, was a failure of a wife. What kind of woman, she intoned, could only sit helpless and watch her sick husband suffer? She was a smart woman, and she knew he didn't go to the hospital because he refused to leave her alone.

"I couldn't have asked for a better, more caring woman to put up with me for sixty years," he'd said, his head spinning when he got out of bed to dry her eyes. "You forget, I wasn't one of these new age men who share the load in the house. You did it all, and you kept me and the boys healthy, clean, and happy. If anyone deserves a rest, it's you. Now, no more crying, my sweet. One more tear, and I'll be forced to sing you a lullaby to sleep."

Mary sniffled. "Please, not that."

"One . . . more . . . tear."

Doyle liked to tell everyone that Pat sang like an amputee—he couldn't hold a note or carry a tune. Tact was not one of Doyle's strong suits.

Though he was right. Pat's voice could bring down the house, and not in a good way.

Pat pulled up a chair that night, and he and Mary talked about the old days, recalling vacations to Gettysburg and Tampa, and the time Pat fell overboard in their rented boat and almost couldn't get back in. He fell asleep in the chair, his head on Mary's lap.

Two days later, he felt no better. His chest hurt, and coughing was difficult. Mary needed to be bathed. He'd almost dropped her taking her to the bathroom in the morning.

As much as he hated to admit it, they needed help.

Mustering up his strength, he went downstairs, pulled his coat out of the closet, and found the postcard from We Care. He broached the subject with Mary, regretting his decision as he heard the words coming out of his mouth, but what else could he do? Heaven knew how long this would drag on. Johnnie and Joe had their own lives and careers. They couldn't put them on hold just to play nursemaids to him and Mary.

"It's about time," Mary said, relieved. "I wasn't going to bring it up because I know what a pigheaded old fool you can be. You should have listened to Father Biglin when he first told you about it."

"I didn't have pneumonia then," he said, a short, painful cough stabbing his lungs.

"You weren't exactly doing cartwheels, either." Mary fussed with her rosary beads. He had a feeling there'd be a prayer of thanks for making her mule of a husband finally see the light. "Take a nap now, and call them in the afternoon."

Pat felt as if he had bags of sand on his shoulders. "That's exactly what I'll do. If I can figure out the speakerphone, we can talk to them together."

"Deciphering technology?" Mary said, an eyebrow arched. "You better make that a long nap, then."

Pat slept for close to two hours.

And then he called We Care, sans speakerphone. He

gave them enough information to fill a book. They said someone would come out the day after next to meet with them and evaluate their needs. He spent that time coughing, struggling to cater to Mary's needs, and sleeping.

The woman who came was pleasant and professional. Her name was Bethany. She was on the far side of middle age, and had the air of someone who had been doing this for years. Dressed in a skirt that went to her mid-calf and a blue blazer, she had several files prepared with information in her briefcase. She sat with Pat and Mary in the bedroom and went over the various tasks that a home aide could do for them. She also wanted to know what duties they didn't want to share with an aide. Both Pat and Mary thought that was considerate. It made them feel in charge, not just a couple of overgrown, dependent children. Best of all, it was affordable.

Two days later, Isabelle came into their lives.

Isabelle Perez was from Guatemala. In her late twenties, she had coal-black hair and chestnut skin that made her stick out like a sore thumb in the Woodlean neighborhood. Pat had waited by the front window that first day, peering through the blinds like Doyle. The agency said Isabelle didn't drive and would be taking the bus. There was a convenient stop two blocks away. He watched her walk down the street, his neighbors pausing to stare at her as she breezed past. It was a sure thing that he and Mary would be the talk of the town as reports of her going into their house spread like wildfire.

Pat had been skeptical, but Isabelle's smile and calm demeanor set him at ease right away. She came carrying two reusable shopping bags that she set down on the floor. The first thing she said to him was, "Do you remember the story about the shoemaker and the elves?"

A bit confused, Pat said, "Of course. We told it to our boys a thousand times."

Patting his shoulder, she said, "I may not have new shoes for you, but I promise that after you take a nice, re-laxing nap, you'll think elves came in and took care of everything in the house."

Her teeth were white as marble, and she spoke English fluently, with just a hint of an accent. Pat assumed she had been in America since she was young. And he didn't miss her hint that he looked as bad as he felt and should lie down and rest.

He took her up to meet Mary, and the two of them got into a conversation about the latest exploits of some movie star who had left his wife for his ex-wife. Isabelle had seen the pile of gossip rags on Mary's table, and Pat left them to become instant friends. The moment his body hit the bed, he felt as if he'd sunk into it so deep, he'd need a line to pull him out. He was feverish and bone weary, and before he knew it, he was asleep.

Hours later, he awoke to a room that smelled spring fresh. Mary was dressed in clean pajamas, her hair brushed and styled the way she used to wear it, before she had to rely on Pat to be a hairdresser of sorts. He noticed her sheets had been changed. The garbage pails had been emptied, and everything was tidied up.

"How long was I out?" he said, his throat feeling raw.

"As long as you needed to be," Mary said.

"She really is an elf."

"What was that?"

He rubbed his knuckles into his eyes, trying to get his bearings. His head was still soupy. "Nothing. Is Isabelle still here?"

Mary smiled. "Yes. She's downstairs making us dinner as well as something to heat up for breakfast tomorrow before she gets here. She is such a doll."

"Mmm-hmm."

"And pretty, too."

Pat knew enough not to say anything to that. They may have been married for longer than the Cold War, but that didn't make either of them immune to tiny pangs of jealousy.

"What's she cooking?" he asked instead. The aroma coming from downstairs was unfamiliar to him.

Mary had to think for a moment. "I think she said it was chicken pepian."

"What in the name of all that's holy is a chicken pepian?"

"She said it's like a stew. It's a big thing where her family is from. Oh, and she's making rice to go with it."

Now, Pat's culinary adventures usually went as exotic as Italian food. He'd never had, or seen, Guatemalan food. But he had to admit it did smell good. And it was chicken. He liked chicken.

Isabelle served them dinner in bed, and Pat had to admit it was delicious. She stayed long enough to clean up and make sure they had everything they needed for the night. Despite his aching bones, Pat walked her to the door and thanked her for everything.

"It was my pleasure," Isabelle said. "Your wife is a wonderful woman. And so funny."

"You should catch her act when she's making fun of me."

Isabelle covered her mouth when she laughed. "I look

forward to it. I'll be back the day after tomorrow. Unless, of course, you've changed your mind. It's not easy letting a stranger into your house. Believe me, it's not easy being the stranger. I'll understand, no matter what you decide."

"Thank you, Isabelle. You have a safe ride home."

He stayed at the door as she walked to the bus stop. There was a nip in the air, and it sent him into a coughing fit. The walk up to the bedroom seemed to take forever, but at least he could rest knowing everything had been taken care of.

Isabelle was welcome back. That nap he'd taken was the best he'd had in a long while, knowing Mary had company and was being tended to.

It made him wonder why he hadn't done this long ago.

CHAPTER EIGHT

"So, how are things going with your Mexican chippie?"

It felt good to talk to Doyle, and feeling good was something in short supply for Pat Knox. His immune system was having a hard time overcoming the pneumonia, and the medication only seemed to be making him worse. His brain was in a fog for most of the day, especially in the hours after taking his pills. He'd made it a point to call Doyle before his first dose. A pair of chickadees chirped from the tree outside his and Mary's bedroom window. The sun was out, and it promised to be a seasonable, sunny day. If he'd been feeling well at all, he would have felt guilty for staying in bed.

"She's not Mexican. She's from Guatemala," Pat said.

"It's all the same."

"I don't think she'd agree with you."

Doyle clucked his tongue. Pat pulled the phone away from his ear. "They all speak Spanish, don't they?"

"So that would make you the same as someone from Scotland, right?"

"Don't be obstinate," Doyle grumbled.

"Coming from you, that may be the funniest thing I've

heard in weeks. Isabelle has been great. I don't know what we would have done without her. So, how is the rehab going? When are they showing you the door?"

Doyle was still in the nursing home, the recovery from his fractured hip and pelvis slow going. Like most things in their lives.

"Ah, who the hell knows? As long as there's a red cent to be made off me, they'll keep me trapped in this godforsaken place. I think they want me to demonstrate I can do the twist before I can set sail."

Pat knew that Doyle, despite his moaning, was not in any shape to come home. If he was, the old codger would have walked home on his own by now.

"I'm not sure you could have ever done the twist. You're about as rigid as a steel pole."

Pat's laugh turned into a wet, rumbling coughing fit.

"You sound like you should be in the bed next to me," Doyle said, his voice laced with concern. "Why the hell aren't you in a hospital yourself?"

Pat's lungs felt as if he had inhaled fire. Settling his breathing, he said, "You know why."

"Sure, before you had the Mexican girl."

"Guatemalan."

"Whatever. Pat, if you don't take care of yourself, you're not going to be there for Mary anyway."

"There's nothing they could do in a hospital that isn't being done here." Pat knew he was being defensive. The last thing he wanted to talk about was the hospital.

Doyle must have picked up on it, because he changed tracks. "Did you hear about Annie Fahey?"

"I haven't heard about anything other than what's on the news."

"It sounds like Bridgett Monahan all over again. They say she was removed from her house, though poor Annie couldn't put up a fight. It took an ambulance to remove her on a stretcher. The next day, a truck came and a bunch of men removed everything from her house. Aggie says it's like she was never there at all. Jesus, Mary, and Joseph, she lived her entire life in that house."

Aggie Firth was both Doyle's neighbor and the head of what they called the Widows' Brigade. The neighborhood was comprised of mostly women, the husbands having met their Maker long before them. The Widows' Brigade made it a point to visit the sick and care for the single men when needed. Doyle might have been a royal pain in the ass, but he was a lonely, single man, and the Widows' Brigade made it a point to take him under their wing. Aggie, or one of the other many widows in the neighborhood, stopped by the nursing home every two to three days to check on Doyle, bringing him food and the latest gossip. So even though Doyle was "trapped" in a nursing home all the way across town, he was still more plugged into things than Pat.

"Does anyone know where Annie is now?" Pat said, recalling that day outside Bridgett's house. The pang of shame felt like a knife twisting in his gut.

"No. Aggie and her gang are trying to track her down. For all we know, she was shipped to some home in Maryland."

"But do you know if she was evicted?"

"I'm sure of it," Doyle said.

"You can't be sure of it. Annie has been bedridden for, what, the past five years? Maybe her health took a turn."

Sounding impatient, Doyle replied, "Sure, things were

only going to get worse for the poor girl. It was either the home or the morgue at that point. But if it was time to go to a home or a hospital, why was her house emptied out less than twenty-four hours later? Something's not right, Pat. They wiped her off the face of the earth, just like Bridgett."

Pat hoped that was not the case and that Annie was still very much around, preferably safe and with people to look after her. He looked across at Mary. She'd fallen asleep reading a magazine that had been clipped to a board so she didn't have to hold it upright. He pictured what happened to Annie befalling his wife. It made him sick with worry and hot with anger.

Doyle continued talking, but Pat couldn't hear him over his own troubled thoughts.

"Mr. Knox?"

Pat pulled himself from a deep, unsettling dream. Already the sounds and images that had made his heart race were falling away like a spiderweb in a nor'easter.

Isabelle stood over his bed, smiling as always. She had a small plastic cup in one hand and a glass of water in another. She put them down on the table and went to the bathroom, returning with a cold, wet washcloth. Isabelle dabbed at his forehead and face, wiping his sweat and chasing the burning sensation just under his skin away.

"Are you all right?" Mary said. "You were mumbling in your sleep and tossing and turning. I tried to wake you up, but you didn't hear me."

Pat felt a flush of embarrassment. Shifting so he could

sit up in bed, he took the washcloth from Isabelle and set it on the edge of his night table.

"I'm fine. I'm fine. Must be the fever again."

"Can you take his temperature?" Mary said.

"Yes, of course." Isabelle went back into the bathroom.

"I'm not having something stuck under my tongue. My mouth feels like it's filled with paste."

"It's up to you," Mary said. "Choose an end, because you're having your temperature taken."

Her teasing grin melted his resolve. He might have felt helpless, but he couldn't fight Mary. Even trapped in her bed, she was still a force to be reckoned with. And now she had the very able-bodied Isabelle to carry out her dirty work.

When Isabelle came into the room with the thermometer, Pat opened his mouth wide, lifting his tongue.

"Thank you, Mrs. Knox," Isabelle said, inserting the thermometer.

"Thank Pat for saving you both a world of embarrassment."

"Ha, ha," Pat said, making sure the thermometer stayed in place.

"Almost a hundred and two," Isabelle said.

"You should see Dr. Murphy," Mary said.

"I don't think I could make it out the bedroom door today."

"I can carry you, if I need to," Isabelle said. The girl couldn't weigh more than a hundred and twenty pounds soaking wet with rocks in her pockets. She lifted her arms in a weight lifter's pose. "I'm stronger than I look. I used to whip my older brother in wrestling."

"Then I'll make it a point not to wrestle you," Pat said.

"Tomorrow. I'll see him tomorrow. Just give me a day to rest and sweat this fever out."

"I've given you weeks, Pat. You're not getting any better. If Dr. Murphy wants to admit you this time, you let him," Mary said sharply. "I mean it. I'll be fine. Isabelle will take care of me, won't you, sweetie?"

Isabelle adjusted the sheet and blankets around Pat and lifted his head so she could fluff his pillows. "I sure will. And I can bring you anything you need in the hospital, Mr. Knox. You won't have to worry about a thing."

If that were only the case. Sometimes, Pat felt that worry was the only thing keeping him going. If he ended up in the hospital, Mary would be left behind in the house, bedridden, just like Annie Fahey. He wished to hell Doyle hadn't told him about that. It made his stance of staying out of the hospital all the more solid.

"Ladies, I promise it won't come to that. By tomorrow, I'll be on the mend."

It sounded false even to his ears.

"Well, today that means you have to take your medicine," Isabelle said, handing him the cup of pills and water. He tossed them onto the back of his tongue and swallowed the lot with a small sip like a veteran pill taker. Thinking about it, Pat was hard pressed to come up with anyone his age who wasn't on enough pills to choke a horse.

"As you can see, I can be an obedient patient," he said. His head throbbed, and every breath felt like a chore. Still, he smiled for Mary.

"When you choose to be," Mary said. "Is there anything you want to watch? I saw there's a Natalie Wood and

Warren Beatty movie on in a few minutes." She turned to Isabelle. "He loves Natalie Wood."

"Didn't everyone?" he quipped.

"Who's Natalie Wood?" Isabelle said.

Pat winced. "I won't hold that against you. At least, I think I won't."

"She was well before your time," Mary said.

"Oh. Was she pretty?"

Mary nodded. "Very. Right, Pat?"

"Fair to middling compared to you, my dear," he said, trying to hide how desperately ill he felt.

Isabelle helped Mary with her own pills. "I didn't forget about you. I was thinking grilled cheese and maybe some tomato soup for lunch?"

"That sounds delicious," Mary said.

"Just soup for me. If I'm hungry by then," Pat said. His throat was scratchy, and his glands were swollen. He wasn't sure he would be able to swallow a sandwich today.

"Anything you want, I'll make sure you have it," Isabelle said. "You just rest today. Do you want me to open the window?"

Pat shook his head. The fever made him cold, his body on the cusp of shivering under the sheet and blankets. "Maybe later. We can air the room out a bit, or I can take a flying leap and put myself out of my misery."

"Oh, Pat," Mary tsked.

"Not to worry, my sweet. You'll never get rid of me that easy."

"Who says anything about you is easy?"

Isabelle was about to leave, when she paused at the

door and turned. "I hope you don't mind my saying this, but I . . . I never knew my grandparents. They passed away before I was born. I like to think that if they were here, they would have been as nice . . . and funny . . . as the both of you. I'm so glad We Care assigned me to you."

"And I'm glad I was able to convince the old mule over there to bring you here. I need someone I can talk to about the fashion at the Oscars," Mary said.

She'd really taken a shine to Isabelle. That made Pat happy. He'd heard that most home aides stole from the people they cared for. He'd made it a point to keep the jar of quarters he'd been saving out in the open on the mantel downstairs. So far, it looked like nary a quarter was taken. Everything was in its place . . . and in a more organized place, too, now that Isabelle had gotten things shipshape.

Maybe he didn't look at her like a granddaughter—he had one already, and she was an absolute jewel—but he liked her a lot. If she weren't here, he and Mary would be in a world of trouble.

His vision got fuzzy, and it was suddenly hard to think in full sentences.

Pat forgot about the burning in his lungs and the pain in his joints. Mary turned the movie on, and he caught a glimpse of Natalie Wood before settling into a dull fog.

CHAPTER NINE

Mary's heart fluttered when her cell phone rang. It was a rainy Sunday. Pat was fast asleep even though it was noon, the sound of his labored breathing keeping her on edge. He'd even slept through Veronica Cleary ringing the bell to give Mary the Eucharist from the day's mass. Mary would have to call her later to apologize.

The phone display read "Johnnie Boy."

Like clockwork, her son called them every Sunday, usually after he and Marion got home from church. She touched the speakerphone button.

"Hello."

"Hey, Mom. Greetings from Maine." Johnnie sounded a little out of breath.

"Did you just run a marathon?"

"Close. I was hacking away at the fresh layer of ice on our steps. It's what we do up here in the early spring. The snowmelt from the awning always leaves me a nice present the next day. One of these years, I may just take the whole thing down and save myself the trouble. So, how are you feeling? Get into any trouble since we last spoke."

Mary stifled a laugh. "So much trouble. I'm fine." She

looked over at Pat, his face so pale, mouth hanging open. "It's your father I'm worried about."

"He needs to go to the hospital, Ma. This is his life he's playing around with."

"I know, I know. But he's so headstrong. He thinks I'll wither up like an old flower if he's not right beside me."

Johnnie sighed huskily. "Then have him declared mentally unfit and force him to check into St. Luke's."

Mary slipped her hand over the phone, too late to make much difference. She didn't want Pat to hear that, even though she knew Johnnie wasn't serious. At least, she thought he wasn't.

"I'll do no such thing. Would you ever do that to Marion?"

Without hesitation, he said, "Yes, if it meant saving her life."

"Now, don't go trying to make me feel guilty for *not* betraying your father." She felt her dander rise, which was very unusual when it came to talking to Johnnie. They had always been close, and even seven hundred miles of physical separation couldn't change that.

"That's the last thing I want to do. I'm just worried and frustrated, that's all," he said.

"That makes two of us."

"How about I come down next weekend and try to talk some sense into him? I'll personally take him to St. Luke's."

"You know that will never work," Mary said.

"I actually don't, until I try."

As much as Mary was sure Johnnie's in-person persuasions wouldn't amount to a hill of beans, she had to admit she'd love having him here.

"Marion's going to a seminar for new foster parents next week, and I still have vacation days left over from last year. If I don't take them soon, I lose them."

Johnnie and Marion were between foster children at the moment. The pretty young girl, Hayley was her name, had returned to her mother's home after spending four months with Mary's son and daughter-in-law. Hayley was nine and in need of a loving home after her mother had been arrested for her third DUI and sent to rehab. Johnnie said the woman was clean and sober for the first time in years, and though it hurt to let Hayley go—it always hurt— he and Marion were happy that things had taken a turn for the better. As much as they loved Hayley, she needed her mother.

"You know we always want to see you," Mary said.

"Then consider it done. I'll be there Saturday and stay until Wednesday."

"That would be wonderful. And you'll get to meet Isabelle. I know we won't really need her with you in the house, but I don't want her to lose any money over it."

"Looking forward to it," Johnnie said. "I'll call later to talk to Dad when he's awake."

"You do that. He needs a little pick-me-up."

No sooner had Mary hung up with Johnnie than Joe made his check-in call. He sounded off. It was three hours earlier in Sacramento. Joe wasn't a churchgoer, preferring to golf on Sunday mornings. He usually called her later in the day.

"Did it finally rain out there?" Mary asked. "I'm sure a little rain will be good for the greens. So, how are Stella and my grandchildren?" She liked to watch golf on TV, though despite having several golf courses nearby she'd never tried to play. And now it was simply too late.

"No rain. Look, there's something I need to tell you. I probably should have told you months ago. I just didn't know how to break it to you."

Mary went rigid. Joe had had a health scare a couple of years back, only telling them after the worst was over.

She was so scared, she couldn't find her voice.

Joe said, "It's about Stella."

Mary gasped. "What about Stella?"

She could hear the hesitation in Joe's voice. "She left— no, that's not quite right. I left because she cheated on me."

Head swooning, Mary said, "What do you mean she cheated on you?"

"I found out she was sl . . . keeping company with a guy she works with. They've been together for over a year. He's married, too."

"Dear God."

"It came from left field, or at least I thought so at first. But the more time I've had to think about it, there were signs. Instead of putting the kids through the trauma of me throwing their mother out, I left. I've been living in an apartment near my office since January."

"Why didn't you tell me then?" Mary's chest hurt from her heart breaking. Joe may be a grown man of fifty-two, but he still needed his mother's love and comfort.

Joe took a moment, then said, "I was embarrassed. And angry. Too angry to be able to talk civilly about it. I guess I just needed some time for everything to shake out. I'm sorry."

"You don't have to apologize to me, Joe. God in heaven, what you must have gone through."

"Going through," he said. "I just had her served with divorce papers the other day."

Divorce.

No Knox had ever gotten a divorce. Then again, she'd been witness to some pretty terrible Knox marriages that should have been brought to a merciful end. How could Stella have done such a thing? She'd not only cheated on Joe. She cheated on their children, Tyler and Emma, too.

They talked for the better part of an hour, Joe, through Mary's prodding, recounting as much as he felt comfortable. Mary kept expecting Pat to wake up so she could not only share the devastating news, but have him settle down her nerves. Pat barely moved the entire time.

When Joe hung up, Mary waved her fingers to make the sign of the cross, praying for her son and grandchildren. She even prayed for Stella, hoping she'd come to realize the fullness of what she'd done and ask forgiveness.

Pat awoke in a haze, a racking cough making him see spots. When it calmed down, he looked over at Mary. She was crying.

"Mary, what's wrong?" he croaked, his throat filled with phlegm.

Her lips quivered. "I was so worried about you. Do you know what time it is?"

He scratched his head and looked at the electric clock on the table. Was that six a.m. or p.m.?

"I called Isabelle. I know it's her day off, but I didn't know what to do."

"I was just sleeping, Mary."

"For seventeen hours."

"Seventeen hours?"

"Yes. I was so worried. But that's not even why I'm crying."

Pat was having a hard time focusing his eyes. His ribs ached. The concept of sleeping seventeen hours was hard to grasp. Everything was a mixed-up jumble in his head.

Crying. If he could concentrate on that, he could work his way through the rest.

"So why on earth are you crying?"

Her head rolled back and forth on the pillow. "It's Joe and Stella. They're getting a divorce."

"A divorce?" That broke through the miasma. "What do you mean, they're getting a divorce?"

Mary sniffled, a fat tear leaking from the corner of her eye absorbing into the pillowcase. "Joe found out she'd been seeing another man. He moved out in January. He sounds so hurt, Pat."

He would be hurt. Pat couldn't imagine the weight of such a betrayal. He tried to ask Mary about the kids, but another coughing fit swarmed over him. As hard as it was for him to admit, he wasn't getting any better. It felt like an elephant was standing on his chest.

Never mind that. His son had just had his life turned upside down.

Getting out of bed was no easy task. He had to stand for a minute and make sure he wasn't going to fall. The first thing he did was get Mary her rosary beads. Pulling down the bed rail, he scooted in next to her and held her while she recounted her call with Joe. Isabelle came in to find them snuggled against one another.

"Can we just have a few minutes?" he asked her kindly.

"Of course. Just call out when you need me."

Isabelle closed the door, and he heard her walk down the stairs.

Mary needed to talk herself out. If she'd been well, he knew she would have spun around the house organizing things, the act of moving about helping to release her tension. All she had now was her voice, and Pat fought through the pain and brain fog until she calmed down, the beads no longer clicking frantically.

CHAPTER TEN

Now Pat was slurring. He was trying to tell Isabelle what they needed from the store, but the words were coming out wrong. Mary watched in quiet horror as his eyes rolled up to the top of his head. He paused, took a breath, and started talking about something completely unrelated to the store.

"Pat, we can't understand you," Mary said.

Isabelle stood beside his bed, notepad in hand, a look of concern on her face.

"Wha—?" Pat said, swiveling to look at her.

One word kept repeating in Mary's head: stroke. He was talking like he'd had a stroke.

"You're not making any sense," Mary said, wishing she could get herself out of bed and go to him. He was only a few feet away, but it might as well have been a thousand miles.

"I certainly am making sense," he quickly rebutted, the word *sense* coming out like "sensh."

"No, you're not. I'm about to call nine-one-one."

Isabelle flinched slightly.

Pat sat up, waving his hands. "Now, just hold your horses. There's no need to overreact."

"You can't hear yourself," Mary said, encouraged that he seemed to be coming around, his irritation—or was it fear?—slicing through whatever dull haze had him in its grip. "You sound like a crazy drunk."

"I'm not totally deaf yet," Pat protested. His eyes had more focus now. He was wheezing, but that had become an unfortunate constant. "And I haven't been drunk in ages."

"I'm not saying you are drunk. I said you were sounding *like* a drunk," Mary said.

"In a pig's eye," Pat grumbled.

"I think he's okay," Isabelle said to Mary.

Pat smiled at their aide. "At least someone is paying attention."

Mary had to suck on her teeth to keep a small smile from her lips. Riling him up a bit did the trick. She didn't want him to guess what she had done. Okay, so he hadn't had a stroke. But the fact that he wasn't getting any better, not to mention all the sleeping lately, did little to diminish her concerns.

"I guess you were just a wee groggy," Mary said to her husband.

"Grogginess doesn't call for an ambulance," Pat said. He rose and shuffled into the bathroom, muttering every step of the way.

"I could still call the doctor," Isabelle whispered.

"Not for this," Mary replied. "But if I can talk him into going to see Dr. Murphy today, would you take him? I'd call a cab to take you both."

"Of course. I'll go to the store and be right back, unless you need me for anything else."

Isabelle wore a gray and red track suit today, her black hair tied in a long ponytail. She had on a little red lipstick and eyeliner. Isabelle was a very pretty girl. Mary wondered if Pat still remembered when she was young and pretty. "No. If you can make sense of what he asked for, that should be all."

Isabelle nodded. "Be back in ten, fifteen minutes."

"Bye now."

The sound of sirens passing by made Mary crane her neck to look out the window. Isabelle had pulled the blinds up to let in the sunlight. Mary just caught a glimpse of a police car cruising by, making a right turn and disappearing out of sight. It didn't go far, because she could still hear the siren. In fact, it sounded like it was right around the corner.

Pat came out of the bathroom, the toilet running. He'd attempted to comb his wiry gray hair. His pajama top was askew. Mary noticed he'd buttoned it wrong.

"I hear the cavalry," Pat said.

"I saw a police car outside. I think it's stopped on Lassiter."

"Let me see." He tottered down the hall to the back bedroom that used to be Johnnie's. The windows in that room had a view of their yard and the houses on Lassiter Avenue. "I think it's parked outside O'Malley's house."

The O'Malleys had lived in the house behind Pat and Mary's for going on fifty years. The low fence separating the yards made it easy to chat to one another when the weather was nice. One year, Pat had cut out part of the fence and installed a waist-high swinging door to make it easy for both families to walk to and from each other's yards. Pat and Archie O'Malley loved to grill over cold Rheingolds and cringeworthy jokes. Nora O'Malley had been a talented seamstress and one of Mary's closest friends. As soon as the weather got nice, they practically lived in the yard, the common meeting place for the Knox and O'Malley clans. Nora and Archie had had a daughter, but she had passed away several years ago from breast cancer. Neither had been the same after the tragedy. Happy, smiling Nora withered away and slowly lost her mind. She had been a resident at the Harlan Rest Home for going on five years now. Heartbroken and lonely, Archie took to drinking in a slow quest to reunite with his daughter. It was hard to watch.

"There's a heck of a commotion," Pat announced just as Mary heard the wail of more sirens.

He came back into the room and rummaged through his drawers, finding a shirt and socks. "Is Isabelle gone?"

"She's at the store, like you asked."

Pat stripped out of his pajamas and got dressed with their bedroom door open.

"What in the name of all that's holy do you think you're doing?" Mary said.

"I'm going to see what's happened. There's a fire engine and an ambulance now."

"Maybe you shouldn't. You're not well."

He waved her off. "I'm well enough to walk a few feet to check on a friend. I'll be back before you know it."

And with that, he left. Mary worried after him, but at least he had the strength to go, which was a sight better than what she'd been thinking just minutes earlier.

* * *

A seasonal breeze met Pat as he walked out his back door. He carefully made his way across the dormant lawn, last fall's leaves crunching under his feet. He could smell the diesel of the idling fire engine that had now joined the police. The hinge on the small gate whined, flakes of rust sprinkling the ground. There was a time it swung back and forth far too often to ever seize up and rust.

Entering the O'Malleys' yard confirmed that all of this attention was on Archie's house. Pat saw a man in uniform walk past the kitchen window.

"Archie."

The last he'd seen Archie was maybe two months ago. They'd run into one another at the stationery store, both out to get the newspaper, though Archie had a large brown paper bag tucked under his arm. His face had been bloated, his eyes gray and rheumy, the smell of alcohol seeping from his pores. Pat had kept his old friend from darting back to his house to continue toward his aim of drinking himself to death. Somehow, he'd convinced Archie to walk with him to the coffee shop, where they talked about old times after Pat asked him about Nora. They'd managed to have a quick laugh or two, Archie lamenting that no matter how hard you wished, you couldn't turn the hands of time back. Feigning that he had something important to do, Archie got up to leave.

"I couldn't have asked for a better neighbor and friend," Archie said.

"Same here, Arch. Same here."

There was a feeling that Archie was saying goodbye that day.

As Pat walked down the narrow alley between houses, he thought, *I guess he was*.

A throng of people had gathered. The front door was wide open. Pat crossed the small patch of dead grass that passed for a front yard and walked up the three steps onto the porch. An EMT saw him and held a hand out.

"Sorry, but you can't go in there."

"That's my friend in there. Is he all right?"

"I understand, sir, but I have to ask you to get on the sidewalk."

The EMT sounded all business, but he looked pained to order an old man onto the curb.

Pat shifted to look beyond the EMT. The house was full of bustling police and EMTs.

"Can you at least tell me if he's alive or dead?" Pat asked.

"I'm sorry, there's nothing I can do for you at the moment." He took a step closer to Pat and whispered, "It's probably best you don't see."

An icy waterfall crashed down Pat's spine. He said, "I fought in Vietnam, son. Believe me, I can handle it."

With a heavy sigh, the EMT stepped aside and said, "Please promise me you'll step away . . . after."

Pat was pretty sure he said, "I promise." What he saw ripped his soul from his body.

Archie O'Malley lay on the floor, one foot on the bottom step of the staircase leading to the second floor that used to be home to their daughter's bedroom and Nora's sewing room. There was blood on the floor. Blood on Archie's face.

Except Archie's face had been turned the wrong way. With the way his body was positioned at the foot of the stairs, his chest on the floor, his face should not have been staring up at the ceiling, eyes cold and vacant.

"Jesus, Mary, and Joseph," Pat muttered.

"It must have been a hell of a fall," the EMT said, moving to block Pat's view. "I assume your friend drank. We found empty bottles all throughout the house."

Pat was too stunned to speak.

"I'm sorry for your loss. Do you need help getting down the stairs?"

Pat looked down, saw the man's hand on his arm but couldn't feel it. He must have nodded, because the EMT walked him down the steps. Instead of joining the crowd gathered outside Archie O'Malley's house—so many familiar faces, all of them curious and worried—Pat turned to walk down the side of the house and back to his yard.

"I live . . . I live behind," he said, feeling as if he were in a dream.

The EMT stayed with him halfway down the alley before going back to his post.

Pat touched the fence separating the two yards and had to stop to take several deep breaths. He pictured the yard the way it used to be. Mary and Nora sitting on lawn chairs, talking and laughing. The kids running through the fine spray given off by the sprinkler. The smell of steaks on the grill. Archie handing him a cold beer, both men making plans to work on Pat's front porch the following weekend and finally replace some of the rotting boards. Archie had always been good with a hammer.

Archie had always been good. Period. A good man who had been the first to lend a hand.

Now that good man was gone. A drunken fall down the stairs that nearly twisted his head clean off.

Pat's stomach lurched, and he threw up onto the brown scrub of his lawn.

He didn't remember going back into the house. One moment he was leaning on the fence, wiping his mouth with his sleeve, the next he was in the bedroom, Mary peppering him with questions. Answers fell from his mouth like lead balls. Mary wept. Pat sat on the edge of his bed, suddenly more tired than he'd ever felt.

"But is he dead?" The man said found a speck of lint on the cuff of his shirt and flicked it off.

"As dead as they come."

Christ, what a mess. Why was nothing going easy lately?

"Please tell me some good news," he said.

The official on the other end of the line cleared his throat. "The guy was a drunk. You should see all the damn empties in his house. Well, they're there now, at least. No one will think it's anything but accidental."

"They better not, because if they do, everyone's ass is on the line. Are we clear on that?"

"Crystal." He didn't sound happy to be threatened, but all of this was too big to be handled with kid gloves. Threats and intimidation were the name of the game on every level here.

"Good. Ditch your phone and buy another. If I see this number call me again, we're going to have a problem."

The line went dead.

Pushing away from his desk, the man got out of his leather chair and walked to the tacked-up map of Woodlean on his wall. Recalling the address, he found the appropriate house on the map, uncapped a red marker, and wrote the letter E over the drawing of the house.

"One more down." He normally celebrated with a glass of expensive brandy and a cigar. But today had been messy, and he wanted answers. Most of all, he wanted someone held accountable. That sense of unease warranted a lesser toast to himself—just a glass of mid-level scotch. He'd save something better for the next one.

CHAPTER ELEVEN

Between the exertion of going out to see what had become of Archie O'Malley and the stress of processing the horror of what he'd seen, Pat spiraled into a tailspin. He felt worse than ever, the pneumonia seeming to be a sentient thing taking glee in his misery and using it as an opportunity to entrench itself even deeper in his lungs. Breathing was a chore, and Pat's heart raced nonstop as his body struggled to take in air. Blinding headaches made being awake something to avoid. Pat knew his blood pressure was through the roof. Doctors called high blood pressure the silent killer, but there was nothing silent about the way he felt.

How he had gotten downstairs was a mystery to him. At least he was in his ratty chair and not the floor.

A light, early spring shower pelted the windows. Pat's breath came in a phlegmy rattle. He looked around the empty living room, the grandfather clock—one of Mary's family hcirlooms ticking quietly in the corner.

Why was he down here?

He turned his head, saw the stairway to the second

floor, and felt his spirits sag even deeper. There was no way he could go up those stairs now.

"Mary," he wheezed.

When she didn't call back, he tried again, quickly realizing he couldn't shout loud enough for her to hear. It wasn't as if either of them had good hearing anymore.

The shape coming out of the kitchen startled him. His eyes had misted over, and he had to rub them with his knuckles to clear his vision.

Isabelle was kneeling beside his chair.

"Are you all right, Mr. Knox?" Her tan, slender hand was on his knee.

He didn't remember Isabelle being in the house. But then again, he couldn't recall walking down the stairs and settling in his chair for a nap.

"How did I get here?"

Isabelle shrugged her shoulders. "Mrs. Knox and I think you came down during the night. When I walked in this morning, you were sleeping, and I didn't want to disturb you."

"Great. Now I'm sleepwalking."

"Mrs. Knox said you were coughing a lot. She assumed you came down here so you didn't keep her awake."

When he winked at her, a bolt of pain shot across his forehead. "Good to know I can be chivalrous in my delirium."

Pat started shivering. Isabelle rose, plucked the afghan off the couch, and covered him with it. She rubbed his shoulders, trying to warm him.

"I'm sorry, I should have put a blanket on you this morning. It was so hot in the house, I didn't think you'd need it. Plus, you were sweating so much."

It was true, Pat did keep the house on the warm side. The oil man loved him for it.

"No need to apologize. It happens to me sometimes, and more since I came down with this damn pneumonia. It'll pass."

She looked at her watch. "It's time for your medicine. Now, don't you move." Isabelle smiled.

"I don't think that's going to be a problem."

He heard her run the kitchen faucet and the sound of pills being shaken out of the amber bottles. She returned with a palm full of pills. Pat took them all in one swallow, having to drink more water than usual to wash them down when a few caught in his cough-ravaged throat.

"Bless your heart and all your parts," he said, handing the glass back to her.

"Do you want anything to eat? I'm making Mrs. Knox an egg salad sandwich."

The thought of food made him wince.

"I'll pass. And I keep telling you to call us Pat and Mary."

"I know. It's just so hard for me. Where I come from, you have to show respect to your . . . well, your . . ."

"Trust me, I'm not offended by being called an elder. The only thing around here older than me is the pine tree out front."

That seemed to confuse her, but he was too tired to explain.

She whisked away back to the kitchen and then upstairs, the floorboards creaking as she tended to his wife.

Awake and alone, Pat was troubled by thoughts of Archie. And before that, there was Bridgett Monahan and Annie Fahey. What in the name of God was happening to his neighborhood? Even Doyle was gone now, stuck in a rehab he might never return from. At least Doyle's absence made sense.

Thinking about his lost friends and neighbors was a poor substitute for bemoaning his illness. It didn't last long, as his mind started to drift. Distorted images and sounds warped his perception until he could no longer tell whether he was asleep or awake.

At several points he thought he saw Isabelle, talked with Isabelle, but he couldn't be sure. It was comforting to know she was there. Or was she?

One question did work its way through the fuzz in his brain.

How long would it be until the neighborhood was minus one more—him?

The ringing of the doorbell dragged Pat from yet another troubled sleep. He was even more confused to find himself in bed. His legs instinctively slipped out from under the sheets, his bare feet touching down on the worn bedroom carpet.

Mary said, "Back to bed, mister. Isabelle will get it."

Pat looked down at his pajamas. "I was just downstairs."

"Yes, you were . . . yesterday," Mary said. Even through his confusion, Pat could clearly see the look of dread in her face. "You don't remember anything since then?"

He scratched his scalp, trying hard to think. "To be honest, no." And then he started to cough.

"Isabelle helped you up the stairs early last night. You

and I talked for quite a while before you went back to sleep."

"We did?"

Mary's eyes watered with collected tears. "We did. You talked to me about the boys and how proud you were of them. How we would do anything we could to help Joe. You were so sweet. I should have known you were delirious." She tried to laugh, but it came out as a pained huff.

Pat cringed. It was disconcerting to hear. He'd never walked or talked in his sleep before, if he was technically asleep when all of this happened. He had a hard time imagining himself doing it.

You're not doing it. The pneumonia is.

He was well aware that it was getting critical now. He needed to see the doctor, and Pat knew once he did, the hospital was next.

Looking over at Mary as she struggled to dab her tears with the edge of her sheet, Pat felt the internal struggle wage once more, the battle ushering him from his fugue. If he ignored things much longer, he was going to leave her, permanently. It was painfully obvious that the medication wasn't working. If he did go to the doctor, he would still have to leave her, but maybe not for good.

Or had he waited too long, sealing Mary's fate as a crippled widow?

A knock at the door saved him from his tortured thoughts.

"Mind if I come in?"

Father Biglin waved at them, his coat draped over an arm. He wore his black shirt, pants, and white collar, which meant he was on the clock, so to speak.

"Hello Father," Mary said, quickly composing herself. "You're a sight for sore eyes."

He gestured toward the chair, and when Mary nodded, he sat between them. "Now that's something I don't hear very often. At least, not from the fairer sex." He winked at Pat.

"What brings you around?" Pat asked, coughing again. This time he coughed so much, he had to grab a tissue to collect what was coming out of him.

"I just wanted to see my two favorite parishioners. You know, Pat, some of these replacement ushers need guidance. We need you back up and on your feet."

Pat noticed Father Biglin was having a hard time keeping the smile on his face when he looked at him. *I must look a mess*, Pat thought.

"I'm trying, Father. I'm trying."

Isabelle came in with her morning plastic cups of pills.

"I'm not taking those anymore," Pat said.

"But you have to," Isabelle said. "You need them."

Pat waved the proffered cup off. "They haven't done a bit of good. In fact, I think they've only made me worse. I'm sick to death of pills."

"Now Pat," Mary said, keeping her tone light in front of the priest, but with enough undertone to let him know she was not happy.

"The doctor said it was important to finish your prescriptions," Isabelle said. She wore jeans and a red cardigan over a white crewneck shirt. Pat was glad she wasn't wearing one of her formfitting jogging suits. Not with Father Biglin in the house. It was ridiculous, but he was as old as he was old-fashioned.

"I tell you, I'm not taking any more," Pat insisted. The

moment he took them, he felt terrible. "Please, just let me skip a day and see how I feel."

Isabelle looked to Mary, who looked to Father Biglin.

The priest said, "It may not be my business, but I can't see that skipping a day would hurt much. Sometimes the body needs a little time to gather itself. And then it's ready to begin again the next day. Right, Pat?"

Pat never thought he'd be grateful to have a priest in his bedroom, but he sure was at this moment.

"That's it exactly, Father. Just give me a day."

Neither of the women looked happy, but they weren't going to argue with a man of the cloth. Isabelle gave Mary her medication, asked if anyone needed anything, and went downstairs.

"Now, on to the meat of things," Father Biglin said. "Mary, I wanted to personally serve you the Eucharist and say some prayers with you. Pat, feel free to join in. I also wanted to let you know that Archie O'Malley's funeral is set for the day after tomorrow, and you are not to come."

He looked directly at Pat.

"Archie was a good, dear friend," Pat said.

"I know that very well, which is why I felt I should tell you in person that I don't want you pushing yourself to go to the service. Archie knows you're mourning him, and I think he'd be the first one to tell you to stay home and get better."

And that was that. Pat wasn't even sure if he could make it to church, but he also knew he would have tried. Some things were too important to miss.

"It's just so terrible," Mary said. "We both worried so much about him these last few years."

Father Biglin sighed. "I came to see him several months

back. He hadn't been to church in quite a while. He wasn't in good shape. He needed help. I was able to convince him to let me bring in someone from We Care. Just a couple of days a week, for the companionship more than anything. Yes, he needed some help, especially when he'd had too much to drink, but I thought having someone else beside him, someone young and caring and capable, would have done him a world of good."

Something scratched at the back of Pat's brain. "Did he still have an aide coming to the house?"

"I believe so. I saw a woman leave his front door just two weeks ago."

Pat recalled what the EMT had said, and how there were empty liquor bottles all over the house. If Archie's aide was anything like Isabelle, the place should have been spotless.

"I saw him," Pat said.

The priest arched an eyebrow. "When?"

"That day. I went to the house to see what had happened. When I looked in the house, I saw him lying at the bottom of the stairs."

Father Biglin rested his elbows on his knees, leaning toward Pat. "I'm so sorry you had to see that."

Pat wasn't going to tell him about the way Archie's head had been turned nearly around. Not in front of Mary. "I was, and I wasn't," he said instead. "At least I got to see him one last time."

"The important thing is that you remember him as he was when he was alive. Hold on to the good memories," the priest said.

Pat's throat hitched, only this time, it wasn't from an

oncoming cough. He closed his eyes for a moment to quell his rising emotions. "I have plenty to choose from."

"Has a mass been dedicated to Archie?" Mary asked.

"Several, as a matter of fact."

"The pews are getting emptier and emptier, especially lately," Pat said, staring past Father Biglin and Mary to somewhere far, far off.

The priest nodded solemnly. "I'm afraid they are. Too much high drama for our quiet neighborhood."

"And too many unanswered questions," Pat said. He wasn't feeling loopy and exhausted . . . just plain worn out.

Sensing Pat's strength, if not interest, was flagging, Father Biglin turned his chair toward Mary, and together they said the Lord's Prayer and went through the rites to receive the sacrament. After that, they prayed aloud for Archie O'Malley and a host of others in need of divine assistance.

Pat sat silently through it all, enjoying a brief moment of clarity, wondering how so much grief had suddenly fallen upon his friends and neighbors.

CHAPTER TWELVE

After resuming his medication regimen, Pat had gone back to feeling like a two-dollar steak that had been dragged behind a tractor trailer.

Needing a change of scenery, he had asked Isabelle to help him down to his chair. Mary had been up all night with him and his wheezing and coughing, and he was tired of the constant chatter of the television. He wanted her to get rest, and for him to sit quietly for a spell.

When the doorbell rang, he assumed it was the Jehovah's Witnesses making their rounds. They loved to make pests of themselves on the weekends. He'd always been polite but had been firm in reminding them he was a life-long Catholic and there was no chance of that changing. There was a stack of their pamphlets in a basket by the couch. If he still used the fireplace, they would make good kindling.

Isabelle hustled down the stairs, dressed in her coat because it was getting late and she was heading home to have dinner with a friend. When she answered the door, he heard her say, "I'm sorry, you are?"

"Just the guy who painted this door as a punishment. Twice."

At the sound of that voice, Pat's entire body perked up. "Johnnie!"

Johnnie Knox strode into the room, dropping his suitcase on the floor the same way he used to toss his backpack when he came home from school. At a couple of years shy of fifty, he still had a full head of black hair and his belly defied the middle-age paunch, making him look ten years younger than his age. He was a little on the pale side, but he was living up in Maine and probably hadn't seen much of the sun since September.

"Don't get up," Johnnie said. He got on a knee and squeezed Pat's shoulder. "How are you feeling, Dad?"

"As good as I look," Pat replied, watching Isabelle close the door and move Johnnie's suitcase out of the way.

Johnnie smiled and shook his head. "That bad, huh?"

Pat's chest rumbled as he spoke. "I didn't know you were coming. I would have baked a cake. Or at least gotten your favorite beer."

In a complete role reversal, Johnnie put the back of his hand against Pat's forehead. "I could bake a loaf of soda bread on your skin."

"Where's your better half?" Pat asked.

"Lady Marion is off at a conference. It's a paid speaking gig. She's very excited. She says hello and she loves you and wishes she could have come down to see you."

"So, I won't be getting any of Marion's special reverse chocolate chip cookies?"

Johnnie nodded toward his suitcase. "I have two dozen in the bag, just for you."

"Bless that wife of yours." Before Isabelle could slip into the kitchen, Pat said, "Johnnie, the woman you so rudely walked around is Isabelle." It was the perfect distraction from talking about his illness. He was surprised and happy at the moment, and it was best to keep it that way.

Johnnie stood and said, "Sorry about that. I guess I got a little anxious." He shook her hand. "John Knox, this geezer's youngest son. My mother's told me a lot about you. I just want to thank you for all you've done."

Isabelle gave a faltering smile. She looked uncomfortable, as if she were intruding on something private. "It's very nice to meet you. Mrs. Knox talks about you and your brother all the time." She cast a quick glance at the ceiling. "Speaking of which, I have to get a snack up to her now."

"You look like you're headed to parts unknown, and hopefully fun. I'll bring it up to her," Johnnie said. "Now, what was she having?"

"Crackers and ginger ale," Isabelle said.

"Some things never change. Thank God for that. Will you be here tomorrow?" He was already dashing into the kitchen, bottles on the refrigerator door tinkling against one another when he yanked the door open.

Isabelle looked to Pat.

Pat said, "Sundays are her day off. The poor dear can't be cooped up in here with Bonnie and Clyde all the time."

The aide's shoulders sagged with obvious relief.

"Okay, then," Johnnie said, popping his head out of the kitchen. "I'll see you Monday. I promise you, I'm far less hectic normally."

"Is he really?" she asked Pat.

"Yes," both men replied in unison.

Isabelle wished them good night and left, locking the door behind her. Johnnie strode into the living room with a plate of crackers and a bottle of soda. "She's quite the looker."

Pat said, "I haven't noticed."

Johnnie burst out laughing. The sound of his laughter bouncing off the old house's walls warmed Pat's soul.

"I'm sure you haven't," Johnnie said. "Let me go say hi to Mom, and then I'm coming back down. Are the Caps on tonight? I'm so tired of Bruins games."

"I'll check the paper. Now, don't make a big production out of surprising your mother. At our age, we have just so many surprises left that we can take."

His son arched an eyebrow. "Oh, she knew I was coming. The surprise was for you."

With that, Johnnie bounded up the stairs, taking them two at a time. Pat listened to Mary exclaim with pure joy when their son walked into the room. The two of them— lifelong motormouths when they got together—chatted in rapid-fire bursts. Pat reached for the paper to find the sports listing. Watching a hockey game with Johnnie would be better than any medicine he'd been prescribed.

Johnnie was the breath of fresh air he and Mary desperately needed. He fell asleep long before his son was able to tear himself away from his mother, only this time, he slept with a smile on his face.

When Pat awoke with his usual coughing attack, he found himself still in his chair, only the leg rest was raised, a pillow was under his head, and a blanket was draped across his body.

Johnnie was also sitting on the couch opposite him. It was apparent he'd slept downstairs instead of in his old bedroom. On the couch beside him were a couple of pillows, a rumpled sheet, and the old blue and gold afghan Mary had crocheted many moons ago.

"I don't know how Mom does it," Johnnie said. He had a steaming cup of coffee in his hands. Sunlight streamed through the slats of the partially open blinds.

Once Pat hacked up half a lung and caught his breath, he said, "Does what?"

"Sleeps next to those very alarming sounds you make. I almost called nine-one-one several times last night. You can't let this keep going on."

Pat sighed, then wheezed. "I'll assume you and your mother cooked up this visit to drag me to the hospital."

His son chuckled. "I'm hoping it won't come to dragging. A peaceable trip to your local medicine man will suffice."

With a loud crank and a thunk, the leg rest came down, the chair gently rocking. Pat tried, but he couldn't come up with a valid argument against his son taking him to get the help he needed. "You're right. I know you're right."

"So why haven't you done it yet?"

Pat hung his head. "You know I don't want to leave your mother alone."

"Isn't that why you hired Isabelle?"

Johnnie got up, went to the kitchen, and returned with a cup of coffee, setting it on the table next to Pat.

"The girl is here for a few hours a day. Your mother needs assistance all day and night."

Taking a sip from his own mug—in fact, it was the very same *Star Wars* mug he used to drink chocolate milk out of when he was a kid—Johnnie winced from the heat and said, "You don't look like you've been up to doing much for her. And it's only going to get worse. A lot worse."

"I know that." Pat should have been angry, defensive, but he was just too damn tired. One thing he was not going to confide in his son was the growing fear that once he went into the hospital, he wasn't getting out. He'd let things drag on too long, and now there was no turning back. His refusal to leave his wife was most certainly going to lead to his departing her for good, and he had no one to blame but himself.

Johnnie's tone softened. "Look, it's Sunday, the worst day to go to the emergency room. If they need to admit you, it'll take forever to get a bed. So why don't we have a nice, relaxing Sunday, and I'll take you first thing tomorrow?"

Pat smiled weakly.

A nice, relaxing Sunday.

A last day with Mary and his son.

A last meal.

A last look at the house he'd bought through his sweat and tears, had raised a family and grown old within.

There was no shame in being melancholy.

Pat was Irish, after all. It was his birthright.

"Sure, that would be nice," Pat said, putting on as brave a face as he could muster.

Johnnie spent the morning changing bedsheets, making breakfast, and cleaning the dishes. Then he went out to get the Sunday paper, no longer near as hefty as it used to be. Settling them all into the bedroom, he sat between his parents' beds and talked, telling stories about his job, life in Maine, and his and Marion's plans to foster another child. Unlike his brother, Johnnie was loquacious, high energy and quick to laugh. Since he was a little boy, he always filled a room with his presence.

There were several times he made Pat forget what he was going to be facing. Mary never took her eyes off him, listening to old stories that were different now that he was here to tell them in person rather than on the phone.

For dinner, Johnnie went out and brought back a full steak dinner with all the fixings from Pat and Mary's favorite restaurant. They hadn't been there since Mary's illness, which had been too many years to count. Pat wasn't very hungry, but he did enjoy the little he ate. He'd requested another break from the damn pills, just so he could keep his wits about him. If this truly was his last day in his home with his wife, he wanted to be awake to savor every moment.

By eight o'clock, though, he was exhausted, and he fell asleep to the sound of Johnnie and Mary yapping about whatever show was just about to start on the television.

It felt as if he'd just nodded off when his shoulder was nudged.

"The early bird gets the good nurses," Johnnie said.

"What time is it?" Pat grumbled, the fluids in his lungs churning painfully. Sunlight poured through the open blinds.

"I let you sleep until nine," Johnnie said. "Figured there was no sense to rush you out in the wee morning hours."

"How are you feeling?" Mary said. Pat looked across the small divide into her pale blue eyes. He knew she wasn't asking about the pneumonia.

"I'd be lying if I said right as rain."

"Take your time," Mary said. "Do you want something to eat before you go?"

Pat shook his head. His body hurt all over, and he already felt like going back to sleep. Johnnie was right. It was time.

"Mom, you need anything before we head out?"

"Isabelle will be here at eleven. I'll be fine. You just make sure you call me as soon as you hear anything at the hospital. My phone is not leaving my hand until you do."

Pat could tell she was just as nervous as he was, both of them knowing where today's trip could lead.

"I'll call you with updates all throughout the day," Johnnie said.

With Pat's guidance, Johnnie had packed a bag for him to have on hand if and when Pat was admitted. Johnnie plucked the bag from the chair and carried it downstairs. Pat went to the bathroom to get himself ready.

When he came out, Johnnie was still downstairs, having the presence of mind to give his parents time alone to say goodbye.

Pat shuffled to Mary's bedside. "I'm off on an adventure."

Mary was trying hard to keep a stoic face, but he saw the quivering beginning of tears.

"You best make it a short one and come back home," she said. "You know I don't like to watch *Wheel of Fortune* alone."

He cupped her face in his thick, arthritic hand. "If I'm in the hospital tonight, I'll call you so we can watch it together. I know you enjoy beating me to the puzzles more than gawking at Vanna's dresses."

"That I do."

He took her rosary beads and placed them in her free hand. "I know you'll be wanting these."

Pat kissed her forehead and left, warning himself not to look back, because if he did, he might not be able to leave.

CHAPTER THIRTEEN

J erry Banner was confused.

This was nothing new. He was often confused, sometimes not even remembering what day it was or his own address. On good days, when there were periods of clear thoughts, he was painfully aware of the Alzheimer's that had robbed him of more than any one man could count in a lifetime.

No, that wasn't exactly right. A lifetime was exactly what Alzheimer's had taken from him.

A former phlebotomist, Jerry had always been a man who preferred a brainteaser to watching sports. He studied philosophy in his spare time and traveled to New York City every summer to spend a week soaking in the arts. From Broadway plays to concerts at Lincoln Center, trips to the Metropolitan Museum of Art and even lectures on anthropology and political science, he loved it all. Woodlean was his home, and he wouldn't have traded it for all the world, but it wasn't exactly the epicenter of art and learning.

Now, he couldn't recall the name of a single play he'd

attended, let alone simple snippets from Descartes or Hobbes.

It was all gone now, bled into the ether—a source of vexation that sometimes drove him into a rage.

He was not raging now.

How had he gotten here?

The back seat of the car smelled like old fast food. Wrappers and crushed takeout cups littered the floor. A woman piled into the front seat, slamming the door.

"Where am I?" he asked, his voice a reedy whisper.

The woman turned around and fiddled with his seat belt. She didn't answer him.

"Who are you?"

The car started, and Jerry flinched. They were moving. But to where? The last he recalled . . .

There was no last time he could recall.

Suddenly he was here, in a strange car being driven by a strange woman.

They passed by houses that looked familiar, but he couldn't grasp their significance. Jerry was scared, so scared he was afraid he might wet himself.

"Pull over, please," he said. "I have to go to the bathroom."

The woman adjusted the rearview mirror so she could see him. "Make in your pants. I put pads down."

The thought repulsed him. Had there been accidents before? Why would she put a pad under him if there hadn't? No matter. He wasn't going to willfully piss himself.

"I want to know where you're taking me."

The car rocked when she hit the brake a little too hard

at a stoplight. Jerry was instantly afraid she was going to hit him. Or worse.

"Where you need to go, Mr. Banner," she simply said.

Where did he need to go?

They drove for a long while. Maybe. It felt like a long while. He'd fallen asleep. Or at least, he thought he had. It was impossible to tell. They pulled in front of a big building surrounded by trees and rolling lawns.

"Who are you?" he asked as another woman he'd never seen before opened his door and unbuckled his seat belt.

"Come with me," she said. It was an order, not a request.

He followed the strange woman, leaving the strange car behind, and shuffled up the stairs into the strange building.

Jerry Banner, the man who preferred his books and plays over people, was never seen in Woodlean again. A moving truck removed his furniture—what little there was in his small, two-bedroom house, save the prodigious number of boxes of books—the following night. Within twenty-four hours, it was as vacant as the mind that once reveled in an evening reading Plato while Mozart played softly in the background of his small corner of the world.

John Knox was exhausted. The hospital still hadn't found a vacant room for his father. It was seven in the evening and neither of them had eaten a thing all day. Before then, they'd been stuffed into a kind of communal waiting room within the emergency room with three beds on either side, all of them full. His dad was hooked up to so many monitors and IVs, a nurse had to set him up with a catheter because there was no way he could manage getting out of bed and into a bathroom.

What frightened John more than anything was the kind of quiet, grim acceptance of his old man, saying very little, not even complaining about the catheter. He had just given in. John had had to endure it once when his appendix had burst, back when he was stationed at Fort Bliss. It didn't take much to recall the squeamish feeling he'd gotten while the tube was being inserted.

He'd called his mother throughout the day, doing his best to soothe her fears. They were both relieved that his father was in the hospital, but now that the moment was here, their worry only increased. Isabelle was nice enough to stay later than usual, but she had to leave at nine.

John turned to his father. "You want me to get you something to eat? The cafeteria might be closed, but there's an all-night diner down the street."

His only reply was a heavy snore. The old man was out like a light.

Going to the nurses' station, he asked the nurse who had been assigned to his father if they would transfer him to a more permanent room soon.

"It doesn't look like it will happen tonight. But there will be a bed for him in the morning. Trust me, he has everything he needs for now. In fact, he should pretty much sleep through the night."

John watched a woman carry her sick daughter past him into a triage room. "I don't want to leave him, but my mother needs someone to look after her." He was bone weary and conflicted.

It must have shone in his face, because the nurse put a hand on his arm and said, "He'll be fine. Go look after your mom. When you come back in the morning, just ask the person at the front desk for his room number. I'm on duty for another ten hours. I'll take good care of your father."

She had such a reassuring smile, he had no reason not to trust her.

"Can I borrow a pen and some paper?" he asked.

"You sure can."

John wrote a note, saying he was going home and would be back in the morning. He left his cell phone number to call if his father needed anything, stressing that the nurses could call him at any time. Folding the paper over so it could stand upright, he left it on the tray table beside the bed.

Stomach growling, he slumped into his car, telling his empty gut it could wait until he got home. As he pulled out of the mostly empty lot, he dialed his brother, who sounded just as tired as he was when he answered.

"Dad's in the hospital," John said, stopping at a red light.

"Jesus. What happened?"

"I came down to take him to St. Luke's. His pneumonia is real bad. He should have been here weeks ago, but you know how he is."

Joe sighed heavily into the phone. "Oh, I know. How is he?"

"Honest? Terrible. I mean, I know he's old, but he looks like he aged twenty years since I saw him a few months ago. It's just weird, seeing him like that. And now he's got more tubes and wires running in and out of him than I can count."

"What did the doctor say?"

"That Dad was foolish to let it go on this long. He'd

wanted to admit him a while ago. Now, who knows? Pneumonia at Dad's age, especially an advanced case like this . . ." John was too afraid to finish.

"I kept telling them to sell the house and move into one of those assisted living places. You know, the ones where you get your own apartment, and they cater the care you get to your needs."

"It's too late for that now," John said. He drove by a Taco Bell and had to resist the urge to pull into the drive-through and order a half-dozen tacos. The older he had gotten, the less fast food agreed with his stomach. It might seem like a good idea at the moment, but he'd pay for it later. "We have to talk about what we're going to do with Mom if Dad doesn't make it out. Or even if he does and can't take care of her and the house anymore. They can't afford full-time home care."

"All of this would be easier if they'd listened to me and we all sat down to map things out for the future."

John felt his dander rise. He was tired, and hungry, and deeply worried. The last thing he needed was to listen to his brother spout a bunch of "I told you sos." "But it didn't happen, so now we have to figure it out."

There was a pause, then Joe said, "We will. We will. Right now, we have to stay positive and hope the doctors can get Dad better."

John chewed on the inside of his cheek, the taste of metal on his tongue. "I'm finding it hard to stay positive after the day I just had. If you saw him . . ."

There was a hint of accusation in his tone. Whether it was intentional or not, even John couldn't be sure. While Joe spent decades trying to find himself, it had always been up to John to be the steady Eddie, the first call their parents made when they needed help. He didn't begrudge them. In fact, he'd been trying to get his job to relocate him to Virginia for years now so he could be closer to them. But dammit, he was the younger brother. It would be nice for his big brother to step up to the plate for once. John had made sure to keep these feelings to himself, to not let them poison his relationship with Joe. Days like today, though, it was hard to keep it bottled up.

"Don't you think I wish I was there to help?" Joe said.

"Trust me, I do. Look, I'll know more in a day or two. It looks like I'm extending my stay here. I'll call you every day, and maybe, if things aren't looking good, you can fly out here."

He heard Joe's microwave chirp in the background. "Or I can just come now. It's not like I have anything holding me here."

John frowned as he made a turn, wondering if he had misheard his brother. "What does that mean?"

Now Joe was chewing . . . loudly. "Nothing. It's been a long day for me, too, though nothing like yours. I don't think I'm going to get much sleep tonight, either."

Not one to believe in miracles, John did find an open parking spot right outside his parents' house. The narrow street crammed with houses was notorious for scarce parking. "All right, your chewing is making me even hungrier, if that's possible. You go eat. I'll call you after I talk to the doctor tomorrow."

"Deal. And John?"

"Yeah."

"Thanks. For everything."

John tromped up the wooden steps and went inside. The house smelled like a mélange of cleaning products.

Isabelle had been busy. His mother was awake in her bedroom, watching a reality show. When she saw John, she said, "Your father said he would call to watch *Wheel* with me."

She looked more worried than he'd ever seen her. "He was worn out. It took me a while to realize I was talking to myself until I saw he'd passed out."

Her rosary beads tinkled as she worked them with her thumb and index finger. "Thank God. I was worried they had him hooked into one of those ventilators and he couldn't talk."

John sat on the bed and put his arm around her shoulders. She was so frail. It was like holding a baby bird. "No ventilator. Just a lot of fluids and meds going through IVs, and the usual monitors to measure his heart and oxygen levels. He's exactly where he needs to be. I'm sure by tomorrow night, he'll be feeling better than he has for weeks."

"I hope so." Her eyes were on the television, but John knew she wasn't seeing or hearing a thing. His mother was lost in her unsettled thoughts.

"Did you have your crackers and ginger ale yet?" he asked.

"Isabelle brought them to me. I couldn't eat."

He kissed the top of her head. "Well, I'm so hungry, I could eat Dad's cooking. I'm going downstairs to make a sandwich or four."

She leaned her head against him. "You look tired. Go eat and get to bed. You need the rest. I'll be fine. If I need anything, I'll call out to you."

In anticipation of a long, brutal stint waiting in the hospital, John had loaded up on cold cuts and bread the day before. He made a monster turkey sandwich with lettuce, thick slices of tomato, Swiss cheese, and mayo. For an appetizer, he also made a bologna and cheese sandwich with a liberal spread of spicy brown mustard. He took the plate of sandwiches and beer with him to sit in his father's chair. Turning the television on to an old episode of *The X-Files*, he finished the bologna sandwich in three bites. He was about to attack the turkey when he spotted the pile of mail on the coffee table.

There was obvious junk mail on top. He'd throw it out later.

It felt strange going through his parents' mail, and the thought that this might become a common thing sent a chill through his body.

One envelope had been stamped with a red "URGENT." That's usually how those phony letters offering a line of credit for a new car got your attention. Taking a bite of the turkey sandwich, he slid his thumb under the flap and shook the letter out.

Unfolding the paper, he read the notice, his hunger suddenly forgotten.

His free hand finding his phone in his pocket, John called his brother.

"I think you may need to come here after all."

CHAPTER FOURTEEN

John's sleep had been troubled and sporadic, so he was grateful when the alarm he'd set on his phone went off at seven. He stretched in his father's chair, his back and shoulders aching from the host of uncomfortable positions he'd tossed and turned into during the long night. The smart thing would have been to move to the bed, but being in the chair kept him tethered to his father. He looked at the open letter on the table and grunted.

As if I didn't already have enough to worry about.

The television blared away upstairs, which meant his mother was awake. There was no time to wrestle with his thoughts, as he had to go up and take care of her. That in itself was a blessing.

"Did you ever come up to bed?" she asked. She was practically in the same position he'd left her in the night before.

"I kinda passed out in Dad's chair. My back is already paying for it."

"Well, tonight your old bed will be waiting for you. Take a couple of Motrin with your breakfast."

"Oh, I will."

With very little effort despite his aching back, he lifted her out of the bed and set her up in the bathroom. When she'd first been diagnosed with MD and things had gotten bad quickly, John and his mother had had their share of awkward moments when he assisted her with . . . private things. As much as his father wanted to do it all, John had known there might come a day when he'd need to know what to do, so he'd insisted every time he visited.

Now, years later, there was no embarrassment. As his mother said, the moment you got sick, shame went right out the window.

After the bathroom, he sat her in a chair and fixed her bed. "How about a change of scenery?" he asked.

Her smile made his heart ache. Here she was, bed-ridden and worried sick about Dad, and the suggestion of getting out of the room was enough to bring a smile to her face.

"That would be lovely," she said.

John carried her downstairs and was about to set her on the couch when she said, "Your dad's chair will be perfect."

He understood exactly what she meant.

No novice in the kitchen, John made them a breakfast of bacon and poached eggs with wheat toast. They ate in the living room, John opening the blinds wide so his mother could look out at the front of the house. A few people walked by, several of them older women pushing metal collapsible carts.

"Is that June?" his mother said, squinting to peer at a tiny woman dressed in black carrying several plastic bags.

John followed her gaze. "I have no idea. With that scarf on her head, I can't tell."

"June always walked hunched over. I'm sure it's her. I'd heard she was going to live with her daughter in St. Petersburg. I guess I heard wrong."

Clearing their dishes away, John said, "Or June changed her mind. I understand firsthand how hard it is to get your parents to move."

His mother tsked. "This is our home, Johnnie. It's where we belong."

It's used to be where you belong, he thought, but wisely kept it to himself.

He'd made sure to bring the letter into the kitchen and tuck it away under a serving dish in the cabinet. He didn't want his mother, or Isabelle, when she came later, to see it. He hadn't been able to wrap his head around it just yet, and the last thing he needed was for his mother to read it.

"You want to go back upstairs?" he asked.

"I'd like to stay down here, if you don't mind. It's been a while, and I like to see my friends, even if they can't see me."

Again, she broke his heart.

"I'm going to pick up a few things, and then I have to call in to work, let them know I won't be back later this week."

"There's no need to do that. Your father and I are both going to be well taken care of."

John shook his head. "No way. I'm here for the foreseeable future." He caught the glint of relief in her eyes that she didn't give voice to. "Which means I want to get some more food and a few things for Dad. And, of course, whatever you need."

She rattled off some gossip magazines and, of all things, a bag of popcorn.

After making sure she was okay, John changed and left the house, enjoying a walk around the old neighborhood. There was the tree he and Joe had climbed almost every day in summers, until Joe fell and broke his arm. They were forbidden to climb it from that point on, but that didn't stop John from carving their initials in the bark. He ran his fingers across the old trunk now, seeing the faint impressions of his and his friends' initials. He wondered where they were now. After enlisting in the army, he lost touch with the old gang, all of them moving on and out of Woodlean. The little park two blocks away hadn't changed much. The monkey bars had been torn down ages ago, but the rusty swings were still there, along with the seesaw. The splintered wood of the seesaw of John's youth had been replaced by metal with cushioned seats. Black rubber had been laid down over the concrete in the play area, and the park was lined with long benches. It was sad to see no children running around. Just the old guard out for some fresh air, several feeding pigeons from bags filled with crumbled bits of bread.

Bridge Avenue, their idea of Main Street, had seen its fair share of changes, as was normal in any neighborhood, per the rules of commerce. Gone was the narrow bookstore where John and Joe bought their comic books. Frank's Pizza had been replaced by Tony's Pizza. The five-and-dime where his mother worked part time for a couple of years was now a Laundromat. The only five-and-dime that John knew that still existed was in North Conway, New Hampshire. He and Marion often took their foster children to the town to take them on the scenic railroad tour and shopping along the quaint main road. They'd yet to see a child who wasn't enthralled with the old five-and-dime, perusing unique old toys and begging for a bag of fresh-made taffy.

John got some groceries at the little IGA market and stopped at O'Toole's Stationery to get two papers—one for his mother and one for his father—along with a copy of the *Irish Echo* and some gum.

Walking along the street, he was hard pressed to recognize anyone, but several women paused and stared hard at him. They were all older, his former neighbors hidden by time and wrinkles. John himself was a far cry from the boy who went hauling ass around the streets on his Huffy bike, shouting that he was Evel Knievel about to jump the Snake River Canyon with nothing but his three speed and sheer determination.

He stopped when he saw a pile of black garbage bags and furniture outside the Owens' two-family house. The door was wide open, the windows naked of blinds or curtains. The sounds of men moving things around inside filtered into the street.

When two guys in blue overalls came outside carrying an old sofa that they unceremoniously dumped on the curb, John asked them, "Where are the people who live here?"

John knew from talking to his mother than Fred and Nancy Owens still lived in the house, though the apartment upstairs had been vacant for some time.

The man wearing a sweat-stained red bandana on his head said, "How would I know? We're just here to clear the place out."

"Do you know when they moved out?" John asked, though it didn't seem like Fred and Nancy had moved. In fact, it looked like most of their stuff was either out here waiting to be thrown in the back of a garbage truck or being manhandled inside.

The other one, a shorter guy with five days of stubble but kind eyes, added, "I don't know for sure, but I think it was recent."

"He don't know nothing," bandana guy said before heading back into the house.

"We get called to these all the time," the other man said. "It's usually someone died or was evicted."

Died or evicted. Fred and Nancy were old, but he couldn't imagine them dying at the same time.

"Thanks," John said. "I was just curious."

He was more than curious, and growing alarmed.

John asked his mother what had become of the Owenses, and she looked at him quizzically. As far as she knew, they were fine and expecting their granddaughter to stay with them for spring break. He told her about the men and the house being emptied, and immediately regretted it. The knot of worry in the center of her forehead was something she didn't need now. As sick as his father was, his mother's health was no great shakes, either.

After assuring her that they were most likely fine—a failed assurance, at that, because she still looked upset as he left—he drove over to St. Luke's.

Pausing outside his father's room for just a moment, he steeled himself for the worst. Bad things happened in hospitals overnight. There was a chance his father would be hooked up to a respirator, or worse.

Turning the corner, he exhaled with relief at seeing

nothing untoward had occurred while he'd been gone. At least, not visibly. His father was just as he'd left him. He was still sleeping. John quietly put the things he'd brought on the windowsill. The view of the closely packed trees behind the hospital, blue sky strung with wispy clouds, was as good as it got in St. Luke's. If he'd been on the other side of the floor, he'd look out into the street, hearing the rumble of buses and cars going by.

John sat in a visitor's chair and took out his phone, scrolling through the texts Marion had sent him this morning. She was nervous about the presentation she had to give that afternoon and needed some words of encouragement. Plus, she demanded a full update on the man she considered her father.

"You must be John."

A burly man in a white coat, maybe ten or so years older than John, held out his hand. John gripped it, feeling skin so soft, it was like holding smooth calfskin.

"Dr. Murphy. Your father told me this morning I have you to thank for getting him here. I'm sorry I wasn't around yesterday. I was with my wife in Delaware for our anniversary. Don't ask why Delaware." He had a mischievous glint in his eyes.

"Nice to meet you. So, he was up earlier?"

"For a little while. I had to wake him to ask some questions. Kick the tires, so to speak."

"How bad is it?"

Dr. Murphy thrust his hands in his pockets and stared at the occupied bed. "I'll be honest with you. It's not good. When people get pneumonia, especially when they're older, it's not the congestion in the lungs that causes the most concern. It's the stress it puts on the heart. Your father's heart has been through a lot, and there may be permanent damage. Right now, I have a cocktail of antibiotics to treat the pneumonia on the one hand and a whole separate regimen to address his heart."

"I saw that his BP was through the roof when we brought him in. I just assumed it was the stress."

"It's stress, just not emotional."

"What's your prognosis?"

The doctor shook his head. "He's stable for now, but that can change. I honestly can't tell you what tomorrow will bring, but he will be here for a while. I can give him all the medicine in our arsenal, but it's ultimately up to him. Your father is a pretty stubborn guy, and that's something in his favor."

John gazed at his father, sleeping what appeared to be peacefully, but fighting a war deep inside.

Just keep fighting. I know you want to get home to Mom. Fight it with all you've got.

CHAPTER FIFTEEN

On the drive home, John stopped outside Fred and Nancy Owens' house. A trash collector must have come by during the afternoon, because all of the furniture and bags were gone. The house stared back at John, dark and empty. Whenever Nancy baked chocolate chip cookies, ones as big and round as his face, she'd called him and Joe in to be her official taste testers. Just looking at their home brought back the smell of those cookies.

"What the heck happened to you?"

He wasn't so lucky finding parking this time. It was near dusk and the streets were filled. John finally found a space four blocks away.

It was too cold out yet for the old-timers to be sitting in their folding chairs or on their porches. The walk was chilly, but John was lost in a million thoughts.

Which was why he was taken aback when he opened the front gate to his parents' house to find three women standing outside the front door.

"Can I help you?" he asked.

The trio turned around, obviously startled.

Three blue hairs, as his father would say. John grinned.

The woman in the middle, tiny and wearing a thick coat buttoned up to her neck and down past her knees, a black hat pulled low on her head, saw him and said, "If it isn't little Johnnie. What a pleasant surprise."

The other two women smiled and clucked for a few seconds.

Aggie Firth. That was a woman John couldn't forget. She had a sizeable wart—or was it a mole?—on the side of her nose. Had been there for as long as he knew her. He and his friends used to say she was a witch. As he got older, he realized she was far from it. She might have been a bit of a busybody, but she meant no harm.

"Hello, Mrs. Firth."

She motioned to the women on either side of her. "Do you remember Kate Maguire and Carol McInerny?"

He vaguely recalled their names. But he did remember what his father called Aggie's band of neighborhood watchers.

The Widows' Brigade.

"I do. So nice to see you," he said, fumbling for the keys. "So, what brings you around?"

Aggie moved in close, as if she were about to reveal a deep secret. "We heard about your father, and I was hoping we'd catch your mom before that girl who comes by left for the day. It looks like we're too late."

"I'm sure Mom will be thrilled to see you," he said, opening the door, and he meant it.

His mother was still downstairs, a blanket over her lap, the TV remote in her hand. When she saw the Widows' Brigade stream in behind him, her eyes lit up.

"Isn't this a nice surprise," she said. She attempted to straighten her hair, but her arms failed her.

John got to her before the Brigade and whispered in her ear, "Just say the word, and I'll give them the old heave-ho."

She shook him off and smirked. "You'll do no such thing."

Suddenly, they were upon her. John took coats and hats, and they pulled chairs up to be close to his mother.

Luckily, he had already filled his mother in on the latest from the doctor while he was at the hospital, so there was no urgent news she needed from him. John slipped into the kitchen, but not before asking if anyone needed a drink. It was no surprise that he was asked to put a kettle on. The house was awash with loud talking (because most of them were hard of hearing) and laughter. John leaned against the counter, drinking a beer, feeling disoriented. He'd been through so many emotional swings the past few days, he either needed ten hours of sleep or ten hours of drinking.

The Widows' Brigade peppered his mother with questions about his father's condition with equal parts concern and need to gather intel to spread throughout the neighborhood. He heard Aggie say she would start a special prayer circle for him, and that took some of the edge off the way he felt about them. As he listened to them update his mother on all the latest in the neighborhood, he couldn't stop himself from interjecting.

"Do you ladies know what happened to Fred and Nancy Owen?"

Aggie paled. Swallowing with a dry click in her throat, she said, "The same as happened to Bridgett Monahan, only it happened later in the day when no one was around."

His mother, along with Carol and Kate, bowed their heads and shook them sadly.

"What happened to Mrs. Monahan?" John asked.

"Thrown out of her house like a piece of trash," Aggie said forcefully. "I was there to witness the awful thing. Bridgett was upset, naturally, but that sheriff and his deputy wouldn't leave her be. She died, right there in the street."

"She died?"

"Yes. From the stress of the humiliation, I would say."

"And you say Fred and Nancy were evicted?"

He hoped to God they hadn't died in the process, as well.

Carol McInerny piped in. "The man who lives across the street, he saw it. He came at night, that fat sheriff, and just took them away. Fred hadn't been well, and he looked a sight being led out of his house."

John looked back into the kitchen, at the cabinet where he'd hidden the letter. His stomach, grumbling with hunger just minutes earlier, was twisted in a knot.

"Where are they now?"

"No one knows," Kate said, making the sign of the cross.

"They're not the only ones," Aggie said. "It's like a plague running rampant through the neighborhood. Believe me, we're trying to get to the bottom of it, but there's just only so much we can do. I just got word about Jerry Banner's house being suddenly vacant, but I haven't seen it for myself yet."

"Jerry Banner," his mother said. "He was always a quiet one. In all the years he's been here, I think I spoke to him once."

Carol bobbed her head. "He was a queer one. Liked to keep to himself. I saw him in the library often. He's had the Alzheimer's these past few years, or so I've heard."

Now John had joined the circle, sitting on the edge of the coffee table. He noticed that Kate smelled strongly of peppermint, the scent making him remember her. She was the woman who grabbed the free mints in the coffee shop by the handful, much to the dismay of the owner. "About how many people have been removed from their houses?"

Aggie Firth closed her eyes for a moment, her lips moving silently, and said, "Seven. And by that, I mean seven houses."

Seven houses? That was a lot, considering the size of the neighborhood.

John wondered if she was including Archie O'Malley in her count. No, Mr. O'Malley had died. He hadn't been evicted. Still, that did leave behind an empty house. "All in this neighborhood, and not bleeding over into McLaren Heights?"

The three heads of the Widows' Brigade nodded. His mother was aghast.

"What kind of time line are we talking here?" John asked.

Aggie leaned in closer. "That's what has everyone so frightened. It's all happened within the last month or so."

That alarmed John more than anything. It's not like Woodlean was some crumbling suburb, suffering from extreme poverty. These were working-class retirees. They might not be rich, but they had done well enough to live comfortably. Woodlean had more than its share of former union workers, many of them lifelong civil servants with the good fortune of having been valued by their employers and nice pensions waiting for them at the ends of their careers. It was all so unlike the experience of John's own generation, where constant layoffs, company hopping, and weak 401(k)s were the norm, not the exception. John was in a good company now, but that could change in a moment. There was no loyalty, and no promises made to make sure he was taken care of when he retired. Whatever happened to the American dream of parents leaving behind a better world for their children? And now even his parents' generation was seeing the fruits of their own dreams ripped out from under them.

John didn't realize he was grinding his teeth until his jaw made a loud pop.

"Someone has to call the police about this," he said. "Something doesn't seem right."

Aggie looked at him as if he had just spouted a line of baby talk. "Who do you think is taking people from their homes?"

"I don't mean the sheriff."

He had a hard time processing everything. Nothing made sense or added up. How would all of these people suddenly lose their homes? It made no sense. He couldn't even blame a bank for being behind it all, because he was pretty sure all of the homes had been mortgage-free for quite some time. Sure, one of them might have taken out a second mortgage, but all seven? And each and every one of them having their numbers called at the same time? Impossible. Yet it was happening.

"Follow the money," he whispered.

"What was that, dear?" his mother said.

He rubbed his eyes. "Nothing." Addressing the Widows' Brigade, he said, "Look, while I'm in town, I'll do some digging and see what I can find out."

"Oh, bless you," Aggie said.

His mother smiled, mouthing, *Thank you.*

She didn't realize he wasn't volunteering his assistance just to settle the fears of the Widows' Brigade.

The letter he'd stashed in the cabinet had made it imperative he find out what was going on in Woodlean. If he didn't get to the bottom of things soon, his parents would be joining Fred and Nancy, wherever they might be.

After tea and cookies, John ushered the Widows' Brigade out of the house, offering to drive them home. They preferred to walk while they still could, and he didn't press them. That was followed by carrying his mother upstairs and helping her get ready for bed. Despite the earlier tension over her disappearing neighbors, she seemed happy, the unexpected visit taking her mind off his father.

Wheel of Fortune was just starting when he got her fully situated. "Your father is just awful at *Wheel,*" she said. "You want to try to solve the puzzles? You can't be any worse."

His brain buzzed as if a hive of bees had been crammed in his ears.

"I'd love to, but I better call Marion."

She leaned her head so it rested on his arm as he fluffed the pillows. "Go, call her. Tell her I said hello."

"I will. When I come back, we'll watch anything you want."

John stopped in his room, found the crushed pack of cigarettes he'd tucked into the outer pocket of his suitcase, stuffed them in his pocket, and went outside to make his call. Only he wasn't calling his wife. Not yet.

Lighting up his first cigarette in months, John inhaled

deeply, making sure he was well away from his mother's window. He'd told her—and everyone—that he'd quit years ago. John was no quitter. Besides, he only smoked when he was feeling unduly stressed. Like he was this very moment.

He dialed his brother.

"Hey, Johnnie boy."

"You get your ticket?"

Joe coughed into the phone. "Wait. What?"

"This isn't a drill. You have to come out here." It was dark and quiet in the backyard, reminding John of the soft solitude of his home in Maine. He wondered how long it would be until he returned to his home and wife.

"I thought you said that notice was probably fake," Joe said.

"That's what I was hoping. But I was just informed by the Widows' Brigade that there has been a rash of evictions over the past month. And here I have an eviction notice from some damn lawyer hidden away so it won't upset Mom. Dad isn't doing so well and is barely conscious, and I need some help here."

"You have to call that lawyer."

"Thanks. I had no idea."

"Be careful, your sarcasm is showing," Joe said.

"If this lawyer tries to railroad Mom and Dad out of their home, it's not the only thing that's going to show." John ground the cigarette butt out into the dirt and lit a second cancer stick.

As John exhaled, Joe said, "Hey, are you smoking?"

John looked around the yard. "You have cameras hidden somewhere?"

"They don't call us Big Brothers for nothing. Look, you

take care of Mom and Dad. Take a picture of the notice and send it to me. I'll call the lawyer tomorrow. If I don't like what I hear, I'm on the next plane to Virginia."

A cold breeze went right through John, making him regret not putting on his coat. He couldn't be sure if that was the only thing making him shiver. "Start looking for tickets tonight. Something doesn't feel right here."

Joe promised to check for tickets and reminded him to send the picture of the notice.

Not right at all, Joe thought, feeling something vital slipping away not just from him, but from the interconnected lives of everyone in Woodlean.

CHAPTER SIXTEEN

Joe Knox decided to make it a work-from-home day, if he could even call this apartment home. He'd been trying to call the lawyer's office all morning, to no avail. With Joe on the West Coast, the man behind the eviction notice should be in his office. It was getting Joe exceedingly agitated, which told him he'd made the right decision not to go in to work today. He wasn't in the headspace to make office small talk. Or big talk.

As his brother had suggested, he'd gone to a few travel websites, looking for the lowest-priced ticket to Virginia. Money was tight, but not so tight that he couldn't fly out to see his parents. No matter what happened during his call with the lawyer today, he was leaving on a red-eye tonight.

The sun was out, as it always was, and he had the window open to let in the barest of a breeze. If things heated up any more, he'd have to turn on the AC, which meant further damage to his electric bill. He paced the apartment. Just a few months ago he was living in a beautiful but modest house with his wife and kids, not counting pennies.

He considered calling his own lawyer. Stella still hadn't signed the divorce papers. Maybe he shouldn't have been as kind as he'd been. She was the one who had cheated on him, for Christ's sake. Trying to take the high road, understanding that she wouldn't have cheated if there hadn't been serious problems to begin with, and knowing the kids would stay with her, he'd asked for very little. Now he realized maybe it was too little.

Joe grabbed his phone, which was next to his laptop, work emails coming in but not being read, and swiped until he found his lawyer's number. His thumb hovered over the dial button, but thoughts of more legal bills stopped him. He eyed the clock on the wall above the refrigerator. It was almost eleven thirty. Close enough to noon for him.

The beer was cold, and went down fast.

Last night, he'd forwarded the picture John had sent of the eviction notice to his computer so he could blow up the image and read it easier. He opened the file and read it over for at least the tenth time. It was brief, a simple statement that Patrick and Mary Knox had two weeks to vacate the premises, as they were in a house that did not belong to them.

Did not belong to them?

Joe's father had bought that house two years before Joe was born. He'd paid it off over thirty years ago. What the hell was this crook lawyer talking about?

Grabbing another beer, he dialed the lawyer's number for the tenth time.

The phone rang and rang while he sipped his beer. After six rings, his call went to voicemail. A pleasant-sounding woman informed him of the office's hours and to leave a message so they could call him back. Joe hung up. There was no sense leaving a message. What he wanted to say was best spoken to a live person, not a machine.

He looked back at the notice.

The law office of Anthony Kramer.

"Let's see who you are, Mr. Kramer."

He typed the lawyer's name in a search engine and got back a single result, which was the flimsy website for what appeared to be Kramer's one-man operation. That in itself set off an alarm bell. In today's information age, newborn babies had a wider internet presence. This guy had somehow managed to keep such a low profile that the only shred of information on him was a web page controlled by him. Hmm.

There wasn't a picture of Anthony Kramer or his office. In fact, the only image was a professional shot of the interior of an office—windows overlooking a cityscape, a large oak desk, and several leather chairs. Joe knew a generic picture when he saw one. There were endless places you could buy images like this online.

Next, he typed in the lawyer's address, mapping the location.

If the address was correct, Mr. Kramer, esquire, worked out of his house in Virginia Beach. The street view showed him a sketchy ranch house close to the beach.

Leaning back so hard in his chair the old wood protested, he closed his eyes and took a few deep breaths. He was glad he'd bought that ticket. John shouldn't have to handle all of this by himself. By remaining on the same coast as their parents, John had been the de facto go-to child for everything. Joe felt bad for that. He really did, no matter what his kid brother might think. Joe missed his parents, and even the old neighborhood, very much. With each passing year, he grew more nostalgic, wondering whether moving the family to Virginia would help him recapture some of the youth, bravado, and exuberance that filled his soul to the brim when he was the kid who slept in the top bunk. Quiet moments found him often thinking back to his and John's exploits when they were kids, family vacations, the sound of his mother washing the dishes while listening to what she called "old country music" on the local college radio station. He missed the smell of fresh sawdust when his father worked in the basement, always building something.

Reminiscing about the old days kept him from thinking about how his mother could no longer even stand at the sink and his father's arthritis had kept him out of his tiny wood shop for more years than Joe had spent in the house. They were all getting old, and John knew with sinking despair that his parents wouldn't be around much longer. He needed to see them. He needed to find out who the hell Anthony Kramer was and why he thought he could kick Joe's parents out of their home.

And if he didn't like the answer, he was happy to make the lawyer wish he'd never stumbled upon the Knox boys. Because for all their current domestication, Joe and John had once been world-class scrappers, John funneling his need for confrontation into the armed services, Joe scratching that itch in bars around the country. They might not have looked for fights, but they sure as hell never backed down from them, either.

Joe had been battered and beaten these past few months. He needed someone to take it out on.

Anthony Kramer had just appointed himself that someone.

Richmond International Airport was surprisingly crowded for just after six in the morning. Joe had slept soundly on the plane, his eyes closed and brain shut down almost the moment he'd taken his seat. The beer he'd been drinking all day helped.

Now he was feeling a little hungover, but he had to find where to pick up his rental car before he could take care of that. His lone suitcase trailing behind him, Joe navigated his way around the airport, going through the baggage claim area and out the door to the rental area. It had been over a year since his last visit home, and the guilt was hard to ignore. In a way, he was thankful for the hangover as a sort of price to pay for his absence.

He was a big man at a shade under six foot four, which made him a target for people to crash into as they zipped about, most of them either with their noses glued to their phones or ears crammed with earbuds, oblivious to the world around them. By the time the fourth person clipped him, he was ready to yank the phone out of the young man's hand and toss it under a passing bus.

Willfully clueless, he thought. Everyone had become so plugged in to their devices, they were unaware they'd unplugged themselves from society. His own son and daughter barely looked up from their phones, even during meals. It infuriated him. Stella had told him repeatedly to lay off Hayley and Matt. They were good kids, just a product of their generation. He had to roll with the times, not fight against them. All he was going to do was alienate himself, prematurely becoming the old fogey who no one paid attention to. When he considered the way things were going, he was perfectly happy being the crank bemoaning the state of the world.

Locating the rental lot, he had no problem finding his car. The new Chrysler was waiting for him in space 147. Joe tossed his suitcase in the trunk and set out to find a place to get something to eat and some aspirin. He came across a diner off Route 64 and had pancakes with sausage, along with two cups of coffee and a glass of water. They had little packets of headache pills behind the counter. He bought two packets and downed one of them.

Listening to the radio on the drive to the old neighborhood, Joe went into autopilot mode, barely noting landmarks as he got closer. With fresh air blowing through the window, the pounding in his skull abated. As he pulled up in front of the house, he briefly wondered how he'd gotten from the diner to home.

Home.

He'd been gone more than thirty years, but this was still very much home.

Now someone wanted to take it away.

Gripping the steering wheel until his knuckles turned white, he went in search of a parking space. The neighborhood looked the same, if not a little more run-down. Parking was still an issue, which to him was a good thing, a tether to the past when the area was vibrant and alive.

He found a space around the corner and two blocks down. It was an overcast day but unseasonably warm. When Joe was growing up, the streets were alive from sunup to sundown. Kids played Wiffle Ball or football or just rode around on their bikes, looking for planks of wood to use as ramps. A lot of broken bones, bruises, and road rash came about from those rickety ramps and misguided attempts at being a daredevil.

Today, the walk to his parents' house was quiet. He only passed by one man shuffling slowly with his cane, his hat pulled low over his eyes. Joe wouldn't have been surprised to see a tumbleweed rolling down the suburban street.

He rang the bell and dropped his bag, remembering that John was probably at St. Luke's or on his way. Fumbling for his keys, he was stunned when the door flew open.

"Am I getting so old I can't remember if you told me you were definitely coming?" John said, holding a bowl of cereal in one hand.

"Surprise," Joe said. It had been a while since he'd last seen his brother. The kid—well, not so much a kid anymore—looked the same. Joe was well aware that he'd put a few pounds on, the stress of the past few months adding a fresh shock of gray to his hair, as well. He looked as old as he felt, but John didn't seem to notice.

They shook hands, their matching grips strong and sure.

"I like what you've done to the place," Joe said. Everything was clean and in order. The last time he'd come here, it had started to look and smell, to be honest, like an old person's house, which it was. Now, the place had hints of pine and lemon cleaner, the windows open to let a cross breeze through.

John closed the door, scooping dry cereal into his

mouth. He had always hated soggy cereal. In between mouthfuls, he said, "I take no credit. That all goes to Isabelle."

"Who's Isabelle?"

"The home aide. Mom didn't tell you?"

Joe tossed his jacket on the couch. "She might have, but I've been distracted lately."

"Who was at the door?" their mother called out from upstairs.

"Just the Fuller Brush man," John said, cupping his hand to the side of his mouth.

"The Fuller Brush man?" she said.

Joe and John snickered like little kids.

"You better go up there and see if she wants to buy anything," John said. "I'll bring your bag up."

Joe climbed the stairs and looked down the hall to his parents' bedroom. He saw the bottom half of his mother's hospital bed and her stick-thin legs. He cursed the disease that had stolen so much from her.

Stepping into the room, seeing the shock and joy in her pale blue eyes, he was just grateful that she was still here for him to see and hold.

CHAPTER SEVENTEEN

John hated to break up the happy reunion between his brother and mother. She had managed to lift her arms, her hands on either side of Joe's face.

"You want to come with me to see Dad?" John asked.

Joe gently took their mother's hands and laid them on her chest. "You park any closer than me?"

"Just up the block."

"Good. You drive."

John looked at his watch, then his mother. "Are you going to be all right without us? Isabelle comes in a half hour, right?"

She nodded. "I'll be just fine. You two go. When your father sees you both, that will make him better more than any medicine."

They kissed her cheek and headed for John's car.

John said, "Before we go to St. Luke's, I want to show you something."

Now that they were away from the house, the gravity of the situation and the reason for their reunion had dulled their spirits. The smiles had left their faces as they walked through the quiet neighborhood.

Getting in the car, John said, "You put on some weight there, big guy."

Joe patted his paunch. "Beer and stress eating. I'll have my bikini body back in time for summer. Don't you worry."

Grinning, John said, "If I saw you in a bikini, I'd go blind."

"You and anyone else around."

They went up and down all the neighboring streets, John stopping the car in the middle of the street from time to time to point out yet another empty house. Bridgett Monahan's big house looked as if it had been abandoned for decades.

"Mrs. Monahan died?" Joe said, leaning forward, his nose practically touching the windshield.

"Right in the street, Dad said. And Doyle broke his hip when he got pushed down the stairs."

"What the hell? That doesn't make any sense. Mrs. Monahan had to be almost ninety. Why would they feel she needed to be manhandled out the door? And how did it come to her getting evicted?"

John checked the rearview mirror to make sure no one was coming down the street. He wasn't ready to leave just yet. He tried to picture the chaos in his mind, the fear and confusion and most likely anger Mrs. Monahan felt. To die being dragged from your home in front of everyone. It was unthinkable. What had this world come to? Whatever happened to respecting your elders? It seemed that the moment you became too old to be just another rat in the daily race, you were forgotten, your value dipping so low as to be utterly inconsequential.

Two short taps on a horn made him pull away. He showed his brother the other empty houses and filled him in on how they had become vacant. Joe took it all in quietly, as was his nature.

"What did the lawyer say?" John said.

"You're implying I got to speak to the bastard. I've called at least a dozen times. All I get is a voicemail. You might assume he's on vacation or maybe out sick, but I'm thinking I can call until the cows come home and no one will ever pick up. I think we should go to his office over in Virginia Beach. Again, I don't expect him to be there, but I have to see it for myself."

John left Woodlean, heading for St. Luke's Hospital. "I'm with you on that. Maybe we'll get lucky and catch him in the act of typing out another one of his eviction notices."

Joe sat with his arms crossed. "Then that would be a very unlucky day . . . for him."

Seeing his father sitting up in bed and spooning orange Jell-O from a tiny cup put a spring in John's step when he entered the room.

"You're up," he said.

His father needed a shave, and the hospital gown hung on his shrinking frame awkwardly. He pointed the spoon in his trembling hand at John and said, "You always were observant."

Awake and with his sense of humor. For the first time, John saw light at the end of the tunnel, and there weren't harps playing in the background.

"How do you feel?"

His father put the Jell-O down. "Like I was hit by a

Mack truck." He patted his chest. "Hurts to breathe, but I'm tired of sleeping."

"And hungry, it appears."

"You miss nothing," his father said with a wink.

John held up a finger. "Ah, but I know something you've missed."

"Your mother? My home? Health? The Capitals game?"

Smiling, John said, "Okay, nothing as good as that."

"Way to downplay my entrance," Joe said, striding into the room.

Their father leaned into his pillows as if he were physically bowled over. "Joseph?" he rasped.

"In the flesh." Joe leaned down to hug him, which took John by surprise. He couldn't remember the last time he'd seen his brother hug their dad. In the Knox family, an outward showing of affection between men involved a hearty handshake or a clap on the back.

Joe must have really been worried about him, John thought. Of course, they all were. He just didn't think it would hit his brother, who had been around so little all these years, so hard. It wasn't quite a case of out of sight, out of mind, but close.

"And there's a lot more flesh than usual," John joked.

"Wait until you hit fifty, smart mouth. You'll see."

John sat in the chair at the foot of the bed, allowing them time to catch up. The television was tuned to a morning talk show. His father hated that kind of stuff, which meant he must have lost the remote. John looked under the bed and found it dangling from its cord. He flipped through the channels until he found a game show.

His father turned away from Joe and said, "Johnnie, how's your mother?"

"Very happy now that the gang is all here," John said.

"Is Isabelle with her?"

John nodded. She should definitely be there by now.

"You want something more substantial than orange slime?" Joe asked. "I could get you a Danish and real coffee from the café downstairs."

"I don't think I could handle it. Best to take it slow."

John leaned an arm on the bed's bottom rail. "The word is out about you."

His father raised a bushy eyebrow.

"The Widows' Brigade paid Mom a visit. Naturally, they have a mass dedicated to you and will be adding you in their daily prayers. Expect a visit from them soon."

"Jesus, if you can hear me, get me out of here before that happens."

"The Widows' Brigade is real?" Joe said.

"Of course it is," John said.

Joe chuckled. "I just thought it was a general term Dad made up about the busybody old biddies in the neighborhood."

"Now that they're on my scent, I can only wish."

Two orderlies came an hour later to take the Knox patriarch down to X-ray for some tests. He was already growing visibly tired, but he managed to make one last joke. "I'm ready for my close-up."

Joe and John followed them to the elevator, waving as the doors closed.

Joe heaved a big sigh of relief. "That was a lot better than I expected."

"You should have seen him yesterday. It's likc night and day. He wants to get home to Mom. That's what's going to get him to pull through."

"He'll need some sleep when they take him back to his room. We should go home and be with Mom. We can come back and maybe bring him some dinner later," Joe said, already heading for the visitor elevators. If John had been alone, he would have stayed, but his brother made sense. Their father had had enough excitement for now.

They caught up on things on the ride home, John doing most of the talking. Something was on Joe's mind, but there was no sense trying to pry it out of him—yet.

John's eyes skimmed the road for parking as they reached the house, but he slammed the brakes when he saw the front door wide open. "You see Isabelle putting out the garbage on the side of the house?"

Joe got out of the car and checked. He turned back to John and said, "No, and I don't think she's playing hide-and-seek."

"So why is the front door open?"

John double-parked the car, not bothering to consider whether anyone would be able to sneak past it. He and Joe ran up the steps and into the house. Joe spotted the paper stapled to the door. He ripped it off and scanned it. "A formal notice of eviction."

"Mom!"

John took the steps three at a time, his heart thundering so hard he was dizzy. At the landing, he turned left and darted into her room. She lay fast asleep, the television on low.

Or was she asleep?

Joe stumbled into him. "Oh, thank Christ."

John couldn't breathe. He stared at his mother's chest, afraid to check her neck for a pulse. The sheet atop her body hadn't moved. He and Joe had made a ruckus rushing up the stairs. Surely she should have heard them?

Joe, satisfied that she was where she was supposed to be, had retreated back downstairs, reading the eviction notice aloud to himself.

Steeling himself, John reached down for his mother's wrist. Her skin was as soft and brittle as old tracing paper. His fingers searched for her pulse.

When her eyes flew open, he nearly jumped.

At first, she looked horrified, but that gradually melted away to mild but welcome surprise. "Oh, it's you, Johnnie. I must have nodded off."

John had to swallow several times and clear his throat before he could answer. "Joe and I just got back from the hospital. We made a ton of noise coming in. You were really out."

"It happens to me. My sleep cycles are a mess, so when I do fall asleep, I'm out like a light."

He heard the floorboard pop below as Joe paced the living room.

"Hey Mom, where's Isabelle?"

"She's still not here?"

"No."

"Can you check my phone and see if she left a message? That's so unlike her."

John went through her cell phone but found no messages.

"Maybe she's sick or had a family emergency," John said.

"Oh, I hope shc's all right."

"I'm sure she is. My main concern is you. I'm sorry for waking you up."

"Don't you dare apologize. I don't want to sleep through my time with you and your brother."

She asked him how his father was and he gave the positive update, but his mind was on the door. Could he and Joe have forgotten to close it? That seemed unlikely. The eviction notice was clear proof that someone had been here.

Had they been inside the house, as well? While his mother was sleeping?

Anger crept up and started to take hold. He excused himself under the guise of going downstairs and talking to Joe about what to make for lunch.

His brother sat at the kitchen table, his head in his hands, reading the letter over. When he heard John, he looked up and said, "This is bullshit."

"You and I both know that."

"I'm going to that lawyer's office, and when I find him, I'm going to make him wish he never took the bar exam."

John took the chair opposite him and said, "Before you go all Rambo on the guy, we have to address the door. Do you think someone broke into the house while we were away?"

"Maybe it was the aide."

"Mom said Isabelle never came today."

Joe finally looked up from the notice. "She could have stopped by but gotten called away and forgot to close the door." Even he didn't sound so sure of that.

When his mother had told him that they had given Isabelle a set of keys to let herself in, John had been un-comfortable. Yes, his parents seemed to have taken to her, but really, who was she? They didn't know a blessed thing about her. Had his parents let a criminal into their home and their lives?

"We should look around the house and make sure nothing's been taken." John's chair squeaked against the linoleum.

"I don't even know what belongs here anymore," Joe said.

"This is Mom and Dad we're talking about. Nothing much has changed. Our *Star Wars* mugs are still on the shelf over there."

"Good point. I'll look upstairs, you look down here?"

John went straight to the living room. Joe bounded up the stairs, stopping in to say hello to their mother so as not to alarm her. They did a quick scan of the rooms, making sure the few things worth any money were still where they belonged. Their father's gold watch was on the little table next to his chair. All of the china was in the hutch, untouched for many a year. When Joe came back downstairs, he said his and John's electronics—John's laptop and Joe's tablet—were still on the dresser.

"Maybe I'm overreacting," John said, gazing at the now-closed front door.

"Or maybe we should call the cops."

"But nothing was taken. They'll think we've lost our minds."

Joe stomped into the kitchen and swiped the eviction note off the table. "According to this, someone's trying to take a whole hell of a lot. Maybe they wanted to poke their head in and have a little look-see."

The eviction. Ever since John had arrived, everything had gone haywire. He took a moment to calm himself.

"If the cops come here, Mom will know something's up," John said.

"Something *is* up. This isn't like when we were kids and saw Greg Egan smoking behind the rectory and promised not to tell Mom or Dad because we knew he'd fight us for squealing. Someone is trying to take their house away from them. She's going to know sooner or later, and if she finds out we were keeping her in the dark, she'll be pissed." Joe sat in their father's chair and pulled out his phone. John stood with his hands on his hips, looking at the ceiling, picturing his mother lying in bed, waiting for that lunch he promised.

John said, "She won't be mad. Worse. She'll be disappointed."

"That's why I'm calling them now. I'll dial the non-emergency number and hope they show up before midnight. And after that, I'm calling my lawyer. Maybe he can refer me to someone in Virginia who can help us out with this eviction nonsense. The clock is ticking."

When the door whisked open without a preceding knock, the mayor's dart sailed wide and left of the bulls-eye. It missed the previous darts, nestled smack in the center of the dartboard, by several inches.

Viktor Bennett, mayor of Woodlean for two terms, scowled at the intruder. Not only had he missed his mark, he'd almost spilled the glass of scotch on the rocks. Seeing that the person who had broken his concentration was Jeremy Brown, his city clerk, only doubled his irritation.

"Do you see what you made me do?" Bennett grumbled,

pointing with his glass of scotch at the dart board. "I guess knocking isn't a thing in your family."

A flustered Brown adjusted his tie and was quick to apologize. "I'm so sorry. I thought Myrna had buzzed me in."

Mayor Bennett sauntered to his couch and settled into the plush leather. The couch had been a gift from his now deceased mother for winning his very first election as councilman. It was worth more than the entire contents of the office. "Did we have a meeting scheduled?"

"Um, yes. You wanted to me to review the minutes from last week's City Council meeting."

The mayor sipped his scotch and rested his head back. "How could I forget something so exciting? It's a good thing I started drinking. You want a drink? I just bought a bottle of premium vodka that I think you'll like. I liked it a little too much last night, which is why I'm enjoying this eighteen-year-old Oban single malt."

Jeremy Brown cast a quick glance at the fully stocked bar and declined. "I'm more of a beer drinker, and not much at that."

"Your loss. Okay, please try to make this quick and painless."

Brown put his briefcase on the round table in the corner of the room and removed his tablet. "Just bear with me. This thing is getting a little old and take a bit to get going."

"Trust me, I'm in no rush to be bored to tears."

While they were waiting, Brown said, "It's a shame what happened to that woman. I've never been a fan of Sheriff Justice. You think this could be grounds for dismissal?"

Mayor Bennett knew exactly what Brown was referring to. The old lady dying during her eviction was a terrible moment that he had been able to keep out of the press. Accidents happened. Evictions were never pretty, or easy. Unfortunately, in this case, the woman was old and frail and, from the intel he'd gathered, didn't make things any easier on herself by resisting the inevitable. Yes, Justice was a bull in a china shop and would never be asked to join Mensa, but for every alpha, there needed to be numerous betas to do the dirty work that needed doing.

"I think it was tragic, but it's not like he went out there to kill her. Maybe it can be seen as a lesson for others to respect authority a little more."

Brown eyed him skeptically. "That seems a bit harsh. A woman lost her life."

"She would still be here, drinking weak tea and watching game shows, if she didn't put up such a fight. People want law and order until their lives are impacted. Then they rebel. If you let them push too far, you get chaos. I don't want chaos in my city." Bennett rose from the couch and went to the window. It was a sunny day without even a hint of a cloud. The ice tinkled in his glass. "Justice is just fine where he is, doing what he does. Unless you want to take over evictions?"

Blanching, Brown's concentration went back to his tablet. "Ah, here we go. Nothing major, but here are some of the key takeaways."

While Brown droned on, Mayor Bennett watched a hawk circling in the sky and smiled.

CHAPTER EIGHTEEN

Maybe it was guilt for not being around for so long, or maybe it was his big brother DNA kicking in. Either way, Joe was taking the bull by the horns. After calling the police, he spoke to his lawyer, who didn't know anyone personally but agreed to ask around. Joe was sure the bastard would charge him for every second and triple for each phone call, but no matter. He was already in debt to the man. Why not throw a few more logs on the fire?

He also took it upon himself to explain everything to his mother. John was in the room, but Joe took the lead. It reminded him of the time John had accidentally broken the statue of Mary their mother kept in the yard. He'd been kicking a ball around and went full Pelé on the little statue. Joe found him in the yard panicked, tears rolling down his chubby cheeks. Joe took his hand and explained everything to their mother, John's shoulders heaving with each sob. No one got in trouble that day, though poor Mary's head was never the same after their father did his best to patch her up.

After being told about the eviction notice, even seeing

the letter, Mary said, "How can this be? This is our house. We don't have a penny of outstanding debt."

To her credit, she looked more angry than afraid. Joe was glad. Anger was something they could work with.

"I have no idea, Mom. For all I know, whoever this lawyer is has the wrong address. I already informed the police, and I'm also going to have a legitimate lawyer look into it." He patted her arm. "Trust me, you and Dad aren't going anywhere."

Hadn't he and John had a conversation two months back about how to get them out of the house and into a better living situation? Now here he was vowing to keep them in it.

She weakly grabbed his hand. "Don't tell your father. Not while he's in the hospital. We'll take care of it. The three of us."

Joe was more impressed with his mother than he'd ever been. They didn't make them like her anymore.

"I won't. Promise."

"I'll be damned if I let some shill run me out of my house."

Joe looked to John, both of them stunned. They'd never heard her utter anything close to a curse before.

She caught the silent communication between them. "Well, I'm upset. And I didn't take the Lord's name in vain. He'd say the same thing if he were my shoes."

That broke the tension in the room. They shared a much-needed laugh.

When the bell rang, John said, "You think it's the cops already?"

"Must be a slow crime day."

"We'll come back up to give you the scoop once they leave," John said.

"You better."

Joe and John had agreed to hide one thing from their mother—the fact that the door being open was the real reason they wanted the cops to come. For all they knew, it was the result of one of them being careless. They didn't need to add to her worry.

Pulling the curtain covering the small pane of glass high in the door, Joe saw it was indeed Woodlean's finest. Two of them, as a matter of fact. He opened the door just as one of them was about to ring again. A male and a female officer stood side by side, hands on their belts.

"Joe Knox?" the female cop said. The auburn hair that was showing under her cap had streaks of gray. She had prominent cheekbones and just a hint of creasing at the corner of her eyes that made it difficult to place her age.

"Yes," he said, ushering them inside. "Thanks for coming."

The male cop, a young kid who looked like he drank too many protein shakes and lived in a gym, strode into the house.

"You don't recognize me, do you?"

Joe looked at the name tag affixed above the pocket on her blue shirt. "Claire Dennehy. Wait, Claire Dennehy from St. Brendan's?"

"The one who split my Twinkie with you all of fourth grade so you'd let me play punchball with the boys."

Joe smiled. "After they saw how good you were, they would have let you play anytime. I just wanted Twinkies."

She came inside and removed her cap. "I always had

my suspicions about that. Good to solve a cold case."

Then she saw his brother, and her eyes lit up. "Is that you, John?"

"How have you been, Claire?"

"Little Johnnie Knox. I used to tell my parents I wanted a little brother like Johnnie Knox. They gave me a pain-in-the-ass sister instead."

"And how is Stacey?"

She rolled her eyes. "Still a pain in the ass. When I heard the address, I made sure to take the call. I just didn't expect to see you two."

The muscular cop remained silent, taking everything in and, of all things, flexing the considerable cords of muscles from his forearms to his biceps. He was most likely less than thrilled at the middle-aged reunion.

Joe said, "I never expected to have you ring the bell. I didn't even know you were a cop."

"Yeah, well, it beat a lot of the alternatives. I'm looking to retire soon."

"Can I get you guys something to drink?" John said. "We have water and soda in the fridge."

The muscular cop said, "I'm good. So, you think you had a break-in?"

He looked like he wanted to get this over with as soon as possible.

Claire Dennehy flicked a quick glance at him and gave a slight shake of her head.

"We were visiting our father at the hospital and came home to find the front door open," Joe said.

"Does anyone else live here?" he asked.

"Our mother," Joe said.

The young cop looked at him as if he were a slow child. "Is it possible she could have left the door open by mistake?"

Claire said, "Don't—"

John narrowed his eyes and was quick to add, "Our mother is bedridden. So, unless Jesus stopped by to perform a miracle, no, she couldn't have even come down the stairs, much less opened the door."

The cop stared at John, as if he were challenging him.

Joe had to defuse the situation. He showed Claire the notice that had been tacked to the door. "We know someone was here. This was on the door. Our concern is that they broke in to look around."

Claire took her time reading the notice. "We've been seeing a lot of these lately."

"So I've heard," John said. "Sounds like an epidemic."

"Makes me gad I convinced my parents to move to Fort Myers a few years back. They live in a small condo a block from the beach. Aside from the occasional tropical storm, it's been great."

"The only problem is," Joe said, getting close to Claire, "my parents haven't done a thing to lose their house. It's been paid off for a long time. My father was never rich, but he prepared himself for the future."

"Did you call a lawyer?" Claire said.

"Working on that right now," Joe said.

"There's not much I can do about that. But I'll see what we can do about a possible break-in. Is anything missing?" She checked the door to make sure the lock hadn't been jimmied or broken.

"Not as far as we can tell," John said. The muscle head

cop shot him another look. John didn't back down. "Have there been any burglaries in the neighborhood lately?"

On her knee, eye level with the locking mechanism in the door, Claire said, "Believe it or not, no. Thieves know there are fatter pickings elsewhere, I guess. Did you look around the house, see if anything seemed out of place? Burglars usually aren't the tidiest people in the world."

Joe shook his head. "No, everything seems fine."

She stood up and adjusted her heavy utility belt. "You mind if we look around?"

"Not at all. I just ask that you don't go upstairs. We don't want to alarm my mother."

She nodded. "Gotcha."

Joe and John remained in the living room while Claire and muscle head poked around, checking the back door and windows. Joe didn't expect them to dust for fingerprints or bring out a forensic team. Still, it seemed to him that they weren't doing enough.

At least Claire seemed to be taking it seriously. But really, what more could she do?

"Look," she said to the brothers, "I'm not saying someone didn't break in, but there's not much to go on. Now, if some items had been taken or things were thrown around, that's another story. Talk to your lawyer about that notice, and make sure everything's locked up tight."

Her partner left without saying a word, almost bumping into John on the way out the door. Claire looked after him. "These kids. I swear, they act like thugs because that's what video games and movies tell them they need to do to look hard. I'm sorry about him."

John waved it off.

She pointed at the eviction note in Joe's hand. "I'm

not going to lie, that bothers me. I don't know what's going on around here, but it's got me on edge. I'm glad you're both here to look into it. A lot of these other people don't have that support system." She gave Joe her card. "If anything doesn't look right, call me. There may be something lurking underneath all this, but no one at the station cares . . . at the moment. Things change."

Joe watched her get into the driver's side of her patrol car.

Claire Dennehy, a cop.

Yep. Things certainly do change.

CHAPTER NINETEEN

John was surprised to see old man Doyle sitting beside his father's bed. His mother had told him that Doyle was in a nursing home, recovering from a broken hip.

"Well, if it isn't himself," Doyle said when he saw him.

The curmudgeon still wore that awful hat, even indoors. John noticed the walker beside his chair.

"Look who's come to bring sunshine to a dreary day," his father joked. Doyle, who for a moment had been happy to see John, reaffixed his permanent scowl.

"Hey, Dad, Mr. Doyle. Does the staff know the dynamic duo is in the house? There could be trouble."

Doyle clicked his dentures together. "There sure was trouble earlier today. They thought they were going to keep me in that prison. I dared them to stop me from leaving. The whole damn place smells like an outhouse, and half the people are off their rocker. How is anyone expected to recuperate in a place like that?"

"Doyle, I don't think the people in the room above us could hear you," John's father said. Doyle was hard of hearing but refused to invest in a hearing aid. When he spoke, especially when he was feeling ornery, his voice carried . . . far.

"Well, it's the truth. I have my walker and their pills. Now I just need to be home in my own damn bed."

"How did you get here?" John asked, handing his father a cup of hot coffee and bag of donuts. His father loved chocolate glazed donuts, even more so as he got older. Whenever John was at the supermarket, he marveled at all the sweets older folks loaded in their carts. Advancing age must revitalize the sweet tooth. He looked forward to guilt-free slices of crumb cake at night.

"I took the bus. The driver harassed me about not having the card, as if my money is no good."

"I'm sure you talked reason into him," Pat said, a chuckle leading to a bout of terrific hacking.

"Suffice to say, he let me stay," Doyle said.

"I'll take you home," John said. "Your money is good with me."

Doyle looked at him, not getting the joke. He said, "So when do we break your father out? He looks fine to me."

The man looked very far from fine, even though he was markedly better than a couple of days ago.

"It's up to the doctor," John said.

"Eh," Doyle said, scowling. "All they want is more money. Once you hit a certain age, you can be healthy as a horse, but they're going to test you seven ways to Sunday so they can make a fast buck off your old bones. It's all a scam."

John's father settled down enough to take a sip of coffee. "That will cut through all the crud. Nice and strong."

"You see Dr. Murphy yet?"

"No, but the pretty morning nurse said he'd come by in the early afternoon."

"Oh, she's a nice one," Doyle said. "All hips and—"

"That's enough out of you," Pat cut in, though he was smiling.

Doyle struggled to get out of his chair, hands grasping at the walker. John went to help him, but a sharp look from Doyle pulled him back.

"Well, let's go then," Doyle said.

"Go where?" John said.

"Home."

"He just got here, you crazy old fool," Pat said.

"And he can just as easily come right back." Doyle tugged on John's jacket as he pushed past. "Come on, son."

John looked at his father, unsure what to do.

"It's easier to just do what he says," he said. "If I'm asleep when you get back, wake me up. Pill time is coming soon."

"I will. Don't eat all those donuts at once. I want one for later."

Doyle was already out the door and pushing his walker toward the elevators. John had to jog to catch up to him. It seemed that Doyle's hip had mended pretty darn well.

Once they were in the elevator, Doyle turned to him and said, "First we have to make a stop at Ida Benson's house."

John pushed the button for the lobby. "Who's Ida Benson?"

Doyle winked. "Oh, you'll remember her. She's part of the reason I left today. Aggie called me this morning, said something's up with the Pigeon Lady. Seeing as I'm one of the few people she'll talk to, it was time to say goodbye to that awful place."

John pinched the bridge of his nose. The Pigeon Lady. He remembered her, all right.

Joe saw the text from his divorce attorney with the name and number of a local real estate lawyer who might be able to help them. He immediately called the number and made an appointment to see her in two days.

Going through his pants pockets before he added them to the washing machine, he found Claire Dennehy's card. There was a time, when they were both sophomores in high school, that he'd had a major crush on her. Claire was a popular girl, but not stuck up like some of the others in her orbit. Even with braces, she'd had a smile that made his heart do backflips. Too awkward and afraid to do anything like ask her out, he instead joined the drama club just to be in her presence. Back then, she wanted to be an actress. He remembered she talked a lot about being the next Debra Winger. Claire was fearless and raw and tended to overact, the same as everyone else in the club. Joe, who would rather eat dirt than act, mumbled through his lines and kept his head down. He told everyone he really wanted to be a stage hand and joined the club just because he loved everything about theater.

He cringed just thinking about it.

Claire had been the ultimate girly girl. Seeing her in uniform had really set him on his heels. She was still as beautiful as ever, though older and a little thicker around the middle. Then again, who their age besides John wasn't?

Joe slipped the card in his shirt pocket and clucked his tongue. His eye caught the wedding ring he still wore and slipped it off his finger. Wearing it was a habit he'd have to break, just as Stella had broken his heart and their family.

The basement steps creaked so loud, he worried they might break. It was after eleven. Isabelle should be here already. He went up to talk to his mother.

"Hey, Ma, you hear from Isabelle yet?"

She looked concerned. "Not a thing."

John straightened the sheet around his mother. "Maybe I should call the agency. I bet they'll charge you for the days she's not here unless you tell them. They might also know where she is."

"You think she just quit?"

"The people who work for these places aren't always the most reliable."

Probably got pinched by immigration services, Joe thought. He and his brother had talked a lot about their concerns over this stranger in their parents' house. John said she seemed to be nice, but really, how well could you know someone from meeting them once? Hell, Joe thought he knew Stella, and they'd been married for almost two decades.

"But she was such a nice girl. The house hasn't been this clean since all this happened to me. And she makes wonderful food. Your father can't handle some of the spice, but I eat everything she puts in front of me. Oh, I really hope she hasn't left. I don't think your father would allow We Care, or anyone, for that matter, to send someone else."

Which was a concern, Joe thought. His parents needed help—if not full time, at least most of the week. Knowing his father, he'd swear up and down he was right as rain and could reclaim his role as caretaker for the Knox home.

Joe really hoped Isabelle had come down with the flu or something.

"You have the number for We Care?" he asked.

"It should be on your father's dresser."

His father's dresser was littered with spare change, opened mail, a dish with tie tacks that he hadn't used in decades, an old coffee mug filled with pennies, eyeglass cases, and a small wire basket where he tossed cards and brochures he wanted to keep. The brochure for We Care was mercifully at the top of the heap.

Joe went to his old bedroom to make the call.

A man with a soft voice and a slight Eastern European accent answered on the fourth ring.

"Hello, We Care, how can I assist you?"

Pacing the room, Joe said, "Hello, I'm calling for my parents, Patrick and Mary Knox. They have a home aide named Isabelle Perez." He heard the tapping of keys.

"Ah yes, I see. How has Isabelle been working out?"

"Great, at least until a couple of days ago. She hasn't shown up or called since."

"Oh, that is not good. I apologize. Let me check her status and see if she's spoken to anyone here. Do you mind holding for a moment?"

"That would be fine. Thanks."

Joe looked across the hall into his parents' room. His mother was watching a morning talk show, but he knew she wasn't into it. She bore the brunt of her worries like a soldier. He hoped the person at We Care, whoever they were, could alleviate one of them.

It took them a long time to get back, the awful hold music grating on Joe's nerves. "I'm sorry, I just needed to double-check. We haven't heard from Isabelle, either, so right now, I am not sure what to say. Until and if she comes back, I can send another aide by as soon as early afternoon today."

Joe sagged. Could they catch one single break?

"No, there's no need. If Isabelle has disappeared, we're likely not to go with another aide for now."

The person at We Cares breathed a short huff into the phone. "I wouldn't say she disappeared."

"Neither of us know where she is, and she didn't leave word as to her whereabouts, so that qualifies as disappearing," Joe said, bristling. "I'd appreciate it if you make sure the past two days aren't billed."

"I will make a note of that."

Something about this customer service's tone wore thin on Joe. As if his call was a nuisance that had to be quickly dealt with. Joe realized some of his frustration had nothing to do with the person on the other end of the line, but there was only so much he could handle right now.

"Please," Joe said, practically having to bite his tongue, "make *sure* of it."

Joe hung up before he said something he'd regret.

And now he had the unpleasant task of telling his mother that the woman, who in a short amount of time had come to mean so much to her, had most likely moved on.

It might have been politically incorrect to think such a thing, but Joe thought it was for the best if she *had* been deported, like he'd suspected. And he wasn't in the mood for political correctness. Not when reality had to be faced.

Taking a few deep breaths, he walked down the hall that had seemed to grow exponentially longer.

CHAPTER TWENTY

John followed Doyle's barked directions, catching hell for making a wrong turn and having to make a broken U in the middle of the narrow street.

All this to see the Pigeon Lady.

Growing up, the neighborhood had a Cat Lady who left food and milk out every night behind a bench in the little park for a posse of stray cats, a Dog Lady who had an uncanny knack for finding runaway dogs (John had suspected she walked off with the dogs, returning them when there was a reward), and even a Squirrel Lady who didn't have anything to do with the little critters, she just had the same furtive movements as a squirrel and bushy gray hair like a squirrel's tail.

The Cat Lady, Dog Lady, and Squirrel Lady had all gone to meet their Maker right around the time John left for the service.

The Pigeon Lady was another animal, so to speak, altogether. She'd always been the crazy old Pigeon Lady, even as a much younger woman. Finally having a real name for her, Ida Benson, made her seem less like a living bit of Woodlean folklore. As far as he knew, all Ida did from sunup to sundown was feed and care for the wild pigeons that did their best to make their mark on every nook and cranny of the neighborhood. She collected stale bread from the local stores, crushed it into small crumbs, and went from spot to spot casting the bread crumbs around for the pigeons. If one was ever hurt, she'd take it to her home, tucking it in the pocket of her enormous black coat, even in summer, and nurse it back to health.

What set the Pigeon Lady apart from the others was the fact that she was a little off. Or more like *very* off. She spoke to the pigeons as she fed them, cooing and clucking. In fact, in all the times John had seen her, she spoke to the birds far more than people. She had no family or means of support, yet she managed to survive, a woman and her bags of bread crumbs.

As a child, he'd often wondered where she lived. There were rumors she squatted in the abandoned two-family house over on Deekman Street. When that was torn down, his friends said she'd been spotted sleeping in trees among her beloved pigeons. John never believed that, but he never thought much more about it. What did a young boy care about a woman who liked to feed birds? He had ramps to make and mischief to get into.

"Right there, right there," Doyle said, pointing to a nice-looking ranch house on a small plot of land on Bain Avenue, just a few blocks from John's parents' house. Seeing it now, he realized it was the perfect place for the woman to hide. No one would suspect she lived in such a place. Abandoned homes and trees were far more intriguing.

"Really?" John said, stopping in the middle of the street. Of course, there was nowhere to park. Doyle was already getting out of the car. John reached into the back seat to get his walker and hand it to him.

"I know what you and your friends thought," Doyle said. "No one lives in a tree."

John chuckled. "I didn't think so."

"I'm sure you didn't. Just pull across that fire hydrant and follow me."

That was easy for Doyle to say. He wouldn't have to be the one to pay the ticket. But John knew there was no point arguing with the man. Hopefully it would be a short visit.

Instead of going to the front door, Doyle wheeled his walker down the side of the house.

"Where are we going?" John asked.

Doyle didn't answer.

They came upon a postage stamp of a yard with a red-leaf Japanese maple tree in the center of the perfectly square lawn. John had the very same tree in his own yard. He noticed the limbs were heavy with bird feeders. A cooling wind made the tiny birdhouses and feeders sway back and forth.

Doyle didn't even look up at the tree, heading instead for the aluminum shed in the corner of the yard. He knocked on the thin door. John thought he heard quiet sobbing.

"Ida, it's me," Doyle said, his usual tone sounding less than soft and soothing.

They heard the fumbling of metal on metal, the door inching open, screeching along the rusted track.

Ida Benson, the infamous Pigeon Lady, peered at them from the darkened shed. Time and age had whittled her down to the size of a bird. Her dark eyes were clouded by tears. A combination lock dangled from one of her long, thin fingers.

"People are looking for you, you know," Doyle said.

John's eyes adjusted to the darkness in the shed. Ida was sitting on an overturned bucket. She wore her heavy black coat and had a blanket draped over her shoulder.

"I can't go back in there," she said, staring at John.

"I'm John Knox. Not sure if you know my parents, Pat and Mary." He felt uneasy under her steady gaze. He'd never been this close to the Pigeon Lady before. Suddenly, John was back to being six, doing his best to keep her in his periphery in case she made a sudden movement.

"I know your parents," she said. "You have a brother, too."

It shouldn't have startled him, what with everyone being in everyone's business in the neighborhood, but still. This was the Pigeon Lady, who didn't care one bit about people.

Or so he'd thought.

Doyle ignored them. "Well, Ida, you can't spend your life hiding in your shed."

"I can if I have to."

"You'll have to leave eventually. Who else is going to feed the pigeons?"

Ida poked her head out the door and took a furtive look at her house. "They're trying to kill me."

"Who's trying to kill you?" Doyle asked.

"Them."

"I don't know who they are."

"The ones that come. There's two of them. They take turns. They hurt me."

Doyle stepped forward, almost in the shed with her,

while John shuffled back. This was Doyle's show, and he didn't want to get in the way. With the way Ida kept flicking nervous glances around, he worried she would slam the door in their faces and lock them out.

"How do they hurt you?" Doyle sounded genuinely concerned, but there was also that undercurrent of simmering anger. John wondered whether the man was more upset with Ida for having him drag himself out of rehab for this, or the mysterious *they* who were trying to hurt her. It was hard to peel away the layers of Doyle's general frustration.

She tapped the side of her head in reply. "Always saying things. Trying to get me to do things."

"Do they put their hands on you?"

"Sometimes."

"To hurt you?"

Doyle's knuckles went white from gripping the walker's handles.

"No. Only inside. They whisper when I sleep. They say things, lots of things, when I don't feel right."

"I want to help you, Ida, but you have to tell me who is saying these things. What are they saying that has you so scared?" Doyle put a hand on the edge of the aluminum door to make sure she couldn't shut it.

Fresh tears sprang to Ida's eyes. "The ones the priest sent. They're in there now. If they see you, they'll hurt you, too!"

John dropped Doyle off at his house along with Ida Benson. They hadn't bothered going into her house to get any of her things. Just the mere suggestion almost sent her into a panic. She was silent the entire ride to Doyle's house. As John opened the door for her, Aggie Firth spotted them and came running over.

"Ida, are you all right, dear?"

The Pigeon Lady looked at her with nervous eyes but didn't answer. Instead, a pair of pigeons sitting on the telephone line overhead captured her attention.

"She's been through something," Doyle said, "though I'm scratching my head to understand exactly what it is. She was terrified to go back inside her house, so I told her she can stay with me for now."

Aggie squeezed his arm, a hand over her heart. "You're a good, good man, Sam."

He waved her off, making his way to his front door.

"Better watch out," John said. "I don't think he wants that getting around."

Aggie smiled, though when she turned to Ida, her mouth morphed to a frown. "It's too late for that. I know he's about as cuddly as a cactus on the outside, but he does a lot for people in his own way. I feel better just knowing he's back."

John's eyes wandered to Bridgett Monahan's empty house. There wasn't even a FOR SALE sign. It was as if she'd been kicked out for nothing, the place just left behind to rot while Bridgett spent eternity in a narrow box under six feet of dirt. John felt his neck grow hot, and he hadn't realized he'd been grinding his teeth until a needle of pain shot from his cheek to his eye.

"Come on inside, Ida. I promise you won't get hurt while I'm around," Doyle called out, waving her into the house from the open doorway.

John thought he heard her coo at the pigeons before hurrying into Doyle's house.

"Do you need me to get anything for you, Mr. Doyle?" John asked.

"I'll get what I need later. The walking will do me good. Now get your father the hell out of that hospital as fast as you can, before there's nothing left of this neighborhood to come home to."

With that, he closed the door, the heavy slam echoing in the calm street.

"I don't know if I should feel sorry for the Pigeon La— uh, Ida—or happy that she can at least turn to Doyle. What an odd pair," John said, getting into his car.

Aggie Firth said, "Everyone talks to Sam because they know he'll always give it to them straight and he'll fight for them if a fight is what's needed. Hopefully, Ida will open up to him once she's had time to settle down."

Keying the ignition, John said, "She kept saying something about them hurting her mind and having been sent by the priest. Do you know what that can mean?"

Aggie screwed up her face in concentration, tapping her bottom lip. "Well, I wouldn't suppose she'll be needing an exorcism. What a queer thing for her to say. Sam will get it out of her."

Smooth-talking Sam Doyle, John thought, then corrected himself. His opinion of Doyle had been thrown on its head this afternoon. Maybe Doyle was the only one who could pry the truth from Ida's mouth.

Hurting the mind.

The priest.

The two seemingly opposing concepts bothered him all the way to the hospital.

Chapter Twenty-one

After Joe carried their mother downstairs into the living room, they all ate Chinese takeout, John finding an old scrapbook on the bookshelf. They looked at pictures taken sometime in the mid-1970s, the boys dressed in a lot of plaid and paisley. Each turning of the page elicited more laughter, and that was something they needed desperately. The nostalgia train stopped for *Wheel of Fortune*, of course, but got rolling again when the show was over. Joe beat his mother at solving one of the puzzles, getting a nod of encouragement in return. "You're much better than your father at this."

The Chinese food was terrible, but Joe's taste buds had been spoiled by the superior Asian cuisine of California. The four years he'd lived in San Francisco alone had ruined him forever for East Coast takeout.

Joe was washing the dishes when John came into the kitchen carrying an armful of empty white boxes. "Mom's out," he whispered. He'd lain a blanket over her on the couch, the scrapbook still on her lap, close to falling.

"Yeah, well, defending the fashion choices she'd made for us would take a lot out of anyone."

John went to the cabinet where the mugs and glasses were stored, stretching his arm to the top shelf, carefully shifting things around. "There it is."

He pulled out an unopened bottle of Glenlivet, angling the bottle so Joe could read the label.

"Eighteen-year-old scotch. When did Dad buy that?"

"He didn't," John said. "I did, the day I came home from the service. I put it up there so I could grab it later but forgot about it until now."

"How do you forget a bottle of top-shelf, eighteen-year-old whiskey?" Joe turned off the faucet, flipping the dishtowel on his shoulder to the dish drainer.

"I was young and dumb and easily distracted. Think it's time we cracked this bad boy open?"

"I'll get the glasses. Let's go out back so we don't wake Mom up."

It was dark and cool in the yard, a little chilly for sitting outside, but the whiskey would warm them. Joe rustled up two folding chairs from the shed and set them by the back door so they could hear their mother if she called out for them. John uncorked the bottle, waving it under Joe's nose so he could savor the aroma.

"I haven't had scotch that good since they took away my unlimited expense account three jobs ago," Joe said.

"I've never had anything over twelve years, so this is new for me." He poured a finger's worth in each glass. "I didn't want to say anything while we were around Mom, but I had a super weird experience with Sam Doyle and the Pigeon Lady today."

Joe nearly choked on his first sip of scotch. "The Pigeon Lady? Where on earth did you dig her up? Was she living in a nest somewhere?"

John closed his eyes, taking a moment to savor the Glenlivet. "Oh, that's good. Turns out her name is Ida Benson. Doyle found her locked up in the shed in her yard."

"Someone locked her in a shed?"

"No, she locked herself in there. She was afraid of what the people in her house were doing to her. I looked in the windows but didn't see anyone inside."

"That is weird." Joe looked up, the night sky obscured by clouds too high and dark to be seen, the only proof of their presence the absence of stars.

"Here's something else to chew on. Doyle is also the patron saint of the neighborhood. I get the feeling he's the self-appointed watchdog and fixer of all problems."

"Cranky, get-off-my-lawn Doyle?"

John swallowed the rest of the whiskey. "The very same."

He poured them each another round, and they drank in silence. Joe remembered being out here with John when they were little, their tent set up, full canteens, flashlights, and comic books all they needed for a night of camping. This was also where he'd first felt a girl up, making out with Maura Marone under the cover of darkness during his junior year. Joe wondered what memories were playing in his brother's head.

"Stella left me for another man. We're getting a divorce. Hell, for all I know, the papers are already signed," Joe said in a rush.

His brother's mouth dropped open. "Wait. What?"

Joe pinched the bridge of his nose to chase the faint flicker of a headache away. "Who would have thought she'd be the one to blow it, huh? I found out just after the

New Year. I'm living in a crap apartment while Stella, the cheater, stays in our house with the kids."

John put an arm over his shoulders. "Christ, I'm so sorry. Why didn't you tell me before?"

Heaving a weighty sigh, Joe said, "Because I was embarrassed. Knoxes don't get divorced."

"Well, someone had to break the mold. You were always good for that." John poured some more scotch in Joe's glass. "Are you all right? How did it happen?"

"I'm fine . . . most days. You know, I'm still not sure what led to all of this. Whenever I try to picture how things were, my memories get clouded by anger."

His brother let it stop there, for which he was grateful.

Feeling a bit of the weight on his chest and shoulders lightening, Joe said, "You want to come with me to see the lawyer day after tomorrow?"

"Hell yes."

A car gave two quick beeps the next street over, breaking the silence of the night. With most everyone around being older, the day was done and the streets were empty. A few windows burned blue from the flicker of televisions.

Joe told his brother about Isabelle and his conversation with We Care customer service.

"So, she's gone?" John said.

"It appears."

"Just like everybody else around here," John said, rolling the now empty glass between his hands.

"Something's not right," Joe said.

"No shit."

"People like the Pigeon Lady are scared of something,

and for good reason. This thing with Mom and Dad's house isn't going to be a clerical error."

John poured another round. "I don't think so, either."

Joe knocked it back and sucked in the night air. "We can't leave here until we know Mom and Dad are going to be okay."

"That might mean looking out for more than just them."

"It might."

"Been a long time since I've had a chance to fight the good fight."

Joe stood up, his back cracking. "Been a long time since I've been in any fight, good or bad. Unless you count the divorce."

John picked up a rock and tossed it into the bushes. "You ready for this?"

Joe's smile fell a fathom short of his eyes. "Oh, yes. I'm ready."

John woke to find Joe had already gotten up, showered, and left the house. Where he had gone, John had no idea, but the remnants of steam and scent of soap still lingered in the bathroom.

His head was pounding. They had really put a hurt on that bottle of scotch last night. John couldn't remember the last time he'd had a hangover.

Coffee.

Checking in on his mother first, he was relieved to see she was still asleep. He didn't remember bringing her back up to bed and hoped Joe, who had a far better tolerance for alcohol, had been the one to carry her.

He whipped up a quick cup of instant coffee, downing a bottle of water before it was ready. His stomach was fine, so he wolfed down some scrambled eggs and four slices of wheat toast. An hour after rising, he started to feel back to normal. The throbbing at his temples had ceased, and the caffeine had whisked the lull of exhaustion out of his system.

It was still early, but not too early to call his wife. She was home now, the conference a success. He missed her terribly. They had never been apart for this long before. He got her caught up on his father's status and told her about the eviction notice.

"That just doesn't seem possible," Marion said.

"Joe and I are going to see a real estate lawyer tomorrow to get to the bottom of it. I want Dad to get out of the hospital, but we need to make sure he has a home to come back to."

"I'm sure there's just been some kind of mix-up. Any lawyer worth his salt can fix it."

"I hope so."

Marion then gave him a rundown of the conference and how she had been asked to speak at several more events. Best part was, they were paid speaking gigs. She was bubbling with enthusiasm. "I heard from Kevin yesterday. He got a job in the IT department of a company in Bangor. He's over the moon. I told him we'd go up for a visit soon and take him out to dinner to celebrate."

"Wow, good for Kev. Definitely. I miss that kid."

They'd fostered Kevin Woodman seven years ago when he was an angry thirteen-year-old without a father and a mother entering rehab for the fourth time. It took a long time for John and Marion to break down his walls and find the scared but loving child beneath all that justified fury. It hadn't been easy. He'd tried to run away twice, and they'd had to transfer him to a new school after he wore his welcome out with his mouth and fists. John and Marion had shown him that unconditional love and stability were possible, and he in turn became a totally different person, growing into a bright young man with an even brighter future.

"He asked if his mother could come," Marion said.

"Of course. The more the merrier." Kevin's mom had been clean and sober for close to five years now. She might have taken a lot of wrong turns in life, but John once told her she could always look at Kevin and know she'd done something good. Damn good.

John talked to his wife for a little while longer and then got the idea to go to St. Brendan's for the eight o'clock mass. His emotions were a mess of gratefulness and trepidation. It would be good to give thanks and ask for guidance. He was no Holy Roller, but he appreciated the warm comfort that church and prayer brought.

His mother was awake when he went upstairs to put on nicer clothes. When he told her he was going to morning mass, her eyes twinkled.

"I miss the eight o'clock. Such a calm and quiet service. I'm proud of you."

"For what?"

"For keeping your faith. It's too easy in this world to be distracted. There's so much out there just waiting to rob people of any sense of belief and wonder. You're a good boy."

John reddened, feeling like he was five and bringing home macaroni art he made for his mom on Mother's Day.

All that was missing was the pat on the head and kiss on the cheek. Looking at her rail-thin arms, he would give anything for that pat.

Instead, he kissed her cheek and double-timed it to St. Brendan's, three blocks away. The old church was the same as ever. Nothing had been changed since the days he'd been an altar boy. The crowd of eight o'clock regulars— six women and two men, all of them looking to be older than Noah—sat in the first few pews, most reading from their personal prayer books. John lit a candle for his father's speedy recovery, as well as one for Bridgett Monahan and another for Archie O'Malley, a man who had always treated him like a member of the family.

When John was walking across the back rows of the pews, his thigh clipped the corner of a narrow table. On it were an assortment of pamphlets and business cards, presumably left there by parishioners looking for local business. Half of the papers slid off the table, making what sounded to John like a riotous commotion in the silent, echoing church. He dropped to a knee to gather them up, putting them back in appropriate piles on the table.

He stared at a particular stack of postcards, struck by their familiarity.

It was an ad for We Care, the same home aide service that his parents employed.

The service Isabelle had disappeared from.

John looked down the aisle at the crucifix hanging above the altar.

Ida Benson's voice suddenly whispered in his mind: *The ones the priest sent*.

His eyes slid back down to the We Care postcard just as Father Biglin entered the church with the ringing of a bell.

Making the sign of the cross, John tucked the card in his pocket and left the church in a hurry.

Running back to the house, lost in thought, he was stopped cold by the blaring of a horn. Caught between two parked cars and about to cross the street, John realized he'd almost been run down by a sheriff's car. The portly man behind the wheel flashed him a dirty look before moving on, making a right at the end of the block.

John hoped the sheriff wasn't on another call to remove someone from their house. The man was in charge of this whole region, but it sounded as if he was in Woodlean so much lately, he might as well set up shop in the little park so he never had far to go.

Joe Knox had one hand on the wheel, the car set on cruise control, GPS showing that he was only thirty miles from his destination in Virginia Beach. He'd snuck out early assuming his brother would be nursing a hell of a hangover, mostly because he wanted to do this alone.

He hadn't realized it until last night, but Joe had been angry for a long time. He hadn't been happy with his job. The culture had seemed to change overnight. He was getting tired of watching every word that came out of his mouth or was written in an email. The largest department in the company was now human resources, not sales and support. A day in the office was like tap-dancing around land mines. Listening to his younger colleagues spew radical liberal ideals they'd likely been force-fed in college almost made him bite his tongue until it bled. It was mad-dening, and isolating. As much as he wanted to tell them the truth about the world, he couldn't. He was trapped there because he had a family to support, a mortgage to pay, college and weddings to save for. He supposed—no, he knew—that dissatisfaction and frustration seeped into every corner of his life, eventually driving his wife into the arms of another man. He wasn't about to take all of the blame for her infidelity, but for the first time, he wasn't dumping all of it on her, either.

Feeling burned out and ashamed these past few months had done little to alter his take on the life he'd been dealt.

You deal your own cards, buddy, he thought, turning up the radio to distract himself from his thoughts.

Okay, so maybe he was a crappy dealer. It was time to reshuffle the deck and dole out a better hand.

But it was hard to shuffle angry. He needed to release some of that rage. What better way to do so than on the lawyer behind his parents' eviction, Anthony Kramer of Virginia Beach? Joe knew he could not, no matter how much he'd want it to, let things devolve into physical violence. Kramer was a lawyer, after all. He'd make sure Joe was put behind bars. So much had been taken from him over the past decade, the great evil white middle-aged man that he was, but he'd be damned to hand over his freedom.

No, Joe wanted to use what his kids used to call his "Big Voice" and maybe see if he could get the crooked bastard to pee himself, just a little.

Just the thought of it brought a big smile to Joe's face. That and listening to a Dire Straits playlist made the long drive fly by. Before he knew it, the stilted, robotic GPS voice was taking him down side streets, the lawyer's office just a few blocks away. He was so close to the beach, Joe could smell the salt air through the small crack in his window.

He took a quick detour to the beach itself, parking the

car and getting out. It was windy by the water, the beach itself mostly empty save for a few joggers. By the first days of summer, the beach would be an unbroken sea of bodies, people flocking to one of the most famous beaches on the East Coast. His parents used to take him and John here for a long weekend every summer. He couldn't remember his mother ever going in the water, preferring to sit on a towel under a beach umbrella, reading a book while wearing a big, embarrassing straw hat, making sure not a single ray of sun kissed her fair Irish skin. Joe and John used to beg her to join them in the water, letting the waves crash over them, but she was steadfast in her refusal. It wasn't until years later that he learned his mother didn't know how to swim and had a deep fear of the water. That made him love her even more, knowing she'd overcome her fear without grumbling or protestation to take her sons to one of their favorite places.

Dad was another story. If he wasn't sleeping on his towel, he was horsing around with them in the cold ocean water, tossing them over the frothing waves or playing shark attack, diving under the murky water to grab their ankles.

Joe looked out over the still beach, the pounding of the waves settling him, his eyes not seeing the present but the cherished memories of his past.

There was one other recollection that was funny to think of now, though it hadn't been when it had happened. That memory was one of pure pain.

He and John had been doing their best to bodysurf, the flesh of their stomachs red and raw from gliding over the sand. A series of waves were chock-full of brown strips of seaweed, the seagrass sticking to every part of their bodies and everyone around them.

Except it wasn't seaweed. They'd been overtaken by a floating mass of jellyfish. Hundreds of stingers brought sharp jabs of pain to every inch of their bodies. People screamed. They fled the water in a panicked mass. John got run over by a woman carrying her wailing baby. Joe had to grab his arm to keep his head above water, both of them yowling from the pain. They sprinted to their parents, strips of jellyfish flapping in the wind, their skin blossoming with red welts.

Well, that was the end of that trip. On the advice of the lifeguards, they'd bought meat tenderizer from the little market by their hotel, rubbing it into the dizzying array of stings. It soothed the pain, but neither Joe nor John were going back in the water after that. Not that summer.

Having walked down memory lane long enough—he didn't want to take too much of the edge off his anger—Joe got back in the car and pulled up in front of the lawyer's office. The ranch house had seen better days, the gray siding warped and pitted from the elements. It didn't look like anyone had lived or worked there for twenty years or more. There was no sign saying it was a law office. As far as Joe knew, even lawyers in private practice put out a shingle.

He rang the bell, the chorus of chimes echoing behind the closed door. It sounded like the house was empty—not just devoid of people, but furniture, as well. Leaning over the rail of the small porch, he tried to peer through the window, but the blinds were down. He rang the bell again and rapped on the door with his fist.

Maybe he had the wrong address.

He looked at his phone, swiping until he pulled up the image of the notice that John had sent him.

No, this was the right place.

It was also, Joe finally admitted to himself, a phony address. Just like the number he'd called that only took voicemails, which he was sure no one ever listened to.

Whatever calm the beach had given him was swept away like grains of sand on the shoreline.

Joe scrabbled down the steps and stormed to the back of the house, checking out every window but frustrated every time by closed shades and blinds. He pounded on the back door, no longer expecting to have someone answer, but needing to use his fist on something.

"Nobody's home," a voice said, startling him.

Joe turned to see a woman in the adjacent yard. She was young, maybe in her early thirties, wearing a baseball cap and jogging clothes, earbuds tucked over her ears.

"Nobody's ever home there," she said, eyeing him warily.

Realizing he looked this side of a lunatic (he knew his face and neck blushed crimson when he was angry, his hair going askew as if it had a life of its own), Joe stuffed his hand in his pocket and did his best to give an apologetic smile.

"Sorry if I bothered you," he said.

A sea breeze lifted the blond ponytail she'd pulled through the back of her cap. "No bother. I just didn't want you to waste your time. You can knock until the cows come home, and no one's gonna answer."

He slowly approached her, chest-high hedges separating them. "Do you know who lives here?"

She cast a glance at the vacant house. "I've been here

two years, and as far as I know, nobody. Who were you looking for?"

Joe sighed. "I was told this is where a lawyer had his office."

Her eyes widened. "You need a lawyer?"

Joe chuckled. "I already have one, and that's one more than I ever wanted to have. No, I needed to speak to the lawyer that supposedly resides here. I get the feeling he doesn't want to be found."

"Hmm, a shady lawyer? Never heard that one before." Her smile, with teeth so white they reflected the sun, quickened his pulse.

"Yeah, well, I'll find him."

"Good luck."

"Thanks. I think I'll need it."

She slipped one of the earbuds into her ear. "Well, it was nice meeting you."

"You, too."

She jogged away, most likely heading toward the beach.

Joe walked back to his car, fuming. Even a pretty girl couldn't tamp down the roiling fire in his belly.

Where the hell was this Anthony Kramer?

Hitting the road, another thought made him punch the dashboard.

What if there was no Anthony Kramer?

CHAPTER TWENTY-TWO

"Shouldn't we wait until later?" Deputy Sheriff Kenny Carlson asked his boss. He looked out the window at the bright day, a squirrel leaping from limb to limb in the dogwood tree at the back of the station where an old picnic table had been set up.

Sheriff Justice swiped his hat off the desk and fastened it onto his considerable head. "We don't have that luxury. You-know-who is riding herd on my ass to get this done right away."

Carlson cast another wary look outside. "It's just, it being so early and all, we could get another crowd."

"That's why we're taking your car."

"My car?"

"Yes. No one will bat an eye at an old Nissan pulling up to the house. Think of it as undercover work."

"If it's undercover, shouldn't we change?"

The sheriff waddled past him, heading for the front door. "No time. Lock up and meet me at your car."

Carlson had made the drive to the Woodlean neighborhood so often lately, he was pretty sure the car could get there without him. They pulled up to a gray colonial in need of some major TLC. The man who lived there, a widower named Jonas Hamm, had two bad knees, his mobility in short supply. He mostly stayed inside, having moved his bedroom into the living room so he had everything on one floor. Stairs were no longer an option. After two months of persuasion, Hamm had agreed to leave, today, without complaint. Sheriff Justice explained this, as well as his concern that the old coot would change his mind if they didn't strike now, on the drive over. Hence, the unusual daytime rush.

Parking beside a fire hydrant, the two men scampered up the steps, furtively looking around to make sure no one was watching. Any feelings that they were acting like thieves more than men of the law had long been flushed from both their systems. They were just hurrying along the inevitable, all for a much greater good. At least, for them and select others. Not so much people like Jonas Hamm. Then again, the man wasn't in any shape to even enjoy life's simple pleasures, much less the rewards coming to Carlson and Justice for following their orders.

Sheriff Justice rang the bell with a stubby, sausage-like finger. A harried woman in her late thirties, dirty blond with ancient eyes, answered. "He's in the living room. I have his bag packed over there."

It was clear Hamm had been crying. The old man looked up from his perch on the edge of the couch. The place smelled like dirty laundry. Carlson cringed.

"You ready, Mr. Hamm?" the sheriff said, his tone hiding his urgent need to get this done as quickly as possible.

Jonas Hamm looked around his home, his hands shaking in his lap. The woman practically lifted him off his feet, her hand gripping his elbow. "He is."

"Get the bag," Sheriff Justice said to Carlson. He walked Hamm as quickly as he could to the Nissan. It took a while to get down the steps, every wasted second pregnant with the potential of being spotted by a nosy neighbor. Carlson sighed with relief once they were all in the car. Nice and easy. No drama. If only they could all go this way. Well, pretty soon, this would all be behind them. He looked up to see the woman on the porch locking the door. She breezed past their car without even looking their way.

As Carlson started the car, Sheriff Justice angled his body so he could look Hamm in the eye in the back seat. "You remember everything she told you?"

The old man pulled his lips back in a tight line, the beginnings of defiance deflating quickly under Justice's cold stare.

"Yes."

"Well, remember this. Those are all promises. Not threats. We're taking you to a nice place. It won't stink to high heaven."

Oh, it will stink, Carlson thought. *Just not like the inside of his house.*

He drove quickly out of Woodlean, the two-hour drive out of town as familiar as the back of his hand.

After checking on his mother and calling his father to let him know he'd swing by the hospital around lunchtime, John jogged to Doyle's house. He hadn't gone for a run since he'd driven down to Virginia, and his body was in sore need of a workout. It wasn't much of one, what with Doyle only living a few blocks away, but it was better than nothing. He rang Doyle's bell and waited. The mornings were busier in the neighborhood than the nights, folks walking either to the store or going to the park to get some air.

When no one answered, he rang again. Odds were, Doyle was out making his morning rounds, whatever that comprised.

"Jesus, Mary, and Joseph, I hear you," Doyle shouted from behind the door. He yanked it open, his hat *not* perched on his balding head, the white hairs he had left long and wild. "Oh, Johnnie, I didn't expect you. Thought you were some damn fool trying to sell me something."

"Is Ida still with you?" he asked, the muscles in his legs twitching.

Doyle raised a brow. "Yes. You come to visit her?"

"I need to ask her a question. Did she tell you anything more about why she locked herself in the shed?"

Doyle ushered him inside. The house had the faint aroma that all old people's houses had. It was impossible to give a proper name to it that didn't sound insulting. Whenever he and Joe used to visit their grandparents in Kentucky, they would just call it "old smell." John wondered how many years he and Marion had until their house was infused with the inevitable old smell. Would they be too old to foster when that happened?

"I didn't want to bother her last night," Doyle said, walking down the hallway into the kitchen. A pot of coffee was on the stove, the radio tuned to the all-news station. The morning paper was spread out on the table. "In fact, I haven't heard a peep from her since I set her up in the guest bedroom. Poor woman was exhausted."

"Any chance she's awake now?"

Doyle looked at the clock above the sink. "I'm sure she

is. She may have been tired, but she didn't magically turn into a lazy teenager."

John took the We Care postcard out of his pocket and handed it to Doyle. "I want to ask her about this."

"You want to sign her up for a home aide?"

"No, I want to ask her if she already had one through this company."

"Why would you want to do that?"

"Call it a hunch. Maybe we should knock on her door."

Doyle put a hand on John's chest. "Now, don't go banging on my doors. I'll get her, since you seem all fired up. Have a coffee, and sit."

John didn't even think not to obey the old man's commands. As Doyle left to get Ida, John found a clean mug in the draining board, poured a cup of coffee that, from the smell, was burned, and took a seat at the kitchen table. Doyle had the paper open to the sports page. John tried to read an article about some baseball player for the Nationals who had been suspended for using performance-enhancing drugs, but he couldn't concentrate.

The stairs in Doyle's house creaked mightily as the pair came down to the kitchen. Ida wore a black, ankle-length dress and gray blouse, her hair tucked into a black beret. She gripped several plastic shopping bags. Doyle must have caught her getting ready to go out to get the bread to feed the pigeons.

"Hello, Johnnie," she said, her voice sounded clearer, more sure of herself than the day before. He was initially shocked she knew his name, but then realized that even though she might have been an oddball mystery to him and his friends, she was more than just the Pigeon Lady and probably knew everyone in the neighborhood, just the way his father and Doyle did.

"Good morning, Ida," John said. "Feeling better today?"

"Oh yes, much better. I haven't had a good night's sleep like that in—oh, I don't know how long."

Doyle pulled a chair out for her to sit. He also got her a cup of coffee and took the seat between them. He put the We Care card on the table. "Johnnie came by to ask you about this."

Ida's face darkened. She touched the edge of the card with her shaky fingertips, treating it as if it were screaming hot.

"Have you heard of We Care?" John asked. From the expression in her eyes, he feared they were going to lose her. She'd be back to the barely coherent woman they found yesterday.

Her mouth pulled into a grim line. She nodded.

"Did you have someone from We Care coming to your house?"

Again, she nodded.

Doyle scowled at him. "You're making her upset, Johnnie. Maybe you shouldn't have come by."

John pressed on. "Did you find out about their service through the church?"

Her eyes flicked away, beginning to water.

"Ida, my parents had someone from We Care coming to their house, too. Except she disappeared a few days ago."

Now she looked at him. "Father Biglin said they could help me. Two of them. There were two of them."

The ones the priest sent.

John reached across the table to hold her hand. It was so cold. "They sent two aides to your house?"

She nodded furtively, like one of her beloved pigeons. "One for the day, one for the night. They said terrible things to me."

Doyle caught John's gaze. He could see the fire burning behind the old man's stare.

"What did they say?" Doyle asked.

Ida pulled her hands to her chest, sinking into the chair as if she were trying to make herself small enough to disappear.

To John's surprise, she spoke, her eyes glassed over, no longer seeing the interior of Doyle's kitchen. "They tried to feed me, but I wouldn't let them. I just needed help around the house, you see. I can feed myself. Oh, but they tried and tried to force me. I promised I would scream. They said they could have a doctor put me away. That if I didn't act normal, they could easily say I was crazy. And crazy people don't get to live alone. Not when they're old and weak and vulnerable." She choked back a sob, a lone tear wending its way through the deep lines in her face. "If I just did what they asked, I would never have to go away."

John felt terrible pressing her, but he had to ask, "What did they ask you to do, besides eat?"

She looked to Doyle, then John. "To give them everything. If I gave them what they asked for, they would share with me and take care of me. If I didn't, I would be sent away to a place where there were no pigeons. They would take all of my friends away."

Doyle's chair scraped across the floor as he excused himself, taking some big strides for a man recovering from a fractured hip.

John said, "Ida, you don't have to be afraid of them anymore. We can call the police—"

Ida's eyes went wide as she pulled away from him. "Don't call the police! They told me never to call the police!"

John did his best to calm her. "It's okay. It's okay. The people We Care sent are bad people. We're going to deal with them." He thought about Isabelle and how she had been the polar opposite. The again, he was never one to paint with a broad brush. The people assigned to care for Ida had been some very bad apples, by the sound of it. That didn't mean the whole bunch was spoiled.

"No police," she said again.

"I promise. No police."

Doyle came back into the kitchen, a little out of breath. "Ida, help yourself to anything you want for breakfast. When you go out, just close the door behind you. It has an automatic lock. Johnnie here can make himself useful by taking me out to pick up some things."

"I'll just have some toast," Ida said, getting up to get the loaf of bread sitting atop Doyle's refrigerator. It was as if she had completely forgotten her momentary freak-out when John had mentioned contacting the police.

Doyle motioned for him to follow.

"Shouldn't you have your walker?" John said as they stepped onto the sidewalk.

Doyle winced with each step.

"Walkers make you look weak. Come on, we're going to Ida's."

* * *

Pat Knox woke up feeling better than he had in weeks. His bladder, which had seen better days, forced him out of bed. He'd been grateful when they'd removed the catheter because it was uncomfortable as hell. He also wasn't keen about having the nurses fiddling with him down there.

He vaguely recalled Johnnie's call earlier, his mind still in a fog from whatever goofballs they'd been feeding him. He'd fallen back to sleep quickly, but now he was up and ready for the day. His morning cough hadn't been so bad, and his lungs no longer felt like they were both on fire and in a vise.

Janet, the always-smiling nurse who worked the early shift, came into the room just as he was settling back into bed. "You're looking pretty chipper today," she said, adjusting his covers before checking his IV lines.

"Feeling right as rain," he replied. "Any chance I can get a few of these tubes taken out of me today?"

She wrote something down on her newfangled tablet. "That's for Dr. Murphy to decide. You think you can handle breakfast?"

In fact, Pat was starving. "Give me everything you've got."

Janet laughed. "We'll start with half of everything and see how you do."

Before she left, he asked her, "Can you show me how to make a phone call? I'd like to call my wife."

She moved the old phone onto the tray and angled it over the bed. "Just dial nine, then her number."

"Bless your heart and all your parts," Pat said, eliciting another smile. Janet hustled off to check the next patient. He was glad he had taken the time to memorize Mary's cell phone number. With the way everyone programmed things nowadays, no one could remember a single phone number. Their heads were too full of important PINs. Mary answered on the fifth ring because he knew working her hands to do so was never a quick and easy thing.

"Hello?" she said, sounding cautious.

"Greetings and salutations to the woman who gives Vanna White a run for her money!"

"My, you sound spry this morning."

"Because I am." He coughed a bit, but nothing like the wet chest rattling from before.

"It's so good to hear your voice," Mary said.

"Not as good as it is to hear yours. How are you faring without me around to make sure things are run efficiently?"

"Just fine. Don't overestimate your abilities."

Pat chuckled. "I forget, you not only have Isabelle but the boys to pick up my slack."

Mary hesitated. Pat could sense trouble even across the phone. He knew Mary better than she knew herself.

"What is it?" he asked.

"It looks like Isabelle quit on us."

"Quit? Did she say why? I don't think we were that bad."

"No, she didn't give a reason. She just stopped coming. The boys called her company, and they haven't heard from her, either."

Pat scratched at his head, feeling in desperate need of a shower. "Well, she's a bright girl. She probably got a better offer somewhere else." Though, he thought, it wasn't polite or professional to just up and leave.

"That's probably the case," Mary said, not sounding so sure.

"Are you worried about her?"

"I just hope she's all right."

Mary had always been a world-class worrier. She came from a long line of worriers, better known as Irish women. "I'm sure she's just fine. What does she need with two old wrinklies anyway?" She snorted a short laugh in response, but he could tell something else was bothering her. "How are the boys treating you?" he asked.

Now she brightened. "I love having them here. We raised two good ones."

"It was touch and go with Joe for a while there," Pat said, smiling. "Johnnie called me earlier and said he'd see me around lunch. What's he up to?"

Again, there was a hesitation. "He went out for a bit. Oh, but he did go to church this morning."

"And Joe?"

"I'm not sure where he is. Johnnie said Joe was already gone by the time he woke up."

"So, they left you all alone?" One of Pat's legs reflexively slipped out from under the covers, his foot inches above the floor as if his body was going to walk right out of the hospital.

"Not before I was well taken care of," Mary assured him. "They'll be back soon. Until then, I have a movie to watch. That one with Marilyn Monroe and Clark Gable where they have the horses."

Pat couldn't recall the movie, but he was too busy wondering what on earth was going on while he lay around in his rented bed. Because through it all, he had a gut feeling that Mary's concern wasn't about the boys; nor was it all about Isabelle. There was something else she wasn't telling him. Experience taught him he'd have no luck prying it out of her if she wasn't in the mood to spill the beans.

He looked at the big clock on the wall opposite the bed, wondering when Dr. Murphy would come around. He also wondered if he could convince the quack to let him go home. Suddenly, he had a pressing need to leave this hospital behind.

Mayor Viktor Bennett stood before the painting of his father, once the mayor of Woodlean, a kind and benevolent man who people still spoke about, even though he had been dead for decades.

They did not speak of Viktor with the same reverence, though they had reelected him with a resounding majority vote two years ago. He may not have been as warm and fuzzy as his father, but he got things done. Including the many things that the public would never know about.

He was exhausted. It had been a long day of meetings, all of them international and complex. All of this speaking in code because they were using online virtual meeting software that could be compromised made his head spin.

"It will all be worth it," he said to his father's portrait. "Mom would be proud."

CHAPTER TWENTY-THREE

John walked beside Doyle, waiting for the man to take a breather. It was obvious his hip was hurting bad. Everyone they passed knew Doyle and said hello, the old crank giving a quick nod in response and moving on.

"I know Ida was upset when I mentioned it, but we should absolutely call the police," John said. Ida's house was the next block over.

"We'll do no such thing," Doyle huffed. "Whoever these people are already broke her trust. I'm not about to do it, as well. And neither are you."

With Ida missing, John didn't expect them to find anyone in her house. He had no idea what Doyle planned to do. For now, John was simply in tagalong mode, though he had to get back to his mother's house soon.

Doyle didn't bother knocking or ringing the bell. He simply turned the knob on the front door and pushed. To their surprise, the door opened.

They stepped right into Ida's living room. Piles of newspapers, cardboard boxes, and bags of bread crumbs covered every surface. It was like walking into one of those hoarder houses, the smell of mildew and, as best as John could guess, pigeon excrement a tad difficult to take in. Now this was exactly what young John expected the Pigeon Lady to live in.

"Hello," John called out.

Doyle elbowed him in the ribs and whispered, "Quiet. I want to catch these people in the act."

"In the act of what?"

Doyle didn't respond. Instead, he crept into the dining room. The table and chairs were hidden beneath mounds of clothes.

John thought if We Care had sent aides to Ida's to get things in order, they hadn't done a very good job. Or maybe they had, making him wince at the thought of the interior having been worse.

Both men stopped when the floorboards above them creaked.

Someone was upstairs, slowly walking around.

"Come on," Doyle hissed.

The stairs were carpeted and mercifully quiet as they made their way to the second floor. Doyle pointed to an open door at the end of the hallway. A shadow passed across the rectangle of light painted on the floor.

Reaching into his pocket, Doyle's hand came out gripping a pistol.

John tugged at his arm. "What the hell are you doing with that?" he said close to Doyle's ear.

The man paid him no mind, suddenly striding down the hall. He used the gun to batter the door all the way open, John on his heels.

A young woman in torn-up jeans and a black T-shirt

was taking a video of Ida's bedroom. All of the dresser and night table drawers had been opened, their contents blatantly rifled through.

"Put that phone down right now, missy," Doyle barked, pointing the gun smack at the middle of her forehead.

The woman's eyes nearly popped out of her skull for a moment. She quickly got control of herself, slipping the phone into her back pocket. She was tall and pale, with angular cheekbones and narrow eyes. When she spoke, John detected an Eastern European accent. "Put the gun down before you hurt yourself."

That only made Doyle take a step closer, moving the gun so close, if he pulled the trigger, the police would be picking up pieces of her skull for days. "You don't tell me what to do. I have a mind to shoot first and ask questions later."

"Doyle," John snapped. "She's right, put the gun down." How had things gone to DEFCON 1 so quickly?

"You like scaring old ladies?" Doyle asked. John was shocked by the rock steadiness of his gun hand.

"Who the fuck are you to come in here waving a gun at me?" she said, hands on her hips. John couldn't believe it. Any other person would be a shaking mess. This woman either had nerves of steel or this somehow wasn't the first time someone had put a gun to her head. No matter what she had been up to, Doyle was now the criminal, and John was beginning to worry.

"Nice mouth on you," Doyle said. "I'll give you five seconds to get out of here. And tell your little partner in crime they better not come back here. I won't give you the consideration of a warning next time."

She sucked her teeth at him, refusing to move.

John said, "Miss, why don't you just come with me downstairs, and we can clear this whole thing up?"

She stared at him with cold cobalt eyes.

"You pull trigger, it will be biggest mistake of your life," she said.

"I seriously doubt that," Doyle said. "By the way, I'm down to three."

"Sam!" John said, using his first name to hopefully gain his attention. "You can't just run up and shoot a defenseless woman."

"Just like I can't allow some criminal to drive a poor defenseless woman out of her home . . . and her mind." To the woman, he said, "Time's up."

She was about to open her mouth when Doyle pulled the trigger. The percussion in the small room sounded like a cannon had gone off. Plaster rained down on the woman from where Doyle had fired into the ceiling. That got her to break into a run, wedging herself between them as she hustled out the door. John was pushed into the hallway as she headed for the stairs. Before she left, she turned to him and sneered, "You'll regret this. You don't know who you are dealing with."

He hadn't realized Doyle had stepped into the hallway, the gun still aimed at the woman.

"And I don't think you know who you're dealing with," Doyle said. "Though I think you're starting to learn a little."

She clambered down the stairs, slamming the front door so hard it shook the house.

John needed a moment to catch his breath. What the hell had just happened?

He looked to Doyle. "Well, you didn't want the police involved, but it's too late for that now. I'm sure they'll be here any minute. What were you thinking shooting a damn gun in the house?"

Doyle slipped the pistol back in his pocket. "It worked, didn't it? Besides, everyone within earshot is hard of hearing. No one's calling the cops."

John wanted to wring the man's neck. He had just been roped into a potential crime.

As Doyle made his way downstairs, John slipped back into the bedroom to assess the damage. The hole in the ceiling wasn't much, but the ancient plaster around it had cracked and splintered as if it had been bashed with a sledgehammer. Ida's bed was covered in dust and plaster.

He thought of the fearless woman.

What was she doing in here?

How on earth wasn't she the least bit terrified of having a gun trained on her?

One thing was for sure. She was no mere home health aide.

This was a person with a backstory miles apart from that of a person who dedicated themselves to helping the elderly. She was someone who had seen some dark things, so dark that looking down the barrel of a gun meant nothing to her.

A lead ball in his gut told him that something had just been started that wouldn't end quietly or easily.

Muttering a string of curses, he went down to talk to Doyle.

Joe Knox found himself staring at his brother and Sam Doyle sitting at the kitchen table nursing cups of coffee. Doyle looked angrier than usual, and John wasn't faring much better.

"What happened?" he said, tossing his jacket on the couch.

"We have a problem," John said.

"That I took care of," Doyle piped up.

John gave Doyle a look that dared him to keep talking. To Joe's surprise, Doyle turned away and screwed his face up tight.

His stomach already topsy-turvy from discovering that the lawyer didn't exist—not in Virginia Beach, at least— Joe declined a coffee, preferring to stand leaning against the refrigerator with his arms folded. "Okay, John, spill it."

John told him about going to church and finding the flyer, how it clicked into place with what the Pigeon Lady had said the day before, and how he'd gone to Doyle's to ask her about it. Things took off from there, ending with a shooting and waiting around for an hour for the police, who never showed.

"I told him no one would hear it," Doyle said.

Like his brother, Joe wasn't so much concerned with the warning shot as he was by the reaction of the aide. "We can't let Ida go back home. Not until this is settled."

"Or I can stay with her, wait for that nasty woman or anyone else to just try to step foot inside the house," Doyle said. Joe looked at the man and saw the bulge of the pistol in his pocket.

"I think it's best everyone stays away from her house," Joe said.

John leaned back in his chair and said, "We could call We Care and give some negative feedback on their services. Maybe even write a scathing Yelp review."

At first, Joe didn't realize he was joking. John's sarcastic smile stopped him from asking him if he'd lost his mind.

"No calling the police. We have to respect Ida's wishes," Doyle added.

"You know that sometimes you have to do something against a person's wishes for their own good, right?" John said. He got up to put his empty mug in the sink.

Doyle got up, too. "I'm not an idiot. Just give me a day. I need to talk to some people and do some snooping around first. Now, before I go, I'm going to say hello to your mother. And no, I'm not going to tell her what happened. She had one of those people in her home, too. I don't want her thinking the same thing could have happened to her."

Joe watched Doyle navigate the stairs, pausing with each step to massage his hip. Isabelle might not have been like Ida's aide, but he no longer thought it was a coincidence that his parents received an eviction notice around the same time she started working for them.

When Doyle was out of sight, John asked, "So where were you this morning?"

Joe flipped the folded eviction notice on the table. "I went to Virginia Beach to pay a visit to the lawyer who was listed on that. Turns out, there is no lawyer at that address."

John started to pace the kitchen, hands thrust in his pockets.

"For all I know," Joe said, "the man's website and phone line are bogus, too. Which could be good news. That piece of paper may be equally bogus."

"If there's any truth to the luck o' the Irish, you're right about that."

Joe smirked. "You know Irish luck is mostly bad. Gives us a reason to drink and moan." He ran upstairs to his bedroom to grab his phone, listening to his mother and Doyle talking as if nothing crazy had been happening. She sounded happy to see him, though she kept worrying that he'd left the rehab too soon.

"You have to take better care of yourself, Sam," Joe heard her say.

"I've outlived every one of my doctors, so I think I'm doing all right."

Back downstairs, Joe slumped onto the couch and looked at his phone.

"Who are you calling?" John asked.

Joe raised an eyebrow. "Doyle said we can't call the cops. He didn't say I can't call *a* cop."

Before his brother could protest, Joe dialed Claire Dennehy. As luck would have it, she was off duty. He asked her to meet him at the Bridge Coffee Shop in an hour. She didn't hesitate to say yes.

"You do realize Claire's not a reporter. It's not like you can tell her things and keep it off the record," John said. He had his coat on, about to head to the hospital.

"I also realize that she's Claire, the girl who used to push you around in a stroller and pretend you were her baby. Neighborhood blood is thicker than blue blood."

Shaking his head, John said, "Did you just make that up?"

Joe got up so he could sit with his mother for a while, knowing Doyle had things to do and people to see. "I did, and don't quote me on that."

"Off the record?"

"Exactly."

CHAPTER TWENTY-FOUR

John had walked Doyle to the door and volunteered to drop him off wherever he needed to go on his way to the hospital. He didn't pry about what the man's plans were. Doyle would just snap at him like a mangy dog anyway.

"I'll walk," Doyle said.

Keeping his voice low, John said, "Keep that gun tucked away."

Doyle cut him in two with a withering look before heading off in his own direction. John sighed and headed for his car.

It was later than John had intended, but his father was a captive audience and would forgive him his tardiness, especially after stopping to get the paper and a grilled Reuben at the diner, along with a side of coleslaw and fries.

The guard at St. Luke's front desk recognized him, handing him a pass without his needing to tell him what room. John took the stairs to the fifth floor instead of the elevator. Aside from his muscles needing a workout, he now needed to burn off all that nervous energy. So much was happening. How was it possible in a neighborhood once so damn quiet and insular? These people should be relaxing and enjoying their golden years, as long as they were healthy. They shouldn't be thrown out of their homes, threatened and intimidated.

At least Doyle seemed to be enjoying his role in things.

"Hey, Dad, I got your favorite."

He nearly dropped the bag when he saw his father sitting in a chair, dressed in the clothes he'd worn when he'd been admitted. There was one IV still in his arm, the pole standing next to the chair.

"What do you think you're doing?" John said, forgetting about the bag of hot food in his hand.

"Going home where I belong," his father said, using both of his arms to push himself up and out of the chair. He looked a little better today, with some color in his cheeks, but he was far from well enough to go home.

John was quick to rush to his side, worried that his father might fall. His legs wobbled a bit, but he steadied himself.

John said, "Unless you had a visit from Jesus himself last night, there's no way you're ready to go home. Have you seen Dr. Murphy?"

His father patted his hand. "I feel much, much better. And no, I haven't seen the Murph. I know what he'll say. But it's my body, and I know I'll be even better when I'm in my own bed and not getting woken up every half hour so people can check my blood pressure, poke me with needles, or fiddle with those machines that never shut up."

As he went to get his coat from the slim closet, John stepped in his way. "Okay, slow your roll. You can't just walk out of a hospital."

"I can and I am. I already signed the ADW papers." He plucked the IV out of his arm and John winced.

"A nurse is supposed to do that."

"I think I handled it just fine."

John said, "And what are ADW papers?"

His father shrugged his coat on. "It means against doctor's wishes. It's not like I'm committed to some asylum. Patients have the freedom to come and go. And speaking of that, let's go."

John was too stunned at first to follow. He just watched his father walk out of the room, bidding a loud farewell to the nurses as he passed by their station. Snapping out of it, he jogged down the hall.

Once in the elevator, his father looked at the brown paper bag. "Smells delicious. Is that what I think it is?"

"Yes, but I shouldn't reward you for bad behavior."

Taking the bag and opening it so he could inhale the savory aroma, his father said, "You can punish me when we get home. Until then, I'm eating this."

Joe felt guilty for not going to see his father, but getting a chance to talk to Claire Dennehy was important. He'd swing by the hospital right after.

The Bridge Coffee Shop had been remodeled since the last time he'd been inside. Back in the day, it served two types of coffee—black or with milk and sugar. They sold prewrapped muffins and cookies and offered the folks in the neighborhood a place to sit a spell and take a break or catch up with friends.

Now, the board above the counter was chock-full of more varieties of coffee than Joe could count.

"They caved to the pressure from Starbucks," a voice said just behind his ear. He turned to see Claire Dennehy dressed in faded blue jeans and a light flannel shirt tucked into said jeans, the fabric pulled taut over all the right curves. Her hair was down, natural waves spilling over her shoulders.

"I was hoping there'd be one last holdout," Joe said, trying to decide what to get.

"The new owner came and took over, oh, about four years ago. He went full tilt, expecting to capture a younger crowd without doing some research and finding out there really isn't much of a younger crowd around to get. But to his surprise, and mine, the older regulars love it. Makes them feel hip."

Joe couldn't help snickering. He also couldn't help but notice Claire's beautiful smile. He remembered her as a kid in perpetual braces. Her orthodontist must have been proud.

Stepping up to the counter, Joe ordered a vanilla latte with a dash of cinnamon.

Claire looked at him as if he'd just stepped off a spaceship.

"I live in California," he said.

"Ahhh."

That explained everything. Claire had a large black coffee with five sugars.

As they waited for their coffee, stepping to the side, Joe said, "Five sugars?"

"No diabetics in my family, so I'm safe. Hey, everyone has to have a vice."

"At least one."

"Oh, and how many do you have?"

Joe thanked the girl behind the counter when she handed him his coffee. "You don't have that kind of time."

He found them a seat, wanting to kick himself for implying that he had a deep streak of depravity. Did he think that would impress her? She was a cop, for crying out loud. Joe thought he'd left that awkwardness around the fairer sex decades ago.

Claire pulled her chair out before he could do it for her, his hand swiping at air.

"Oh, sorry," she said, smiling.

"Chivalry is not dead, just a little slow."

"It's been a long time since anyone even attempted to pull out my chair, so I'll award you the proper points." She sipped her coffee. "I'm all for equality, but sometimes I miss being treated like a lady."

They sat across from one another, their table by the window overlooking the aging main thoroughfare of Woodlean. Everyone around them was old enough to collect social security. Joe himself could see those deposits on his own horizon.

So why did he all of a sudden feel like a clueless teenager again?

Thankfully, Claire broke the ice. "So, Joe, tell me what you've been up to since we last hung out."

"Hmm, you want a rundown of all thirty-plus years?"

"Bullet points will do."

He knew he should just get right to the reason he'd called her, but he found himself recounting his travels across the country in an attempt to find himself, all the way to his marriage, career he wasn't all that enamored with, and impending divorce. When he was done, he exhaled loudly, took a sip of his latte, and sat back, feeling as if he'd just gone through therapy.

Claire, to her credit, took it all in without batting an eye.

"Wow, I think that's pretty incredible," she said.

Joe looked at her, confused. "What? My divorce?"

Her eyes went wide and she apologized, laughing behind her hand. "No, not that. Divorce is a bitch and a half. I should know. I've been through two of them. I meant that you got to leave this place and see America."

Joe fiddled with his coffee cup. "Yeah, but I was broke and lost most of that time."

She swatted at his arm. "So what? You got to live, Joe. You did what a lot of people wish they could have done. You got to see and experience America. All of it. That's pretty special."

He'd never looked at it that way. In his eyes, he'd been an itinerant failure, at least until he'd met Stella.

"Well, that's nice of you to say."

"I mean it."

"Okay, I gave you my story. What's yours? How did you get to be a cop? I always thought you'd end up a ballerina or something."

Claire dropped her elbow on the table, her hand cupping her chin. "Oh God, you remember my ballet lessons? You know, I could have been a prima ballerina if I didn't have two left feet and weak arches." She tipped back her cup and finished the rest of her coffee. "Beneath all the girly-girl pink and makeup, I always secretly wanted to be a cop. After college, I tried to work in an office for a few years, but I hated it. So when I saw the posting for the exam, I took it and passed with flying colors. It nearly killed my mother, but she got over it. Now, she brags to all her friends about her daughter the big bad police officer. Though lately she keeps asking me when I'm going to retire. I think she wants me to move down to Florida to be close to them, which isn't a bad idea."

"Wow. With two divorces, you should be ready to live the easy life," Joe said, wishing he could dislodge his foot from his mouth.

Claire didn't flinch. "I married two bums, one in my twenties and one in my thirties. Not much to divide after those disasters."

"No kids?"

"Thank God, no. You?"

"Two. A boy and a girl. They're living with their mother now."

"I'm so sorry."

The last thing Joe wanted to do was get into the horror of his flamed-out marriage with Claire. So he changed the subject. "I might as well just jump right into it. I need to tell you about something and for you to listen as an old friend who has experience with the law, but not as a cop on duty. Does that make sense?"

"Kinda. Now I'm intrigued." She leaned closer to him.

"It's about the Pigeon Lady. Well, for starters."

"Ida Benson? What has she gotten herself up to? She's not setting pigeons free from Frank Moody's coop again, is she?"

"I wish it was that." Joe took a deep breath and told her about Ida locking herself in the shed, afraid of what her aides were trying to get her to do. He mentioned Doyle and John confronting the aide in Ida's house, neglecting to mention Doyle's warning shot. He didn't want to test her limits, not now.

"Jesus," Claire said. "That they scared her so much she's afraid to go to the police just burns me up."

Joe looked around and saw the crowd had thinned out. He and Claire were just about the last people left. "I'm sure we can convince her to call the police eventually, just not yet. And Doyle is hell-bent on sticking to her wishes."

"Trust me, I get it. Until then, you should call the Better Business Bureau and report We Care. It's not much, but it's a start. Any chance your brother and Doyle can get me a description of the woman? Maybe she's local and has priors."

"I could ask. John said she had a heavy accent, like Russian or something." He'd just come to talk about Ida, but now he felt comfortable enough to share what was happening with his own parents. "There's something else."

"I'm all ears. Only thing I have to do today is clean my bathroom and do a few loads of laundry. Not something I want to rush home for."

He explained to her about his research into the lawyer named on the eviction notice for his parents.

"It looks like the lawyer behind it is a total fake. I take that with what I've heard is going on around the neighborhood, and I'm beginning to wonder if it's all connected somehow."

Claire started tearing pieces off the lip of her coffee cup, a nervous tic he remembered from school, when she used to shred her milk cartons. "You know, I've been concerned about the things I've seen around here for weeks now. I keep seeing more and more empty houses, but nothing is for sale. It makes you wonder what's going to happen next. I know a lot of them need some work, but you'd think a couple would be on the market as is. Once the old guard is gone, who will be the new? All of Woodlean could be unrecognizable in a few years."

"That would be a crying shame," Joe said.

"It would. I know most of the kids we grew up with flew the coop and never looked back. But I'll bet they'd be pretty upset to see their childhood homes turned upside down."

Claire leaned back in her chair, her face clouded with concern.

Joe said, "Are you cool with keeping this between us for now?"

She nodded slowly, her mind chewing on heavy thoughts. "I am. You could be right. I'm going to look into We Care myself. Just some background digging. You might also want to talk to your parents' neighbors. There may be others who are too afraid to talk about it or are housebound and have no one to talk to."

Joe hadn't realized he was clenching his fists under the table until his knuckles started to ache.

"What kind of animals prey on the elderly?" he said, watching a pair of octogenarians walk hand in hand past the coffee shop. The man wore a Korean War veteran cap, his beloved using her cane to tap his leg when he said something that made them both laugh.

"You'd be surprised how common it is," Claire said. "Elder abuse is rampant, not just in this county but everywhere. They're easy targets, and there's no shortage of lowlife assholes out there looking for a quick score."

"Yeah, but this is more than a quick score. What's the endgame here?"

Claire's demeanor had changed, morphing into what Joe imagined was her hardened cop face. "I don't know, but we're going to find out."

The got up, tossed their cups, and promised to call one another the next day after Joe's appointment with a legitimate lawyer.

Outside the shop, gray clouds had crept in, obscuring the sun.

"Good luck tomorrow," Claire said.

"Thanks. I think I'll need it."

He went to shake her hand as she went to give him a hug. They then reversed, resulting in an awkward chest bump that had them both laughing.

From the corner of his eye, Joe saw the sheriff's car idling across the street. The man at the wheel, presumably the sheriff, seemed to be staring right at them.

"A friend of yours?" he said to Claire, nodding his head toward the sheriff.

She cut a sharp glance at the car. "That pig? Not a chance."

"Sounds like some unpleasant history," he said. The sheriff wore reflective sunglasses even though it had become a gloomy day.

"You could say that," Claire said. "He's ex number one with a bullet."

CHAPTER TWENTY-FIVE

Pat Knox sat in his favorite chair, exhausted but quite happy to be home. John had carried Mary downstairs and set her up on the couch. It was the first time they'd all been together in the living room in as long as he could remember.

All of this would have been a wonderful homecoming if not for the news he'd wrangled out of Mary. Well, not really wrangled. She'd been prepared to tell him, and since he was now back in the house, there'd be no way to hide it.

When Joe walked in, the look on his face was priceless. Pat imagined he'd worn that same look many moons back when he'd stay up to wait for their restless and wild son to come home in the middle of the night.

"How?" was all Joe could say.

"Sheer force of Knox will," Johnnie said from his spot on the end of the couch.

Joe went to drop his coat on the chair by the door but stopped. How many times had Pat yelled at him when he was a boy to hang it on the hook? It looked like all that effort had finally paid off.

"Are you even well enough to be home?" Joe said.

"I'm here, aren't I?" Pat said, giving Mary a wink.

"Are you hungry, Joe?" Mary said. "John bought a nice pound cake from the bakery."

"No, Ma, I'm fine." He stood over Pat. "You don't look so good. I can't believe they let you out."

"It was a hospital, not a gulag," Pat said. His head was feeling a little soupy, and visions of sleeping in his bed were a constant siren call. "Now take a seat, and let's talk."

Joe's brows knit in confusion, but he did sit down in the rickety wooden chair that Pat had found in the basement when he'd bought the house. He'd restained and fixed the legs several times over the years. It wasn't the height of decorative fashion, but he refused to give up on it.

"He knows," Johnnie said, sipping from a bottle of water.

"Knows what?" Joe said.

"About the notice."

Joe sat back, the chair making a racket, and took a deep breath. "Look, Dad, we weren't hiding it from you because we didn't think you could handle it."

Pat raised his hand to stop him. "I'm not upset. Well, whoever is behind this has my dander up, but that's not directed at you. Your mother and I had a nice talk earlier. I understand. But I need you to understand that I'm back and better—at least, better than I was before—and we're going to handle this together. No secrets. Your mother and I may be old, but we can hold our own."

Joe folded his hands, arms resting on his legs. "Then you know I'm seeing a lawyer tomorrow. It's very likely this whole thing is a scam."

Pat nodded, feeling a cough coming on but able to keep it at bay. "I do. I'm not going to insist I come. Your mother has made it clear she'll kill me if I even think of leaving the house."

"That I did," she said.

"But when you get back, you have to tell me everything."

"I will. I promise. I'm actually relieved. I didn't feel comfortable doing all this stuff behind your back, even though we had a valid reason. I'm glad you understand." He leaned forward, looking at Pat as if he were a doctor inspecting his face for moles. "Are you sure you're Patrick Knox?"

Pat waved him off. "Maybe I'm getting soft in my dotage."

Johnnie got up and started fiddling with the framed pictures on the mantel. "We might as well tell him everything."

"There's more?" Pat said. He already knew that Isabelle had gone like the wind. It was disappointing, but he would worry about what they'd do after the boys went back home.

"It's about your buddy Doyle. And Ida Benson," Johnnie said.

"And Claire Dennehy," Joe chimed in. "You remember her? We went to St. Brendan's together."

"I heard she became a cop," Pat said.

"Boy, the information flows better and faster around here than it does on the internet," Joe said. "We just met for coffee so I could talk to her about everything and get her professional take on things."

Pat saw the furtive look in his son's eyes. *I'll bet that's not the only reason he asked her for coffee.* Joe might have technically still been married, but after what Stella had done to him, to their family, well, Pat didn't begrudge the man a cup of coffee with an old friend who just happened to be female. He wondered wryly if she still had her braces.

Johnnie perked up. "Have you heard the one about Doyle and his gun?"

"A gun? Okay, let's take this back to the beginning," Pat said, though hearing about Doyle with one of his guns wasn't so shocking.

Johnnie and Joe started talking over one another, stopped, and Johnnie went into his adventure with Doyle rescuing Ida. The part about the aide not being the least bit afraid of having a gun in her face worried Pat, while also making him grateful Isabelle was out of the picture. He couldn't imagine her being like that, but he didn't want strangers in his house from here on, thank you very much. Joe then went into how he'd driven to Virginia Beach only to find the lawyer behind the eviction notice didn't exist, not at that address.

As much as it pained him to recall that day, he thought back to what Bridgett Monahan had shouted as the sheriff and his deputy had struggled to remove her from her home.

Thieves! You're nothing but thieves!

Okay, maybe the sheriff wasn't a thief, but someone could have somehow stolen that house right out from under her. Like they were trying to do to him.

Except he wasn't some terrified old woman with no one to turn to.

He and Mary had Johnnie and Joe.

"I'm glad you told Claire," Pat said when the boys were done. He was bone weary and really needed to sleep. He knew his eyelids were drooping.

Mary cocked an eyebrow and sniffed the air. "Does anyone else smell smoke?"

Joe got up and went into the kitchen, checking the burners. "Nothing in here, but I smell it."

Johnnie walked around the first floor, taking deep breaths like a bloodhound. "Anyone around here use a fireplace?"

Pat shook his head. "Not for a long, long time."

Joe strolled over to the front window and shouted, "The garbage cans are on fire!"

He ran out of the house, Johnnie on his heels. A second later, Johnnie burst back through the door, ran to the kitchen, and unhooked the small fire extinguisher from its holder on the wall.

The terrified look on Mary's face got Pat out of his chair, his legs wobbling as he looked to see if the entire house had caught fire.

Joe had removed his shirt and was beating at the flames in one of the trash cans, sending up spirals of dancing fireflies. John cringed as they touched the house.

"Move back!" he shouted at his brother. Pulling the pin on the extinguisher, he aimed it at the first can, the fire crackling well over his head. The white foam smothered it quickly. He then moved on to the other before dousing the side of the house for good measure.

When he turned around, Joe was gone.

His father was on the porch, his arm wrapped around the post. "Is it out?"

John looked into the pails, bubbling with foam, the acrid stench of burning garbage stinging his nose. He gave it another blast just to be sure.

"Yeah, crisis averted."

Anna McCurty, their neighbor, was on her porch, as were several others who must have smelled the smoke and heard the commotion.

"Was your house on fire, Pat?" Anna said, one hand at her stomach, the other her mouth.

"Thank God, no," his father said. "Just the garbage cans."

"The garbage cans? Were you burning leaves?"

"We were in the house. I don't know what started it."

John found a stick and poked around the bubbling goo in one of the pails. "More like who started it."

He lifted a wad of newspaper from the mess and brought it to his nose. There was a definite hint of accelerant, like barbecue lighter fluid. Since he was the one who had been taking out the garbage, he knew they hadn't thrown away any old bottles of lighter fluid.

"Should I call the fire department?" Anna said.

John did his best to look like everything was fine. "No need. We caught it in time. I'll hose down the house a bit just to be sure."

"Could you do mine, too, Johnnie? I don't want to take any chances."

"Absolutely."

Then she looked at his father. "Aren't you supposed to be in the hospital?"

"I had to come home sometime," he replied.

"You still don't look well."

"Compliments are always accepted."

"Men," Anna muttered, taking one last look at the garbage pails before heading back inside. That was the cue for everyone else to return to their homes, too. The show was over.

But not for John.

Someone had doused the pails and set them on fire. The lids were stacked atop one another in the narrow alley between the two houses.

"Where's your brother?" John's father said.

"I was going to ask you that."

As if hearing his name, Joe came jogging back into the front yard, huffing and puffing. He bent at the waist, hands on his knees, getting his breath back.

"Where the heck did you go?" John asked.

"To see if I could find . . . the prick who . . . started the fire." He straightened up, looking up and down the street. "It didn't just start . . . by itself. Jesus, I'm out of shape."

John looked to his father, who really should get back inside. "You have any miscreant teens around who like to start fires?"

"Not since your brother left."

Joe said, "That was one time."

"Why don't you guys go back inside? I'll get the hose out, just in case there are some embers I can't see," John said.

Joe took one look at their father and forgot he was in pain from his sprint through the neighborhood. "Good idea."

After the door closed, John went to the yard to fetch the hose. Thankfully it was long enough to reach all the way to the front. Anna watched him from her window as he doused the part of her house that was closest to the garbage cans.

Whoever had started the fires did so for one of two reasons: a prank, or a warning.

It didn't take much for him to eliminate it being a prank. Their house was someone's target. If they wanted to take it away from his parents, why burn it down?

Unless they knew John and Joe were inside and would put it out. Hell, they hadn't even bothered to make sure no one would smell the lighter fluid. Those pails had been thoroughly doused.

No, it was a message, and the message was clear.

Get out.

Chapter Twenty-six

It had been a long, long night. John had opted to sleep on the couch, but he did very little sleeping. Instead, he spent the whole night prowling around the house, looking out every window, even going outside several times to make sure no one was hiding in the shadows. The old coffeepot was called into service again and again. He'd dragged the pails to the curb so they were away from the house, but that did little to alleviate his concerns.

When Joe came down at seven, he looked at John and said, "Did you get any sleep? I heard you banging around all night."

"Wasn't my first time pulling sentry duty," John said, recalling his years in the military. He'd once considered staying in the army and becoming a lifer, but then he'd met Marion, and she was a woman who needed stability. He never once regretted his decision, but he also never begrudged a moment of his time in the service. Now that he was older and could look back, he realized it had given him much more than he ever could have expected. Serving his country had been an honor.

"Yeah, I had a crap night, too. Kept looking in at Mom and Dad all night as if they were kids."

"Role reversal," John said. "We knew it was going to come someday. It just seems weird."

"Very."

"Coffee's on the stove."

Joe gave him a fist bump. "Gotta look alive and make myself decent. You catch anyone lighting fires?"

"Thankfully, no."

Joe went to the closet by the front door and found his old baseball bat. It was a genuine Louisville Slugger his father had given him when he made the baseball team in high school. He handed it to his brother. "You see someone, hit them so hard we can read the insignia on their forehead."

Joe and John decided it was best that one of them stay at the house at all times. Since Joe was the one to make the call to the real estate lawyer, he left his exhausted brother at home.

The law firm's office was located in an office park on the third floor of a building that was a clone of the other three around it. The sign for Woodbein, Scheir, and Billingsly, plated in faux gold, was the first thing Joe saw when he stepped off the elevator.

"I'm here to see Caitlin Scheir," he said to the pretty receptionist. She offered him coffee, which he gladly took, and he was shown to a comfortable couch in the small waiting area.

"She'll be with you in a moment. She's just wrapping up a call."

"Thank you."

The coffee was hot and tasty, with just a hint of hazel-nut. He flipped through a surprisingly current *Sports Illustrated* magazine, not comprehending a single thing he was reading. It didn't take long until he heard his name called.

"Joseph Knox?"

The woman before him wore a navy blue belted dress with sensible heels, her dirty-blond hair hanging loose around her shoulders.

"I'm Caitlin. So nice to meet you."

Joe got up and shook her hand. She was younger than he'd expected, maybe her mid-thirties, with an easy smile that went straight to her eyes.

"Thanks for seeing me on such short notice."

He followed her to her office, forgetting his coffee. Caitlin Scheir had a modest corner office overlooking the back parking lot. The walls were lined with framed degrees and awards mingled with pictures of her and her family. It was cozy but professional.

After they took their seats, Caitlin opting to sit next to him rather than behind her desk, she said, "So. How can I help? I have a little bit of information, but I always find it better to get the story straight from my clients."

Joe had been nervous. Not because he was meeting with a lawyer, but from the fear of what they might find. Caitlin put him at ease right away. He opened the file folder he'd been carrying and gave her the eviction notice.

"It says my parents have to vacate their home, but it doesn't make sense. They've owned that house since I was a kid. It was paid off years and years ago. No one, and I mean no one else, can lay claim to their home. Well, other than my brother and I, but we're in no rush to get our inheritance because, well, you know."

Caitlin took her time reading the letter, one leg crossing the other.

"This is unusual, but not unheard of," she said.

"What is?"

Joe's heart started to thud.

"Normally, a person would receive a thirty-day notice to vacate. I've only seen one other case when it was less. This says two weeks."

"With the end date coming up fast."

She nodded. "Like I said, it's not the norm, but not enough to send up any red flags. Maybe a yellow one."

"The time line concerns me, but what I'm really curious about is finding out if this is legitimate. I tried contacting the lawyer mentioned in the letter, but he's nowhere to be found."

Her eyebrow arched. "Now *that's* a red flag."

"So you think this could be a scam?"

She bit at her bottom lip. "I don't have enough yet to make a judgment like that. Some scams are still legal. It all depends on the expertise and intelligence of the scammer."

"Look, no one else owns that house other than my father. No stranger has the right to throw him out of his home."

"If there's one thing that gets my blood pressure up, it's elder abuse. Criminals see them as easy prey, and often those targets are too weak, scared, or confused to fight back. I'm not saying this is a case of elder abuse, but if I were a doctor ticking off symptoms, there's a couple right here."

Joe decided to tell her the rest. "I don't think it's just us. There's been a rash of evictions in the neighborhood. Houses are being left vacant left and right."

"Really?"

"Yes."

"Tick another one on the list. It would be helpful if you can email me some of the names and addresses so I can do some digging."

"I'll put that together for you as soon as I get back."

He almost told her about the burning trash cans but decided against it. That info was more for Claire.

She asked, "You mind if I keep this? I'll have my assistant make a copy for you."

"Please."

"The first thing I need to do is contact the county clerk and check the land records. You're sure your father hasn't made any changes recently? As people get older, they tend to get more active with making sure their affairs are in order. Sometimes, through no fault of the professionals brought in to help them—considering they have to be impartial—mistakes or misjudgments are made."

Joe felt the back of his neck get hot. Caitlin must have seen the frustration in his eyes, because she was quick to add, "I'm not saying your father is incompetent. It's a question I have to ask. Believe me, you never know. I've seen just about everything."

Joe sighed. "No, he says he hasn't done a single thing with the house or his will. That was all drawn up over twenty years ago. He may be in his eighties, but he's in full control of his faculties. I wish I had the energy to do what he does every day."

He gave a nervous chuckle that made Caitlin smile, though he supposed mostly out of pity for him.

"Okay, so I know where to start. I'm also going to find this Anthony Kramer."

Joe looked out the window, his eyes catching a crow as it dove into one of the trees in the parking lot.

"How long will it take?" he asked.

"Not long."

"Before the date of the eviction?"

"Yes."

"Good."

"One thing," she said. "If this is some kind of scam, they may try to get your parents to leave before the date on this notice. Whatever they do, they should not take a step out of that house. Not until we know what this is really about."

Joe flexed the fingers on his right hand, knuckles popping. "No worries there. My brother and I are in the house. No one's going anywhere. Even if this whole thing is somehow magically on the up-and-up, my parents aren't leaving their home. I don't care who comes knocking."

Caitlin shot him a look of quiet approval. "In that case, I'll make sure we have a different kind of legal counsel waiting in the wings for you."

CHAPTER TWENTY-SEVEN

Pat Knox had managed to roll out of bed the day after Joe's visit with the lawyer. Leaving the hospital when he did might not have been his wisest move, considering he'd slept most of the previous day. But he was feeling stronger now, strong enough to go downstairs and have breakfast with his sons. Johnnie made sunny-side-up eggs, sausage, baked beans, home-fried potatoes, and toast. Pat's mouth watered at the smells coming from the kitchen. He was served in the living room, sitting in his chair so he could watch the morning news on Fox.

"You want your pills now?" Johnnie asked from the kitchen. He'd picked them up from the pharmacy the other day on the way home. Four amber bottles filled with pills big enough to choke a cow.

"Not especially," Pat said, his mouth full of egg and beans. "But I might as well."

Joe was tucking into his Irish breakfast from his seat on the couch, hunched over the full plate on the coffee table. He said, "When did you become such a good cook?"

John handed his father his pills. "Remember when Marion and I fostered Kayla?"

"Cute kid," Joe said, piling a slice of toast with sausage, eggs, and potatoes. "I always got the feeling she was afraid of me."

"She was terrified of all men. Her father was a piece of garbage. He's a three-time offender. Won't be out of prison unless it's in a box. Anyway, Kayla loved watching all those cooking shows. I was having a tough time getting her to be comfortable with me, so one day I signed us up for a cooking class. Marion had to take us because Kayla was too scared to be alone in a car, or anywhere, with a man. That class was the turning point. She got so lost in having fun and learning how to make a layer cake, she forgot about her fear. I signed us up for classes every other week, and in between, we bonded in the kitchen. You have Kayla to thank for breakfast."

"If I see her again, I surely will," Pat said. He'd only met her once when John and Marion brought her down for a long weekend. The shy girl spent most of her time playing alone in the yard.

"You just might," John said. "She's working as a sous-chef in a restaurant in Delaware. I was thinking of having a little reunion down here someday."

"That would be grand. Now, which one of you wants to run a plate up to your mother? I feel guilty eating like a king."

"I've got it," Joe said, scooping the prepared plate off the kitchen table and running upstairs.

Pat was about to tuck into his coffee when there was a pounding at the door. He looked at John, who had stopped mid-stride on his way to the kitchen.

Pat couldn't get up with the laden tray on his lap. Not that John would have let him.

Bam, bam, bam!

"I know you're awake. I can smell food."

Pat relaxed. "It's Doyle. Let him in before he breaks the door."

Johnnie was nearly knocked aside as Doyle rushed in, Ida Benson trailing behind him holding two bulging shopping bags. Pat saw a trail of bread crumbs drip out of a hole in one of the bags.

"I'd heard you were home," Doyle said.

"And good morning to you," Pat said. "Hello, Ida." He didn't wonder how Doyle knew about his leaving the hospital. Anna next door must have spread the word.

"We have to talk," Doyle said. He looked more agitated than usual, his holey cap perched high on his spotted forehead.

"Have a seat," Pat said. "Either of you want anything? Johnnie cooked enough to feed the Palm Sunday crowd."

"Breakfast?" Doyle scowled. "I already ate. I'll have a coffee, though."

Ida politely shook her head, staring wistfully out the window. The poor woman looked to be trapped in Doyle's orbit, just along for the ride. Though with what had happened to her, Pat suspected his friend wouldn't let her out of his sight.

Doyle pulled up the old chair so he was practically knee to knee with Pat. "We have a problem."

"Do tell," Pat said.

Doyle stuck a finger through one of the holes in his cap and scratched his head. "Ida isn't the only one."

Pat stared wistfully at his plate. His stomach screamed at him to finish it, but it would be rude in front of company. "You have more people living at your house?"

"No. Don't be daft. I've been poking around, along with Aggie and the Widows' Brigade. Did you know that more than half the people in the neighborhood have We Care people working for them?"

"That makes sense, considering we're all older than Methuselah."

"It's not just that. When we asked them how they were being treated . . . well, I didn't like the responses or the way they looked around, as if they were afraid of something. Or someone."

Pat looked at Ida hovering behind Doyle, the pyramid of bread crumbs growing on the carpet, and said, "Ida, why don't you have a seat? Johnnie can take your bags." He glanced at his son, then the crumbs, and Johnnie quickly escorted her to the couch and moved her bags to the kitchen, where he slipped the one with a hole into another bag.

"Are the other We Care aides threatening them?" Pat asked.

Doyle chewed on it for a while before responding. "They didn't come right out and say it. But I'm telling you, something is wrong. Aggie says the church has been empty the past month. People aren't coming out of their homes anymore. I think it's because they're not allowed to come out. Not until they're kicked out for good. Just like they did to Bridgett and the others."

"You forget that Mary and I had a We Care aide. Isabelle was nothing but good to us."

Ida spoke up. "I think they're making people sick. They want us to take pills that are bad for us." She tapped the side of her head with a gnarled finger.

"You think they tried to poison you?" Pat asked.

"I know they tried to poison me. And when I wouldn't

take their pills, they threatened me." Tears brimmed in her eyes. Pat didn't want to press her any further.

Doyle, on the other hand, had fire in his eyes. "It would be easy to do. We're all on so many pills, it's hard to keep count."

Pat motioned for Johnnie to take the tray off his lap so he could sit up farther. "This sounds crazy, you know that, right? Why on earth would people from a home health aide company try to poison everyone? If we're all dead, they're out of work."

"How do you explain all of the mysterious evictions lately?"

Just hearing the word "evictions" made Pat lose his appetite. He wavered on whether he should tell Doyle about his own, but the man already had a big enough head of steam.

Doyle continued, "And what about Archie O'Malley?"

"Archie had a drinking problem. Leave that alone, Doyle. He fell."

"Are you one hundred percent sure that no one pushed him? He hated pills, which is why he self-medicated. They couldn't control him, so they killed him."

Pat closed his eyes and gestured for Doyle to calm down. "Now you're accusing them of murder. Doyle, I ask again: Why? What good does a slew of empty old houses do anyone?"

"It clears the way for new houses, condos, strip malls, you name it," Johnnie said. He was suddenly pacing the room. "Follow the money. There's a ton of money to be made in gentrification. If Doyle's right . . ."

"You're all headed for the loony bin," Pat said, despite little alarm bells going off in his head.

"Pat, what kind of medication were you on when Isabelle was here?"

"The ones the doctor prescribed. They weren't poison, I assure you."

"Where are they?"

Joe came down the stairs, looking concerned. "What's going on?"

Pat said, "Can you grab my pill bottles from the kitchen? They should be the ones in the little yellow plastic bin by the blender. That's where Isabelle was keeping them."

"Ooookay," Joe said, retrieving them and handing them to Pat.

Ida gasped. "Where are the labels?"

Pat looked at the bottles. The usual prescription labels were missing, and there weren't any signs they'd been torn off. He shook them, the few pills rattling around.

"What was the prescription for?" Doyle said, swiping the bottles out of his hand.

"Antibiotics," Pat said, feeling his assuredness becoming unmoored.

Doyle opened the bottles and spilled the pills onto the coffee table. Half were round white pills with no markings, the others yellow and shaped like little footballs. He looked to Johnnie and Joe. "Either of you able to look these up on a computer or something and find out what they are?"

Pat interjected, "If they were poison, wouldn't I have been poisoned? I would think the hospital would have uncovered that with all of the blood they took out of me."

Johnnie grabbed his tablet from the kitchen and started searching.

"I do recall you getting sicker and sicker from the moment Isabelle arrived," Doyle said.

A knot twisted in Pat's stomach. "That's what happens when people our age get pneumonia. I'm lucky I pulled through."

Doyle scowled. "Maybe."

"Jesus," Johnnie said, holding one of the yellow pills. "Dad, did the doctor put you on any antidepressants?"

"Not a chance. I wouldn't have the need to take such a thing."

Johnnie showed them the image on the tablet of a matching pill to the one in his hand. "Because this is clonazepam, or Klonopin. It's a heavy-duty benzo drug that's given to treat anxiety. I can't tell the dose here, but if you were taking a lot, it could have put you in a permanent fog. Maureen and I have taken classes on prescription meds addiction so we'd know what to look out for with the teens we've taken in. Stuff like Klonopin and Xanax are abused often, and highly addictive."

"I was taking those four times a day," Pat said, his head swimming with the memory of being out of it all the time. He'd thought it was because of the pneumonia.

"I don't know what the other ones are. They're too generic," Johnnie said. Joe and Doyle both looked ready to crush bricks with their bare hands.

Doyle scooped the white pills into a bottle. "I'm taking these over to Hank at the pharmacy and asking him what the hell they are. Come on, Ida."

Ida shuffled to the kitchen to get her bags and followed Doyle out the door.

Pat looked at the stunned faces of his sons. "God help us if Doyle is right."

CHAPTER TWENTY-EIGHT

Joe Knox fumed at the thought that Isabelle had been dosing his father with anxiety meds, and God knows what else. Had she tinkered with his mother's medication, as well? What kind of heartless creature would do such a thing to an old man and a disabled woman?

He'd been raised to never, ever lay a hand on a woman, but he was beginning to think Isabelle wasn't even human, much less a member of the fairer sex. Feeling his anger bubbling up, he went out back and walked up and down the yard, pausing a moment to kick a lawn chair ten feet into the air.

John came outside after a few minutes, looking like he felt the same way.

"What the hell, Joe?" Hands on his hips, John's jaws flexed as he ground his molars.

"I'm trying to wrap my head around all of this. Every day, it just seems to get worse. I mean, who's targeting this neighborhood, and why?"

"Pure evil," John said, staring at the back of the now empty O'Malley house. "Whoever is behind this is as evil as they come. I'd normally blow off Doyle's theory that

Archie was murdered, especially because the police don't think so, but now I don't know. There are too many strange things happening here for it all to be random."

Joe picked up the chair he'd kicked and noticed he'd bent one of the legs. The last thing he wanted to do was break his father's stuff, but it was either that or bust his hand when he punched a wall. "No, none of this is random. I'm almost hoping someone comes early and tries to evict Mom and Dad today. Might be a good way to work out my frustration."

John put a steadying hand on Joe's shoulder. "And spend some time in jail."

Joe shrugged. "With the way things have been going with me, prison would be a welcome break. My kids only care about their phones, and Stella's in love with another man. Hell, my boss barely even says hello to me in the morning. At least in prison I'd have no responsibilities, and all of my meals would be provided, free of charge. I could catch up on a lot of reading I've been putting off, finally have time to work out and get in shape."

With a half-smile, John added, "And have eyes in the back of your head in the shower, worry about what gang you need to join to stay safe, and kiss women goodbye. Because let's face it, you wouldn't be going to some country club prison. You'd be thrown in with the rank and file."

"I'd hold my own," he said, and he meant it.

A robin landed on the awning over the back door, looking right at them. Joe wasn't a bird fan, but for that moment, he envied the robin's ability to simply live its life without worrying about other corrupt robins conspiring to destroy it.

"You supposed to hear from that lawyer today?" John said.

In his red-hot anger, Joe had completely forgotten about Caitlin Scheir, esquire. He was supposed to check in around this time. Maybe she'd have good news. Lord knows, they were overdue for some. "Thanks for reminding me. I'll give her a call now. I never bothered to ask her what her rate is." He massaged the back of his neck, kneading the knot of tension. "I'll burn that bridge when I get to it."

"That's my bridge to burn. You did the legwork, the least I can do is foot the bill. I know divorce doesn't come cheap."

Joe patted his brother's cheek. "Big brothers are supposed to take care of little brothers. So why does it always feel like the other way around?"

"Family takes care of family. Period," John said, opening the door and letting Joe through. "You want me to run up to St. Brendan's and light a dozen candles before you call?"

"Ha. We're gonna need more than candles."

As Joe walked into the living room, he stopped and stared at his father.

"You okay?" he said.

His father turned his eyes to him as if he hadn't heard him enter the room, his mind far, far away. "What is it people say nowadays? I'm trying to process everything."

"It's a lot to process."

"I can't stop thinking about Archie being murdered in his own house. By someone he paid to help him. It can't be. Can it?"

"I really hope it can't. Why don't you try to take a nap

until Doyle comes barging back through the door? You're not magically all better just because you're home."

His father nodded, his eyes at half-mast. "You're right. You're right. Never pass up an opportunity to take a nap." He pulled the lever on the side of the chair to swing the leg rest up.

"Or a piss," Joe said, recalling the sage advice his father had given to him in a far simpler time.

"Or a piss," his father repeated said, smiling.

No matter what was going on, nothing changed the fact that the man still had pneumonia and was not getting any younger. Joe worried that stress would hamper his ability to recover. And maybe, depending on what that other mystery pill actually was, he was recovering from more than just the illness.

Upstairs, he looked in on his mother.

"Something's going on," she said. "I'm not deaf, but I couldn't make out what everyone was saying."

"Can I tell you in a minute?"

"You can tell me now. And hand me my rosary beads."

Anxious to get on the phone, he obeyed his mother, sitting on the corner of her bed as he recounted the fresh madness Doyle had introduced. Her fingers worked the beads as he spoke. He knew she was both listening and praying for guidance. To his surprise, it wasn't the possible medication swap that concerned her most.

"They're devils if they killed Archie," she said in a half-whisper. "I know I'm supposed to forgive, but how? How can I find forgiveness in my heart for someone who murdered poor Archie?"

He leaned in and hugged her, her tiny bones feeling like brittle straws in his embrace. "I don't know. That was one of the things that never made sense to me. But Doyle might be wrong, and maybe we're getting worked up for nothing."

As he got up to go to his room to call Caitlin, his mother said, "It's not for nothing. I'm sorry you and Joe have to be here to deal with it, away from your homes and families. But I'm also grateful to God that you're here."

Joe said, "I'm glad we're here, too. It's time for us to take care of you. You and Dad earned it."

He closed the door to his old room, picked up Caitlin Scheir's card, and called her office. He was put on hold for a couple of minutes, listening to terrible generic music.

"Mr. Knox?" Caitlin said, putting a merciful end to the concert in his ear.

"Yes, it's Joe. I was wondering if you made any headway with the land records."

She paused for an interminably long moment before she replied, "I hope you're sitting down."

Sheriff Justice cruised past the Knox house, making sure not to linger in case one of the busybodies happened to be looking out their window.

The sons are going to be trouble.

He especially wasn't thrilled with the older one, the one he'd spotted spending time with Claire in the coffee shop. Claire hadn't been his wife for going on twenty years now, but he still didn't like seeing her with anybody else, not even that dipwad second husband of hers. It was with great pride that he recalled tailing the main and anonymously reporting to Claire all of the man's indiscretions, from sleeping with clients to buying pot from a gang of local teens who were destined for prison or death. The divorce had come quickly after Justice had slipped the envelope into her mail slot, a special delivery with a list of dates, times, and names relating to the man's secret life.

He could read Claire like a book, and when she had emerged from the coffee shop with Knox, he knew she was attracted to the fly in the ointment. The last thing this operation needed was someone on the force getting involved. It was made all the worse by that someone being his ex-wife. Despite all of that, it was the look she had given Knox that burned him up the most. Setting fire to their trash cans had been ill-advised. He was smart enough to know and admit that. But he was angry, and when he was angry . . .

He'd watched Knox run out back looking for the culprit. Justice had hidden in the empty house behind the Knox place, careful to peek through the blinds and follow Knox as he jogged around the house and down the block. It took Justice a while, too long a while, to catch his breath. Running was not his thing. Hadn't been for a many a year. There was no rush. Things needed to settle down, night needed to fall, before he could step out of the house and walk to his personal car, not the patrol car, parked several blocks away.

Justice was in his patrol car now, and it was a quiet day. Nothing lined up for him and Carlson to do. Behind the closed doors of Woodlean, the aides were doing all the work today. He was usually given a one-day heads-up when it was time to take action. For now, it was up to the women to do what they had been brought here to do.

There was no shame in admitting that some of them

made him nervous. Especially the Russian ones. Or at least the ones who sounded Russian. They might have been able to plaster smiles on their faces and add a sing-song lilt to their voices when they spoke to the people in their care, but their eyes were deader than Elvis. He'd once asked, out of curiosity, for their rap sheets, if such a thing were available for these undocumented cons. He was quickly told to shut up and do his job.

That was okay by him. He didn't need some document to tell him that these broads were bad news. So, he stayed out of their way and did as he was told. He hadn't grown up in Woodlean. There was no love for this place.

Oh, but to see Claire's neighborhood destroyed . . . Well, that was a far better incentive than the money.

John had no sooner put all of the breakfast dishes away than Doyle came knocking again, this time rapping the door with what sounded like an aluminum bat.

His father startled awake before John could get the door.

Doyle stood there holding a new cane up high, ready to hammer the door some more.

"Why are you using a cane to hit the door?" John said. "We have a bell."

Doyle lowered the cane, looking apologetic. "I'm used to it just being your father on the other side. Some days, he can't hear an elephant trumpeting."

"You didn't have a cane before, did you?"

"Nah. Hank insisted I use it when he saw I didn't have my walker. Since I was asking him to do me a favor, I didn't fight it."

John thought he must appreciate the cane to still be using it, far from the disapproving eyes of Hank the friendly neighborhood pharmacist.

John looked over Doyle's shoulder. "Where's Ida?"

"Feeding pigeons."

Doyle returned to the chair he'd sat on before, his hands resting on the cane's handle. "Well, Pat, we know what that pill is now. And it's no wonder you just got sicker and sicker."

John's father put the leg rest down, leaning toward Doyle. "I'm almost afraid to ask. What is it?"

"Nothing."

"Nothing?" John and his father said at the same time.

Doyle gave a slow nod. "Exactly. It was nothing but a sugar pill. What did Hank call it? Oh, a placebo."

"I hope you didn't give them all to Hank," John said. "We may need them as evidence."

His father rubbed his hand on his chest, looking very much his age and then some. "Isabelle was trying to keep me sick."

"She was trying to kill you, is what she was doing."

John felt ill. "Then what was the Klonopin about?"

Doyle shrugged. "To keep him loopy, pliant. If he was out of it most of the time, he wouldn't question her."

"Jesus, Mary, and Joseph," John's father said. "It all makes sense. And here I was sad that she'd left us."

"Like a thief in the night, which is what she was," Doyle added. "You can bet I'm going to see Father Biglin next to ask him how he came to be in bed with this We Care outfit. We have to tell everyone who has an aide with them to get rid of them. They're not going to just listen to me. Well, some will. But to make it stick, Father is going to have to come with me."

John thought about Doyle's hip and wondered just how much the man could push himself. "What about the Widows' Brigade? Since they're already canvassing the neighborhood, they can spell you for a bit and knock on some doors with Father Biglin. If this is going to be all hands on deck, we can't have you run yourself ragged. Plus, Joe and I can help, though I'm not sure if most people will remember or recognize us."

"We should tell Claire Dennehy, too," Pat said. "This is a matter for the police."

Joe came down the stairs looking like he could chew iron bars.

"It's more than that. Way more."

CHAPTER TWENTY-NINE

Two more days until eviction.

John looked around the house he'd grown up in, so much of it unchanged since he'd left to carve out his own life. Yesterday's bombshells had rocked them all. But they didn't stay stunned for long. Doyle had called Aggie Firth, who then called her brigade, Kate Maguire and Carol McInerny, all of them rushing to the church—well, rushing as fast as they could—to confront Father Biglin. Not a one of them thought he was in on some scheme to defraud his parishioners of their family homes and lives. The priest was a good man, through and through.

Though, if they were being honest with themselves, history was riddled with good men doing terrible things. John was old enough to realize that you never truly knew most people. Father Biglin had been a positive influence on their lives over the years. Like it or not, that influence equaled power and power could be corrupted.

Regardless, it was important Father Biglin knew what was happening. If he was hiding something, the Widows' Brigade would detect it better than any polygraph machine.

It was a great relief when Doyle returned and said the

news made Father Biglin paler than a bowl of milk. He'd grabbed the edges of his desk, his legs wobbly, before collapsing in his chair to hear the whole story. From there, it became an old-fashioned door-knocking campaign. John accompanied them for a spell when they'd marched down their street, mostly as a spectator, while Joe stayed home to make sure nothing untoward happened to their parents. Anna McCurty had joined the ranks by then, along with William Campbell. John remembered Mr. Campbell having a funny nickname but couldn't recall what—not until the octogenarian got to close talking. Then he remembered in a moment that they used to call him Onion Breath.

The whole scene reminded John of something from an old Western, the town folk gathering everyone for a shoot-out at high noon. Except in this case, a lot of the people called to action were too sick or frightened to come out. That's where Father Biglin came in handy. A good Catholic couldn't refuse to let a priest enter their home.

The aide at Mr. Ginty's home, a young blonde with hard eyes, tried to slam the door in their faces, but Doyle was quick with his cane, wedging it between the door and the frame. The Widows' Brigade practically pushed her aside, calling out for Ginty, who was upstairs in his bed. The living conditions were deplorable, the man cowering under a sheet in his own filth.

Not surprisingly, the aide fled while everyone was gathered around Ginty.

She wasn't the only one that day. Three other aides slipped away, using the commotion as a distraction to skedaddle.

At other stops, the aides were gone, and the sick (or,

in many cases, spacey) occupants were told what was happening by either Doyle, because everyone seemed to trust him, or Father Biglin. John couldn't believe the state these people were in. He shuddered at the thought of what would have become of his parents if he and Joe hadn't shown up. Calls were made to We Care, their services canceled. John was pretty sure word would be getting around the offices of We Care, or whatever the company really was, that people were onto them. Everyone who had employed an aide with We Care had been dosed with meds that weren't prescribed by their doctors. It explained the hollow-eyed look on so many faces. They had been sick and scared for so long. Now, they were angry.

There was worse news to come for the Knox boys the next day. John and Joe, especially Joe, were fit to be tied after learning that their father had been tricked into sign-ing the deed to the house over to Isabelle Perez, who was nowhere to be found. According to Caitlin, the lawyer Joe had consulted, everything on the surface appeared to be on the up-and-up. It had been properly notarized and filed, and, for all intents and purposes, Isabelle was now the sole owner—an owner who was morally fine with kicking Joe's parents from their rightful home. Their father had been so high on the pills she was feeding him that he had no recollection of signing anything. Just thinking about everything that had gone on under this roof made John shiver and boil with anger. He chastised himself for not convincing his parents years ago to move up to Maine to be near him.

No matter what you said, they wouldn't have come to Maine. John knew in his heart that truer words were never spoken, but it didn't give him any comfort. A stranger had invaded his parents' home and stolen it out from under them. He had to console himself with realizing it could have been worse. They didn't end up in a morgue like the others.

It wasn't a stretch to think Isabelle would in turn flip the house over to whatever shady person or organization was behind the cleansing of the Woodlean neighborhood. The aides were merely tools sent to gain trust, manipulate, terrorize, or perhaps even kill to gain ownership over many of the homes.

Now they waited for Claire Dennehy to arrive so they could lay it all out for her. She came to the door in jeans and a sweater, having gone off duty an hour earlier.

"This doesn't look good," she said to Joe as she entered the house. Even his mother was in the living room, dressed in what she called her "Sunday clothes," because this was deadly serious business.

"Thanks for coming. Please, have a seat," John said, casting a furtive glance out the door. All day, he'd been waiting for something to happen. If they'd nearly set fire to the house as a simple warning, what would the criminals behind this do knowing they'd been exposed?

"Hello, Mr. and Mrs. Knox, John," Claire said, taking the seat next to Joe. "I could tell by your voicemail that this was pretty serious."

"We need to talk to you. We know we can trust you, Claire," John's father said.

"And after you hear what we have to say, you'll realize we can't say that about most people at this point," his mother added. Her rosary beads were intertwined with her fingers.

Claire looked wary, and who could blame her? It had

been decided that Joe would take the lead because he had the closest relationship with her, even if that relationship had lapsed over thirty years ago.

Joe turned to her, his chair creaking, and said, "You remember what we talked about at the coffee shop?"

"I do, and I've been doing a little digging, but we're so short-staffed I haven't had much time. We had two guys retire last year, and one up and quit with no sign of replacing him. Sometimes I feel like I'm in Mayberry. Except most of the time, I'm Barney."

John looked to his brother, exchanging a knowing glance. Maybe it wasn't a coincidence that the Woodlean police were so short-staffed.

Claire took a deep breath and put a hand on Joe's knee. It wasn't hard to miss the tension that was holding him together. Joe's face and neck were flushed beet red. He'd been like that ever since he found out about the deed. "Tell me what else has happened," she said.

Joe detailed everything they knew so far, from their father being drugged and tricked into signing over the house to the fire and finding out that aides from We Care were all throughout the neighborhood doing their damnedest to get rid of everyone. Claire didn't interrupt, but she pulled a small pad from her pocket and took notes. When Joe finished, he was a little less crimson.

"You don't remember signing anything, Mr. Knox?" she asked.

"Not a thing. I barely remember being awake the whole time. I thought it was the pneumonia, but it was worse."

"Did you save any of the pills?"

"We did," John said, pointing to the bottles on the coffee table.

"My question is why didn't you and everyone else just call the station?"

Joe got up and walked to the mantel, resting his arm on it. "Because we don't know if the police have been compromised."

"I think I'd know if I was working with dirty cops," Claire said, bristling a bit.

"What about the sheriff's office?" Joe said.

Now Claire stood. "Look, I know my ex is a jerk, but I can't see him being in on a grand scheme to swindle senior citizens out of their homes."

"But he is the one who has removed everyone from their homes," Pat said.

"Yes, because that's his job."

"That's what the Nazis said," Mary said, cutting Claire's rationale off at the knees.

Claire sighed, taking a moment to look everyone in the eye. "Look, part of being a sheriff means you have to take people out of their homes if they refuse to obey an eviction notice. Even the lawyer you spoke to says the paperwork is all legal."

"But not how they obtained it," Joe interjected. "You know as well as I do that my father would never sign his house over to a freaking health care aide."

After a pause, Claire's shoulders drooped, and she plopped back into the chair. "You're right about that."

John said, "I've been trying to look into We Care's background, but it's all smoke and mirrors. Up until yesterday, they had a website and phone line, but both are

244 William W. Johnstone

down. I can't find mention of them anywhere. Not even a review. It's like they never existed."

"Then how did they get here?" Claire said.

Mary spoke up. "Through the church." Her eyes shimmered with tears. "They came to Father Biglin and told him all the wonderful things they could do for the parish. From what we can gather, they started with Fiona Muldoon, the Father checking in on her every week to see if they were treating her well."

"I thought I heard Mrs. Muldoon passed a few months ago," Claire said.

"She did, she did. But according to Father Biglin, the aide who cared for her until the end was wonderful. Of course, if you'll notice, Fiona's house is still vacant. She never had children. I'll bet we all know who owns the house now." John sat beside his mother and helped her dab her eyes and cheeks with a tissue. "They used our church, the most sacred place in the neighborhood, like a Trojan horse. How could they?"

Joe said, "Look, Claire, do you still talk to your ex?"

"God no. It's bad enough I have to run into him on the job from time to time. We were like oil and water from the start. I was just too young and dumb at the time to realize it."

"And you divorced, what, twenty-five years ago?"

"About that, yes."

"So in truth you don't really know him anymore. How do you think he's doing financially?"

Claire arched an eyebrow. "That's a weird question."

"Actually, it isn't. From my vantage point, all of this is a land grab, and land equals money. Big money. You want someone to look the other way or worse, find people who need money and fill their heads with dollar signs. Any chance your ex has had some recent financial troubles?"

"Abe," Claire said.

"Huh?"

"His name is Abe. Actually, his name is Abner Justice, but he goes by Abe."

"His last name is Justice? That's a little on the nose," John said.

"He used to tell me that's why he went into law enforcement. He wanted to live up to his name. When it came to money, he couldn't hold on to a dollar with superglue. Being a sheriff doesn't exactly pay a lot, either."

"Now that's a name I would remember," Mary said. "Where's he from, dear?"

"West Virginia. He came here out of college to visit his cousin in Roanoke. We met in a bar, and he never went back. I always thought he would after we split up, but he never had anything nice to say about his family. They didn't even come to our wedding."

She was clearly conflicted. John felt he should add, "Look, we're not saying he's in on it. We have to consider every possibility. It's just that he's the pair of boots on the ground every time it happens, so we can't ignore it."

Claire nodded. "No, trust me, I understand. It's just— I don't want to think I ever loved someone who has that kind of evil in their heart, you know?"

Joe sidled up next to her and rested his hand on her shoulder. "No matter what, it's no reflection on you."

She reached up and gave his hand a squeeze. "Thanks, Joe."

"Well, our eviction is tomorrow," Pat said. "And we

have no intention of stepping one foot outside this house. I suppose we'll be seeing your Abe soon enough."

"I can't tell you to break the law and resist," Claire said. "But I can tell you to call me if and when he does come by. I want to have a word with him. He was always a terrible liar. I'll know the truth soon enough. And if he knows anything about what's going on, I'll drag it out of him whether he wants me to or not."

Chapter Thirty

Sam Doyle had just gotten off the phone with Pat Knox, his friend telling him about their meeting with Claire Dennehy and how she was once married to the fat, remorseless sheriff who had killed Bridgett Monahan.

Abe Justice.

Well, if there was any justice in this world, that porky bastard would meet the same fate as Bridgett.

The radio was tuned to an all-news station, and the kitchen smelled like frying bacon. Dusk was starting to settle outside the lone kitchen window. One of the many stray cats in the neighborhood, a scruffy piebald that Doyle secretly called Spot, lounged in the grass, his tail twitching back and forth as the birds sang good night. Doyle winced when he walked. His hip was hurting seven ways to Sunday. Even the anti-inflammatory pills couldn't cut through it. He eyed the walker, folded up and leaning against the wall in the hallway.

No. To get the walker was to give in to the pain. Since he'd turned seventy, there had always been pain somewhere—his back, his joints, his neck, stomach pains from not being regular, and cramps from being too regular. What was one more?

After everyone had gotten rid of their We Care aides, Ida Benson had told Doyle she wanted to go back to her house. He could tell being in his home made her nervous, but he made it clear his door was open any time, day or night, if she felt nervous or scared. It took him a while to clean up the bread crumbs that littered the guest room floor.

When the bacon was done, he loaded four slices of bread into the toaster. It had been a long, wild couple of days, and he was famished. Slathering the toast with thick slabs of sweet Irish butter, he cut each slice in half, loaded them with crispy strips of bacon, and folded them over. The first two bacon and butter halves went down quickly while he listened to the latest liberal nonsense railing against the president.

"Let the man do his job," he barked. "He's making it work, and it's eating you alive!"

Since becoming a widower, he had gotten to talking out loud to himself often, but only when he was alone in the house. It wasn't the best company in the world, but it beat the silence. He sipped his strong black coffee and took his time eating the next slice.

Needless to say, he was not pleased when his phone started ringing.

Getting up from his chair was a chore. He had to use his cane and the edge of the table to pull himself up. The phone clattered away like a fire engine, Doyle having turned the ringer up as high as he could go since his hearing was no longer as good as it used to be.

"I'm coming, I'm coming! Hold your water!"

He grabbed the wall phone, the long cord curled by his feet.

"Yeah?"

There was silence, then a whispered voice. "Sam?"

His heart skipped a beat. It wasn't Ida. It sounded like Edna Moore. He hadn't seen her since the day he and Pat had taken her home, the woman in no condition to be out and about. She hadn't answered her door when he'd gone knocking along with Aggie Firth and her posse. But he had talked to her on the phone yesterday, and she had assured him she didn't have a home health aide and would never allow such a thing.

"Edna? Is that you?"

"Yes. You have to help me." It sounded as if her hand was cupped over the phone, her voice a breathy whisper laced with panic.

"What's the matter?"

The plastic receiver cracked under Doyle's tightening grip.

"I hear them downstairs. I locked my bedroom door, but they're going to come in, I just know it."

"Who's in the house?"

"The aides. I hear at least two of them."

His heart dropped. "I thought you said you didn't have an aide?"

"They were right next to me when you called."

She didn't need to say more.

"I put the latch on the door before, but they broke through it. I think they're going to hurt me."

Edna sobbed quietly. Her house was only four blocks away.

"If you can, put a chair under the doorknob," Doyle said. "I'll be right there. Don't you worry."

"It's just that my chest . . ."

"Edna, hang up and wedge a chair under the knob, and wait until you hear me. Okay?"

"Y-yes, Sam."

The line went dead. Doyle made one more quick call, grabbed his pistol from the gun safe, and stormed out of the house.

Joe Knox got Doyle's call, quickly told John what was going down, and grabbed the keys to their father's car because it was parked right outside. He rushed to Doyle's house, the old man already limping down the block.

"Get in," Joe said.

Doyle slammed the door so hard, he though the window would shatter.

"Make a right, then a left, and Edna's house is on the right," Doyle said. His hat was at an awkward angle on his head, practically covering his left eye.

Joe jammed on the brakes when Doyle shouted, "Stop!"

The old man had the door open and one foot out while the car was still rocking. Joe parked in the street and got ahead of Doyle. The front door was closed, the windows in the front of the house dark. He was about to ring the bell when Doyle grabbed his wrist.

"We don't need you announcing that we're here, you idiot."

A few choice words died on Joe's tongue. There was no sense arguing with Doyle. Besides, the man was right.

Doyle turned the knob, and the door swung open. Thankfully, the hinges were well oiled and it didn't make a sound.

A heavy thud above their heads was followed by a desperate cry.

The ambient light coming through the open door gave enough illumination for Joe to see the gun in Doyle's hand. He remembered John telling him how quick Doyle was to fire off a warning shot in Ida's house. In the dark, he might kill someone, including Edna, by mistake.

They stood at the foot of the stairs, the house growing eerily quiet.

"Maybe I should have the gun," Joe whispered.

Doyle flashed a dismissive look. "Maybe not."

The old man had just put his foot on the first creaky step when Joe was tackled from the side. He thudded onto the floor, his breath escaping in a painful rush. A fist as hard and heavy as a cinder block pounded the side of his face, rocketing his head off the hardwood floor.

Joe saw stars.

Doyle shouted, "Step back! Back away or I'll shoot!"

Struggling to get up, Joe made it to his hands and knees, a dull throb already pulsing on the side of his head.

He turned to face the enormous shadow standing over him, its fists clenched, shoulders heaving.

Doyle pointed his pistol at the shadow, his arm remarkably steady.

"Get up, Joe," he said.

Joe hadn't been tackled like that since he'd been on the varsity football team. He had been punched plenty of times in his life, but never with a shot so hard and out of the blue. It had dazed him, that's for sure. But his anger was starting to take command.

"Who the hell are you?" Joe spat.

There was a sharp click, and the overhead light came on. Doyle had inched toward the wall switch, the gun still dead center in his target's chest.

Joe had been prepared to give his attacker a little payback. Except now, under the harsh glare of the light, he felt handcuffed, conflicted.

Before them stood a woman over six feet tall and broad as a barn. Her long hair was in a braid that draped over her shoulder, coming down to her waist. She had a wide nose, a boxer's nose, and a ring of tattoos around her neck. The woman might have looked tougher than old shoe leather—and the power behind her punch told Joe she would put up more of a fight than just about anyone he'd ever tussled with—but there was still no way he was going to hit a woman.

"What are you doing here?" Joe said.

She sneered at him.

The floor groaned overhead. When Joe and Doyle looked up, the massive woman bolted for the door. Joe saw that Doyle was going to take a shot at her retreating back. He grabbed Doyle's forearm and aimed the gun at the floor. Thankfully, he didn't pull the trigger.

"Upstairs," Doyle said, clearly unhappy Joe had spoiled his chance at taking down the woman. He limp-hopped up the stairs. An older woman whimpered, speeding them on.

Edna Moore was on the floor in the hallway, her nightgown bunched up past her knees. Her hands were clasped together as if in prayer, but they were pressed to the center of her chest. Her eyes were squeezed shut, her lips quivering.

"Edna, are you all right?" Doyle asked, hustling as fast as he could to her. He dropped to a knee, which couldn't have been easy, and put his free hand over hers.

Joe saw the crack in her bedroom door.

"Are they in there?" he asked.

She opened her eyes and nodded. Joe plucked the gun from Doyle's hand and ran into her bedroom. The sheets had been ripped off her bed, most likely from Edna being dragged off it. It was a small room, Spartanly furnished, without a closet. No one was in the room.

There was only one place to hide.

Without thinking that the intruder might be armed, Joe grabbed the edge of the bed and heaved the box spring and mattress, pointing the gun at the floor.

The empty floor.

"Where the hell . . . ?"

It was then that he felt the soft night breeze chilling the sweat on his face. The diaphanous curtains billowed out from the open window. He dropped the bed and thrust his head out the window.

It was a short drop into Edna's garden. A rosebush, too early to have been in bloom, had been crushed. Whoever had jumped out the window was long gone by now.

He startled when Doyle ran into the room, eyeing the pill bottles on Edna's dresser. "Damn my eyes. Joe, find the bottle with her nitro pills."

He quickly found the bottle. Doyle popped it open and spilled some pills into his palm. Edna took one and slipped it under her tongue while Doyle grabbed a pillow from the floor and placed it under her head. Joe, his adrenaline pumping and head pounding, didn't hear Doyle telling him to get a blanket for Edna until the man was shouting. He scooped it off the floor and covered Edna.

"You feeling a little better?" Doyle said.

She took a trembling breath and nodded. "Thank you, Sam." Tears leaked from the corners of her eyes. "I don't know what would have happened if you hadn't come."

"I do," Doyle said.

So did Joe.

On the way over, Doyle had told him that Edna was recovering from a massive heart attack. She was weak, her heart damaged and tender. The people who broke into her house were doing their best to scare her to death. Edna's waxy complexion worried Joe that they might still succeed.

If she died, that was one more empty house.

He wondered who held the deed to her home.

Dollars to donuts, it wasn't someone she knew.

CHAPTER THIRTY-ONE

When Joe had come back from Edna Moore's house, a shiner budding on his eye and a knot on his head, Pat was the first to the freezer, finding the ice pack under a box of ham steaks for his son's head and a bag of peas for his eye.

"Damn, Joe, what happened?" Johnnie said.

Joe plopped onto the couch next to Mary. She told him to move closer so she could look at his bruise.

"Would you believe me if I told you I got decked by a woman?"

Johnnie started to grin, and Joe cut him off. "I'm serious. And it's not funny. She could probably whip both of us with her hands tied behind her back. Man, what a punch."

Mary gasped. "Please don't tell me you fought a woman, Joe."

He shook his head. "No. Thanks to you guys raising me right, I instead had my butt handed to me. That's not the worst part."

"Is Edna okay?" Pat asked.

"She's fine now. There was someone else in the house.

Another woman, she said. She broke down the door to Edna's room and dragged her out of bed. We think she was trying to give her a heart attack, but Edna wasn't cooperating as planned. By the time we got there, the other woman jumped out the window."

Mary muttered something and made the sign of the cross with the fingers of her right hand.

Pat wrung his hands together. If he'd been put in the hospital earlier and the boys hadn't been able to come here, that could easily have been Mary.

"Did she recognize them?" Johnnie asked. "Did she have an aide through We Care?"

"Yes and no," Joe replied. "She only saw the one, and she was someone Edna had never seen before. She's had an aide through We Care for several weeks now. A very nice woman from Ecuador, she says. These were not that nice woman."

"Where is Edna now?" Pat asked.

"With Doyle. We also stopped at Ida's house and brought her back."

"Now that leaves these crooks exactly what they want— two empty houses." Johnnie said, pacing around the coffee table, making Pat more nervous.

"Can you please sit, or at least be still?" Pat said. Johnnie sat in Pat's recliner. "Two empty houses are better than two dead women."

"Agreed," Joe said. "We've spooked them. They're going to make a last-ditch effort to get what they want. They might be tired of playing the long game."

"They can't think they'll get away with breaking into people's houses and terrorizing them," Mary said. Pat saw her rosary beads on the table, picked them up, and folded her hand over them. They were her comfort, and the look in her eyes said she needed comforting.

"Okay, now we need to call the police," Johnnie said, heading for the phone in the kitchen. "Last time I heard, breaking and entering is a crime."

Joe leaned back, the bag of peas rustling. "Good luck. We tried. The emergency line is busy."

Pat said, "That's impossible."

"Go ahead, give it a try. Someone on the force knows about it and is basically telling us we're on our own," Joe said.

"Shit," Johnnie spat.

"Please, Johnnie, language," Mary said.

"Ma, bad language is the least of our worries. I think this moment calls for a suspension of the Knox house rules."

"There's no need to take that tone with your mother," Pat said. Johnnie was upset, which was understandable. They all were. But they had to stick together. It was the only way to get through this.

"I'm gonna try anyway. Maybe the lines were temporarily down," Johnnie said. Before he did, he kissed his mother's cheek. "I'm sorry."

Mary said, "You were right. This isn't the time for an old church biddy playing manners police."

They watched Johnnie dial the phone. His face said it all. "A busy signal. I can't remember the last time I heard a busy signal."

"So now what do we do?" Mary said. Pat could feel the helplessness coming off her. They were going to have to defend their house, without the assistance of the police, and there was nothing she could do to help them but offer advice and encouragement.

Joe got up, dropping the ice and peas on the kitchen table. "We prepare for tomorrow. Good old Sheriff Justice should be waddling up our steps first thing in the morning. He may come while it's still dark. John and I will take turns on watch. Doyle said he's stopping by tonight with something that could help us."

Pat didn't need to ask what that something could be. He'd known Doyle for longer than he could remember. Sam Doyle had fought in the last year of the Korean War, becoming enamored with guns of all makes and models. He'd volunteered for Vietnam, but a heart murmur kept him out of those cursed jungles, while Pat had served a tour early in the conflict. In Doyle's words, if he couldn't fight a war, he'd prepare for one, because an evil, envious society, whether it was the Russians or Chinese or Iranians, was eventually going to try to take his country away from him. Pat had seen his collection. It was impressive. It took three gun safes to hold it all.

Well, someone wasn't trying to take their country, but taking their homes was just as bad. Or perhaps this *was* just the first step to something larger. Foreigners and brain-dead liberals had already started the eradication of true American culture, Pat thought with disdain.

"Excuse me," Pat said, his guts churning.

Pat took his time getting down the basement steps. His lungs were better than they'd been, but he was still wheezing and tired. Past the covered pool table and behind his workbench was a long metal locker. He found the key under a coffee can filled with nails and opened the lock.

The old rifle looked practically new, thanks to his

taking it out to clean and oil it every month. He'd bought it at Doyle's insistence when both men were in their thirties and wondering if they should build a bomb shelter under their houses. The Cold War weighed heavily on their minds back then. Everyone felt vulnerable, scared. For Pat, buying the rifle gave him a measure of peace, even though it would be next to useless in a nuclear war. But if it came to a boots-on-the ground invasion, he could protect his home and family.

Who would have thought it wouldn't be Russians but female aides from a home health care company who would swoop in to take it all away?

Joe texted Claire Dennehy. She said she was on the job and cleaning up a big car wreck and would get back to him.

"At least someone's doing some policing," he said to his brother.

Johnnie stood at the top of the basement steps, his arms folded across his chest. "You need any help down there?"

Their father coughed for a moment and replied. "Nope. I'm fine."

"What's he doing?" John said.

"Beats me. You have any ideas, Mom?"

She rolled her eyes. "I haven't been in that basement for years. He could have a rocket ship down there, for all I know."

"We could use a rocket right about now," John said. "One we could aim at the We Care headquarters, if they even have one. I'll bet whoever's running it is doing so out of a basement somewhere."

"I think if we went to look for them, we'd find nothing but false leads and thin air, just like that so-called lawyer in Virginia Beach," Joe replied.

When the bell rang, they all jumped.

"Too early for the sheriff," their mother said, the rosary beads clacking together.

"Or too late," John said, checking to see who was on the porch before opening the door. "It's Doyle."

Sam Doyle came barging in carrying a bulging olive duffel bag. It must have weighed a ton, because the floor vibrated when he dropped it. "Dammit," he cursed. He looked to Mary. "My apologies. I take good care of my stuff. Didn't mean to drop it, but my arm was getting tired."

John lifted the bag. "Did someone drive you here? This weighs a ton."

"I walked, but you can drive me back home to Ida and Edna. And it *should* weigh a ton. There's a lot in there."

Joe joined his brother's side as they opened the bag.

"You've gotta be kidding me," Joe said.

John reached in and pulled out a formidable-looking rifle. "An M4. I haven't seen one of these since the army. I hated to turn that baby in."

Doyle seemed surprised.

Mary said, "Johnnie was a marksman in the service."

John shrugged. "Yeah, but I could never hold a candle to old dead-eye over there," he said, motioning toward his brother. "Remember when we used to go to the shooting range? I swear, Joe could shoot the eye out of a passing hummingbird."

"I was a lucky shot," Joe said, finding a pistol and checking to make sure it wasn't loaded.

"Everyone should have your luck," John said.

The duffel bag was filled with rifles and handguns. Knowing Doyle, they were all legally purchased from reputable dealers at the gun shows that came around every year. Boxes of ammo were at the bottom of the bag. He'd brought enough to hold off a SWAT team.

To Joe's surprise, his mother didn't even bat an eye at the military-grade haul they laid out on the coffee table. Doyle stood over the table, admiring his weapons. "Now, I know you're most likely not going to need them, but sometimes a show of force is more than enough."

"We don't have the proper licenses to carry these," John said.

"And the people trying to run us out of our homes don't have the proper authority to do so, either," Doyle shot back. "They're as crooked as the day is long. Well, my guns shoot straight as an arrow."

Joe hefted the weight of the .44 in his hand, appreciating the feel of it. Back in California, even hinting you were pro-gun would get you run out of town by a mob who used social media instead of torches and pitchforks. Holding one now reminded him of how much he missed going to the range, especially with John, both of them laying bets on who could make the better shot. His brother was right. Joe almost never missed. He wondered how rusty he was and if he still had it in him. Unfortunately, there wasn't time to find a range and discover if it was truly like riding a bike. His eyesight was good, but not like in his twenties. That alone would dampen his skills.

"Visual deterrent," John said.

"I hope that's all it needs to be," their mother said.

The sound of footsteps and wheezing made them all turn toward the cellar door.

"Dad, you look really pale. Come on, sit down."

Their father shuffled to his chair, his eyes fixing on the gun collection. His gaze shifted to Doyle. "You know, one apiece would suffice. The guns don't need to outnumber the people."

Doyle scowled. "You forget Vietnam? I'm sure your young self would have loved to have his hands on all of this down in those jungles and rice paddies."

"That was a war."

"And so is this, except this time it really means something. I wanted your boys to be prepared. We just need Sheriff Justice to wet himself a bit, buy some time. They may have isolated the neighborhood and cut us off from help, but it won't last forever."

Pat sagged in his chair, his face waxen but his eyes sharp and clear. "I hope you're right. And I hope no one gets hurt."

Doyle pointed to the direction of the empty O'Malley house. "They may already have. And don't forget Bridgett Monahan. Edna would have been added to the list if we didn't get there in time."

"I could never forget Bridgett. I wish I could be sure about Archie."

Waving a dismissive hand at Pat, Doyle said, "Do you need the truth to smack you upside the head, Pat? You can't hide from the truth or wish it away."

Joe said, "Lay off him, Doyle. He's still sick, and now he has to deal with all of this."

"I'm okay, Joe. And Doyle is right. I'm not afraid for myself. I'm worried about you and your brother and mother. If something happens to any of you, I have a feeling Jesus won't look at me the same way again."

"Yeah, he might actually like ya," Doyle said, flashing a rare smile. "The big man loves an underdog."

"Mary, maybe we should take you to a nice hotel away from all of this," Pat said.

"Don't you dare even think of it. You want to kill me with worry?" she snapped.

"Maybe you both should go to a hotel until this is over," John said.

"This is more than just our house. It's our home. We've lived the majority of our lives in it, and we'll die in it if that's what God has planned," Mary said. "I honestly don't think my heart could take being separated from you and not knowing what was happening. And I know your stubborn mule of a father isn't leaving the fighting to you, either. My place is here. It always has been and always will be. Right, Pat?"

He tenderly placed his hand on her shoulder. "You heard your mother. Any objections better be the stuff of legend if you think you're going to change her mind."

Joe and John both opened their mouths, then quickly closed them. When their mother spoke and took a stand, that was that. The Knox boys, their father included, knew better than to try and contradict her. They would just need to make sure she was kept safe from harm.

A sudden strobe of red and white lights penetrated the closed blinds. Joe ran to the window, his heart thundering.

"Looks like I was wrong."

CHAPTER THIRTY-TWO

"Who is it?" Pat asked. What he wanted most right now was to go to sleep. His body, not to mention his mind, had hit a wall. Tomorrow would be a big, stressful day.

It looked like tomorrow had come early.

"It's Justice," Joe said, eyeing the man through the window.

Pat struggled to get out of his chair. He took Doyle's offered hand. His friend didn't look like he was faring much better. There was only so much men their age could do.

That's what they've been counting on, Pat thought.

"What's he doing?" Pat asked.

"Just looking at the house."

Johnnie joined Joe at the window. Pat had to squeeze between the two of them. Sure enough, the round sheriff was standing on the sidewalk, looking the house up and down, hands on his hips.

Pat turned to Mary. She'd gone white as a ghost. "I don't think he's planning on doing anything. Not now."

"No," Johnnie said. "He's trying to intimidate us."

"It isn't working," Joe said. "He looks like he'd be out of breath if he had to make a slow jog up the porch steps."

Johnnie was still gripping the M4. "And our guns are bigger than his."

Pat knew the sheriff could see them looking back at him. Even though it was night, Justice wore his sunglasses. He must have seen people do that in movies and thought it made him look intimidating. To Pat's thinking, it made him look like an ass.

Sheriff Justice just stood there, minute after minute, barely moving a muscle.

Mary's cell phone rang. Pat helped her answer it, switching it to speakerphone.

"What's he doing out there?" their neighbor Anna McCurty said.

"We don't rightfully know," Mary said.

"I don't like it. It's not right."

"No, it isn't. But don't you worry, Anna. Everything will be all right. And my boys are here to protect us both."

Johnnie and Joe turned to her, and she smiled.

Anna hung up.

Doyle opened the front door. No one had noticed him taking up one of the rifles. He held it against his chest rather than pointing it at Justice, for which Pat was grateful. The last thing they needed was a justifiable self-defense situation, with the sheriff shooting Doyle right on Pat's doorstep.

"You like what you see?" Doyle barked.

There was a startled shift in the sheriff's body language. He hadn't expected this. Pat wondered if he'd done this same tactic to the others he'd evicted. Most likely not. They were unwell and shut-ins by that point. They didn't need any further threats.

Justice didn't respond.

Joe brushed past Pat.

"Son, don't."

It was too late. Joe joined Doyle, making sure the sheriff saw his own gun. Johnnie mentioned something about checking out back and ran to the door leading to the back-yard.

"You're a little too early," Joe said.

Finally, Justice spoke. "Early for what?"

"I'd tell you not to play dumb, but with you, I don't think it's playing," Doyle said.

"You may want to talk to the people whose pockets you're in and tell them to call tomorrow off. You won't be dragging any sick old people into the street. Not this time. Not ever again."

Justice's lips pulled into a straight, tight line. "You think you can flash a weapon at a man of the law and get away with it?"

"Feel free to arrest us, then," Doyle said. "But to do that, you'll need to get your fat ass up here and cuff us."

Pat stayed at the window because it was closest to Mary. He held her hand while she prayed, her eyes closed, lips moving soundlessly.

"Maybe I should draw my own weapon," Justice said.

"It's a free country," Doyle said.

Pat dropped Mary's hand when he heard Johnnie ex-claim, "Stop! Identify yourself!"

Someone was in their yard!

Pat hustled to the back door. Johnnie was in the yard, his rifle raised and pointed at a shadow. His hands shak-ing, Pat tried to turn on the outdoor lights. When he hit the switch, there was a flare of light, then darkness. The damn bulb had blown out.

"You shoot, and you're making the mistake of a lifetime," the shadow said.

"Hands in the air. Now!" Johnnie shouted.

The shadow complied.

Pat went into the kitchen and opened the junk drawer, searching for a flashlight, his chest feeling as if someone were crushing it.

He peeked at the front door. Doyle and Joe were still there, though they'd both gone silent.

Just as Pat stepped into the backyard, a walkie-talkie squawked to life. "Let's go."

Pat flicked the flashlight on. The strong beam revealed the sheriff's deputy. He squinted against the light. It was the same one who had dragged Bridgett Monahan out of her home.

The deputy lowered his arms, tapping a finger against the badge clipped to his chest. "You see who you're pointing a gun at, son?"

The man was maybe thirty at best. Johnnie was no son to this snot-nosed son of a bitch.

"I see a man creeping around my backyard while his partner created a distraction out front. What were you planning on doing?" Johnnie said.

The deputy sucked on his teeth. "You heard the man. I best be going now."

Johnnie kept his rifle trained on the deputy as he walked out of the yard. He followed him for a bit, making sure he went all the way down the side of the house and into the car. Pat trailed behind him. When Pat saw Justice, the sheriff lowered his glasses and said, "Mr. Knox. This house no longer belongs to you. As of tomorrow, you won't be able to stay here. Do us all a favor and use the extra help you have on hand to move your stuff out before I get back."

He turned and waddled to his car.

Pat had never felt so furious in his life. He shouted to get his attention. "Justice!"

The sheriff paused, turning on a heel to face him.

"If you know what's good for you, you won't come back."

"Is that a threat?"

"Take it any way you want. But take it away from my home."

"Well, that was about as subtle as a hammer to the head," Joe Knox exclaimed after watching the cruiser disappear around the corner.

Doyle patted his shoulder. "You did fine, son. Shows that son of a bitch that he can't get you and your family to just roll over."

"I'm going to check on your mother," his father said.

Joe looked up and down the street for several minutes, expecting the sheriff and his deputy to return. When they didn't, he finally exhaled and went back inside, Doyle still talking about putting one over on the sheriff.

His father sat next to his mother on the couch. They were holding hands and exchanging worried looks. John was pacing, as usual. It was odd to see all of the rifles and guns strewn about the same living room where they used to watch cartoons when Joe was a kid.

"Do you think they'll come back tomorrow?" his mother asked. Her voice trembled slightly, and there were beads of sweat on her forehead.

"I'm sure they will," Joe said. "But no one is going anywhere."

"Maybe we should," she said, stunning them all to stillness.

"Mary, you don't mean that," Pat said. He rubbed her hand between his own.

"I . . . I think I do. Our sons could get hurt, Pat. Do you want to live with that? I know I couldn't."

John took to a knee and grabbed her other hand. "That's exactly how they want you to feel. They know they can't drag you and Dad out of the house like they have with the others. So, they have to scare you enough to simply give up."

Tears shimmered in her eyes. "No matter how corrupt they may be, they still have the law on their side. Who's to say how far up this goes? We can't fight that. And they have guns, Johnnie! What if you or your brother were wounded . . . or worse?" She turned to Pat. "Maybe it's just time. We can go to one of those extended-stay hotels until we find a retirement home."

Pat sadly shook his head. "All of our equity is in this house. If they take this from us, there's not much left."

Mary leaned forward until their heads were touching. "So we wouldn't spend what's left of our days in a four-star facility. So what? Our family would be safe."

No one spoke. The only sound in the room was Mary's quiet sobbing.

Joe's anger bubbled into rage.

They had done it. They had scared his mother so much,

she was willing to die in some state-run home not fit for a dog in order to save them. These bastards were nothing but bullies with a badge. And like all bullies, they preyed on the weak.

"You're not going anywhere," Joe grumbled.

His parents looked to him as if he were ten again and had disobeyed an order.

"Joe's right," John said. "Whatever's been going on around here ends now. Besides, they wouldn't have the guts to pull on us. You can probably see the yellow streak on them from space."

"Pull on us?" Joe said.

"Someone's watched too many Westerns," Doyle said with a smile. He limped to the couch and rested his hand on Pat's shoulder. "Something tells me this is going to extend far beyond your house. We've stirred up the hornet's nest, and they're going to attack. One of your boys can take me home so I can make the rounds on the phone and check on everybody. We all have to be prepared. If you leave, that will take the heart—and fight—out of everyone else. We don't just lose our homes, we lose our neighborhood *and* our history. If that's not worth fighting for, I don't know what is."

"Not at the expense of my sons," Mary replied, defiant.

Doyle looked at Joe and John and clucked his tongue. "I used to watch those boys try their damnedest to meet their Maker when they were young, and the worst that came out of it was a broken bone or two. They'll be just fine. They've got brains, and firepower, and ability. That puts them well ahead of Justice and whoever he's working for."

He tugged Joe's wrist and told him to get the car keys. Doyle carried his rifle out of the house for all to see. Joe suspected it was to show the neighbors, who he was sure were all at their windows, that the fight was still very much on.

Joe made sure the front and back doors were locked while his parents talked in muted whispers. He really needed a belt of that good scotch. His brain and nerves were humming like live wires. While Joe was searching in the high cabinet, his father said, "So you boys finally found Johnnie's hooch?"

"You knew about it?"

"Do you think your mother and I never clean the cabinets?" For the first time that night, he smiled. "Pour me a finger's worth while you're at it."

"And one for me, as well," his mother said.

Joe paused with the bottle in his hand. "What? I've never seen you drink before."

She sighed, slowly closing her eyes for a moment. "Yes, well, maybe it's time I found out what I've been missing. If we're going to make our stand, we should toast properly to our success."

He had no idea what his father had said to her, and he wasn't going to ask. As a father himself, he knew there were layers of his relationship with Stella that had never been revealed to their children. That's exactly how it should be. There was too much oversharing nowadays. Too many parents were so concerned with being liked and hip, they strove to be friends, not parents.

Joe brought the glasses over, and his mother said a small prayer asking for God to support them and carry them safely through tomorrow. His mother winced when she took a small sip.

"It's not exactly my cup of tea. How do you decide to drink something like this?"

"It takes practice, my dear," Pat said. "Years of practice."

The scotch scratched the itch in Joe's belly. "We forgot about John," he said, finishing his glass.

His father motioned toward the bottle on the kitchen table. "That's what the second toast will be for when he gets back."

CHAPTER THIRTY-THREE

"I thought you said you had a handle on things?"

Sheriff Justice stood with his hat in hand, surrounded by bookshelves and furniture more expensive than his entire one-bedroom house outside of town. He'd left Carlson in the car. Better one voice than two in this case, even if he had to have his ass handed to him.

"We do, sir," Justice replied, doing his best to sound confident. "I guarantee you that family will be long gone before we even get there tomorrow."

"And what makes you so cocksure?"

"You have to admit, I know what I'm doing with these people. They have their sons, sure, but the parents will want to keep them out of harm's way. By the time they regroup and are ready to put up a fight—from a distance, mind you—it'll all be over."

He failed to mention that the Knox sons and that cantankerous old crank, Sam Doyle, were armed. No matter. Justice knew human nature, and this whole operation had taught him how to play these old fogies like a fiddle.

Mayor Viktor Bennett sat behind his mahogany desk, his fingers steepled in front of his face. He was still in his suit, but his tie was on the desk. He stared at Justice with his fiery emerald eyes. "And I suppose everyone putting their aides on notice is part of your plan, as well?"

"It'll be dealt with once we get these Knox irritants out of the area."

The mayor spread his hands wide. "Oh, it's as simple as that, huh? They'll just welcome the aides back with open arms like nothing ever happened?"

Justice felt his resolve begin to waver. Bennett was not a man to be trifled with. He was the son of one of Wood-lean's most successful businessmen, Harvey Bennett, and his bride, Anya Avramova, a woman Harvey had met on a trip to eastern Europe when he was working in the import-export industry. The affable Harvey Bennett had passed away when Viktor was just eight, the young boy's mother raising him to be the best at everything, from youth sports to school and now politics. Anya Bennett had been a force to be reckoned with, right until cancer had taken her several years back. Viktor was the perfect union of his parents—a warm, smiling face to the public, and a ruthless, sometimes terrifying manipulator behind the scenes.

In essence, he was the model of a successful politician in today's world.

Sheriff Justice would bet his right arm that this whole scheme had been concocted by the late Anya Bennett, a deathbed wish for her son. It wasn't lost on Justice that so many of the so-called aides were from Russia and its former states. Sure, there were a few South Americans thrown in, but all of them, no matter what country of origin, were ex-cons as slick as goose fat and heartless as the Tin Man. Some just hid it better than others.

Word was that Anya Bennett hated Woodlean but liked the life her husband afforded her. She never tried to fit in with the predominantly Irish community, and from Justice's few interactions with Anya, he understood why they kept their distance from her. The chill that came off that woman could have rivaled the core of an iceberg.

Viktor Bennett was very much like his mother at the moment.

"Look," Justice began, feeling like the back of his neck was on fire, "these people are scared and have nowhere to turn. Things just need to settle down for a spell. Maybe we can change the name from We Care to something else, just switch the aides around and no one will be the wiser."

Without warning, Bennett grabbed a book from his desk and launched it at Justice, then grabbed another. The sheriff barely had time to duck away from the onslaught, the edge of a book parting his hair.

"And how long do you think that's going to take? There's a time line we've been working on here, you imbecile! There is no wiggle room for delays. You might answer to me, but I answer to someone else. And they're not nearly as benevolent as I am!"

He threw pens and his phone at Justice. The sheriff flinched, but he wasn't quick enough to avoid the phone clanging off the side of his head. Justice pressed his hand to his temple, momentarily woozy.

"I promise, I'll fix it," Justice said, any trace of steel in his voice vanishing.

"No, you won't," Mayor Bennett said. "I'm going to do what I should have done in the first place. If I had, this would all be over by now. This is what happens when I try to use the American system against itself. Christ, it doesn't work no matter what side of the fence you're on. I knew better, I *knew* better, but I had to go against my gut."

Justice, his body tense, wary of any more oncoming objects, squeaked out, "What are you going to do?"

Bennett's face morphed into a wolfish grin, his eyes crystal and soulless.

"I'm going to prepare the land for a new, healthy crop. And when all is said and done, I'm going to be the great American hero everyone is always looking for."

The man looked like he'd come unglued. *Prepare the land*? What did that even mean?

Fighting every instinct to leave the mayor's study as quickly as possible, Justice asked, "How will you prepare the land?"

When Bennett jumped from his chair, Justice stumbled back, nearly tripping over his own feet. Instead of looking for something else to hurl at the sheriff, the mayor clasped his hands behind his back and looked out his window. The glass was tinted, and with a sliver of a moon out, there was essentially nothing to see.

"Slash and burn," Viktor Bennett said to his reflection. "We want fertile soil. We need to slash and burn."

No one really slept in the Knox house that night. Everyone stayed in the living room, Mary on the couch, Pat in his chair, and Joe and John taking turns sleeping on the floor and keeping watch. At the first pink rays of dawn, John made a pot of coffee. Everyone's eyes were closed, but he knew they were simply resting, not anywhere near true sleep. His father was the first to get up when the smell wafted out from the kitchen.

"I hope we have a lot of that on hand for today," he said, taking a seat at the kitchen table.

"I bought a fresh can the other day. I think we'll be good," John said. He poured them each a steaming cup. His father blew on it for a few seconds and took a long sip. "You mustn't have any skin left in your mouth. I've always wondered how you did that," John said.

Pat put the mug down, his hands wrapped around it. "When I was in Vietnam, there were bugs the shape and size you can't even imagine. Never saw anything like them before or since. They were everywhere. Nothing we put on kept them away. Hell, some of them were big enough to carry the cans of bug spray off with them. They got into everything. They crawled in our ears, our mouths, our noses, under our clothes. And they especially liked coffee. Those bastards tried their best to drive us insane, but I refused to let them ruin my morning joe. So, I learned to drink it steaming hot, and fast. Every day was a race, and every day I won." He smiled at the remembrance, but the corners of his mouth turned down as other images, the ones he'd spent his adult life trying to forget, muscled their way in.

"And here I bitched about scorpions when I was in El Paso," John said. "There was the heat, too. But I guess a dry heat is better than jungle heat."

His father shook his head. "Heat is heat. It's awful no matter what. Easier to warm up than cool down." He looked back at Joe, who had pushed himself up on his elbow and was rubbing his eyes. "Look, Johnnie, you and your brother can change your minds right now, and we all walk away from this unscathed. Your mother and I are grateful for everything you've done. You've given us a lifetime of love and pride."

Now it was John's turn to shake his head. "Not a chance. Whoever is behind all this is like some old-time land baron. And you know how they settled scores with them in the old west."

"The world, and the law, has come a long way since then. You can't just have a shoot-out at the corral and ride off into the sunset."

John got up and poured his father some more coffee. "Let's hope it's not that dramatic. Not to mention my steel horse is parked in a spot so tight three blocks over, I might never get it out to ride off into the sunset."

Mary stirred next, and Pat brought her a cup of coffee with extra cream and two sugars.

"Today's the big day," she said.

Pat looked into her eyes and thanked the Lord for the life he had blessed them with . . . together. Sure, their marriage had had its ups and downs just like everyone else's, but he never once doubted his love for this beautiful woman. Even seeing her now, her body eroded by time and disease, she was still the most beautiful woman he'd ever laid eyes on. "We've had our share over the years."

"But nothing quite like this," she said. Pat held the mug to her lips so she could take a sip.

"It's true, it's true."

She motioned for him to come close, her lips grazing his ear. "I'm scared, Pat. But I'm even more angry, and that scares me, too."

He kissed her lips, caressing her face. Today would be harder for her than any of them. No matter what went down, she would have to be a bystander. If anything happened to Pat or the boys, with Mary looking on helplessly, it would crush her entirely. Which was reason enough to make sure they emerged from this horrible day not only unscathed, but stronger than ever.

"Well, you get on that direct phone line to Jesus and do your thing. I'm telling you, the big man listens to you more than most."

She shook her head. "That's blasphemy, you old codger. We're all the same in his eyes."

"It would be nice if you could get him to cast those eyes down on this house today. If we're lucky, all will be settled down in time for *Wheel of Fortune*."

The phone rang in the kitchen, and Johnnie answered before it rang twice. "Dad, it's for you."

Pat tensed. "Who is it?"

"Doyle."

Sam Doyle calling at the crack of dawn wasn't a good sign. Joe got up and followed him into the kitchen. His boys drank their coffee but stayed close so they could listen in.

"Is it presumptuous to say good morning, Sam?"

"Something's happening," Doyle said in a rushed whisper.

"Where are you?" Pat asked.

"Home. I just saw three women and two men sneak inside Bridgett Monahan's place. They had keys, so they didn't need to break in."

Pat took a seat. Joe and Johnnie sat on either side. "Is that all?"

"Of course not. They came while it was still dark. I called a few other people living next to abandoned houses to see if they saw anything strange. Women and men are settling in all throughout the neighborhood. It's strange, I tell you. The ones I saw were wearing black, like thieves, and carrying what looked to be gym bags over their shoulders. You should have the boys take a gander at the O'Malley place. I don't like the look of it, Pat."

His throat suddenly dry, Pat replied, "I don't like it, either. I'll let you know if we see anything at Archie's. Just don't go off threatening people with your mouth . . . or your guns. Promise me that."

He could feel Doyle bristling over the line. "I'm not an idiot. But if they come on my property, that'll be a different issue. Call me back."

The line went dead.

"What is it?" Mary asked.

A short coughing fit reminded Pat that he still hadn't recovered from his pneumonia. *Keep it to a dull roar, you,* he commanded the persistent illness. "Doyle says that groups of strange men and women have been taking up residence in the empty houses around the neighborhood. He suggested we take a look out back at the O'Malleys'."

"I'll go," Johnnie said, practically jumping from his chair. "It's been a long time since I did a proper recon. It'll be nice to dust the cobwebs off."

Joe looked like he was about to object, but the look in Johnnie's eyes defied anyone to stop him.

"I'll mind the fort," Joe said. He and Johnnie had slept in their clothes so they'd be prepared for anything. "But if you don't come back in five minutes, I'm going after you."

Johnnie took his phone from the kitchen table and slipped it in his back pocket. "You can't. What if it's a diversion to get us both out of the house so they can drag Mom and Dad out? No, stay here no matter what. I'll keep low. I just want to see if anything's going on there."

"That's asking a lot," Joe said.

"I know."

Johnnie went out the back door before anyone could tell him no. Pat felt his heart stumble as he watched his youngest disappear and prayed he'd come back soon.

CHAPTER THIRTY-FOUR

A lone cricket chirped in the brush between the Knox and O'Malley houses. John's shoes were damp from traipsing through the morning dew. As he'd said to his brother, he hunched low so he'd be hidden from view behind the back gate. It felt good to be doing something rather than waiting for something to happen. He hoped Anna next door didn't happen to spot him out her window and come outside to ask him why he was skulking around.

None of the lights were on in the O'Malleys' house. It was morning, but not exactly bright enough to move around a house without some light. That meant it was either still deserted, or whoever was inside didn't want to be seen. What anyone trying to do something nefarious in Woodlean didn't know was that most of the residents barely slept anymore, and looking out the window to make sure all was well was more than a pastime. It was a vocation. No matter how stealthy they felt they were, they couldn't escape the watchful eyes of Woodlean.

Who were these men and women slipping into the empty houses? If they were carrying bags, what were in them? Knowledge was power, and power was what they needed to win the day.

Getting onto all fours, John reached up and lifted the latch on the gate. The hinge squealed so loudly, he was sure it could be heard three counties over. John stopped, his eyes on the house, looking for any sign that the rusty gate had alerted anyone inside. He watched the windows for what felt like hours, holding his breath. When he didn't see anyone, not even a passing shadow, he finally exhaled.

The gate was partially open, just enough for him to squeeze uncomfortably through. It was slow going, because he didn't want to risk making any more noise. Now his pants and the elbows of his shirt were properly soaked. It was a small price to pay for not being seen. His army days were many moons behind him, but suddenly, he felt like a kid again at Fort Bliss. At least it wasn't hot enough to fry an egg on the sidewalk here.

He made it to the back of the O'Malley place and took a moment to collect himself. With his back against the house, he took a moment to listen. He thought he heard a single pop of a floorboard, evidence of a lone footstep, somewhere inside. If there were multiple people inside, he expected he'd hear the low murmur of voices. Nothing.

Taking a deep breath, he stood, casting a quick glance in the kitchen window. He'd noted on his way over that the blinds had been left open. There was a moment of concern that he would come face-to-face with one of the intruders taking a peek outside. John was relieved to find the kitchen empty, the sink full of empty liquor bottles.

An open loaf of bread was on the counter, the slices blue and green with mold.

Keeping to a corner of the window so as little of himself was exposed as possible, he watched and waited. He could see out of the kitchen and into the hallway that led to the front of the house. John knew the layout of the O'Malley house as well as his own. Past the kitchen was the dining room, a low wall separating it from the living room. In fact, most of the houses in Woodlean had a similar layout, the boom of the Irish flooding into the neighborhood in the thirties leading to quick construction of cookie-cutter houses.

Every now and then, John pulled away from the window and looked around, wary of someone sneaking up on him while he was focused on the interior of the house. So far, so good.

John peered inside and went still.

What was that?

A shadowy blur popped in and out of the kitchen entrance. He waited, but it didn't return.

It might have been nothing, he thought.

But on the off chance it wasn't . . .

John crept to the side of the house, the concrete lining the way between the O'Malleys' and the Shearsons' making the alley an echo chamber. He had to take it real slow.

The blinds in the dining room were closed, but there was some luck of the Irish. On one window, the blinds had been pulled up just enough for him to see inside.

John inched his way up to the window, and what he saw froze him to the spot.

Four men and two women sat around the table as if waiting for Mrs. O'Malley to bring in a Sunday roast. They weren't speaking. Three duffel bags on the table seemed to capture their full attention. One of the men had a gun in his hand. It was too dark to make out any defining features, but he could tell who was who by their build. A woman lined up several white canisters, extracting them one by one from the bag.

This didn't look good. If he didn't know any better, he'd swear they were getting ready for an assault.

Even if the sheriff was in on the scam, why risk getting caught by the police? What was in those canisters?

Making sure the flash was off, John used his camera to take several pictures of the intruders. Angling to get a better shot, he accidentally kicked a rock hard enough for it to bang off the house next door. The sound in the tight alley was like a gunshot.

John froze, jamming his phone in his pocket. Pressing his back against the O'Malleys' house, he listened for the sounds of chairs scraping against the floor, for footsteps or voices. It was silent inside. For all he knew, someone had crept to the window and was looking into the alley. Even though they couldn't see him, John felt like a deer in headlights.

After several minutes of panicked waiting, John checked his watch and saw he'd been gone almost ten minutes now. He'd seen more than enough to confirm what Doyle had said.

As much as he wanted to run back to his house, he had to double back slowly and carefully. Keeping his body pressed to the house, he inched his way to the yard, dropping to his hands and knees. The back of his neck tingled as he made his way home, feeling eyes on him, waiting to feel the burning sting of a gunshot.

His mother must have been praying hard for him, because he made it to the back door unscathed, though possibly not undetected.

When he walked inside, Joe was waiting for him.

"You see anything?"

John brushed off his pants. "Oh yeah. I think we're really going to need those guns. Where's Dad?"

"Keeping an eye on the front of the house. Who's in the O'Malley's?"

John took a moment to settle the pounding of his heart. "Four men, two women. They have guns and something else. I'm not sure what they are. They could be homemade pipe bombs, for all I know."

"Dammit."

"You need to call Claire. Maybe the police can stop things before they even start."

"Woodlean has a force of six. If Doyle is right and every vacant house is filled with four or more people, it's going to be awfully hard for them to contain."

John paced around the cramped vestibule. "Maybe just their presence will get whoever's sent these goons out here to call it all off."

Joe leaned against the wall. He looked tired, but the pulsing in his jaw showed he was spitting mad. "I hope you're right."

Before Joe could get his phone, John grabbed his arm. "One more thing. We need to get Mom into the basement.

If there's any crossfire, that's the only place where she'll be safe."

"She's not going to like it."

"I don't like any of this," John said. "But the walls are solid rock down there, and there are no windows. I'll talk to her and Dad. Call Claire. We need loud sirens and lights to wake the place up."

His father turned expectantly toward him the second he strode into the living room. His mother was still worrying at her rosary.

"Did you see anything?" his father asked. His mother stopped in the middle of a silent prayer.

"Yeah, there are definitely people in there. I even took some pictures." He took out his phone and called up the series of photos he'd snapped. At one of them, his parents gasped.

"What is it?" John asked.

His mother paled. "Heaven help us. That's Isabelle."

The mayor might have told Sheriff Justice to keep out of Woodlean today, but he just couldn't help himself. Curiosity may have killed the cat, but satisfaction brought him back.

Justice wasn't high enough on the food chain to be privy to the mayor's change of plans, but his words, *slash and burn*, buzzed around in his brain to the point of distraction. The streets were quiet and empty, as always at this time of day, but something in the air felt different. Perhaps it was simply because he knew something was coming.

He drove down Bridge Avenue, all of the stores closed except the coffee shop, which was just getting things ready for the day.

"You want a coffee or anything?" Justice asked his deputy.

"Nah, I'm good. My stomach's not feeling right today," Carlson said, his head pressed against the passenger window.

Justice hadn't told Carlson about his meeting with the mayor. Maybe his deputy had been out late last night and had too many beers, but maybe even Carlson, who could be as dense as a redwood, sensed something different about today.

Turning onto Decatur, Justice spotted a black van parked across a fire hydrant. He'd been driving these streets for years and knew just about every car. This wasn't a local. The windows were heavily tinted, the license plate saying it was registered in New York. Carlson noticed it, too, and sat up a little straighter, his head locked on the van as they slowly passed.

A few more blocks away, Justice saw the Knox house coming up. Oh, how he was tempted to knock on their door and pay them a friendly visit. Bennett was right. Those stubborn Irish mules would definitely be home. A smart man would have taken his family to safety. The Knox men underestimated what they had gotten involved in and, in turn, overestimated their ability to put the toothpaste back into the tube.

Justice chuckled, making sure not to pause in front of the Knoxes' and cause a scene. He hoped by some twist of fate he could be there when Joe Knox was led out of the house with his brother and old fogey parents in tow. That would truly make his day—and perhaps ruin Claire's, which was just a bonus.

"Something funny?" Carlson asked.

"Not yet," Justice said. "Not yet."

CHAPTER THIRTY-FIVE

Joe Knox was relieved when Claire Dennehy answered his call on the second ring. She didn't sound groggy or put out. She sounded wide awake and, hopefully, on the job.

"What's wrong?" were the first words out of her mouth. She was smart and knew Joe wouldn't call her this early just to chitchat.

"I think we have a storm brewing," Joe said. "People have been sneaking into the vacant houses around the neighborhood. They're wearing black and carrying bags with guns."

"Are you sure about this?"

Joe grit his teeth. He wished to hell he wasn't. "Very. John even took pictures of the people in the house behind ours."

Claire exhaled heavily into the phone. "Have they done anything other than break into the houses?"

"Not yet. The unofficial neighborhood watch has eyes on every house at the moment. Though I do believe breaking and entering is enough cause to be removed in handcuffs." He heard someone talking in the background. "Are you at the station?"

"Yeah. My shift started an hour ago. I'll grab my partner, and we'll get over there fast as possible." She paused, then asked, "Your brother see how many guns they had?"

"He wasn't able to see everything, but they had a few visible."

"Never thought I'd have to put on my bulletproof vest," Claire said.

Joe instantly felt guilty. Here he was, dragging Claire into this mess—a mess that could get her killed. Even though she was a cop and this was her job, she was still Claire, the girl with braces he'd mooned over throughout his teens.

"You might want to get all hands on deck," he said, realizing there was safety in numbers.

"That's exactly what I was thinking. How many people did John spot in the house?"

"Six. Two women and four men."

"So that makes six that we know of."

Joe looked in at his family. John was showing something to his parents on his phone. "With others skulking about. This is supposed to be a quiet, nowhere town. Why the hell is this happening?"

He could hear Claire moving about the station, her breathing becoming erratic as she fumbled with something. "I don't know, but maybe today's the day we put a stop to it."

There was a loud squawking in the background, and a man shouted for Claire.

"Hold on a sec," Claire said.

Joe's stomach knotted as he heard her talking to

someone in the distance. He couldn't make out what they were saying, but there was no disguising the urgency in their tone.

When Claire came back, she was all business. "There's been a horrific accident on I-70. A fuel delivery truck just plowed into several cars and exploded. There are potential fatalities, including a minivan with a woman and her kids. We have to run. Just hold tight until I call you back. Don't do anything rash. If those people want to lay low, let them. I'll call you back as soon as I can."

She was gone before Joe could say anything.

John glanced at him and jogged over. "What's wrong?"

"A truck blew up on seventy."

"Jesus."

"There may be some kids hurt . . . or worse. Claire has to be there."

John sagged against the wall. "Seventy is way over on the other side of town."

Joe looked out the back door at the O'Malley place. He felt as if he were going to get sick. "Exactly. All first responders will be as far from Woodlean as they can get."

John perked up. "You think it's a diversion?"

Staring at the O'Malleys' back door, Joe said, "I think we're about to find out."

Mayor Viktor Bennett typically woke up after eight in the morning. Sometimes ten, if he had a light schedule. Chronically late to the office, he didn't much care that his detractors mocked him for his tardiness and teenage sleeping habits.

If they could only see me now, he thought.

It was barely six in the morning, and he was not only awake but fully dressed in his gray Armani suit and sipping a mimosa. A dedicated bachelor—why buy any cow when the milk flowed freely for men with power and money?—there was no one to nag him about indulging at this hour. The splash of orange juice made it a breakfast drink, anyway, at least to his mind.

Besides, this was a morning of celebration.

Well, not for the people of Woodlean. For them, this was going to be a descent into hell.

The next few days were going to be busy for him. He despised talking to the press, what little press there was in this nothing town, almost as much as he hated being around his constituents. Unfortunately, he'd have to do both a lot until everything blew over. His lip curled just thinking about it.

But just like stubbing your toe in the dead of night, the pain wouldn't last. When the dust settled, the real work would begin. The Russian consortium his mother had courted and Viktor had sealed the deal with would not only rebuild Woodlean into a shining example of modern America, with beautifully appointed condos, a high-end shopping experience (because *malls* were passé), and a brand-new horse racing track that would attract a younger, newer breed of residents and visitors. All of it would be secretly owned by both Viktor and his Russian counterparts, hidden deep beneath layers of phony holding companies. Hell, the Russians would even make money off the reconstruction. Woodlean wasn't the richest town in the world—far from it—so Russian, nonunion construction would be the only way to go.

Oh, but in five years, the coffers would be overflowing, especially those in Bennett's offshore bank accounts.

The Cold War with its threat of nuclear annihilation might have ended, but there were other ways to conquer a country. Bennett had been told he wasn't the only so-called American currently involved with the Russians to overturn their towns for profit. These were stepping-stones toward a financial and cultural takeover, the people of America too stupid, too focused on following the lives of their celebrities on social media, to even realize what was happening in their own lives. Just as Chinese businesses had become the landlords of every large city in the U.S., the Russians would carve their own slice of the American pie, siphoning billions while the citizens grew deeper and deeper in their debt. The day the Chinese and Russians called in their markers, America would crumble.

Bennett smiled, looking out over his yard at the rising sun. He finished the rest of his mimosa.

He didn't know exactly what was planned for today, nor was he supposed to. Plausible deniability was the name of the game. Besides, it would be all the better to learn the news with everyone else, making it easier to appear shocked and stunned.

One thing he did know was that a Russian heart, like the one beating in his own chest, was resolute in the face of combat. Some might call it cold, brutal, or callous. No matter. Only the weak had hearts that bled.

The police scanner sat on his mantel, daring him to turn it on. His fingers grazed the on switch, but he didn't allow himself to power it up. He was far more disciplined than that.

Pouring another glass of champagne, this time not

bothering with the orange juice, Mayor Viktor Bennett wondered if the plan had begun. He should thank the Knox family and their meddling for drastically stepping up the timetable, but he still hoped the hammer dropped on them first, and fast.

In the end, Pat Knox had to insist that Mary do what the boys said and take cover in the basement.

"I won't be treated like a frightened animal and locked away," Mary protested.

"It's to keep you safe," Pat insisted. "There are a lot of windows in the house, and windows aren't safe to be around if there's gunfire."

His poor wife blanched at the thought, but after a few moments of silent contemplation—Pat knew she had picked up her direct line to the Father—she finally acquiesced. "But you're coming with me," she said.

"I need to be up here with the boys."

Joe and Johnnie had taken up positions at the front and back doors. They knew not to interfere with Pat's delicate situation. His sons would always be his children, and there were times when they needed to steer clear when the "adults" were talking.

"You know I can't do that, Mary."

With great effort, she lifted her arm and brushed his cheek with her dainty fingers. "Yes, you can. You belong with me. We raised our boys right. They can hold their own. They don't need to worry about two old coots getting in the way, or getting hurt."

Pat had never been so torn in his life. Yes, the boys would be concerned about them, but Pat would be equally if not more worried about his sons. He couldn't imagine carrying on if he lost them. Maybe he should go outside and wait for the sheriff to arrive and simply give up.

Mary, who Pat swore could read minds, tugged at his collar. "The Knox family does not give up, or give in. Now, the both of us are going downstairs, and there's nothing you can do about it."

And that was that. Pat knew enough not to argue.

"Boys, can we get some help?"

Joe and Johnnie made quick work of carrying their mother into the basement and setting her on the old couch that used to dominate the living room when they were growing up. Like most old things, Pat just couldn't seem to give it up, offering it a second life in the musty basement. Pat followed them down, grabbing his rifle along the way. He unfolded an old lawn chair and sat beside his wife, the butt of the rifle on the ground resting against his leg.

"Call us if you need anything," Joe said. His expression was firm, his mind obviously cycling through dozens of possible scenarios. Johnnie wasn't pacing for once, his arms folded against his chest, eyes on the stairs.

"And you do the same," Pat said. "Keep the door open. I want to be able to hear what's going on."

As if on cue, the phone started to ring.

"I'll get it," Johnnie said, sprinting up the basement steps.

Pat reached out for Mary's hand as they listened in on Johnnie's side of the conversation.

"Hello . . . Wait, I couldn't hear you . . . Where? . . . What are they doing now? . . . How many are there? . . . Don't open the door . . . Doyle, do not give them access to the house . . . Doyle!"

Pat's heart ticked like a broken clock. He squeezed Mary's hand too tight, the slight click of her bones rubbing together making him stop. They heard Johnnie hang up the phone and walk slowly to the basement doorway.

"Joe, it's happening."

"What happened to Doyle?" Pat asked desperately.

Johnnie's voice drifted down to them. "He said they were hammering on all of his doors and windows. Edna and Ida were screaming so loud, it was hard to hear him. He said he was going to open the front door and put the fear of God in them. That's when I heard the shot, and the line went dead."

CHAPTER THIRTY-SIX

With his brother guarding the front door, Johnnie peered out the back. The sun was out in force, but he knew from the weather report that a storm system was moving in. The steady murmur of his parents talking downstairs centered him. When he was around five, he had a series of nightmares that lasted for months. He remembered listening to his parents talking in their room or downstairs in the living room, their even, calm, everyday tones giving him comfort enough to realize it was just a nightmare and fall back to sleep.

The M4 in his hands felt both strange and natural. His years in the service were some of the best of his life. The army made him a man and set him up for every success. Back then, his M4 was one of his most prized possessions. He cared for it as one would a child.

When he saw someone step out of the O'Malleys' back door, he pointed the rifle at the approaching figure. He was not about to shoot someone in cold blood, but he refused to let his guard down. Maybe if they saw he meant business, they would turn tail and run.

"Someone's coming," he shouted to Joe.

"I'll be right there."

"No, stay where you are. They may be trying to draw us to one side of the house so they can breach the other."

Joe didn't argue.

As the figure got closer, John saw it was a woman, clad all in black and empty handed. And not just any woman.

"Isabelle."

"What's going on up there?" his father said.

"It's Isabelle."

"I'll be right up."

John was about to tell him to stay with his mother when Isabelle came to the door. She could see the rifle pointed at her, but that didn't stop her from gently rapping on the doorframe.

"What do you want?" John asked through the closed door. They could see and hear each other just fine through the pane of glass.

"I need to talk to you," she said. She looked pale, nervous, as anyone with a high-powered rifle pointed at them should. "Please, let me in. If you don't, the others will come."

When he felt a hand fall on his shoulder, John nearly pulled the trigger. His father whispered, "Maybe we should hear her out."

"Remember what she did last time she was in the house?"

"Yes, well, she's certainly not going to drug me or make me do anything against my will," he said with a wet wheeze of his lungs. "At least if we let her in, it will delay the rest from coming over. Maybe we can find out their intentions."

"I think we know their intentions."

Isabelle cast a nervous look at the O'Malley house as if she could feel the anxious stares at her back. She looked like a frightened doe. John wasn't buying it. She was a cold, ruthless villain. How else could she have done what she did to his family?

"Please, you have to hurry," she said.

Pat nudged John aside and unlocked the door. "My son will shoot you if you try anything," he said as she hustled her way inside. Isabelle held up her hands.

"You have to leave here, now," she said. "If you don't, they're going to burn your house down with you in it."

John's stomach went cold. "And I'm sure you'll be part of the bonfire committee."

Tears spilled down her cheeks. "I am so sorry for everything I've done. I never wanted to hurt anyone. But I have no choice. If I don't do what they say, they will kill my family back home."

"Who are *they*?" Pat demanded.

"Pat?" Mary called.

"Give us a moment," he said.

Isabelle looked toward the open basement door and said, "I don't know. I was in prison for stealing food to feed my children. A man met me and spoke to me for a long time. He said my English was very good. Two days later, I was free, but I found myself a captive again, this time with other women who had been taken from prisons around the world. Some of them were very, very dangerous. With so many nationalities involved, it was hard to tell who is in charge, but I believe they are Russian. We're not allowed to know anything more than what we're told to do. If we ask questions, they will kill our families. My babies are only three and five. I would die before I let anyone harm them. These men know that. We've been told that if we kill ourselves, they will murder our children, our husbands, and our parents."

Pat visibly sagged. "Jesus, Mary, and Joseph."

John kept the rifle on her, but the tortured look on her face and gut-wrenching story had him wavering. He looked across the way at Joe, who had obviously been listening in. Snapping his attention back to Isabelle, he said, "How do we know you're not just spinning more lies?"

She put her hands down to wipe the tears from her face. "Because what would be the point? If you don't leave, you'll be dead anyway. All they want is your house and your silence. You and your brother have wives and children. Don't think they're not aware of that."

Marion. John's knees went momentarily weak.

"What the hell did you just say?" Joe barked.

"Are you threatening my family?" Pat asked.

Isabelle shook her head. "No. I'm only telling you what will happen. Please, a house is just a possession. You can find another place to live. Why sacrifice everything?"

"This is more than a house. It's my home," Pat said.

"Is it worth more than your family?" Isabelle said.

John felt the wind go out of his father's sails. If he were being honest with himself, his own resolve had started to crumble. He couldn't fathom doing something that could lead to Marion being hurt, or his niece and nephew, or any of the children he'd fostered over the years. What had they gotten themselves into?

"It wasn't supposed to be like this," Isabelle said.

Pat snorted. "I'm sorry we didn't just let you steal the house out from under us and stick my wife and me in some nursing home."

"You would have recovered. You have good sons who would have taken care of you."

"And what about Bridgett Monahan? Or my friend Archie O'Malley, whose house you're casually using to hide your thieving partners?"

Fresh tears sprang from Isabelle's eyes. "It would never have been that way with you. Your wife is a wonderful woman. I would have made sure it wouldn't have come to that."

"You mean to this," John said.

It was so hard to stay in the moment when he kept worrying about Marion. As much as he didn't want to let these people win, the stakes had suddenly gotten much higher.

"Don't move," John said to Isabelle. She dabbed her tears with the back of her hand. He leaned close to his father's ear. "What should we do?"

Pat cupped his hands around John's ear. "Sometimes it's wiser to know when to surrender rather than fight and lose everything. I'd rather face the fires of hell than let them take my home away, but not at the expense of my family."

John said, "If we decide to leave, will you call the dogs off?"

Isabelle brightened. "Yes. Yes."

"How long do we have?"

"I'll tell them now. I'm sure they would give you at least an hour."

"An hour? How goddamn generous of them," Pat grumbled.

An hour to pack a lifetime, John thought.

"Fine," Pat relented.

Another lone tear snaked down Isabelle's left cheek. Her lips quivered. John thought she might faint from relief. He put the M4 down. "Go on. Tell them." He never felt so defeated in his life.

But at least the family would be safe. He'd take his parents to Maine with him, and they could figure out what to do from there.

Isabelle turned and put her hand on the doorknob. With her back to them, she sobbed, "I'm so sorry. But if I don't do this, my babies will suffer."

"Don't do what?" Pat asked.

Suddenly, she bolted toward the basement. John dropped the M4 and went to grab her, but she was too fast. She sprinted down the steps, wailing all the way.

"Isabelle?" his mother cried.

The explosion rocked the house.

CHAPTER THIRTY-SEVEN

Sam Doyle hadn't shot a man since the Korean War. Even then, it had been from a distance. He hadn't seen the man's face, just the uniform.

The dead man on his porch gazed skyward with graying eyes, the look of surprise forever frozen on his face. Doyle had shot him square in the chest the moment he saw the gun in his hand.

Just like Korea, Doyle did not feel remorse. Back then, it was his duty. Now, it was his life.

The deafening shot had managed to quell Ida and Edna, who were cowering in the living room holding one another. Doyle slammed the door shut and locked it. The others who had surrounded his house, all of them wearing black pants and shirts, had scattered like rats.

Stepping into the living room, he said, "It's okay, it's okay. They're not going to dare come in here now. I'll call the police, and we'll be safe."

Edna was pale as a cloud. He worried about her heart. Ida, he was sure, wished she were one of her beloved pigeons about now, with the ability to fly far away from here. "Do you have your pills?" he asked Edna.

The old woman nodded.

"Best you take one, just to be on the safe side."

She pulled the tiny pill bottle from her pocket and did just that.

Doyle was surprised by how fast he was able to walk, the pain in his hip nearly gone. It was the adrenaline. When it crashed, the pain would flood back, probably twice as bad.

Well, no sense worrying about that now.

Doyle had dropped the phone to warn the man off his porch. He found it still on the foyer floor. He dialed 911 and got a woman from dispatch after several agonizingly long rings.

"I need you to send someone to my house quick," Doyle snapped. "People are trying to break into my house. I just shot one who approached me with a gun."

The woman on the other end sounded shaken.

"Sir, do you know if he's alive?"

"I sure hope not."

"Are you in any danger?"

Doyle almost chuckled. "If I wasn't, I wouldn't be carrying a gun and using it, now would I? Now, please send someone over here as fast as you can."

"Sir, I need you to lock your doors and stay inside. I will get someone to you as soon as I can. We have a major incident out on I-70."

Doyle pressed her for more about the major incident, but she wasn't spilling any beans. She just kept giving him the line about staying locked down until someone could get there.

He never thought he'd see the day where killing a man

wouldn't get top billing with the police. Doyle hung up while she was still talking.

"Ladies, let's get you away from those windows."

Doyle ushered Edna and Ida into what he called his reading room, just off the living room. It wasn't much more than a glorified closet, but it didn't have any windows, which would be some benefit in case the dead man's cohorts decided to start filling the house with lead. The women, both tiny and thin, fit in the lounge chair.

"I want to go home," Ida said.

Doyle rubbed her shoulder. "I know. It's not safe to be out there right now. Help will be here soon."

The crashing of glass ripped his attention away from his friends. Doyle ran into the living room and down the hall. A wall of flame danced along his kitchen floor. Dropping his weapon, Doyle darted into the kitchen, holding his arm over his mouth. The back window was broken, a shattered bottle at his feet.

Molotov cocktail!

Avoiding the flames, Doyle inched along the wall and ripped the small fire extinguisher from its clamp. He pulled the pin and shot a geyser of foam at the fire. One of the walls was burning now, black smoke filling the room. He tried to douse the wall, but the extinguisher ran out. Cursing, he tossed the empty canister on the ground. It bounced off his refrigerator and skidded away.

There was another crash. Then another, this time from upstairs.

Going as fast as he could up the stairs, he saw his worst fear.

His bedroom and the spare were both on fire.

They're burning me out!

Would they shoot him and Ida and Edna the moment they stepped out the door to save themselves? To brazenly shoot the trio in the light of day, in front of all the neighbors—the fire would be too big for them to ignore— would imply something even more terrifying than simply burning an old man's house down.

Well, he'd find out soon enough if they were lying in wait for them. He headed back to the reading room.

"Ladies, we need to skedaddle."

"The house is on fire!" Edna shrieked. The poor woman looked to be on the verge of collapse.

"It is, which is why we have to leave," Doyle said. "Here, take these."

He handed each one a .38 caliber pistol. They weren't the big guns, but anything larger and Ida and Edna might only hurt themselves.

"Why do we need guns?" Ida asked.

Doyle held her under his stare. "Ida, if I have to really answer that for you, maybe you are as far gone as everyone says."

Her expression grew serious. "I'm not crazy."

"I know that. Now let's go."

Edna had to use two hands to hold the gun. Doyle grabbed what guns and ammo he could. "I'll go out first," he said. "You two follow me."

The sound of wood splintering overhead should have made him sad. But his home was going to crash down around them if they stayed any longer.

Since his wife had died, nothing in the house mattered. It had gone from a home to just a roof over his head. He was mad as hell it was meeting its end this way, but he wouldn't wax nostalgic over its loss.

Opening the front door, he wondered if he'd live long enough to have a moment to be nostalgic.

He turned the knob, brought the rifle up, and stepped out into the unknown.

Joe Knox's ears wouldn't stop ringing.

He ran to the back of the house on numb legs, his brain crackling like a fireworks display, all noise and light with little room for coherent thought. He could see John shouting something before disappearing into the basement, but the words were lost to him. His father was on the ground, dazed.

What the hell had happened?

"Dad, are you all right?" he said, his voice a muffled groan in his head.

His father nodded and reached out for him.

It took a little effort to get him back on his feet.

Had the furnace blown?

Smoke billowed out of the basement.

Mom!

Joe nearly fell clambering down the steps.

Inside the basement was pure chaos. From one direction, light filtered in, trying to pierce the gloom. There must be a hole in the top of the basement wall leading to the yard. There were bits of things he'd rather not contemplate on the walls and ceiling. The floor was littered with shattered furniture, at least from what he could see through the roiling smoke. He waved at the air, calling for his mother.

John emerged from the haze cradling their unconscious mother in his arms. She was covered in a layer of soot and dust, her head at an awkward angle. Joe reached for his brother, but John rushed past him as if he didn't see him in the whirling smoke and debris. Joe followed him up the stairs.

Running to the living room, John gently placed their mother on the couch. Joe's hearing started to return in time for him to hear his brother wailing. "Why? Why? *Why?*" His fingers were bunched in his hair as he paced in a small circle beside the couch.

Joe took his father, who was still dazed and leaning against the wall, by the elbow.

The moment he saw his wife, Pat knew she was gone. Her body lay like a broken marionette. Her torso had been ripped apart.

"Oh Jesus, Mary!" Pat shouted, collapsing next to her. He took her face in his hands and rocked, saying her name over and over again through agonizing wails. Tears streamed down John's face, winding in streaks through the grime on his face.

Joe stood at the entrance to the living room, taking everything in in stoic silence. This wasn't happening. He was not staring at his dead mother, his father broken beyond saving. The house groaned and shifted. For a moment he thought it might collapse, but it somehow steadied itself. Even if it was about to come down around them, he wasn't sure he'd be able to move to save himself.

"How?" he murmured.

His brother heard him and said, "Isabelle. She had a bomb on her somewhere. She went down and . . . and . . . and—"

Crippling waves of sorrow should have been swallowing Joe whole now, but all he felt was a volcanic bubbling of pure hate and anger.

There was a sudden and jarring knocking at the door. Joe ran to it, hoping it was one of Isabelle's co-conspirators. He would tear their head from their neck. He ripped the door open, only to startle Anna McCurty. Half the people on the block were standing outside the house.

"Joseph, what on earth happened?" Anna said.

Joe stepped aside to let her in. When she saw his mother lying there, his father crumpled in a ball on the floor, she shrieked and threw her hands in the air. His parents' neighbors heard her and shifted closer to the house.

"You have to get out of here," John said, grabbing the older woman's arms. Joe was too busy scanning the crowd for anyone suspicious to talk the woman down. "Tell everyone to get as far away from here as they can."

"But . . . what . . . I mean . . ." Ann's eyes were wet with tears, her body trembling like a dry leaf in the wind.

"It's not safe here," John said, edging her toward the door. Joe moved aside so his brother could walk Anna to the porch.

"Your mother needs a doctor," she said, her voice sounding far away, lost in shock.

"I know. Help is on the way." John looked to the gathering crowd. "Now, I need you to go back in your house and grab your purse and car keys and drive as far out of town as you can go. Don't stop to gather your things. Just go. Can you promise me you'll do that?"

She nodded, but he wasn't sure she comprehended what he was saying.

Joe interjected, "It's not going to be safe here, Mrs. McCurty. We don't want you or anyone else getting hurt." He looked at the pressing crowd. "That goes for all of you. If you don't want to get hurt, you'll leave now."

Heads whipped around at the sound of gunfire in the near distance. A ripple of panic shot through the elderly gathering. They immediately dispersed, disappearing into their own houses. Joe hoped they were looking for their car keys.

Anna McCurty was among them, moving as fast as she could into her house, slamming the door behind her.

The brothers exchanged knowing looks.

Any chance of backing out quietly had just evaporated like morning dew under the harsh summer sun. Even if the house's foundation had been mortally wounded by the blast and it was nothing but a pile of sticks, they would defend it until their last. Those sons of bitches had taken something far more important than a home from them.

Now they would pay.

CHAPTER THIRTY-EIGHT

Sam Doyle was met by a sea of frightened faces, most of them behind the relative safety of their windows. It was easy to see the dead man on his porch, his blood running down Doyle's steps and pooling on the walk. He suspected there were a lot of calls to 911, though none of them would bring the police anytime soon.

Aggie Firth stepped out of her house when she saw him emerge with Ida and Edna in tow, the women sobbing as they circumnavigated the corpse at their feet.

"Sam, what happened?" Aggie called over to him.

"There's more of them," Doyle said. There was no time for explanations. "Call the Widows' Brigade and have them tell everyone to watch out for people dressed in black. Do not let them inside, no matter what they do."

Doyle went ramrod stiff when he heard the explosion, feeling it reverberate under his feet. "What in Sam Hill was that?" Whatever it was, it had come from several blocks away. He immediately thought of the Knoxes, and his stomach soured.

He looked back at Edna and Ida. "Go inside with

Aggie. And don't move until either the police or I come get you."

The women needed no prodding. Aggie had dipped inside, and he could see she was already on her phone.

A man darted out the side of Bridgett Monahan's empty house. Doyle brought up his rifle and shouted, "Stop right there!"

The man was tall, with pale features and razor-sharp cheekbones. Even from across the street, Doyle could see the sweat covering the man's face. He had a bag slung over his shoulder. Doyle hoped he would reach in that bag and give him an excuse to pull the trigger. This time, he'd try to wound the man so he could be questioned by the police when they eventually came.

The top windows of Doyle's house exploded outward, raining glass on his bare head. He flinched, nearly falling forward as he tried to protect himself.

That was all the distraction the man needed to dip his hand into his bag and extract a hand cannon that looked straight off a movie set. If someone told Doyle the thing held bullets big enough to take down a raging elephant, he wouldn't have been surprised.

Doyle knew it was too late for him. By the time he managed to raise his rifle, he'd be cut in half. Now was as good as any other to die. He only regretted that he wouldn't be around until the end of the assault on his beloved neighborhood.

Resigned to his fate, he stared down the barrel of the gun.

The sharp crack was smaller than he'd expected. It was followed by another, then another.

He looked down at his chest, expecting to see daylight

streaming through a series of holes. He'd heard that some people didn't register the pain of being shot at first.

To his utter shock, he was unscathed. The guy had to be the worst shot in the northern hemisphere. Or maybe that oversized gun was too much to handle.

Doyle looked across the street, the heat from his burning house warming his back, only to see the man face-down on the sidewalk. Ida Benson stood on Aggie's porch, the gun trembling in her hand.

Saved by the Pigeon Lady.

His hip now barking like a crazed hyena, Doyle limped to Aggie Firth's house. Aggie was trying to drag Ida inside, but the woman seemed to be waiting for the man to miraculously get back up just so she could put him down again.

With a light touch on her shoulder, Doyle got Ida to put the gun down.

"You saved my life."

"He was going to kill you."

Doyle looked at the man's cooling corpse. "Yes, he was."

"I couldn't let that happen."

"And I'm mighty grateful for it. You have nothing to feel guilty or sorry for."

She looked to him with a clarity he hadn't seen in her eyes in many a year. "Oh, I don't, Sam. He's with the people who did the bad things to me, isn't he?"

Aggie's phone rang, and she dashed inside, chattering away frantically with whomever had called. He peeked inside and saw Edna on the couch, one hand resting on her chest.

"He is. And if this is any indication, they plan to do a lot worse things to Woodlean before the day is through."

He was itching to get to Pat Knox's house and make

sure they were okay. The flames licking the façade of his house reflected in Ida's gaze. The fire was seconds away from claiming the McDermots' house next door. He saw Tim and Laura McDermot holding one another on the sidewalk, waiting for the inevitable. Doyle supposed it would be too much to hope for a fire engine to come along. No, they were probably out on I-70, along with anyone who could help the people of Woodlean.

Though two men were down, Doyle knew there were others skulking around. "Tim, Laura, over here!"

That was confirmed when he heard a man shout, *"Bystro, takim obrazom!"*

Doyle didn't understand the words, but he knew the cadence of the language.

Goddamn Russians.

Reagan might have frightened the reds into submission, but a succession of weak-kneed commanders in chief had let the enemy grow stronger, bolder. That the Russians were brazen enough to do this was proof that the United States' so-called leadership had made the country grow softer than their padded waistlines. It was a disgrace, but Doyle didn't have time to contemplate the international state of affairs. Right now, he had a neighborhood to defend. He might be old, but he still had fire in his belly and the steady beat of a patriot in his heart.

Tim and Laura McDermot ambled across the street like a pair of sleepwalkers. Doyle escorted them inside Aggie's house. She was still on the phone. Edna looked glad for the company, then disheartened by the vacant looks on their faces. Doyle didn't know what to say, so he said nothing. He went back onto the porch.

"I want to go home," Ida said. She no longer sounded frightened. In fact, it was quite the opposite.

"I told you before, we can't go there now. Not until the police come and I know it's safe."

She walked past him and onto the sidewalk. "No. I won't let them burn my house down. It's *my* house."

"Ida, get back inside," Doyle insisted. His skin crawled thinking that they were in someone's sights at that very moment, a fraction of a second from being blown away.

She ignored him, shuffling down the sidewalk, the gun still clutched in her hand. Doyle sighed with exasperation. Getting down the steps was a chore, his hip feeling as if it were going to snap in two. He limped after her, asking her to slow down. For an old woman, she was incredibly fast.

Casting wary glances behind him, Doyle followed Ida, knowing they had to pass Pat Knox's place to get to hers. He dreaded what they'd find. If they made it that far.

And if they somehow made it through this day, what would he be coming back to? If first responders didn't get here soon, this whole block, with houses built so close to one another, would be nothing but smoking cinders.

Doyle heard the impact of the bullet as it dented the aluminum siding of the house he and Ida were passing. He instinctively ducked, grabbing the back of Ida's coat so she was forced to do the same. A flowerpot exploded, and a window shattered.

They were under fire, with nowhere to go.

Joe Knox had a hard time finding Claire Dennehy's number in his phone. His fingers felt fat and clumsy and numb. Every time he glanced at his mother on the couch, a blanket pulled over her by his brother, he was hit by a blast of anger that made his head spin.

To his surprise, Claire answered quickly. "Joe?"

He could hear the steady bleat of sirens and mayhem in the background. It was painfully clear she was dealing with her own disaster.

"They murdered my mother," he said, his voice cracking.

"I'm sorry, Joe, I didn't hear you."

Someone was shouting, and a fresh set of sirens blared close to Claire. "They came into our house and killed my mother." He tried not to scream, not to take his frustration and pain out on Claire.

"Good God. How did this happen?"

"Her home aide came in to warn us. She said the others would burn the house down with us in it if we didn't leave. We didn't know she had a bomb on her. She blew herself up, right next to my mother."

Joe's phone case started to crack from the pressure of his tightening grip.

"A bomb?" Claire blurted. "What the hell is going on? This place is a disaster area. It looks like ground zero for a missile strike. Every cop and firefighter in the neighboring counties are here." Joe stared out the back door, waiting for someone to make a move. It had been quiet since the detonation. He wondered if they'd left, figuring Isabelle had done her job. No, they would be back. He was counting on it.

Claire barked orders at someone and said, "I'm coming right over. There's nothing I'm doing here that someone else couldn't do instead. Please, don't do anything rash."

"Can you bring anyone else?"

"I'll see."

"We need as many bodies as you can get."

"That's not going to be easy."

"That's why they staged the accident on I-70. They don't want anyone to be here until they've done whatever it is they plan to do."

Breathing heavily, Claire said, "Joe, you're scaring me."

"I'm scaring myself."

"Where are you now?"

"We're still in the house, though I don't know for how long. The bomb did a number on the foundation. I think they're waiting for us to run out of here so they can pick us off."

"Just hold tight. I'm coming."

Joe stuffed the phone in his pocket, cursing himself for calling Claire in the first place. If she came alone, what could she possibly do to help? The last thing he wanted to do was get her hurt. But she was a professional, and they could use every bit of assistance they could get.

Was there more to it?

Perhaps, if he had a clearer mind, he wanted Claire with him because if he was going to die today, he wanted her face to be the last he saw before he claimed his reward in heaven. It had been a long time since he felt this way about a woman other than his soon-to-be ex-wife, and now he might not get a chance to see where it could lead to.

"Someone's coming, seven o'clock!" John shouted, shocking Joe from his momentary contemplation.

Sure enough, a man had stepped into their yard from the O'Malley's. He wore a black ski mask and gloves. But what had them immediately concerned was the flaming bottle in his hand.

"Oh no, you don't," Joe said, kicking open the back door.

As the man reared back to launch the Molotov cocktail at the house, Joe jerked his rifle up and fired. The round went through the man's wrist. The bottle fell behind him, bouncing harmlessly on the grass. He wailed in agony, clutching his damaged wrist. As he turned to run, Joe considered shooting him in the back.

John reached out and lowered the rifle. "No, not like that."

The man scrambled back into the house, leaving a trail of blood behind.

Joe bit his lower lip so hard, he tasted blood instantly. His brother was right, but it didn't help satisfy his need to make them all pay.

"Dad, is there anything out front?" John called out.

Their father had wiped his tears, staggered onto his feet, and grabbed his rifle, taking a post by the front door. There would be time for mourning. Now was the time for fighting.

"All clear," he said.

Much to their chagrin, not many cars had departed the block since the bomb had gone off. People were either too scared to go back out or too stubborn.

"Smoke," John said, pointing to a black plume billowing from between the houses a couple of blocks to the east. It looked like the Knox household wasn't the only one under attack.

The whole neighborhood was going up in flames, and there wasn't anyone to stop it or put them out.

Chapter Thirty-nine

Just when Sam Doyle was about to say his final prayer, the rapid *pop-pop-pop* of gunfire coming from another direction stopped the Lord's Prayer on his lips. He turned his head to see the upstairs window shatter in yet another vacant house across the street.

That was followed by merciful silence.

"Go!" a man shouted.

Doyle nearly stood up and saluted when he spotted old Onion Breath himself, William Campbell, standing on his porch with his deer hunting rifle.

"I saw one of them sneak in there just as your house was going up," Campbell said. He was dressed in camouflage, black boots, and his lucky cap with the brim pierced by fish hooks. "Don't know if I got him, but you and Ida can move on for the moment without worrying about getting a bullet in the gut."

"You're a lifesaver, Bill," Doyle said, helping Ida to her feet.

"Not if you don't get going. I'll cover your backs. If those sons of bitches even think of trying to burn my house, it'll be the last thought that ever crosses their pea-sized brains."

Doyle simply nodded, knowing darn well that Campbell meant it. If he remembered correctly, Onion Breath fought in 'Nam, too, just like Pat Knox. It was good to see there was still the fire of a true soldier burning in his heart.

"Come on, Ida, let's get out of here."

Ida rushed ahead of him. There was no way he could keep up, especially after dropping to the ground and painfully getting back up. His entreaties to slow down went unheard. He didn't want her running into a trap, but all he could do was be there to try and get her out of one if she did. He took one last look at his burning house, wondering how long before the fire department arrived and how extensive the damage would be by then. Campbell might have been willing to kill a person for trying to burn him out, but if the fire didn't get under control soon, there was nothing he could do.

The air was acrid with smoke. The day was turning to dusk early as plumes of smoke throughout the neighborhood obliterated the sun.

They couldn't throw us all out, so they think they'll just get rid of us in one fell swoop.

But maybe not.

These people weren't counting on Doyle's neighbors to fight back. Hell, Ida alone had a confirmed kill. No, there was hope yet.

"Remember, we stop at the Knoxes' first," he called after Ida. She waved her gun in the air to acknowledge she had heard him.

Doyle was out of breath, and his hip and back felt as if

they were going to crumple. Each deep inhalation made him cough as he sucked in more and more smoke.

This wasn't Woodlean anymore. It was a war zone.

Two more blocks until they got to Pat and Mary's. It was the longest two blocks of his life. He heard another gunshot in the distance.

"Down there," he shouted to Ida as they came to the corner of Pat's street.

"I know the way," she replied, keeping the gun pointed straight ahead. He worried she'd shoot an innocent person instead of one of the invaders.

There were no fires, but Doyle could sense something was wrong. Then he spotted the puff of white dust in the still air between Pat and Anna's houses. Was their yard on fire?

Now Ida slowed. Doyle saw faces in windows. Terrified faces.

"It's too quiet," Ida whispered.

She was right. It was like a town that had shut itself up at high noon, the oppressive tension in the air so thick, you could barely walk through it.

Doyle cupped her elbow. "We should take it slow."

Ida gave a slight tug in the other direction, toward her own home, but he urged her to stick by him with a gentle squeeze.

They crept along the parked cars, heads low, protected if someone were to shoot at them from across the street but wide open to any attack on their side of the street. Doyle didn't like it, but what else could he do?

He saw Anna McCurty pull the curtain back, and their eyes met. She pointed at Pat's house, her face heavy with sorrow. Doyle's heart skipped a beat.

"Stay low," he said to Ida and they darted as fast as they could across the street in a crouch. Pausing between two cars, Doyle looked around. He couldn't see any potential danger, but the invaders could be hiding anywhere. For all he knew, they had commandeered even the full homes, duct-taping the residents, and had him and Ida in their sights at this moment.

"You wait here while I go inside," he said.

"I don't want to wait here," Ida protested.

"Please, don't argue with me. I'll come back and get you."

Doyle remembered the lessons of war. The enemy would let the point person walk through unharmed, only to ambush everyone behind him. Ida was safe—well, relatively safe—nestled between the two SUVs.

Gritting his teeth through the pain in his hip, Doyle limped up the porch steps and knocked softly on the door. "It's Doyle."

It was immediately opened, Pat Knox looking like death warmed over. Pat grabbed him by his shirt and hauled him inside, slamming the door closed.

"You're okay," Doyle said, relieved.

The interior of the house was filled with roiling dust and smoke.

Pat's lips were pulled into a grim line. His eyes were red and puffy. Doyle followed his gaze to the shrouded figure on the couch.

"She killed Mary," Pat said.

Doyle willed his legs not to give out.

"How?"

"Isabelle. She came inside, saying she wanted to warn us. We didn't know she had a bomb. She . . . she . . ."

Doyle put a consoling hand on his friend's shoulder. They shared a quiet moment. Then Joe said, "How is it out there?"

Doyle took a breath, making sure he didn't look at Mary on the couch. Doing so would only break him down. "They torched my house. But I did get one of them. Old Ida took another one down before he could get me. It looks like they're intent on razing the entire neighborhood."

Joe had a look of fury in his eyes that would send most men running the other way. "I just shot one that was going to throw a Molotov cocktail at the house."

"Did you kill him?"

"No."

There was no mistaking the sense of a missed opportunity in his reply.

"Where's Ida?" Pat asked.

Doyle went to the window and pointed. "I told her I'd come back and get her. She's desperate to get to her house and stop them from burning it, too."

"I'll get her," Pat said, storming out of the house before anyone could stop him.

He clambered down the steps, his head swiveling all about. When Ida saw him, she popped up and hustled toward him.

That's when Doyle saw two young women, both in black, come tearing around the corner, guns drawn.

Joe Knox saw the women at the same time as Doyle. "Watch my back," he said to his father as he leapt past him off the porch. One of the women, her raven hair loose and wild, stopped to aim at Doyle, who had followed him to the doorway.

Without a moment's pause, Joe fired near the woman, his finger tapping the trigger the way he used to work the controls in the arcade. A line of bullets kicked up asphalt, peppering the women with shrapnel. The both pulled back, shielding their faces, before turning tail and running back around the block.

Doyle winked at him. "Nice shooting, son."

Joe spotted Ida cowering between the two cars. He looped his arm around her waist and lifted her off her feet, whisking her into the house with Doyle close behind. She was so incredibly light, Joe wondered if her bones were hollow, just like those of her beloved birds. He no sooner deposited her beside his father, still standing in the open doorway, than he heard glass smashing.

A man carrying a duffel bag over his shoulder was coming from the other direction, tossing flaming bottles at houses. He didn't appear to be carrying a weapon, though the Molotov cocktails were doing more than their share of damage. The Deevys' front lawn burst into flame. It wouldn't be long until the trail of fire reached their house.

He looked to his father and Doyle.

"Go," his father urged.

It would be easy to shoot the man, but Joe needed the satisfaction of more direct contact.

He ran directly at him, legs pumping, his massive bulk giving him the menace of a charging bull.

As soon as the man saw him, he dashed between two

cars and headed for the other side of the street. Joe, no longer feeling like a tired middle-aged man, slid across the hood of an older Nissan. He wanted him, and he wanted him bad.

Surprisingly, the man was still trying to light the rag sticking out of a fresh bottle. More surprisingly, it caught. But instead of launching it at a house, he stupidly tossed it at Joe.

The bottle, spinning end over end, was easy to dodge. It broke in the street to Joe's left.

Nice try, Joe thought, adrenaline giving him the extra push to tackle the man. Joe leaped at him, wrapping his arms around the guy's midsection and driving him into the concrete sidewalk. He felt a satisfying crack. The duffel bag rolled away, bottles clinking.

Quickly getting to his knees, Joe straddled the man, who was having a hard time catching his breath. Not wanting to make this easy for him, Joe landed a sharp jab to his nose, snapping the cartilage. A pocket of blood exploded, coating Joe's fist.

"Who the hell are you?" he shouted, grabbing the man by his collar and shaking him.

When he didn't reply, Joe rapped the back of his head against the sidewalk. This time, his eyes fluttered, showing mostly whites.

Joe had to be careful. Shooting a man in self-defense was one thing. Beating him to death was another.

Not that anyone in the neighborhood would testify against him.

Still, as angry as he was, he still had a conscience, unlike these destroyers of lives. When the smoke cleared,

Joe would have to live with his conscience for the rest of his life.

"I asked you a question. Who are you working for?"

This time, the man smiled. "You are all . . . so stupid. Clinging to . . . to thinking that . . . you're owed these houses, this land. For that . . . you will all die." His accent pegged him as Russian, or from one of the former Soviet Union's captive countries.

Joe ground his teeth until it hurt. "I didn't ask for your manifesto, comrade. I don't know if anyone told you, but the Cold War ended a long time ago, and you lost."

When the man's eyes flicked to Joe's right, he instantly rolled off him, grabbing his gun. But not fast enough. There was a sharp whine, then it felt as if an invisible monster had punched him in the leg. Joe flopped onto his back. The pain came a second later.

He lifted his head to see a man and woman, each on one knee in a firing position twenty yards away. They worked the bolts on their rifles, ready to finish the job. Joe's brain and vision were flooded by the searing pain in his leg that went all the way from the tips of his toes to the top of his skull. He fired blindly back at them, missing by a country mile.

Before the other two could pull their triggers, the man he'd tackled got to his feet, most likely so he could return the beating. He looked at Joe the way a wolf leered at a trapped rabbit. His timing couldn't have been more perfect. His body absorbed both bullets meant for Joe. The surprise on his face was something Joe would never forget. His arms splaying out to both sides, exit wounds painting the sidewalk red, he fell on his face.

At least he can't break his nose twice, Joe thought with a heavy dose of gallows humor.

He was about to muster whatever strength and coherence he could to sit up and fire at his attackers when the air exploded with the sound of gunfire coming from every direction.

CHAPTER FORTY

Pat Knox damned Isabelle to hell. He damned them all for taking his Mary away. As much as he wanted to sit beside her and let himself come undone, it would have to wait until later, even if later meant when he too was dead and could once again be with her.

At first, he didn't see who had shot his son because the shooters had snuck beside the cars parked across the street. Seeing Joe catapult backward yanked Pat from the haze of grief.

No! Not my son, too!

Pat clambered down the steps faster than he had in decades. Doyle was right beside him. Johnnie shouted after them, but nothing could stop Pat.

There was grim satisfaction watching the man standing over Joe get mowed down by friendly fire. But now that he was down, Joe was a literal sitting duck.

With no regard to his own safety, Pat made it to the other side of the street, facing the shooters. The man and woman lowered their guns for the briefest of moments, alarm registering on their faces. What was going to be an easy kill had just gotten a little more difficult, especially now that Doyle was beside him.

Two on two. Pat liked those odds, especially when he had no fear of dying.

He was about to pull the trigger when the back window of the car the shooters were kneeling beside shattered.

William Campbell came tearing around the corner dressed like a weekend warrior, his pump-action shotgun scattering shot everywhere. The cars took the brunt of the spray, but it was enough to stop the shooters cold.

Alongside Onion Breath were a couple of Woodlean old-timers, including Aggie Firth. Their combined age must have hovered near four hundred. All were armed.

Pat used their unexpected arrival to his full advantage. He aimed at the man and caught him in the neck. The man's head snapped and he fell backward, dead.

Both he and Doyle found it impossible to draw on the woman. As soon as her partner went down, she jumped to her feet, looking for an exit that wouldn't get her killed.

Aggie Firth didn't have the same reservations. Armed with a handgun, she fired after the fleeing woman in black. All of her shots missed, but the woman got the point. She dashed between houses on Pat's side of the street and disappeared.

Grateful for the cavalry, Pat turned his attention to Joe. His son was grimacing in pain, both hands on his wounded thigh. There was a lot of blood.

Straddling over the dead man, Pat said, "Stay with me, Joe."

His heart fluttered when Joe's pale lips pulled back into a pained smile. "I'm not seeing any bright lights at the moment, Dad. Just need to stop the bleeding."

None of them heard Johnnie approach. He was taking off his belt and had it cinched around his brother's upper thigh in seconds. He found the bullet hole and tore Joe's pants wide to get a better look.

"Doesn't look like it nicked an artery." He urged Joe to turn onto his side. Joe complied, but not without a groan of protest. Johnnie ripped his pants all the way around. "Good, there's the exit wound. At least I don't have to heat my knife over the fire and dig lead out of you."

"Not funny," Joe said.

"True, but good news anyway."

"Doyle and I will get him into the house. You think you can put the fire out on the Deevys' lawn?" Pat said to his younger son.

"I'm on it."

Johnnie picked up his M4 and sprinted to the Deevys', passing William Campbell and his posse. Campbell was breathing heavily, his complexion alarmingly waxen. "Looks like . . . we got here just . . . just in time."

He was close to Doyle, who fanned the air between them. "But you still found time to eat an onion, didn't you?"

Campbell ignored the remark. "There are more coming. We saw them darting all around. Looks like they're making this block the focus of their attention. They've set fire to Woodlean's periphery. If the fire department doesn't come soon, it'll just keep coming this way until there's nothing left."

Which was all the more reason they needed to get Joe off the street.

Aggie Firth's hand was trembling so hard, Pat was afraid she'd drop the pistol. Sure, she had loved to go hunting with her husband when they were younger, but shooting at a deer and a person were two totally different things.

"You did good, Ags," Doyle said.

She patted her chest with her other hand. "The Widows' Brigade—as you love to call us—have even bigger guns coming."

What had the Widows' Brigade cooked up? Pat couldn't imagine at the moment because of his overriding concern about his sons.

He said to Campbell, "Keep an eye out for Johnnie while he douses that fire." Johnnie held a garden hose in one hand and the M4 in another. He swept the hose back and forth, trying to put out the fire before it caught the Deevys' porch.

"You up for a walk?" Pat said to Joe.

"Not especially."

"Then we'll do the walking for you," Doyle said, grabbing one of Joe's arms. Pat took the other, and they struggled to lift him up. Joe felt as if he weighed more than the rental car he drove to get here. Luckily, Joe was able to get his good leg under him and hop.

"When you were a kid, I used to say you were big boned," Pat huffed as they walked him across the street. "Now, you're big everything."

Joe's arm was like a log across Pat's shoulder.

"Yeah, well, sitting behind a desk all day will do that to you. With excitement like this, I kind of miss my desk."

They managed to get Joe back inside the house, where Ida, keeping well away from the occupied couch, looked pensive.

"Set me up by the back door," Joe insisted.

"You need to lie down," Pat said.

"I can just as easily sit and keep an eye on things."

Pat wondered how long until the loss of blood rendered his son unconscious, but realizing that they'd taken their attention away from the rear of the house gave Pat cause for alarm. The living room—hell, every room—looked like it had been exposed to falling ash from an exploding volcano. Doyle grabbed a kitchen chair and set it up by the back door. Joe dropped heavily into the chair, eagerly accepting one of the weapons from Doyle's bag of tricks. All looked calm out back, but looks could be deceiving.

"I see police lights!" Ida shouted from the front window.

Pat, his lungs burning something fierce, hobbled to the door.

He saw the cruiser turn the corner, heading their way.

Then he watched it get strafed by an unrelenting assault of gunfire, glass and metal coming undone in seconds.

Sheriff Abner Justice watched the towers of smoke through his field glasses while sitting on the hood of his car. He'd parked on Scrub Hill, a popular, out-of-the-way make-out spot during the evenings. His half-eaten cheeseburger sat on the wrapper, the grease congealing as it got cold.

"Bennett wasn't kidding," he said. "They're burning the whole fucking place down."

His deputy, Kenny Carlson, was in the car, his head back and eyes closed. Ever since the fires had started, he'd grown quiet. The man's paling complexion didn't go unnoticed.

"Don't you wanna see?" Justice said.

"I can see the smoke just fine from here," Carlson said, his eyes still closed.

When Justice hopped off the hood, the car's shocks rocked from the release of the heavy weight. He strode to Carlson's window. It was turning into a gray day, and not just from the smoke. There was rain in the forecast, which meant Bennett's thugs better do their work quickly. Still, Justice kept his sunglasses on. The Woodlean residents weren't the only ones he could intimidate.

"You getting soft on me?" he said.

Now he had Carlson's attention. He opened his eyes and narrowed them at the sheriff. "You kidding me?"

"I didn't see you bat an eye when we dragged those old-timers out of their houses and dumped them in a home. Your hands aren't even dirty on this one, and you look like you're gonna puke in your Wheaties. What's the deal?"

Sitting up straighter, Carlson said, "There is no deal. I'm fine. I just don't see anything exciting about watching burning buildings, especially when they're way over there."

Justice smirked.

"You know what? You're absolutely right. It's time we got to see the action up close."

"The mayor said to keep away."

"I'll bet it's pure chaos down there. We could walk through there wearing tinfoil hats and blowing on a bugle and no one would notice us. No, we're gonna take a look."

Carlson seemed like he was about to protest, but one look from the sheriff cut him at the knees.

Justice started the engine and flicked on the two-way radio. The chatter was still about the debacle on I-70. He knew it wouldn't go on much longer, but from the look of things, neither would Woodlean.

As Justice cruised down the winding hillside, he said to his deputy, "Remember, today's mayday is tomorrow's payday. Let's go see when we can start counting our money."

CHAPTER FORTY-ONE

John Knox had just put out the last of the flames when the hail of gunfire made him drop to the ground. William Campbell, Aggie Firth, and the two men he didn't recognize did the same.

It ended as suddenly as it had begun. John looked up to see a police cruiser stalled in the middle of the street. Only the red revolving light hadn't been blown out. A harsh breeze filled the street with black and gray smoke. It rolled over the cruiser, rendering it, as well as the people who had opened fire on it, near invisible.

He realized with sickening dread who would probably be in that car.

Claire.

Using the smoke as cover, he headed toward the crippled vehicle. Campbell jogged alongside him after telling the others to get inside the Knox house.

As they got closer, John saw the driver's side door was open. The windows were blown out, the steel pocked with hundreds of holes. He dropped to the ground where there was less smoke, looking for the black-clad legs of the assailants behind the cruiser. No one was there, which meant they had fled after accomplishing their cowardly duty.

Swallowing hard, he crept to the side of the car, dreading what he was going to see inside.

To his surprise, the car was empty.

The engine sputtered and died.

"Behind you," a voice whispered.

Claire was on the ground between two parked cars, her service revolver in one hand and a shotgun in the other. Her cap was gone, and her hair draped the side of her face. There was blood on her cheek.

"How the hell?" John said, scampering to nestle beside her. Campbell followed quickly. Somehow, the man's breath cut through the acrid smoke. He'd certainly earned his nickname.

"I bailed the second I heard the first shot. I think one of them grazed my ear, but I'll be fine."

He pulled her hair away and saw that, indeed, the top corner of her left ear was missing. If that was her only injury, she might be the luckiest person alive.

"I had to come when Joe told me about your mother," she said.

"Anyone else with you?"

She gave a grim shake of her head.

"Where's Joe and your father?" she asked, the look on her face expecting the worst.

"Back in the house, at least while it's still standing."

Campbell rose to a crouch and looked around. "Smoke's clearing. We better get inside while we still can."

The trio rushed past the dead car and ran into the house, shoulders hunched, expecting to hear a shot any second. John let Claire and Campbell in first and was about to go in, too, when a woman's voice called out, "I don't want to be alone!"

He looked over to see Anna McCurty on her porch, tears running down her face. Campbell was right, the smoke was thinning out as a fresh wind from the east filtered it out.

Even though he was sure Anna was safer in her own house, at least for now, he couldn't leave her there crying.

"Hurry," he said.

She scampered down her porch steps and made a bee-line for their open door. His father was there to help her inside. John looked around one more time before closing the door. Breathing heavily, he rested his back against the door. The living room was filled with the oddest assortment of gun-toting individuals he could ever have imagined.

They were all here, a united front against the invaders.

So why did he get the feeling they had been corralled?

Mayor Viktor Bennett answered the burner phone that he'd purchased just for today. An hour from now, when all was done, he'd smash it with a hammer, distributing pieces here and there in various garbage pails and sewers over the course of the next week.

"We have a sight problem," the man who called said with a thick Slavic accent.

Bennett's stomach recoiled, the early-morning champagne threatening to spoil. "I don't want to hear that," he said calmly and with enough menace to make the man stammer for a moment.

"They have guns," the man said. "They've killed several of our men. Others are wounded."

What was this? Were his Russian cohorts afraid of some wrinklies waving old relics around? No, this wasn't happening.

"You see someone waving a gun around, you kill them! And make sure you keep the rest scared and in their houses. Let them burn. We'll have to let some free, but make sure your team makes it clear to them they are never to speak of what they saw if they don't want their families to die. Do you understand me?"

The man's breath whooshed into the phone. Bennett pulled the phone away as if the breeze were going directly into his ear.

"Some have military weapons. It looks like they've all retreated into the same house. There was a police car, but it has been neutralized."

That brought a smile to Bennett's face. "Well, then, problem solved. You ever hear the phrase 'shooting fish in a barrel'?"

"No, it is not familiar."

"Well, you have your barrel and your guns. Now go fishing, and call me back soon to tell me it's all done . . ."

He hung up before the man could say anything else to ruin his mood.

Bennett would bet his incoming fortune that he knew exactly what house all of the fish had fled into. All the better. He looked at the portrait of his mother hanging over the mantel and wished she were here to experience this. She would have been so proud.

* * *

The moment Claire Dennehy saw Joe sitting by the back door, a puddle of blood by his leg, she set her weapons down and ran to him. "Jesus, Joe, we need to get you to a hospital."

He was covered in sweat and light-headed, but still very much with it. He reached out and took her hand. Now wasn't the time to be shy.

"It doesn't look like I'll be able to drive on out of here. Even if an ambulance did try to make its way, it would be like signing the EMTs' death warrants. I'll be fine. It looks worse than it is."

Her fingertips grazed his cheek and jaw. "I can't believe this is happening."

Joe looked down the hall at his mother's covered corpse. "This is like something straight out of a town in Afghanistan, not America. How on earth do they think they're going to get away with burning the neighborhood down and killing as many people as they can?"

There were tears in Claire's eyes, but Joe could tell they were tears of rage, not sorrow. "They're not going to get away with it. Not while we're here to tell the world."

Joe wondered how long that would be. He'd spied a lot of movement in the O'Malleys' house. Their assailants were getting ready for a big push.

"I hate just sitting here playing defense," he said. "Not that I have much choice."

John came over holding the bottle of scotch. "In lieu of painkillers, take a few belts of this."

Joe gratefully accepted, the burning in his throat nothing compared to the fire burning in his leg.

"Not too much. We still need you to be able to see straight," John said, taking the bottle away.

"And shoot straight," Joe said.

"That goes without saying. So, what's this about wanting to get off our heels?"

"Joe's not going anywhere," Claire said. "He could bleed out."

Checking his leg (and wincing at the black and red hole), Joe saw that most of the bleeding had stopped. He wasn't sure if it was the scotch or the deadening of his nerves, but the pain had started to subside, as well.

"I may not be able to run a 5K, but I'll be able to get around."

The house made a sudden and terrifying shift, the foundation wailing like a wounded monster. Bits of plaster sprinkled the air as the ceiling and walls cracked.

"Besides, I don't think it's wise to stay in here much longer," Joe said. "I say we take it to them instead of waiting for them to come to us."

"We don't exactly have a crack squad of commandos," John reminded him

Joe looked at his father commiserating with Doyle and Campbell, Aggie, Ida, and the other gentlemen listening in. "I beg to differ. I'll bet all of those guys are war vets. They've seen and done stuff we could never imagine. They may not have talked about it with us, but I'm sure stories that would keep us up at night have been traded quietly in the Post over the years. We may be young, but we don't have an iota of their experience or grit. Way I see it, we're the liabilities."

Claire nudged him with her elbow. "Speak for yourself."

He held up his hand. "Ok, maybe just Joe and I are liabilities."

"You forget my five years in the army?" John said.

Joe looked at his leg and recalled his soft life of wandering and office cubicles. "The point is, we have enough to take them on."

"But we've lost the element of surprise. They know we're armed," John said.

Wagging a finger, Joe said, "Ah, but they think we're going to hole up in here, cowering. That's where we prove them wrong. But we have to move fast, before they make their move or this house collapses."

John went to tell the others their plan. Claire stayed with Joe. Their eyes met, and Joe asked, "When this is over, would you like to go to dinner with me?"

"Are you really asking me on a date?"

He shrugged. "It's too late for the prom. I figure a nice steak dinner will have to do."

"You know, your timing is awful."

"Never was my strong suit."

"Then it's a date."

John returned, along with their father. "Everyone's in, including Ida, who wants to get to her house real bad. But first, I'm going to take Mom to Mrs. McCurty's. I won't be able to think straight knowing she's here in a crumbling house."

As if it heard him, the house grumbled again, zigzag cracks breaking across the wall opposite them.

"You up for this, Dad?" Joe said. His father looked terrible, but there was no denying the blazing inferno in his eyes.

"I have nothing to lose. Let's see if we can save the neighborhood for our friends."

CHAPTER FORTY-TWO

While Johnnie carried his mother to Anna's, Doyle and Pat stood on the porch at the ready. Luckily for Johnnie, the smoke came back like a rolling wave and kept him out of sight. Anna went with him, convinced that her house was safer and a firefight was no place for her. The poor woman was trembling, but they didn't have time to soothe her justified fears.

It had been decided that Joe, Claire, and Campbell, plus Frank and Tom, bachelor brothers who were ushers at St. Brendan's and veterans of both Korea and Vietnam, would storm the O'Malley house.

Pat, Doyle, Johnnie, Aggie, and Ida would head out the front and take it to the invaders wherever they found them. The plan—or, more like, hope—was to meet the next block over.

During the war, Pat had been under heavy fire twice and spent countless days waiting for something to happen, something that usually never did. He was never sure which was worse—waiting for all hell to break out or fighting through it. He'd never gotten used to either, his nerves always a jangled mess. Sometimes it was so bad, he worried he'd shoot himself by accident. But his training and survival instinct had always taken over, delivering him from life-and-death situations time and again. Sometimes he had wondered if he should write to Mary back home and tell her to live her life without him. Maybe it would be easier if he didn't have something to look forward to, something to hope for. And Mary would never have to experience an awful day when she received a telegram or knock on the door to tell her she was now the widow of a United States war veteran.

He was glad he'd never written that letter. In the end, knowing Mary was waiting for him was what saved him.

Today, she was still waiting for him, just in a different place. Any trepidation Pat had in Vietnam was nonexistent now. The worst that could happen to him today would only bring him back to his wife.

Johnnie came back and called across the house to his brother. "Ready?"

Joe gave a thumbs-up. He was standing now and able to walk, though with a pronounced limp. Claire promised not to leave his side.

"Let's go," Pat said.

He was the first to hit the sidewalk, eyes darting back and forth and stinging from the smoke. He stood tall, ready for anything that came his way.

They didn't have long to wait.

Through the haze, they saw an encroaching line of invaders up ahead. One of them tossed Molotov cocktails on two homes across the street from one another. As the flames licked the sides of the houses, a man peeled off from the group, guns raised, waiting outside the burning houses to cut down anyone who tried to leave or, even worse, frighten them too much to evacuate so they burned to death.

Yet another unconscionable, immoral act by the monsters who had infected their town.

Pat didn't think the invaders had spotted them yet. Aiming down the sight of his rifle, Pat pulled the trigger. The man standing guard outside the house on the corner spun, his weapon clattering to the ground. Doyle took his cue and shot the man on the other side of the street, hitting his mark.

That prompted the others into action.

The return fire was tremendous.

Johnnie and the others gave it all they had, taking cover behind cars but doing their best to advance by a car length after expending each round.

Pat didn't take cover.

He felt the rippling of the air as bullets whizzed past him. They didn't concern him in the least. He fired into the advancing line, the smoke obscuring them from one second to the next. There was no way to see if they were hit or not. The air was electric with the steady crack of gunfire.

"Get the hell down, Pat!" Doyle shouted at him.

Pat ignored him.

When the hammer clicked and nothing happened, Pat stopped to find fresh ammo in his pockets. Something tugged at his pants legs, and he saw a hole right through the fabric. A half an inch closer, and he'd be on the ground. Steadily reloading, he fired into the direction he assumed the shot had come from.

"Are there any friendlies up there?" Doyle asked.

Pat turned to see Doyle, Johnnie, Aggie, and Ida

crouched behind a car and firing into the smoke. He had the best, if most reckless, viewpoint. He squinted his eyes and said, "I don't see any."

Doyle put his gun down and fumbled in his pocket.

When Pat saw what his old friend had, he stopped shooting and shouted at everyone else to do the same. He ducked behind the car with everyone else.

Let them think they have the upper hand and regroup.

Sometimes, it was best to play dead for a spell, until it was time to show your enemy that news of your demise had been greatly exaggerated.

Joe and Claire had decided that the best approach was to simply storm the O'Malley house with a show of brute and overwhelming force. Tom and Frank would take the rear because they were slower than even a wounded Joe.

Joe opened the back door and half ran, half hopped through the yard. Everyone else followed. They were met by immediate fire.

"Up there!" Claire shouted.

A woman with an automatic rifle was in the window of one of the upstairs bedrooms. Clods of grass and dirt were kicked up all around Joe and his team.

Claire aimed her service revolver and squeezed off several shots. The woman disappeared from view. Joe was impressed. Hitting a target while running was no small feat.

The commotion alerted the others, who had taken positions behind the downstairs windows. Joe, Campbell, and the rest strafed the windows, making the invaders duck for cover. The idea was to bust through the back door, hoping the shocking turn of events was enough to give their quarry pause and give themselves enough time to make the enemy pay. Finesse was not part of the plan.

Joe, being by far the biggest, volunteered to shoulder his way through the door. The foot of his bad leg hit the single step leading to the door and slipped. His knee buckled, and he merely bounced off the door, having lost his momentum. Shooting from above caught his attention as he struggled to get up. A man hung out of the window, firing down on them.

Frank and Tom turned on the man, hitting him in the head and chest. He slipped out of the window and nearly crushed Claire.

Someone in the house popped up and got a lucky shot that took Frank in the stomach, folding him over. Tom returned fire, and Joe heard the man inside cry out in pain.

"I've got it," Campbell said. He shot the doorknob and kicked the door in. With Claire's help, Joe got up and followed him inside.

A man lay on the kitchen floor writhing in agony. The sounds of retreating footsteps echoed in the house.

"I've got 'em!" Campbell cried, setting off down the hall.

Just as Claire was about to follow, a woman with bright blond hair and wide shoulders came out from behind the basement door and tackled her. The woman had a knife long and wide enough to skin a bear. She stabbed at Claire, who just barely managed to roll away.

Joe lunged at the woman as she brought the knife up again, grabbing her by the arm. The woman spotted his wounded leg and punched the wound with her free hand. Joe saw stars. His body went rigid, and he let go of her arm. She sliced at him, the tip of the sharp blade cutting through his shirt and the top layers of skin on his chest.

Good Christ, it burns!

Still straddling Claire, she grabbed the hilt with both hands with the clear intention of driving it through Claire's breastbone. Claire reached up and grabbed the woman's wrists, and she cursed at Claire in an unknown language. They struggled, the knife inching closer and closer to Claire's heart.

His vision filled with sparks of pain, Joe lashed out with his good leg, kicking the woman's side. It was just enough for Claire to wriggle out from under her, still clutching the woman's wrists.

"We will kill everyone you know," the woman hissed.

With both of them on their sides, Claire brought her knee into the woman's groin. The knife clattered between them. Claire was quick to get atop the woman and cuff her hands behind her back.

"Help me tie her legs," she said to Joe. He found a lamp and ripped the cord free, wrapping it as tight as possible around the invader's ankles. She spit a steady stream of what he assumed were Russian curses their way. Claire grabbed her by the hair and thumped her head against the floor, knocking her out.

"We'll come back for her later," she said.

The house was now quiet. Where had Campbell gone?

John spotted the open front door and ran to it, ignoring the line of fire on his chest and dull throb in his leg. William Campbell was sitting on the front steps. A man lay sprawled out before him, bleeding from the head.

"I introduced him to the butt of my rifle," Campbell

said. "It was better than shooting him in the back, though I think he might have broken his neck in the fall."

Joe touched the man's neck, searching for a nonexistent pulse. He wouldn't be shedding any tears over the loss.

The sound of gunfire from the next street over was deafening.

"We better get back over there," Joe said.

"Where's Tom?" Claire asked.

"Crap." Joe bounded through the house, hopping over the captive woman and out the back door.

Frank wasn't moving. Tom sat beside him. He looked like he was having a hard time breathing.

"I'm sorry," Tom said.

"You have nothing to be sorry for," Joe replied. The man was so pale it was frightening.

"I . . . I can't keep going," Tom said, staring at his fallen brother. Joe thought of the roles being reversed and how that would affect him. He patted the man on the shoulder.

"You've done more than enough. Sit tight. As soon as help arrives, I'll send them your way."

Before he could leave, Tom grabbed hold of his arm. "God bless you, son. Not many young people would stand up and fight for us."

Joe grimaced. "Not many folks your age would do what you and your brother have done today."

As Joe turned to rejoin Claire and Campbell, he heard Tom say, "It's all we can do: 'Rage, rage against the dying of the light.'"

CHAPTER FORTY-THREE

The damn smoke made it hard to see, but Pat was sure their attackers had gathered together once more, emboldened by the silence.

Mary must have been watching over them, because a sudden, strong wind swept the inky smoke away long enough to confirm what Pat had thought. There were at least a dozen of them, with two of them getting more Molotov cocktails ready.

"How's your arm?" Pat whispered to Doyle.

"I can't throw a fastball, but I can sure as hell lob this."

He held out a grenade.

They all stared transfixed at the grenade in Doyle's hand. Pat had no idea where and how his friend had gotten it, but at the moment, he was grateful he had it.

"They're all in the street," Johnnie said softly, keeping an eye on the number of boots on the asphalt through the car's undercarriage. "You'll need to get it at least forty feet. If you want, I can do it."

Doyle shook his head. "This is my neighborhood, and my grenade. I need to be the one. Unless your father the southpaw wants to give it a go."

Pat thought of Mary, and he wanted to throw that grenade and so much more. But no, this was Doyle's moment.

"It's all yours, you crazy curmudgeon," Pat said.

The smile on Doyle's face showed Pat he'd done the right thing by deferring.

Doyle stood, pulled the pin, and chucked it dead in the center of the street. It clattered loudly, but the smoke prevented the invaders from seeing what made the noise.

Doyle motioned for them all to cover their ears.

It did nothing to mute the blast. Pat's ears popped painfully, and he felt the wind punched out of him.

He rose to assess the damage. Several of the invaders were on the ground—some writhing, others still as stones. He looked up just in time to see the manhole cover that had taken flight come crashing down, clipping the shoulder of a woman who had spotted Pat and was about to get a bead on him. Those who had managed to escape unscathed were scurrying for cover like rats.

Johnnie leapt to his feet, the M4 spitting out rounds as he tried to catch them before they were out of sight. Pat followed suit, managing to wing one of the men with the Molotov cocktails. If they kept pressing, they could outflank them. Sensing the end of the nightmare, Pat stepped up his pace, reloading quickly as he walked. The return fire lessened with the invaders pinned to their hiding spots, their numbers greatly depleted. He was sure they had thought today would be easy as pie. Pat and his neighbors might have been part of the Silent Generation, but they had learned much from the Greatest Generation. They were silent no more.

Doyle joined the suppressing fire while Johnnie moved

to the other side of the street. They had the invaders right where they wanted them.

Something stung Pat in his lower back. He stopped for a moment, flicking away what he thought was a bee. When the sting became a spreading pain that went down his leg, he faltered.

They were now taking on fire from behind. What few car windows were left exploded.

"Get down! Get down!" Johnnie yelled, leaping between two houses. Doyle was caught in the middle of the street. Pat couldn't tell if he was hit or simply let his body drop to the ground.

As for Pat, he couldn't get his legs to move anymore. He fell to one knee, then the other, a bullet whining just over his head as his palms hit the concrete.

He knew he'd been hit, but it was hard to tell exactly where because he hurt everywhere.

Unable to do anything but lay on the ground, he searched for Johnnie, praying he'd find a way to escape.

As the periphery of his vision darkened, the sounds of warfare fading, he muttered, "Mary," and closed his eyes.

Sheriff Abner Justice followed the flames and sounds of shooting.

"Maybe we should keep away," Deputy Carlson said. He looked ready to jump out of the moving car.

"We're just gonna cruise by and see what's going on."

Bridge Avenue, the lifeblood of the town, was deserted. People heard the shooting and had either fled or were hiding in their homes. The ones not smart enough to vamoose weren't going to have homes much longer. From what

Justice could see, all of Woodlean was going to be in cinders soon enough.

Two blocks ahead of him, he saw half a dozen people toting mighty powerful rifles making their way down Percy Avenue, the street where the Knox pests lived. Even for a man who had an inkling of what was happening, it was shocking. He stopped the car, the people disappearing into the whirling smoke.

"What the hell, Abner?" Carlson said.

"That sick bastard brought an army in." Well, if that's what he had to do to wipe old Woodlean off the map so it could be rebuilt and certain people, including himself, could get very rich in the process, so be it.

When Justice touched the gas, Carlson protested, "You can't go there. We could get shot!"

"Then get the hell out if you're so scared. I have to see."

Carlson stayed put, crouching low in his seat.

As Justice pulled alongside the entrance to the street, the car was struck by a bullet. Carlson screeched.

The smoke cleared for a moment, and Justice went cold.

What the hell was Claire's squad car doing in the middle of the street?

She'd rather die with Knox than give you the time of day, a voice whispered in his head.

He should just let it go and drive away. There would be plenty of time to view the aftermath and count his money.

Why wasn't Claire out with everyone else on I-70, where she belonged?

Because this was where she wanted to be: with Joe Knox, a man marked for death.

Justice saw red, and it wasn't the red of the flames everywhere.

He put the car in park and got out.

"What do you think you're doing?" Carlson shouted after him.

There was one hell of a firefight going on, but all he could see was Claire's cruiser.

Claire.

I have to find Claire.

She doesn't want me. Fine. I'll make sure no one can have her.

Even though Joe was supposed to wait for his father and brother to meet them around the block, it didn't sound like they'd be able to go anywhere. He, Claire, and Campbell cut through his house. Its dilapidation had gotten worse, the interior now tilting at a dangerous angle.

They hit the front porch just in time to catch sight of reinforcements boxing his family in.

"They don't know we're here," Campbell whispered in his ear.

He was right.

"I'll take the two on the left," Joe said. "Claire, you get the two in the middle, and Campbell will get the two on the right."

Joe needed to take them down quickly before they could react and turn on them. It sounded like they had Uzis. They didn't stand a chance against Uzis.

Even though the cacophony was loud enough to wake the dead, they crept off the porch and onto the sidewalk carefully to avoid making any noise. Joe got into position, pretty sure he could take down his two in a few seconds.

He was about to pull the trigger when someone behind him shouted, "You bitch!"

Joe spun to find the sheriff, Claire's ex-husband, pointing a shotgun at them.

"Abner," she replied, unable to hide the shock she felt.

Joe glanced at the invaders, who mercifully hadn't heard Justice. But they were still advancing on his family.

"Put the peashooter down," Campbell said. "There's three of us and one of you. Don't be stupider than you already are."

Justice laughed. "You couldn't have bunched yourselves up any nicer for my 'peashooter.' All it'll take is one pull of my trigger, and you're all history. Now, put your guns down."

"You don't want to do this," Claire said.

Justice smirked. "I wasn't sure until I saw you. Now I know I want to. Besides, you were about to ruin all our plans. I can't have that. Hell, I may be able to get an even bigger payday for stopping you. For that, I thank you. Now, I'm not going to tell you again. Put your guns down!"

Claire lowered her arm. Campbell did the same with his rifle with great reluctance.

Only Joe refused to comply.

The look of hate in the sheriff's eyes when they lit upon Claire was unlike anything he'd ever seen. No matter what they did, Justice was going to shoot her.

"What kind of a man wants so badly to kill a woman he once loved?" Joe said.

Justice's face reddened, and spittle flew from his mouth as he shouted, "You shut your dirty, stinking mouth! When she dies, it's because of you. You can take knowing that with you to the grave!"

Claire touched his arm. "Just do what he says."

"Don't you dare touch him!"

Sheriff Justice took three strides forward, the barrel of the shotgun pointed at the center of her face. She would bear the brunt of the blast, but Joe and Campbell would take enough shot to have half their heads carved away from this short distance.

But Joe knew something Justice didn't.

"Please, Abner, don't do this," Claire pleaded. Tears snaked down her cheeks.

"I should have done this a long time ago."

"You know what?" Joe said. Justice flicked his eyes to him. "You talk too much."

"To hell with all of you!"

"No!" Claire wailed.

There was a sharp blast.

Claire and Campbell jumped back.

Sheriff Justice's sunglasses flew off his face. He dropped the shotgun, his hands clutching a spreading red stain on the belly of his shirt. His eyes were so wide, Joe thought they might roll out of their sockets. He breathed a gurgling last breath and fell facedown in the street.

Behind him, Deputy Carlson lowered his weapon, his whole body shaking.

"Go," he said to them.

Joe grabbed Claire's hand, and they turned toward the fray, hoping there was anyone left to save.

None of them noticed the approaching cars and vans.

CHAPTER FORTY-FOUR

Whatever advantage they'd had was gone. John Knox pressed his back against a house in the narrow alley. The men they'd had cornered were now up and shooting. That was nothing compared to the flak they were taking from the other direction.

He thought of Marion and their dreams of one day retiring to Arizona, where she could pursue her dream of archaeology and he could finally write the novel he'd been threatening to start for decades. John hoped she never forgot how much he loved her. The loss would crush her, but time would heal the wound. Had he saved enough to keep her comfortable while she healed?

He couldn't see his father, and Doyle hadn't moved. He did catch Ida's terrified face where she was wedged between two cars with Aggie. The old woman would raise her gun over her head and fire blindly every now and then.

They were done.

John wondered what had happened to Joe, assuming the worst.

He could slip between the houses and come out on the other block, away from the madness and certain death.

Would that make him a coward? Or would surviving to tell the world what had happened here be the exact vengeance his family needed? He'd never been so conflicted.

Out of the chaos, he heard a man scream, followed by a woman shrieking in anguish.

Then he saw them.

Out of the soot and mist appeared several dozen men and women, only one of them under seventy years old. Father Biglin led the remnants of his congregation into the fight. John spotted mostly hunting rifles and a few handguns among his rescuers. Even the priest was carrying a rifle.

Several people went down as the intense fire coming from the other end of the street continued.

"Take cover!" John shouted.

The band of oldsters dispersed, finding safe spots among the cars and houses. From there, they fired away. John knew he was witness to something never seen before in modern America. Then again, this is what the country was founded on. When invaders came to take away land and liberty, the citizens united. This was a resistance by a marginalized and forgotten sector of society, a generation that was tired of being pushed around and shut away.

John edged around the house and fired into the roiling smoke, praying he hit someone in black.

It was at that moment when the air rumbled and the sky opened up, dumping buckets of rain on the street-cum-battlefield.

It was difficult to spot the invaders, as they had advanced far enough into the haze to disappear. Joe used his ears to guide him as he pulled the trigger over and over.

"I see one!" Campbell shouted.

Joe saw him, too, a burly man holding his Uzi low against his hip and firing in a moving arc. Campbell went to shoot the man, but his gun was empty. Instead, he raised his rifle as if it were a club and charged. Somehow, the man heard his approach, turned, and burped a barrage of bullets into William Campbell. The old man flew backward and fell atop the trunk of a car.

While the man was fixed on Campbell, Joe shot him in the neck.

Claire darted forward and grabbed the man's Uzi.

Thunder rumbled, and the rains came. The deluge was as savage as it was sudden.

And it drove down the smoke.

For once, Joe could finally see ahead of him.

What he saw had him grabbing Claire and heading for cover.

It looked like most of Woodlean had come out to fight. Bullets filled the air. He and Claire focused their shots, aiming for the black-clad men who scrambled for safety, finding none.

It was over in minutes.

He heard a man shout, "Cease fire!"

When Joe looked, he saw Father Biglin with his rifle raised over his head, commanding everyone to put down their weapons.

John staggered onto the sidewalk, and their eyes met. Joe wanted to run to him, but his wounded leg, sensing the battle was over, felt like a dead log attached to his hip. Claire hugged him fiercely, crying into his shoulder.

Holding her was a dream come true. It was unreal that he had to fight his way through a nightmare to get here.

Looking to the end of the street, he saw the plethora of

news vans. Now that the shooting had stopped, men holding cameras were gathering, others holding cell phones to record the historic event.

He was exhausted. So tired he couldn't keep his eyes open.

Joe slipped into unconsciousness to the sounds of approaching sirens, wondering what had become of his father.

CHAPTER FORTY-FIVE

When Joe Knox awoke, he had no idea where he was. Momentarily panicked, he tried to get out of bed but was thwarted by a solid bed rail. Not to mention the plethora of IVs in his arm. He was about to rip them out when a hand fell on his chest.

"Easy there."

He looked up to see John standing over the bed, a smile of relief on his face.

"Where am I?"

"You mean the bed and IV pole aren't giving it away?" John said sarcastically. "You've been out for days since the surgery. I was starting to get worried."

Out for days? Surgery? What was his brother talking about?

Then he looked down at his leg, now wrapped in yards of gauze, and remembered.

"How bad is it?" Joe asked.

John took the seat next to the bed. "You lost a lot of blood. But the damage to your leg was minimal. You're also going to have a nice scar on your chest."

Joe settled his head into the pillow, slightly dizzy. He felt like dozing off, but suddenly jerked awake. "Dad?"

John sighed. "He's actually across the hall. He was luckier than you. Took a bullet to his, um, posterior. They're ultra-concerned about infection, especially since he hadn't gotten over his pneumonia yet, but he's already harassing the nurses asking about you."

"Well, what are you waiting for? Go tell him I'm among the living."

John patted his arm, got up, and left. Joe used the time to replay the events that had gotten them here, and even he couldn't believe it all. It seemed not just like a dream, but like someone else's dream.

He was about to doze off when he heard his father say, "I knew your mother would never have allowed you to join her. Not this soon. You know that woman and her pipeline to the Big Man."

Pat looked pale and weary, but there was no disguising the love and gratitude on his face. He leaned down and hugged Joe, neither wanting to be the first to break the embrace. Once they did, John helped their father into a chair.

"You're famous now," Pat said.

"Come again?" Joe said.

"Our faces are everywhere," John said. "The Widows' Brigade, knowing all first responders were at the I-70 disaster, called the media. They weren't there for the whole thing, but they caught enough to stun the world. Some of them even livestreamed it on the internet—a completely unfiltered look at what went down. That deputy, what was his name?"

"Carlson," Pat said.

"Yes, Carlson, well, they pounced on him, seeing as he was the only man with a badge at the time. He'd just taken down Justice and was really shaken up. The story he had to tell was this side of unreal. I heard he clammed up when they got him at the station, but his lawyer made a deal where he will get a lighter sentence for giving them the whole story."

Joe was confused. "The whole story? Justice was going to kill Claire, and Carlson shot him first."

John shook his head. "No, that part was cut-and-dried. But it turns out all of this was a grand scheme for Russian infiltration by Woodlean's illustrious mayor."

"I never liked that red bastard," Pat said, crossing his arms over his chest. "Viktor Bennett was a snake in the grass on his best days. I sure as hell never voted for him."

"Russian infiltration?"

"It sounds crazy, right? The plan was to ship all of the Woodlean old-timers to awful rest homes, raze the town, and rebuild it into a modern nightmare using Russian labor and money. They would get rich off our misfortune," John said, taking a sip from a can of soda on the windowsill.

Joe turned to his father. "You said the mayor *was* a snake in the grass."

At this, his father chuckled. "When he heard he was caught red-handed, so to speak, he tried to escape. But his way was blocked by a convoy of news vans and police, those cops mad as hell at the carnage that had been created on I-70. Five children died. If you ask me, they were going to kill him if he resisted arrest. But the snake couldn't even give them that satisfaction. He put a gun in his mouth and ended it right there in his car."

"Coward," Joe seethed.

"Of the highest order," Pat said. "But there's enough of a trail to suss out the bigger plan. Woodlean was a testing ground for more small-town takeovers. The whole thing's become a bit of an international incident. The president is taking a hard line with the Russians, and it's scaring a lot of people. I say good for him! Chickenhearted diplomacy doesn't work against an evil empire . . ."

"Jesus," Joe said.

"Don't blame him," Pat said. "He's the reason we're here to talk about it."

Joe thought of his mother and fought back a surge of tears. Where was she now? When would they have her funeral?

"What about everyone else?" he asked instead, knowing that talking about his mother would crush him.

At that, his brother and father blanched.

"We lost Doyle," John said. "Aggie Firth, too. Shrapnel caught her in the temple. William Campbell died, but I suspect you knew that. There were half a dozen others, and a lot of injured. The hospital is filled with the walking wounded now."

They sat in silence, thinking about all that had been lost.

Pat struggled to get up and squeezed Joe's arm. "You'll be needing your rest. We can talk more tomorrow."

He was about to walk away when Joe said, "Wait! What about the neighborhood? It's destroyed. Where will everyone go?"

"There are volunteers working to rebuild it as we speak," John said. "The president signed a relief fund that will pay for most of it. Multiple charities and just plain good people are going to do the rest. You have no idea of the outpouring of goodwill. Woodlean is in just about everyone's thoughts and prayers. Who would have thought it?"

Joe thought about conversations with John when they were teens and their plans to leave their boring hometown behind. They couldn't imagine themselves spending their lives there.

"What about the house?" Joe said.

Pat raised an eyebrow. "Somehow, it's still standing, but there are plans to take it all down. The foundation took a hell of a beating. It's going to be rebuilt from the ground up. Once it's safe to go inside, John is going with a crew to retrieve all the stuff that's still in one piece."

Sagging with relief, Joe said, "Even the Russians couldn't take your home away."

"Oh, I'm not going back. I'm moving in with Johnnie and Marion. It'll never be the same, and I have to admit, I'm not getting any younger."

The last few weeks had probably aged him a decade— a decade he didn't have.

"And Claire?"

Pat said, "I was wondering when you'd get around to her. She's been a little busy, as you can imagine. But when she's not on the job, she's been sitting vigil with you. I think she's sweet on you."

"Understatement of the year," John added.

"Is there any chance I could move into the house when it's done?" Joe asked.

Chuckling, Pat asked, "It's yours. It was always going to be yours and Johnnie's. Besides, I think you now have a reason to stick around. Get some rest. The Capitals advanced to the Stanley Cup while we were preoccupied. We'll watch the game in your room tomorrow."

Joe watched his brother and father leave the room, missing them already.

Maybe his wanting to move back to Woodlean was an impulse born of trauma.

Then he thought of Claire, and the dinner he owed her.

No, he'd fought for Woodlean, and he wasn't going anywhere ever again.

Turn the page for an exciting preview from

USA TODAY BESTSELLING AUTHORS
WILLIAM W. JOHNSTONE
and **J. A. JOHNSTONE**

*A nation in flames. Freedom under fire. A call to all
heroes to stand up, fight back, or die.
From the bestselling authors of* BLACK FRIDAY,
HOME INVASION, *and* KNOCKDOWN

AMERICA IS BURNING.
It begins in the Pacific Northwest. A deadly wave of
massive wildfires are raging out of control, killing
hundreds in their path, and showing no sign of stopping.
This time, the fires are man-made.

FEAR IS SPREADING.
In Portland, Oregon, a sleeper cell of terrorists have
recruited a disgruntled Forest Service smokejumper
to train their army. To spread the fear coast to coast.
To make America burn.

HEROES ARE RISING.
Those who flee the hot flames are gunned down in cold
blood. But one man—Forestry Service smokejumper
Cory Cantwell—is fighting back.
Leading a team of elite firefighters,
he is determined to stop the destruction.
Not with water. With Glock 19s. With real firepower.
And with no mercy.

THE SCORCHING
by WILLIAM W. JOHNSTONE
and J. A. JOHNSTONE

On sale wherever Pinnacle Books are sold.

Tillamook State Forest, Oregon

There was an intruder in the woods, and the gray squirrel had never seen its like. From its lofty perch on a pine branch the little rodent's black, almond-shaped eyes fixed on the strange creature, assessing its potential as an enemy. The squirrel had no way of knowing that the invader was a man . . . the most dangerous predator on earth.

He had walked far, the last mile on a badly twisted ankle. The Jeep Wrangler he'd driven was hidden in ferns off a hiking trail. After today, he would have no further need for it. Around him the forest was silent in the afternoon heat, and dusty shafts of light filtered through the tree canopy as hushed and hallowed as sunbeams through a stained-glass window. In the distance a couple of scrub jays disturbed the peace as they fussed and quarreled in the bushes.

The sweet, acrid stench of gasoline suddenly spiked into the path of a rising south wind as the man sloshed the gas from a five-gallon plastic can, showering as much of the drought-stricken undergrowth as he could. When that was done, he thumbed a Zippo into flame and set the accelerant alight. The fire took, flared and spread rapidly, burning pine needles, leaves, and grass, gorging on fuel and oxygen. The blaze fed hungrily and with mindless ferocity. Now intensely hot, the flames grew in height, the pines became their food source, and within minutes the entire forest around the man was ablaze.

He screamed in delight. He'd played his part well, and from coast to coast soon all of America would burn to ashes. Only now did the man consider himself a martyr.

The south wind fanned the flames around the man, a roaring, red and yellow wall of fire that closed in on him. With terrible intensity, the heat scorched the skin of his face and hands, he found it hard to breathe, and suddenly he was afraid. The fire burned out his throat and lungs, and he could not even scream.

He had hoped to perish like a martyr, but he died hard, and badly, in terrible pain.

CHAPTER ONE

Indian Wells, Oregon

Big Mike Norris's smoke jumper crew parachuted onto the Indian Wells fire zone without a detailed map of the area. But they'd been told a crack crew was already in place, local hotshot firefighters who knew the terrain and probably had the blaze well in hand.

"It will be a piece of cake, Mike," Norris's base manager had told him. "A walk in the piney woods."

But when they landed on a windswept clearing on top of a high bluff, there was no one in sight. After he dropped his chute harness and most of his hundred pounds of gear, Norris looked around, cursed under his breath, then said, "What the hell? Where is everybody?"

His was a short crew, only fifteen members instead of the usual twenty, but this was supposed to be a mop-up. The heavy smell of wood smoke in the air put the lie to that claim.

Cory Cantwell, the only squad leader present, stepped beside his crew superintendent boss. "They must have seen us make the drop, Mike," he said. "You'd think somebody would stop by and say hi."

"Seems like," Norris said. He looked hard at Cantwell. "How's the shoulder?"

"Bad," the younger man said. "But it will stand up just fine."

"What did the doc say?"

"He told me it's arthritis. I said I was only thirty and how the hell could I have arthritis. He said anybody at any age can have arthritis."

"So what did he give you?"

"Nothing. Told me to quit the weight training. I told him that ain't gonna happen. Maybe I'd get flabby after a while. Well, he shook his head and said that every fire-fighter he ever met wants to be Arnold Schwarzenegger, and that includes the women. Finally, since he knew I was making this jump in an hour, he shot cortisone into the shoulder, though he warned me that since medical school he wasn't very good with a needle."

"And was he?"

"No. He was a butcher with a horse needle. It hurt like hell."

Norris smiled and said, "Come over here. What do you make of this?"

He walked to the edge of the plateau and nodded in the direction of a saddle-backed hill that loomed to one side of the rise, the dark evergreens at its base obscured by a gray haze of smoke.

"We got to get down there, Cory," Norris said. "I have no idea where the hell that other crew is. They ain't fighting fires, that's for damn sure."

Cantwell examined the terrain. A dry, steady wind blew

from the heights of the Cascade Mountains to the desert lowlands below. To the east rose the rocky hills of the high desert, covered with bunch grass and cheatgrass with a few ponderosa pines, that descended to sagebrush-covered flatlands. To the west the foothills of the mountains had a dense cover of Douglas fir.

Just before the team had left base, a Red Flag Watch had been issued, which meant high winds, lightning, and no rain. So far, the smoky fire wasn't crowning, but a sudden gust of wind could whip it into flame.

"Cory, the wind is blowing in the opposite direction from what they told us," Mike said. "They should have dropped us on the flat."

"The fire is in the gulch, so how do we get down there?" Cantwell said.

"I'm not happy being on grass above a fire," Norris said. He removed his scarred white helmet, wiped sweat from his brow with the back of his hand. "We have to get down into the gulch somehow."

"We could call it off, make another jump onto the flat," Cantwell said. He knew Norris would nix that idea, but he felt it was his duty to mention it.

"It's a thought, but it would take too long," Norris said. "The fire could spread a considerable distance by then."

"Then we make our way downhill," Cantwell said.

"Damn, it's going to be rough heading down the slope," Norris said. "Broken leg central, huh?"

"Maybe broken neck central," Cantwell said.

"Yeah, why not look on the bright side?" Norris said. "Mike!"

A young dark-haired man with wide shoulders and earnest brown eyes stood at the edge of the rise and pointed down into the gulch, where smoke curled like a great, gray serpent. "Lookee there. I think I found a game trail."

"Going down?" Norris said.

The young man grinned. "It's going both ways, Mike, up and down."

"Smartass," Norris said. "All right, make like Dan'l Boone and go check it out, Wilson. And be careful."

"Sure thing," Bob Wilson said. He disappeared over the rim of the plateau.

"Good kid that," Norris said. "Needs some weight on him though."

"A few years eating National Wildfire Service grub will bulk him up," Cantwell said.

"Meat loaf."

"Beef stew."

"Plenty of protein."

"And cake and Cool Whip for dessert. Plenty of carbs."

"Sounds good," Norris said. "I'm making myself hungry."

When young Wilson returned five tense minutes later, he stepped beside Norris and said, "It's a game trail all right, probably deer, and I think it goes all the way into the gorge."

"Cory, what do you think?" Norris said. "Should we take a shot at it?"

"Where a deer can go, so we can we," Cantwell answered. "Nothing else is presenting itself, so it's sure worth a try."

Norris nodded. "Right, let's get it done. We got a fire to fight." He looked around, and his gaze fell on a man with a goatee beard and overlong hair. "Connors . . . you're lookout. Stay here until we're safely down and then follow. Okay?"

The man called Connors nodded. "I got it, boss."

"Mike, do you see that?"

This from Cheryl Anderson, at twenty-one the youngest member of his crew. A tall, pretty girl on her first drop, like the rest she'd shucked her heavy jumpsuit and stripped down to boots, a yellow shirt, and olive-green pants. She filled out both shirt and pants beautifully. Her hair was chopped short, a bob that looked like a glossy bronze helmet. The woman pointed to the top of the butte, where stood an abandoned lookout tower, rickety and half-hidden behind a growth of vegetation. Once it had hosted a park ranger, now it was the haunt of owls.

"Yeah, now I see it, Cheryl," Norris said. "That shining example of the National Wildfire Service's folly could be useful as a landmark." He pulled out his cell phone. "Google Maps to the rescue."

There was no reception.

Norris cursed under his breath. One more goddamned techno failure. At thirty-five he was old enough to remember when the firefighters relied on human observations, and old enough to be nostalgic about it. If he'd had some good old-fashioned maps, he'd know exactly where he was, the names, the topography, the contours and elevations. Even better, if the lookout tower had been manned, the ranger probably could have put out the aborning fire—which wasn't that big even now.

Instead, a satellite picked up the blaze. A computer produced the weather forecasts given to him. Norris had been handed the printouts before they left the airbase, and it was all supposedly very up-to-date.

And already he could see they were wrong.

For one thing, the satellite had apparently spotted a larger fire than actually existed. Because of that, fifteen volunteers had been drawn from the several crews that were lounging around the Redmond Airport near the end of the season, hoping for some action. It was a far larger team than necessary. Norris thought about sending some of them back but decided whomever he chose would be pissed. By this late in the season, the overtime wages were welcomed.

It was all pretty messed up. At the very least, they should have been dropped farther down, closer to the fire. Well, now Norris had the game trail. While such trails are predominately used by grazing animals, humans have always found them handy. Lost hikers will follow a well-marked game trail to a waterway that could eventually lead to civilization . . . and they provide a stable path through otherwise impassible terrain.

Norris called his people together and ordered them to pick up their gear and head for the trail, except for Joe Connors, who would remain on the butte as lookout and stay in radio contact.

"Cory Cantwell will take the point, and I'll bring up the rear," he said. Norris waited for comments, and when none came, he said. "All right, we got it to do."

"Break a leg, folks," Cantwell said, grinning.

"That," Mike Norris said, "is not funny."

Visit us online at
KensingtonBooks.com
to read more from your favorite authors,
see books by series, view reading group guides, and more.

BOOK CLUB
BETWEEN THE CHAPTERS

Visit us online for sneak peeks, exclusive giveaways,
special discounts, author content, and engaging
discussions with your fellow readers.

Betweenthechapters.net

Sign up for our newsletters and be the first to get exciting news
and announcements about your favorite authors!
Kensingtonbooks.com/newsletter